RESEARCH INTO
MARGINAL LIVING:
THE SELECTED STORIES OF
JOHN D. KEEFAUVER

RESEARCH INTO MARGINAL LIVING

THE SELECTED STORIES OF
JOHN D. KEEFAUVER

EDITED BY SCOTT NICOLAY

LETHE PRESS

ISBN: 9781590215142

Cover and Interior Design by INKSPIRAL DESIGN

Published by Lethe Press.

Dedicated to Marina Westfield,
who saved her Uncle Johnny's work from oblivion.
Every good author deserves such a great great-niece.

TABLE OF CONTENTS

THE ODD AND WONDERFUL FICTION OF JOHN D. KEEFAUVER

JOE R. LANSDALE

I DIDN'T REALLY KNOW JOHN Keefauver well, and in fact we never met face to face, but we traded letters, back in the days when people wrote them. My letters from John exist, or most of them do, but my letters to him probably do not, unless he kept them and someone ended up with them.

I wrote lots of letters, but rarely if ever made carbons of what I wrote. It didn't occur to me. I don't know if John made carbons of his or not. I have the faint memory that his missives to me always smelled of beer and cigarettes, but that may have been my imagination.

My letters from John are either at the A&M library in College Station, or they are at San Marcos in the Texas State Library. I'm uncertain where they eventually ended up, but one of those archives is the most likely, as I have manuscripts and career artifacts in both. I know I always enjoyed his letters, though they were generally short, and one thing that came through in them was that he seemed as interesting as his stories.

John turned out a lot of material in his writing career, and was published regularly. If he was a writer of novels under his own name, I'm not aware of them.

What I am aware of is this: John was a writer who never got his due, and though he wrote for a number of genre publications, he told me that he really didn't have much interest in what he called goal-oriented fiction. By that, I think he meant plot. The quirkiness of his stories may have had something to do with him not being as well-known as he should be, and the fact that the bulk of his work was short stories, and not goal-oriented in the usual sense of what that might mean, but when it came to short stories, he was undoubtedly, a master.

Like Ray Bradbury, John wrote images, metaphors, and though he certainly wrote some things that could be called more traditional, it always had the Keefauver touch. I think the goal-oriented aversion came to him later in life. I feel that he thought of himself as a serious writer of what I call absurdist fiction. I often wondered if he had been influenced by impressionistic and surreal painters, but I never asked. Wish I had now.

John was a writer whose stories I looked for everywhere, and he was a writer that could turn up anywhere. His stories were always unique and had a way of stirring the juices in the brain, though I was uncertain exactly what was being stirred. His work boiled and bubbled and after reading one of his stories my brain did the same. I still recall fictions of his many years after reading them.

One of my favorites appeared in *Omni* and had to do with a field of stones that were coming out of the wild country and were moving closer and closer to civilization. Instead of civilization encroaching on nature, John took the opposite view.

When I finally became an occasional editor of anthologies, he was one of the first writers I thought of. I felt this guy was just a moment away from greater recognition, and I wanted to help him get there, even though at that point I had about as much impact in the field as a gnat on an elephant's ass.

In the end, I don't think I helped much to expand his readership, but I was certainly glad to have him included in those anthologies.

The first story I bought from him was for a Western anthology. At that time a lot of those anthologies were figurehead anthologies, meaning the publishing company picked the writers they wanted, and the "editor" was merely a name on the cover. I didn't want to do that. I wanted to be involved, and was.

Once it was realized I meant to actually edit the book, I remember I got a call from a couple of noted Western Writers to tell me how to do it and who to have in it.

I appreciated their suggestions, but one of the writers who called me surprised me by becoming angry once he realized I didn't intend to do it the way he wanted. That I planned to also reach outside the membership for some of the stories, and that I didn't have a completely traditional view of the sort of tales I wanted. I felt new blood was needed as well as old blood. I wanted something that could reflect the West without all of it being about gun smoke and saddle leather, the good ole cowboys who were always reining their horse to a halt at the top of a rise. I can't tell you how many older Westerns began that way.

Western short stories at that time were nearly nonexistent due to lack of market, and it was the beginning of the general decline for short stories as a whole. I thought it might be fun to shake things up a little, do something exciting. I bought some traditional stories, and I bought some that weren't. That would be where John D. Keefauver came in. His stories always seemed quietly drunk when they entered a room, but still capable of breaking the furniture, and taking a dump in the corner of the room before passing out. And I mean that in the best way. John wasn't towing the line with his stories. He was a visitor from another dimension.

I was grateful John wrote some tales for the anthologies I edited. He wrote about bears who watched TV, as well as unidentified flying objects that doubled as swimming pools. The best thing about John is he could make the most ridiculous ideas seem logical, at least for the duration of the story. He had things to say, and I could tell you what I think they were saying, but instead of my stuffy explanations of what he meant that in the end might be dead wrong, it's best for you to read the stories and decide for yourself. The thing is, you'll leave happily mystified, like discovering aliens had been living in your basement all along, and that questions as to why things go missing from your refrigerator and your dog is pregnant have suddenly been resolved. John's stories had that kind of feel.

I rank John primarily as a fantasist, and one of the best, right up there on the shelf beside Ray Bradbury, Rod Serling (mostly scripts, but I'm generalizing here), Theodore Sturgeon, Kurt Vonnegut, and well, I could make a longer list. But he fits snuggly there if those guys would move over and quit hogging the shelf and let him in.

Truthfully, John should have a shelf all his own. He would be more comfortable there, for he was definitely his own thing when it came to writing.

I wish John was still around and writing stories. I wish I had known him better. I would have loved to have talked shop with him.

But listen. What's really cool, is you have a fat book of his wonders at your fingertips. This is a broad view of his work and it is a good one.

Please open the book now, along with your mind, and journey into the world of a writer of excellence and inimitable imagination, John D. Keefauver.

EDITOR'S PREFACE

SCOTT NICOLAY

JOHN DAVID KEEFAUVER WAS BORN on December 13, 1923 in Washington D.C. and grew up in College Park, Maryland, where his family owned a general store. He died in his sleep at the age of 90, on December 21, 2013, in Carmel, California, where he had lived for over 60 years. In between he served in the U.S. Army Air Corps from 1943 to 1946, worked as a reporter in Michigan, traveled the world, and published over 900 works of fiction as one of America's last great freelance fiction authors. In his later years he received an inheritance that allowed him to retire from writing, though he continued to pen humorous letters to the editors of his local papers, the *Monterey Herald* and the *Monterey County Weekly*, under the byline "Uncle Coleslaw." A few of these are still available to read on the newspapers' websites, including this micro-fiction that appeared in the *Weekly* on Jan. 1, 2009:

"Every morning Uncle Coleslaw sprinkled on his new toupee a special tonic so powerful that one evening it sprang off his head and scuttled under the stove. He coaxed it out with a warm saucer of Wildroot and with patience eventually trained it to stay on his head during the day. Every night it scuttled back under the stove. It had fallen in love with a female mouse living there, and six weeks later the pair had three babies. All three had long hair, a part in the middle, and liked cheese."

That brief example offers a good introduction to Keefauver's work, all of which is quirky, humorous, ribald, and/or macabre, in varying measures. Sometimes all at once, though generally not to the extreme of any of these aspects. This may explain the difficulty he encountered in publishing his longer works, which neither fit with the mainstream nor fully edged into any other commercial niche. Although Keefauver also wrote at least half a dozen novels, he only ever succeeded in publishing two of them: *Tormented Virgin*, originally published as soft-core porn in 1962 (reprinted in a new scholarly edition by Lethe Press in 2019), and *The Three Day Traffic Jam*, published by Simon & Schuster Books for Young Readers in 1992. Thus he is predominantly remembered—by those who do remember him—for his short fiction.

The first John D. Keefauver story I ever read was "How Henry J. Littlefinger Licked the Hippies' Scheme to Take Over the Country by Tossing Pot in Postage Stamp Glue," in *Alfred Hitchcock Presents: Stories to Be Read with the Door Locked*. I believe I read it when the book was new, so that was probably in 1975. At the time, I was deep into my infatuation with *MAD* magazine, so that tale's whacky title drew me right in. Other stories from that volume have stayed with me as well, notably "A Good Head for Murder," by Charles W. Runyon, and "Royal Jelly," by Roald Dahl, but it was Keefauver's contribution that I read first and which registered most strongly. So strongly that here I am some 45 years later, editing the first collection of his fiction, something long overdue.

At the time, that story immediately shot Keefauver to the top of my list of authors to seek out. Soon I found "The Great Three-Month Super Supersonic Transport Stack-Up Of 1999," which as I recall actually came as somewhat of a disappointment at the time. I stuck with him though, and soon I encountered "Special Handling" and "A Pile of Sand." All of these appeared in additional Hitchcock volumes.

I immediately recognized those last two stories as a sort of "levelling-up." Clearly the author who had caught my attention was indeed capable of real greatness—and genuine weirdness. I continue to assert that "A Pile of Sand" is a neglected masterpiece of Weird Fiction. Thereafter I kept my eyes out for the longer work I felt must be forthcoming—a collection of short stories or perhaps a novel. Like Joe R. Lansdale, I felt certain that Keefauver "was just a moment away from greater recognition." Although I continued to encounter the occasional short story, that longer work never surfaced. For years, I presumed I had missed that longer book. Eventually the internet allowed me to search for it, but the only books I ever found under his name were the two short novels mentioned above. I purchased both and read *The Three Day Traffic Jam* to my daughters as a bedtime story, between installments of Harry Potter and Lemony Snicket. They loved it, but no similar works by the author appeared. By all indications, Keefauver had gone silent.

Later my mentor John Pelan and I located Keefauver's address in Carmel, and I wrote him a letter, suggesting that we would be interested in editing and publishing a volume of his stories. I included a list of those stories that I had already gathered, including the titles mentioned above. His handwritten reply was not encouraging. "The only way I could possibly agree to enter into what you propose" he wrote, "…is with the understanding that I have to do absolutely nothing (including sending you or John Pelan manuscripts if desired) except receive a copy of the published collection. You're about 25 years too late, alas."

I was at a loss for a response, and life took a few turns, so I never wrote back.

A few years later I received a phone call from Margaret Westfield, John's niece. John had passed away, but she and her daughter Marina had traveled to Carmel and recovered his files, including all his manuscripts and a detailed log of all his publications from the early sixties on. His landlady had found my letter on his desk. Was I still interested in editing a volume of his stories? Very much so. It turned out Margaret and Marina lived in New Jersey, my home state, and although I was living in New Mexico at the time, I was due to visit my family back east that summer. We made plans.

For the next few years, every time I visited my family, I also made the trek down to Ms. Westfield's home in Haddon Heights, coincidentally the town where the Jersey Devil allegedly attacked a packed trolley car on January 21, 1909—perhaps the largest mass cryptid sighting in American history. A close high school friend, Christine Boccella Santangelo, always accompanied me on these trips, and she became my assistant editor for this archival work, effectively doubling the work we could accomplish during each visit. Together we sifted through two file cabinets of Keefauver's records, which included copies of all his published work back to the early sixties, along with records of the payments he received. He had also kept a detailed log of his sales.

Many of Keefauver's early stories appeared in the sort of publications that Kurt Vonnegut categorized as "beaver magazines" in *Breakfast of Champions*. Although Keefauver had only kept the pages on which his stories appeared, along with the tables of contents that included his name, these presented interesting time capsules, and meant conducting our editorial efforts while navigating through grainy photos of women unfamiliar with either silicone or the razor. By the mid-seventies he had largely moved on to the Pan and Hitchcock anthologies where I had first encountered him.

Among the surprises were the stories that had appeared in more literary venues, such as "Getting to Lord Jesus Is a Powerfully Important Thing," "The Jam," "The Hunt," and "The Tree," all of which were new to me. Although most of these show a dark side, they are not truly macabre. Together they show a different side of Keefauver, and "The Tree" is among his very best works, one of the stories, that like "The Pile of Sand," deserves a second life in anthologies. Regardless of any future publications, the reader new to Keefauver should find many surprises here.

Thus at last you have that long overdue collection of Keefauver's short fiction. It may be 25, 35, even 45 years too late, alas. John may no longer be around to appreciate it, to add this volume to his little brag shelf atop the file cabinets of yellowing tear-sheets from beaver mags, but *you* have it, dear reader. A well-kept secret is revealed—as Joe R. Lansdale wrote in his introduction, it's like discovering "that aliens had been living in your basement all along." We hope you enjoy this close encounter with Keefauver's work.

OH WELL WHAT THE HELL

(A SORT OF CONEY ISLAND OF THE HIND)

In San Franciscotown
    there's a cooled-up cat
  name of Lawrenched Forgetti
    (or something like that)
      who writes poetry
      street poetry
      walking-along poetry
   not the kind that sits around all day
         looking at its navel
      the oral message kind
      jazz poetry
        of the stepped-
           on
            soul
    beat
    complete

telling you all about the icky square world
      with its
            drunk clotheslines
            grappling with hot legs
            in rollaway beds
    and its beat-up landscape of
            mindless supermarkets
            with steamheated carrots
            protesting
   a honeyless world of square toiletseats
            never sat on
            (even by las vegas virgins
            tampaxed and disowned)
            a world waiting for someone
                        to push a mushroom button
and make bombed cadillacs rain thru trees

For cadillac ashes
         are what that square type man
                   was really wailing about
     when he kept talking and talking
              from that catless place
                   name of Galilee
only trouble was they cooled him
           until he was hanging dead
                a shame
                and we're to blame
so our circus souls go marching on
stuffed soldiers carrying a sawdust cross

Oh well
        what the hell

Like when they were putting up that statue
                in front of a church
                                in San Franciscotown
        and not a goddamn bird was singing

I mean
        oh well
                what the hell

Like that man who painted
                The Horse with Violin in Mouth
        then jumped on the horse
                        and rode away
                                waving that violin
        and then of all the goddamn things to do
                        he gave it to a plugged-up virgin
        and there were no strings attached

I mean
        oh well
                what the hell

What Forgetti of San Franciscotown is trying to
                                        tell you
                                        yell to you
        is that this life ain't supposed to be a circus
        attended by
        governed by
                make-believe monks in silktights
                monkeys with teacuphandle tails
                horny hiawathas
                                drinking out of horny-rimmed glasses
                                lipsticked with yesterday's mud
                                                or dirty suds
                babooned ladies
                and gorillaed men
        ain't
            but it is

We just gotta stop chomping down
                            on these fake
                                    Last Suppers
we gotta
        take the locks off our pants
                        and start slaying old ladies
                                        and
                                            young lays
            and make the old ones young again
            and make the young ones late again
            making them all
                    sweet
                    and oh well
                    what the hell

He says we gotta arise
               even though we're not workers
                              of any world
                              of any thing
          we're not even of
          we're a not
                    without a negative to hang our not on

We're a can of sterno that won't burn
an empty bottle of muscatel
we'd recite from broken bibles
                    but we don't have a tongue
we're sisters in the streets
               with our brassieres on backwards
we're dogs listening for our master's voice
we're Christmas trees with no balls
we're Wise Men praising Lord Calver whiskey
we're Bing Crosby
               groaning
we're hi-ya housewives
          veneered in nylon snobberies
                    trying to lacquer-up all the scenes
we're in a whorehouse
          with no whores
                    just bores
                    sores
                    and unfound doors
we're sunk
     junk
     when we let fall a sock
               it clanks

What we gotta do is goose George Washington
                                     in the seat of his cherry tree
          and then give Joan a pat
                         on her Arc

We have only dishonorable intentions
                              not to mention
                                          disintentions
               we're dis people plainly

In short
we're constipations

But
     as Forgetti says

Oh well
          what the hell

~

NOTES ON "OH WELL WHAT THE HELL"

Originally published in the November 1958 issue of *Playboy* (Vol. 5, No. 11, pp. 30-32). This piece, "The Daring Old Maid on the Flying Trapeze," and "Thanks..." (a.k.a. "The Soap Cat") are the only early Keefauver publications I have been able to identify that do not appear in the meticulous record of his professional sales that he began in 1960 (even his first published novel, *Tormented Virgin,* receives an oblique mention via a note regarding the payment he received for it). Although Keefauver went on to become a regular contributor to *Playboy*'s "Ribald Classics" column, submitting rewritten versions of risqué tales by earlier authors such as Apuleius and Boccaccio, he never again received a byline for his own work in that lucrative venue. Given this auspicious and unusual beginning (a poem no less—how often did *Playboy* run poetry?—and before the centerfold), it may seem strange that he continued only in that limited capacity. As no new information is forthcoming, we must accept this mystery.

Obviously, this piece begins as a parody of Lawrence Ferlinghetti's "A Coney Island of the Mind," but ultimately it stands on its own. The editor (likely Hugh M. Hefner himself) offers an insightful introduction to the poem that remains apt: "Keefauver...has written for us an appreciative parody that not only echoes, joshes and synthesizes the original, but also comes comfortably close to being an insightful poem in its own right." Over 60 years later these words remain an accurate description of the piece. Like *Playboy* itself, Keefauver occupied a liminal space between the true counterculture and the bourgeoisie, satirizing both from an isolated position somewhere in between, and "Oh Well What the Hell" exemplifies that standpoint in all regards.

THE DARING OLD MAID ON THE FLYING TRAPEZE

1 SLEEP

WAKEFULLY FLAT AMID WIDE UNIVERSALS, trying laughter for size, so tired, the dragging end of all, of Gilbert and yes of Sullivan, cobwebbed teeth, memory, hot, the feet of Paris, the pains of Jericho, much hunting on the streets, hunting the color of water, sea and symphony, a ping-pong table in the Eiffel Tower, always hunting, tired hunting, alarm clock and the dull Jazz of sawdust, conversation with a tulip in a teacup, in the river Nile, in an Austin-Healey, the roar of Elvis Presley, and the flying trapeze.

This trapezed earth, the swing of one who flew, rope without knots, bubbled red sweat, bubbled knot, white knots and black clouds, caged ox, ox-tails and Milquetoast with rolled bread baking sleeves, death with no space, Mickey Spillane and Little Orphan Annie, polished mathematics and onion soup, burps, and the flying trapeze.

The sly whistle of an old maid, unseen but seeing, sawdust squall in the circus tent, covering the chess, hushing the queen, ploughing the king, breaking the Titanic, Lords of London weeping, Joe McCarthy, little boy with boots on, tomorrow isn't Monday, no parking in the tent, and the flying trapeze.

O swift moment with the greatest: it is ploughed, the trapezed earth is again now.

2 WAKE

SHE (THE LIVING) DRESSED AND didn't shave, grinning at herself instead of at a mirror. Fat, she said; where is my talcum? Coffee-colored sky, Pacific Ocean and fog, the clank of a passing Austin-Healey, people going to the city, the circusless city, again and again, days and days, scotch and soda.

Dressed in her trapeze clothes, she moved in a fast waddle down the stairs to the street, thinking damn suddenly, it is only in sleep that we live, it is only in sleep that we are awake, only in sleep that we don't sleep, that we meet ourselves and our fathers and our mothers and a whole mess of people, that the upstairs becomes now and last Tuesday becomes here.

She nosed into the day, alert, making a definite trapeze noise with her trapezed heels, seeing plainly with both eyes the unreal real of the surface truth of buildings, the poo-poo truth of superficial reality. She snorted, and her mind helplessly sang, *She flies through the air with the greatest; the daring old maid on the flying trapeze.* Laughing, she belched with all the real might of her being. It was truly a reality morning: coffee-colored, brisk, and briskless, too; a morning for ingrown real; ah, William Saroyan, she said, how I long for your trapezed music.

In a far gutter now she saw a penny near, a penny dated 1923, and she examined it closely, this penny with Lincoln's profile stamped there. This is a real penny, she said; but Lincoln is not real, and at this she shuddered. But it was not a real shudder, because with a penny she could buy anything. I will buy an Austin-Healey, she thought. I will buy a circus tent, or more pennies. Or I will weigh myself. Then, immediately, came another shudder, a real shudder this time. Sawdust, she spat; I've been eating it too much.

It was good to be poor; but it was not good to be hungry. To be hungry was like having an empty stomach, like pennies not having a taste. She tasted the penny. It tasted like Lincoln. It tasted better than sawdust. How hungry she was. Every meal was coffee and cigarettes and circus sawdust, and now she had no more sawdust, and there were no cigarettes in the park that could be cooked as weeds are cooked.

Bluntly, she was starving. Big as she was, she was starving because all she had in her was circus sawdust, and now there were no more circuses. Sawdust had never been enough, either; she knew that now. Yet, she laughed; she laughed at the whole mess of unreal real. But there were still so many *Billboards* she should read before she died. She remembered the young circus press agent in a tented hospital, a small man sick with a lost ear from the sandpaper lick of a real lion, who had said desperately, I would like to see my ear once before I die. And she thought earnestly, I ought at least to read Little Orphan Annie once again, or perhaps *Playboy*.

From a hill she saw the city squatting in the east where once a circus sat, a tent, tents, bursting with her kind, tented people, now gone, and she was outside of it now, pretty damn sure she'd never get into another tent, now that tents were folded and hocked away. Here she was, a fat old maid of 62, tentless, circusless, with nothing but a big belly full of sawdust and coffee. It was a disgusting thing. Yet, peculiarly, it was not saddening, this thought. Pondering, she pondered to herself, pretty damn quick I ought to write *An Application for Permission for an Old Maid to Fly with the Greatest.*

She accepted, though, the thought of dying without pity for herself, or for the young press agent, or for Lincoln, or for Mickey Spillane. Her rent was paid; there was still tomorrow; there would be more pennies. She could always go where other homeless sawdust-filled old maids went. She would go to Madison Avenue. There her life would be a private life.

Through the air on the flying trapeze, her private mind hummed. Extremely amusing it was, hilariously hilarious. (Why, she did not know.) A trapeze over Madison Avenue; between the tents of Madison Avenue she would fly. She laughed, and real sawdust rumbled.

And I have a penny of Lincoln, too, she said. She had always wanted to polish Lincoln, and tonight she would polish him with sawdust (she would find a few crumbs in the secret places of her room) and coffee until he was truly an Abraham.

She had waddled into the city by now, with people, yet without and outside of these people; these were not her people; these were not tented people, fliers and lions; these people were not real; they were reflections in store windows. She saw herself in a store window, herself dressed in trapeze clothes, bulging with sawdust food. It was a disappointing sight. She in-bulged as much as she could; she walked on her trapezed toes. Still, it was a disappointing sight.

With real discipline she passed restaurants without peeking inside, until finally she came to a building which she entered. On the third floor she waddled into the office of an employment agency. The place was jammed with old maids, all dressed in trapeze clothes, all waiting for trapeze interviews. After hours of waiting, she was questioned by a young press agent who had only one ear.

What can you do? he said.

Fly, she said simply.

You mean you are a pilot?

No, I am not a pilot, she said simply.

Then, you mean you have wings?

I do not have wings, she said simply. I mean that I can fly on a trapeze.

She spoke simply. All this was not real, and she was. If it would make him happy, she would get wings.

I see, he said. Unfortunately, he went on, there are no openings for trapeze fliers today. We will get in touch with you, however, if there are. We have your address.

They had her address, she thought as she waddled back onto the street. That was good, that they had her address. She had a penny and a sawdust stomach, and they had her address. The matter was closed for another day. She felt a relief. She was a living old maid in need of money with which to go on being a living old maid, and there was no way of getting money except by flying with the greatest; and there was no greatest. Thus, the matter was closed. She laughed, and the gods rumbled.

Counting, she passed countless restaurants on her way to the Y.M.C.A. She had come to the Y.M.C.A. many times before, when she was younger and was looking looking looking, and she had flown with some of the boys, but they were never the greatest. Now, though, she came to the Y.M.C.A. for ink and paper on which she would write her *Application*.

She worked on her writing for most of an hour, but then the ink turned to sawdust and the paper began to fly, and she felt weak and rumbly (she had eaten little since she had reached the age of 59). Hurriedly, in her waddling way, she left the "Y" and went across the street into a park where she washed her penny in a fountain, then rolled it in the grass. This was good, rolling a Lincoln penny in the grass, but it was not nearly as good as eating. She watched a little young lady wearing a shawl throw sawdust to a group of birds. When the little young lady skipped away, the shawl by itself kept throwing sawdust to the group of birds. She (the living old maid) knew now that something was wrong: it was impossible to ask a shawl for some of the sawdust. Truly her life lacked precision.

She went now into a library and read *Billboard*. But soon *Billboard* dissolved in her hands, and she felt herself dizzily flying, though not with the greatest. She rushed back to the park and began to roll her penny, but the shawl kept throwing sawdust to the birds, and this was a bothering thing. It was time now to begin the long waddle back to her room. She yawned; she'd take a nap as soon as she got home. She was tired; she'd carried her sawdust a long way.

When she arrived home, though, her mind was alert, as if it were a real mind, as if it wanted something real to do. She made coffee, and used it to wash her penny; then she drank the coffee, which was better coffee now, with Lincoln in it. She smiled; she was happy drinking the coffee that Lincoln made. Pennies were good for many things. If she only had more of them. Wasn't there something else she could sell? She looked about her bare room. Her trapeze was gone, the one that had hung so many years from the ceiling. And her net, the one she'd slept on. And the sawdust. And her trapeze clothes. All sold. And all her *Billboards*; forty-nine of them for sixty-five cents. She felt angry and sad and dramatic. Then she ruined the whole damn thing by belching a real belch. And she had to smile.

Smiling, she yawned, and said, There is nothing to do but sleep, and thought, Thank God. She threw the coffee-making penny onto her pallet, then sagged down beside it and waited for her real self to be gone from her body so that it, the self, could turn into something else. Anything; it didn't much matter. She was due for a change.

Fingering her penny, she waited a long time for a change. Waited and waited. But nothing changed. She didn't become a fish, or a rat, or a snake, or a man. Absolutely nothing happened. The city didn't burn. And as far as she knew, there were no rioting crowds. It was quiet as hell, really. Finally, she got disgusted and went to sleep.

~

NOTES ON "THE DARING OLD MAID ON THE FLYING TRAPEZE"

Originally published in the Summer 1959 issue of *Big Table* (No. 2, pp. 7-12). That historic, but short-lived and mostly forgotten journal, whose total run was only five issues, was primarily a vehicle for Beat writers (the title came from a suggestion by Kerouac). As we have already seen, Keefauver kept daylight between himself and the Beats, but in his early work he was clearly "Beat-adjacent"—quite literally in this story, which opened a Table of Contents including Allen Ginsberg, William S. Burroughs, Brother Antoninus, and Paul Blackburn...and closing with Lawrence Ferlinghetti, whose best-known work Keefauver had parodied (or paid homage to) a year earlier, in *Playboy*.

Although Keefuaver's files do not go back to the Fifties, they do include a letter from *Big Table* editor Paul Carroll dated April 1, 1970, offering $25.00 for the rights to reprint the story in the Big Table Reader, planned for later that year. A note at the bottom in the author's handwriting reads: "I gave permission, but book not published."

KALI

I KNOW WHEN IT BEGAN, the nightmare, and I know why. I know its past, its present. And I know its tomorrow. I know it will never end.

This I accept. This I bow to. This is mine to live with.

But what I shall never accept, cannot accept, is the abnormality. Blood gives me warmth. The edge of a knife, used, brings relief. Death is a pleasant thing.

The horror is this: *terrible things give me happiness.*

So strange, so terribly strange: I, who have always had an aversion to blood; I, who have always been a lover of animals; I, a gentle man, a teacher of children. I am these things, I swear it. Yet, for the last few weeks—months, I suppose; time has become meaningless—I have fed, as if it were dope, on a nightmare that, shorn of the occult, the mysticism of India, is nothing more than brutality.

A girl, of course. A woman, a quiet, powerful creature, a mysterious, manila-skinned, syrupy-eyed woman of India. Like a flower she came out of the poverty of the land and drew me down into horror, brutality, blood. This was her present. This is my nightmare.

I suppose I should have suspected something, or, at least, been more hesitant, when she told me her name was Kali. I knew that Kali, to the Hindu, is the goddess of destruction and death as well as of motherhood. But, at the time, I had become too enchanted with her beauty and her gentleness—yes, *gentleness*—to do more than give a passing thought to the name, to the haunting musicality of it.

I met Kali in Calcutta on a hot, summer morning, just under two months ago now. An elementary school teacher in San Francisco, I had saved for many months for a vacation in India. The mysticism, the antiquity, the religion, the humble, unmoving strength of its people had attracted me since childhood, and I had been determined to visit the country. I flew into Calcutta one June evening. The following morning I met Kali next to the Government Tourist Office on Old Court House Street.

I immediately sensed her business. She was an unlicensed guide who simply stood outside the tourist office and collared visitors before they could get inside. Of course, I should have been wary of her because she was not officially connected with the office. But she was a beauty in her sari, an explosion of color. Asphalt-black hair, glittering teeth, eyes like shimmering puddles of warmth. In short, she was a beautiful young woman, and I was a young man—a hungry man, a bachelor, handsome and intelligent enough to be choosy.

She stopped me cold with her brisk yet smiling, "Good morning, sir. May I show you Calcutta?" Her English accent clashed strangely with the India of her sari.

"Perhaps," I said, grinning easily with her. I liked her immediately—unfortunately.

Very quickly then she went through a list of attractions that I, as a tourist, should see, pointing out the merits of each and her qualifications as a first-class guide for them. "I'm cheap too." Her laugh popped in me like a champagne bubble—and right at that point, yes, right then there passed between us an understanding, an empathy, a current—call it what you will. It was the thing that men and women since all time have felt when his or her key fits, *exactly*, the other's lock. I wanted to touch her.

Yet, her professionalism, however unbefitting, did not totally disappear until I told her I wished to visit the Kali Temple. As I look back—as I have done so many times, going over and over each detail of that first meeting and my subsequent deterioration—I realize that of all the tourist attractions she mentioned, she *repeated* only the name of one, Kali Temple, dwelling on it much longer and much more appreciatively than on the others. It was clear that the temple was easily her first choice. Yes, I see it now—too late: she wanted very badly to go there herself.

When I agreed to go with her to the temple, partly to please her and partly because I had read of the goat sacrifices I would see there, she became enchantingly charming and dropped all pretense of professional detachment, and off we went, chatting happily, to Kali Temple.

If only I had retained a sliver of my normal cautiousness (I had, prior to meeting Kali, always considered myself a thinking, rather than an emotional person), I would have hesitated to go with her if for no other reason than that an Indian woman accosting a strange man on the streets, especially a foreigner, was considered, even in a business venture, as a most abnormal and suspicious action in that country. Too, I had shrugged off a negative shake of the head by a tourist office employee; he had come to the door of the office as Kali and I walked away, and I had seen—yet ignored—his glance of warning.

I forget the name of the street the temple was on, but the location is not important. I remember it was some distance from Dalhousie Square, the nerve center of Calcutta, and that, dodging an occasional sacred cow, we went there by taxi through dirty, narrow streets, choked with carts, white-shawled men, and sari-wearing women. A number of raggedy, filthy beggars were in front of the temple, a glittering, ornate building, its walls surfaced with polished bits of gold and silver-colored glass, richly incongruous to the bleak poverty which surrounded it. When the scavengers saw me, a foreigner, getting out of a taxi, they swarmed around me. But, seeing Kali, they immediately shrank back, lowering their eyes, frightened. I was astounded. She had done nothing, said nothing; her expression had not changed. Her very presence frightened the beggars. I was quite impressed at the time: later—now—I curse myself for not recognizing the evil in her. The beggars did; but, of course, they knew her; I did not.

As I look back, I even thought little, if anything of the obeisance and fear shown to Kali (the woman) by the faithful inside the sparkling temple.

When these poorly dressed people shied away from her, evading her eyes, making a way for her approach, I thought it was simply because she was a guide with a rich foreigner. The worshippers quickly laid their *leis*, purchased from flower stalls outside the temple, before goddess Kali and left us relatively alone. It was when I saw Kali's response to the goddess, when I saw the intense, devoted expression that came over the young woman's face, her seeming fusion with the goddess—it was here that I suppose I felt the first real uneasiness about my guide.

The goddess, wife of Shiva the Destroyer, one god of the Hindu trilogy, was a horrible creation. A three-eyed, four-armed, gold-colored, four-foot-high image, she had a gaping mouth and protruding tongue; metal snakes coiled around her, and she danced on what appeared to be a corpse. Her earrings depicted dead men, her necklace a string of skulls; her face and breasts were smeared with blood. Two of her four hands held a sword and a severed head, the other two, quaintly, were extended in protection and blessing. For Kali, strangely, is the goddess of motherhood, *and* destruction and death.

I felt a mingling of disgust, curiosity, excitement, and I suppose, fear when I saw the strange image. But as I glanced at Kali, the woman, uneasiness became easily the dominant emotion. She was gazing at the weird goddess with a look of intense concentration, as if she were detached from me, from the faithful, from the world about her. It was as if, yes, as if Kali the woman felt joined to Kali the goddess, fused, as if they had merged in that glittering temple among the filthy, the ragged, and the poor.

I suppose we would have been standing there yet if I had not finally made a move to leave. With my words she seemed to come out of her trance—partially, anyway. She mumbled something in Hindu to the goddess, then reluctantly led me outside. "She is so lovely," she murmured, not looking at me. Even her voice now seemed detached, as if she were talking to only herself. "So powerful."

"In a weird sort of way," I couldn't help but put in.

Kali's expression still had most of its strange, faraway—godlike?—quality. "We will watch the sacrifice now," she said.

As if she didn't realize I was with her, she started walking across the temple grounds towards a wall that surrounded the area. I followed her, by now thinking that she probably came to the temple every day regardless of whether she had a tourist with her or not.

At the time, I thought my interest in goat sacrifices was purely clinical, intellectual, not emotional, certainly not morbid, or, at least, not any more morbid than the attraction of a highway fatality to the crowd that is drawn to the collision scene. Now, however, weeks later, the nightmare still destroying me, I wonder. Out of all the places I could have chosen to visit in Calcutta that morning with Kali, I chose to see the murder of five black goats to goddess Kali.

Bleating, eyes darting with fright, the young animals, one by one, were brought from a nearby pen by the executioner. He wore a blood-spattered tunic; even his unshaved-face was red-dotted, reminding me of the crimson betel stain you see on the streets of Calcutta, spat out by chewers of the nut. The goats, brought to the temple by the faithful making sacrifices that sunny morning, were placed, one by one, on a wooden contraption so that their necks were stretched for the slice of the knife. Their feet were tied. As each goat was placed on the chopping block, worshippers who had brought that particular animal mumbled prayers in Hindi.

A flash of the knife and the head dropped to the ground, spurting blood. Picking it up, the executioner held the head over small copper cups, letting blood pour into each one. Those who had sacrificed the animal came forward and, dipping their fingers into the blood, each put a crimson spot on his forehead, then went to claim the body of the goat. The body had been hung from a hook in the wall surrounding the temple. Gutted, it was taken home and eaten. "No food is wasted in India," Kali told me.

The area was fogged with flies. And every few seconds starving dogs darted to spilled blood and licked it hungrily. The executioner, before he killed each goat, chased the dogs away.

I was both fascinated and repulsed. But my feelings were nothing compared to those of Kali. Her expression, her intensity during the sacrifices was one of complete absorption. Her whole body seemed to strain towards the bloody mess. She was not a spectator. She was fused with the sacrifice, swallowed by it. It was almost as if she herself were the executioner, or, I thought later, more accurately, as if she herself were Kali the goddess receiving the sacrificed goats.

As if she herself were receiving the sacrificed goats. If only I had realized that at the time. If only I had *half* realized it. If only I had suspected.

Again, I was the one who had to make the move to leave.

She stayed silent as we left the temple and walked up a street looking for a cab. She walking in flowing dignity, her sari fluttering only slightly, her brilliant eyes abstracted, her expression still dreamlike. "Were you disgusted?" she finally asked.

"Some. A little. Mainly I was fascinated."

Although, as a polite guest in a foreign land, I deliberately played down my feeling of disgust at the killings, my statement contained more truth than I realized at the time.

"Really? Most foreigners are horribly disgusted."

"I'm not the average foreigner," I grinned.

At my words, at my seeming acceptance of the sacrifice, she did something I'll never forget. She touched me. It was only a slight pressure on my wrist, a quick, gentle touch: comradeship, empathy, the link again, the same thing I had felt when I met her. But as I look back, I know what she meant to tell me: that we were—God forbid—alike.

Her smile was very gentle. "In the old days," she said, "men, not goats, were sacrificed to Kali."

I nodded. I felt she was waiting for me to say something more— denounce the sacrifice of men? When I said nothing, her smile grew and, glancing at her more closely, I saw in her eyes a glitter, a powerful sparkling quality, a hunger. Her eyes, as if she were a demanding goddess herself, seemed to swallow me.

And, God have mercy, I wanted to be.

"I'm glad...you feel that way," she murmured. "Very glad."

We walked on in silence. Once her hip brushed against me; it was as if fire had touched my soul.

"I want to show you more of Kali," she said after a taxi had passed. She had not tried to hail it. "That is my name."

"Kali?"

She nodded. "I named myself after the goddess." She smiled, very gently. "As I said, the goddess used to like men. This Kali still does.

"Would you like to come to my room?" she said, not immediately.

EVEN NOW I'M NOT SURE if I actually heard the bleat of the goat when I reached Kali's room or if I imagined it, hearing in my mind, remembering, the voices of the doomed animals at the temple. At any rate, after Kali and I got out of the taxi into a horribly poverty riddled part of the city (streets like sewers of misery), she led me into an alleyway so narrow that when a sacred cow came ambling towards us we had to back up into the street in order to let the bulky female by. Kali lived in a small room in (perhaps I should say *under*) one of a number of unpainted wooden structures that appeared to have been nailed to each other by a drunken carpenter. Her windowless room contained only the barest essentials: a saggy cot, a wooden-legged sofa, a few chairs, a table, a scarred bureau, a lamp, which she lit upon entering. One end of the room was curtained off.

"Please," she said, "sit down. I'll bring you a drink."

She disappeared through a doorway and came back in a moment with a lukewarm glass of dark liquid, but not before I definitely heard again the bleat of a goat. The animal seemed to be very near, and at the time I thought it probably belonged to a neighbor. The sound disturbed me more than a little: it reminded me, of course, of the bloody mess I had just seen at the temple.

"Drink," she said.

"Where's yours?"

"Later."

The stuff tasted odd: tangy yet chalky, heavy as milk of magnesia, salty, non-alcoholic. "What is it?"

She shrugged, smiling gently. "It is for you. Drink. It's very good."

She sat on the sofa beside me and carefully watched me drink half of the liquid. When I put the glass down she slid closer to me, her eyes like honey; I felt her cheek brush mine, her breath warm and rapid. She caressed my neck, very gently, "Drink it all," she said, giving her sari a slight pull, showing golden legs, inching it up just a trifle, not really disrobing, or even starting to, but hinting, implying, smiling, saying, "Hurry, drink it all, I want to show you...Kali." Her smile, goddamn her smile!

I drank, I gulped down the liquid. I was trembling. She was so beautiful...and her smile, her hinting, her urging. So I drank, a fool!

A fool! As soon as I had downed the drink she got up from the sofa and went behind the curtained end of the room. "Wait," she said. "I'll be back in a moment."

A moment? An hour? I'm not sure. The drink went to work immediately. No sooner had she disappeared behind the curtain than I began to feel myself change into a—as close as I can describe it—a dreamlike state. The room, the things in it, lost their harshness. I seemed to merge with them. My body seemed to be weightless; when I moved my arm it felt as if it were floating. I felt deliciously warm, particularly in my stomach. I had a great sense of well-being, a godlike quality: all was good and right with the world. I was powerful; I could do anything. I was a god. My sense of smell went wild: my nose was assailed by strange smells, odors totally new to me—except one: I smelled in that room something I had smelled less than an hour ago at Kali Temple: I smelled a goat. A goat was in the room.

I was not at all disturbed by the realization of the animal's presence. It struck me as quite normal; I was a god (Siva?), and to me, unto my most high, most powerful presence came all creatures. Come unto me, goat; let me bless you; come to me and ye shall be saved.

Ridiculous? Perhaps now—to you.

Nothing, I tell you, nothing! was out of place, was beyond normality. I swear it! In my condition I did no wrong! I swear it!

And so when I saw Kali come out from behind the curtain dressed as a horrible Kali the goddess, when I saw that she carried a young black goat, when she handed me the goat and a butcher knife, when she told me I was to sacrifice the animal to her, I saw nothing unusual in it. I was a god and all was right with the world. Blood is warmth. Blood is peace. Blood is milk.

Believe me!

As nearly as possible, Kali the woman had tried to appear as Kali the goddess. I have tried to shut the sight from my mind. I cannot, just as I cannot begin to understand why she would do such a thing, *want* to do such a thing. She gave me a reason (as you will see), but her *real* reason lay buried deep within the mystery of India. Call it insanity, if you wish. Who *really* knows? She had devised a set of arms (they looked to be those of a mannequin), which she had attached to her shoulder blades somehow, thus giving herself four arms. Fastened to her forehead by a band was a glass eye. She kept her tongue protruded, her mouth open. What appeared to be stuffed snakes were wrapped around her arms, her earrings and necklace looked as if they were made of bones. One real hand held a knife, the other a human skull (not hard to find in India), and her artificial hands were extended in what could be called protection and blessing. Other than these attachments, she was naked, golden brown in the light of the lamp, shimmering, shiny. She had oiled her body.

And, oh God, I desired the creature!

I remember the warmth of the baby goat in my hands, his trembling and pitiful whimpers, almost human, his struggles; but I, a god, felt only love for this "child" who had come forth to be sacrificed, voluntarily, out of love for me, his god, out of love for Kali, his goddess. Oh, the power and love for all mankind, I felt. Believe me!

Believe me, as I believed Kali when she pulled back the curtain and stepped upon a small foot-high platform and in a voice musky, muffled, as if she were speaking from a great distance, said, "I am Kali, goddess of motherhood, bride of death and destruction," her eyes raised to the heavens, her beautiful breasts lifting.

I believed! and I was so very, very happy.

"I Kali, accept this sacrifice. In the name of my son, I accept. My only son, my sacrificed son, I accept. I, Kali, goddess of motherhood, bride of death and destruction, accept this goat as I accepted my only son, my sacrificed son."

I believed! I accepted the story of her sacrificed son. To me (then!) it was so normal, so magnificent! A sacrificed son. Of course! Goddess Kali, until about one hundred years ago, accepted men as sacrifices. Of course Kali would sacrifice her own son. What greater glory could there be than this! What greater glory...

Her eyes came down and flowed into me and she said, "Now."

Without hesitation, almost hurrying, feeling great happiness, I pulled the blade of the knife across the throat of the goat.

BUT THIS IS NOT MY NIGHTMARE. This led to my nightmare, true. This *started* the torment that is slowly driving me insane, that has driven me to write this...confession, I suppose it must be called. But this hell itself was not my nightmare.

The torment—the guilt, the shock, the disgust—came immediately with the murder of the goat. As its blood gushed down my hand, dripped onto my clothes, my dreamlike state, my hypnotic condition, abruptly disappeared. It was as if the act of cutting, along with the actual sight and feel of blood, had sliced, too, into my hypnotized soul and let in the brisk air of reality. As if I had awakened out of a dream, I suddenly found myself holding a dead goat in front of a hopelessly insane woman.

From that point on, until I reached my Calcutta hotel, nothing is clear. The shock, the realization of what I had done, numbed me—fortunately, I suppose. I remember, hazily, dropping the still-warm animal (I can, even now, hear the dead thump of it hitting the floor), looking in horror at my bloody hands, then turning, half crazed, and running from the room. Somehow—I have no idea how—I reached my hotel. The next thing I remember is scrubbing blood off my hands, for hours it seems, scrubbing long after all traces of it had disappeared, filling and refilling my bathroom sink, trying to scrub away horror, disgust, guilt.

I failed. Horror, disgust, guilt—they remained, they still remain, now, here in San Francisco. I have stopped teaching. It is impossible for me now to associate with the innocent, to have their minds in my hands—bloody hands. I do nothing now but sit in my room and drink, dreading the coming of night—and sleep. I sit in my room and listen—for the sound of a goat.

It began immediately, the nightmare. (I mean the conventional nightmare, the one of sleep, the lesser one.) That first night, the night after the day with Kali, I'll never forget. A night of sleepless horror. I couldn't pry my mind away from what I had done, from every detail of its terror, from my meeting Kali to my rushing from her room. Asleep or awake, it was all I could think about, feel about. And this night was only the first of many.

I cut short my visit to India and returned to San Francisco. The nightmare persisted. I took sleeping pills. The nightmare continued. I sought out psychiatric help. The nightmare did not stop. Every night. Every night. I saw blood on my hands—imagined it. On my clothes, although I had long ago thrown away *all* the clothing I had worn the day I was with Kali. I gave up my teaching job. I began to drink heavily. The nightmare persisted.

Then I found relief—of sorts. A relief that, though doing away with the conventional nightmare, led to one much more hideous. In brief (I must end this), I stopped the lesser nightmare (if you can call it that) but started one that is now driving me relentlessly insane. Driving me insane *because I find happiness in horror.*

The manner in which I might find relief had been apparent, if not obvious, to me for some time. I, of course, fought doing it—the act—from the very beginning. Each day, however, as my torment increased, I came closer to the act. Finally, after undergoing a number of particularly intense and thorough sessions of psychiatric analysis, all with totally negative results, I decided, my psychiatrist concurring, to try that one thing that might save me.

It didn't. It merely replaced one horror with a far greater one, a horror from which I gained happiness. The second terror did not begin immediately, however. At first, I felt relief, my original nightmare vanished. That first night, after committing the act, I slept soundly, the first such night of sleep I'd had since my day with Kali in Calcutta. The second night after the act, however, I had a trace of my original nightmare; and the third night, an increase of it. By the fourth night after the act the nightmare was back with all its terror.

So I committed the act a second time, in my hotel room again. My reaction to it was repetitious: I gained temporary relief, my nightmare vanished at first, then gradually increased until by the fourth night, it was back in its full horror.

I repeated the act a number of times. Each act brought the same results. It was obvious that the only way I was to find happiness, even temporary, was to continue my barbaric acts *every night for the rest of my life*.

And with this knowledge, this realization of my depravity, I lost all hope.

I am lost. I sit now on the edge of my bathtub, my bare feet inside it. The goat—black, of course—is before me, feet bound, in the tub. I pick up the knife. (What else is there to do?) I bend over the goat. I place the blade against his neck. I cut.

~

NOTES ON "KALI"

Originally published in *The Fifth Pan Book of Horror Stories*, edited by Herbert van Thal (1964, Pan Books, Ltd. pp. 189-200), and reprinted in *Oriental Tales of Terror*, edited by J.J. Strating (1971, Fontana, pp. 115-126). This story marked the beginning of a four-book run in the iconic Pan series, which may well have put Keefauver in the sights of Robert Arthur, who edited the Hitchcock volumes.

I vacillated some on whether to include either "Kali" or "The Most Precious" in this volume. Both stories have their moments, but overall they present obvious examples of the sort of Western othering of Asia and the Middle East that critic Edward W. Said described in his landmark 1978 work *Orientalism*. Ultimately however, I felt it important to include all of Keefauver's Pan stories here, as they represent an important phase of his career in which he engaged more fully with the darker elements of his fiction. These stories also reflect the period when the author had begun traveling extensively, so his descriptions, unlike those of some European and American authors, were based at least in part on personal experience and observation.

GIVE ME YOUR COLD HAND

I T IS THE WAITING THAT is hardest—now that the numbness is wearing off. The waiting, as one shovelful after another of earth is thrown out of the hole, as each swing of a pick digs deeper into the wet, floodlighted ground. Will they never reach the body, if one is actually there? Can't they be satisfied with *one* body, the one that lies, covered now, near the hole? They dig so slowly, these poor sweating cops. I feel sorry for them.

I should feel sorry for myself. Or George. He stands beside me, handcuffed to my left wrist, so excited he seems about to wet his pants. His eyes shine, his large shoulders are hunched and tense, his neck muscles like thick, wet ropes. His hands, easily a third larger than mine, and I'm not a small man, keep jerking, unconsciously, anxiously, as if he is helping the cops dig. His beard glistens with rain. He hasn't shaved since he started hearing the voices. A beard, a body like a giant—yet he is a child, as surely as I am a man, a teacher in the Monterey school system—as surely as I am a fool named Tony!

A fool! Only a fool would have let himself become involved in such a miserable mess. Only a fool would have stayed with Anita—at least as long as I did. Only a fool would be standing among a bunch of digging cops in the middle of the night with summer fog coming in from the Pacific nearby. A fool, with one dead person beside him, waiting to see if another is found.

A fool from the beginning, overwhelmed by a woman, although any man might be overwhelmed—easily—by Anita. What was not forgivable in me was that I stayed with her *after* I knew her evil.

It seems unbelievable now that I met her only a few months ago on Carmel Beach, some hundred miles south of San Francisco on the Monterey Peninsula. Ironically, I was beside another hole then, too, and death was in it. A poor bastard—he must have been a nut—had dug a deep shaft in the sand as a makeshift dressing-room for himself, his wife, and their three children. Childlike, he had tunneled out from the base of the hole later in the afternoon. The tunnel had collapsed while he was inside; he had suffocated.

I was one of the frantic diggers who had tried to save him, and Anita was among the spectators. I noticed her immediately—her body, her expression. She was taller than most women, large-boned, her sun-stained body richly curved, sexually powerful—a strong, proud woman. But it was her expression that stuck like glue, that made me again and again glance at her. All the bystanders carried pity in their faces—*they cared*—but Anita's was cold as the ocean, unchanging except once: a smile, I swear, flicked through her cheeks.

Of course, at the time I thought I had been mistaken. No one could smile at such a horrible death. It wasn't human. Little did I know...

The man's body was removed from the beach, and spectators gradually drifted away, speaking in whispers as if they were afraid death would overhear. Anita didn't leave.

"Men choose stupid ways to die," she said in a husky Scandinavian-accented voice. "So filthy, covered with sand. Sand in his hair, in his eyes, all over his hands. He had such beautiful hands, did you notice?"

Then, for the first time, I saw the darning needle. Glittering in the afternoon sun, it was stuck in the left shoulder strap of her bathing suit, just above one breast. As she spoke, she raised her hand and swiftly—unconsciously, it appeared—stroked her index finger over its long silvery surface, as if she were wetting her finger on her tongue, or, as I came to understand later, as if she were touching her being, her soul, her sex.

Anita took me home with her that afternoon. Within days we were lovers. Even now, months later, I'm not sure why it happened so quickly, or how it came to happen at all. Who knows *exactly* why a certain man at a certain time jumps into the velvet well of a certain woman? Why she wants him there? What is the *exact* combination? Who *really* knows?

No matter now. Too late. It happened. Eyelids pinned, ears plugged, mind shellacked, I jumped into her. She was Swedish, a blonde mountain of sex with ocean-blue eyes. I ached to climb her and swim in those eyes. She had come from Sweden only four years ago; most men she had known there were blonds. I was dark, olive-skinned, black-haired—like her husband, Nelson. Perhaps that was why she wanted me, took me inside. Of course, it was more than this. It *must* be more than this, I kept—keep—telling myself. With Anita, you were never sure of anything.

I reminded her of her husband in another respect: I had large hands. Twenty years of handling footballs, basketballs, the last few years as a physical education instructor, had made them into powerful weapons. "It is nice to have strong hands caress me," she said from the beginning, stroking them over and over. "Nelson beat me with his."

He had left her, she told me. He had gone to San Francisco one morning less than a year ago and had never come back. They had been married not much more than a year when he disappeared. She had never heard from him again. She thought he was dead. And she was glad. He was a bastard, a rich, cruel bastard with a two-hundred-thousand-dollar home in Pebble Beach. He beat her with his million-dollar hands.

Or so she told me.

Of this I was sure—that Nelson had tremendous hands. She showed me a full-length photograph of him, and her. He was a small man, skinny, shorter than Anita, but his hands were hams with knuckles, clubs, abnormally disproportionate to the rest of his body. And nestled in one of the clubs, completely hidden, was one of Anita's hands.

I didn't see the needle the first time I looked at the picture, but, weeks later, after I was beginning to suspect—and fear—the meaning of the piece of glistening steel, I looked at the photograph again and, yes, stuck in the front of her dress was the long darning needle, the same one she had in her bathing suit the day we met on Carmel Beach, the same one she *invariably* had stitched in her clothing.

"Why always the needle?" I finally asked. It had pricked me while I kissed her.

She shrugged and lightly smiled. "It is mine," she said—and that was all, as if that was enough explanation for any man.

I think that it was with that question that I, for the first time, saw in her eyes a hardening, a withdrawal, a shutting-out, like fog coming in to shore from the Pacific. And as I got to know her better—if that is *really* possible—I saw again and again her ability to detach herself from me—and from everybody but herself, I suppose. She'd be talking to me when suddenly— as if a key word of mine, or hers, had unlocked a door that only she could enter—she'd leave me, psychologically, her eyes fogged, her expression appearing as if she were asleep. Even in bed, after a frenzy of loving, I would find myself totally left out of her thoughts, her consciousness. Once it even happened while we were in the act of love. She simply died on me. Even her body seemed to lose its warmth.

Rejection. I felt it even from George—at first. Later, strangely, we became friends of a sort. The day Anita took me home from the beach I felt the man's resentment, his jealousy. I first thought that possibly he might have been her lover, too, but I soon gave the idea up. When we drove up to her Pebble Beach home, near Carmel, and George opened the massive front gate for the Cadillac convertible, his expression immediately became sullen when he saw me in the car with Anita. Childlike resentment was in his voice when he acknowledged Anita's introduction of me.

The shaggy-haired, burly, bearded man—he was so hidden by hair it was difficult to tell if he was twenty or forty years old—lived in a kind of guest house behind the main home. He was the gardener, the handyman, a stupid, childlike gorilla of a man who usually talked in grunted monosyllables.

Anita told me she had hired him a few months before her husband disappeared. "They never did like each other," she said. "Nelson treated him as if he were a dirty shoeshine boy. He wanted to get rid of him." I remember the brightness that came into her eyes then. "But George was mine. (Like her needle? I thought later.) I was the one who had found him. He was working in Monterey on a fishing boat. As soon as I saw him, I knew he was for me. He had such large, strong hands." The brightness in her eyes reached such an extreme then that I felt uncomfortable. "With those hands, I knew he could do anything around the house I wanted him to do. Anything."

Hands. Nelson's, George's, mine. Anita seemed to gain nourishment from them, although I didn't realize the extent of what they meant to her until, I suppose, it was too late. Or so I rationalize, like all men must do. In any event, I realize now that one of the reasons, certainly, that Anita chose me as a lover—as well as other men—was because of my large, powerful hands.

Her home, too, was large and powerful. Built out of stone hauled up from the nearby beach, it reminded me of a castle. Its high, narrow, triangular-topped windows, its four turret-like corners on the roof, its great wooden door with large metal hinges, its moat-like ditch—all were the work of some eccentric during the twenties. Wind moaned through huge pines and cypresses circling the house, except on the ocean side. Inside, ceilings were high, floors and walls were bare stone, and a fireplace was in almost every room. At night, in the main room, firelight danced on a suit of armor.

Anita's bedroom faced the ocean, and there we threw ourselves against each other in a frenzy of lovemaking, violently, like the surf crashing against the shore outside. Afterwards, she would take my hands and press them to her breasts. "Your hands are as strong as waves," she'd say. "Give me their strength."

Yet, once, cupping my hands as usual, she murmured, "Even waves die," and, trembling suddenly, she reached for her needle on the bedstand.

At night she always kept the piece of steel on the stand. Increasingly, I became bothered by its presence. Often it sat gleaming in a puddle of moonlight, naked too. She refused to put it elsewhere, just as she refused not to wear it in her clothing. She would not talk of it. She simply said, "No," to my requests—then pleas—that she put it away. I stopped mentioning it, of course. I realized her sensitivity, its importance—too late.

Anita, the needle, George, hands. If only I had understood these things as I understand them now. Handcuffed to George, watching the poor, sweating cops dig their hole deeper, I feel a great sadness, a loss; so much has been wasted: George, Anita, me—and, yes, Nelson, too. I don't know whether I'll be glad if they find a body at the bottom of the hole, or if they don't. And the covered one lying beside me?—I suppose it is better that it is there.

Fear. It is hard to say when I first felt it. It came slowly, kept back, rationalized out by my passion for Anita. I think it began to nibble on me the first time I heard George moaning outside. I was leaving Anita for the night, walking to my car in the backyard. He was behind the main house, not far from his own quarters; his voice wailed to the moon as I walked towards him and my car. As soon as he heard me, he became silent. He was sitting on the ground next to a newly planted flower garden (not too far from where I stand now, in fact). Beside him, her head on his lap, was Sags, Anita's old bloodhound. I asked him what was the matter. He wouldn't answer. He let his cabbage head drop until his chin was almost on his keg-like chest, his uncut hair matted over the collar of a ragged jacket.

"Is there anything I can do? Are you ill? Do you want me to call Anita?"

"No," he finally said, spitting out the word with disgust. "I don't like her no more. She's bad." Broodingly, he petted Sags with a hand as big as Nelson's, bigger than mine; the dog responded with a feeble wag of her tail. "She told me to do something tonight that's bad."

I let his words pass. They were typical—childlike jealousies, passing angers. Once George told me Anita had chased him with her needle; I, of course, didn't believe him—then. Little did I know...

"You better go to bed, George. You'll catch cold out here."

"I'm listening now." His voice had become sullen.

Stupidly, I asked him to what. If only I had kept my mouth shut; it would have at least kept the fear from starting so soon.

"Mr. Nelson talks to me every night," he said defiantly, as if (I later reasoned) Anita had scolded him for believing—or telling—such a thing.

"Nelson's not here," I reminded George.

Up and down the man's big head rocked. "Yes, he is. I can hear him. It's plain. He's trying to tell me something. He wants me to do something for him. It's plain."

The next day I didn't see Sags. And the dog was not to be seen all that week. I finally asked Anita what had become of her. She told me the dog had died. It wasn't until weeks later that George, in a fit of guilt, told me Anita had made him kill the dog and bury the animal in the backyard. That was the "bad" thing he had been moaning about.

"But why?" I asked Anita, angered. And, yes, fear was there, too; it was beginning, or, more precisely, it had started and I didn't realize it at the time.

She shrugged. "The dog was old. She was useless. Besides, Nelson liked her, she reminded me of him." Her hand darted for the needle in her dress; her voice climbed into an emotional shrillness, a tension that I had never heard. "I can't *stand* anything, anybody—even a dog—that reminds me of him!"

Fear. George waited for me in the yard one night. When I came out of Anita's house I was already shaken. In the middle of our lovemaking, while my world was driving into her, joined in a passion almost unbearable in its intensity, she called out a name, a moaning cry.

"Nelson!" she had cried, then gone cold, her body stilled. Minutes later, reaching for my hand, she murmured, "Nelson was the only one who could ever frighten me. For a moment I thought you were him."

"But why, for God's sake!"

"Your hands," she said. "I felt them suddenly, and for a moment I thought they were his."

"But mine are so much smaller."

"I know. But they are hard, they are strong. Quick, give me one. No, both!" And she took them and held them to her breasts—for almost an hour, murmuring, "They are mine, mine."

Then, later, George grabbed me as I walked out into the yard. He slapped a monstrous hand on my shoulder—it reached almost halfway across my back—and pulled me towards the backyard. "Mr. Nelson wants to talk to you," he said in a whisper that climbed with excitement. Tugging me, babbling all the time, he led me to the spot next to the new garden where he had sat before with poor Sags' head on his lap. "He told me to come get you, Mr. Nelson did. He told me! I heard it *plain*!"

"George, I got to get home."

"Mr. Nelson is talking to me plain now. Every night. He says, 'I want you to help me, George. I want you to get somebody for me.' Listen to him."

"Oh, for God's sake, George, Nelson's not here!" I was tired, very tired.

The man's great cabbage head went up and down in spasm jerks. "Yes, he is! All the time. I hear him. He says, 'George, I want you to help me. I want you to...'"

Of course, I didn't hear anything, any voices. But the very fact that I stood there a moment—*only a moment*—and listened indicated, as I look back, that I was involved with Anita and her life more than I realized.

When I wouldn't "listen" longer with George, he became gruff, resentful, and within his anger said, "She'll get you too, Miss Anita will. She's bad. I don't like her anymore."

I passed this off—or, tried to—as the babbling of a nut. I had previously mentioned to Anita that George had told me of his hearing Nelson's voices. Immediately, alarm had rippled across her face. "I'll speak to him about it," she had said crisply. "You mustn't believe him when he says things like that. He's crippled mentally."

Yet, his words, "She'll get you, too, Miss Anita will," stuck in my mind like glue, sticking so well that I almost didn't give up my apartment in Monterey, as planned, and move in with Anita for the summer vacation. I did it, however, even though at the time I believe I knew I was making a horrible mistake. I simply could not resist her—her rich body, her power. Power. She had power over me—perhaps as she had had over Nelson, and as she had over George. Power that kept me coming back for more of her. And I knew full well that power attracts, then destroys. I was tired then, so very tired, and didn't realize it.

So when school was out I moved in with Anita. We were happy— at first. We went to the beach, we took drives down the coast to Big Sur, we took in the plays in Carmel and Monterey, we sat on the rocks at night outside the house. In bed, she'd take my hands and caress them, whisper to them, tell me how strong they were, like her father's. She had a recurring dream of sitting in her father's palm as a child, laughing as he tossed her up and caught her, over and over. "He *always* catches me," she said, telling me of the dream. "Always. He never lets me fall." The dream was based on fact, she said. Her father had tossed her up and he had never let her fall. Never.

Hands. They were so often on her mind. "Don't ever hit me with your hands," she told me more than once. "Please, Tony. That's what Nelson did." Her fingers flew to her needle as she'd told me, something she did whenever she felt tension, fright, anger. "And my father hit me once, too, with the same hand he used to throw me up with. It was the same as if he'd let me fall. Please, Tony, don't ever hit me, please, with your hand."

One night she angered me. I could no longer stand seeing the needle always in her clothes, always on the stand by the bed at night. Why? I wanted to know, demanding to know this time. Why! in God's name.

"It is mine," she said, her usual answer.

"That is no answer!" I shouted at her.

"I need it," she said. "You have your cigarettes, I have my needle."

"I don't like it, get rid of it!" I shouted, not realizing then how I feared the long, glittering thing.

"No," she said. "It is mine."

I raised my hand to grab it from her dress. In an instant, as if she had made the move many times before, she pulled the needle from her dress and struck out at my hand with it. The point went into my palm.

Even now, handcuffed to George as the police dig ever deeper into the ground, I feel the itch where it healed.

Fear. From that night—only a little over a month ago now—I felt increasing fear, the dull ache of it, not sharp, not slashing, not sudden and intense enough to make me pack up and leave Anita. Little fears, growing.

The wind was right one night and from our bed we heard George outside in the yard, heard his repeated moaning wail: "Yes, Mr. Nelson, yes, Mr. Nelson, I'll help you, I will, just tell me who it is."

"The man is crazy," I told Anita. "I wish you'd get rid of him."

"No," she said. "I brought him here, I found him. He belongs to me, he is mine."

The man's cries were so loud one night that they awakened me out of a deadened sleep. His wails increased to a point where I knew I'd have to go out and shut him up. As I climbed over Anita to leave the bed, she woke up—or, perhaps, only partially woke up. I've never been sure, and I've thought back over the incident so many times my head swims. In any event, her eyes opened. Even in the moonlight I could see—or thought I saw—the fear in them. "Nelson, don't!" she screamed, jerking up so quickly she almost struck me with her forehead.

"It's only me," I said quietly. "Tony."

"Nelson, for God's sake don't!" she screamed again. Automatically, her hand went to her pajama top, to the spot where the needle would be if she were dressed.

I shook her roughly. She must have been awake. Yet, for the third time, she screamed, "Nelson, don't, please! Don't hit me again!"

I snapped on the bedstand light. Still over her, I recoiled at what I saw: her face was literally smeared with terror: lips drawn back, colorless and tight against her teeth; eyes like spurting fountains of fear. Frantically, almost desperately, she searched her pajama top, hunting for her needle. Then, realizing it was on the bedstand, she twisted under me, reaching for it. I grabbed her arm and, angered now, shouted at her that I was Tony, damn it, Tony! "Nelson," she mumbled, "please," staring right into my face.

I finally calmed her enough so that I could let her arm go and get out of bed. Unmoving, she said not another word. She simply stared at me as I threw on a coat, stared at me as I put on shoes, as I went out the bedroom door.

When I got outside George was gone. I heard only the sound of waves dying on the rocks, the wind in the cypresses and pines. But just as I was going back into the house, I thought I heard a distant voice, one pained and crying, "George, help me, help me."

My imagination, of course. The workings of fear. The influence of Anita, George, the needle, hands. My mind—any mind—could take only so much. It was at this point that I realized I definitely had to leave Anita.

But I waited too long.

When I got back into the bedroom, Anita had not changed her position in the bed. Only her eyes, now glazed and dead-like, moved. They followed me, sullenly, as I undressed and got back into bed. When I reached to turn out the bedstand light I noticed the needle was gone from the stand. "What did you do with it?" I asked her quietly. She did not answer. I asked her again. No answer. Then I saw it—stuck in her pajama top. I turned out the light—reluctantly. I slept little that night.

From that night she slept with the needle in her pajama top, in addition to it always being in her daytime clothing. "I feel better with it," she said, "like you do with your cigarettes." At night, in bed, when she took my hand—rarely now—and put it on her breast, I sometimes felt the needle prick my fingers. She never mentioned calling me Nelson, and I (wisely?) never brought it up.

Our relationship deteriorated rapidly. We stopped going out at night, stopped going to the beach, stopped sitting on shore rocks and watching evening fog come in. Our lovemaking stopped. When she went out, she went alone. In the house, she stayed in her room most of the time. Once I found her, needle in hand, slowly, deliberately, punching holes in a package of my cigarettes.

Fear. One night I woke up and found her gone from the bed. I searched the house, calling for her. I found her outside. She was sitting on the ground next to the garden where George sat and wailed. She was rolling the needle between her fingers when I walked up to her.

"What are you doing out here?"

She did not answer.

I asked her to come inside, I asked her what was the matter, I asked her if I had done something wrong. She never answered.

Fear. I told her I was leaving as soon as I could find a place to stay. She shrugged. "As you like," she said. I began to look for an apartment—only a week ago now. I found one—today. I was to move into it tomorrow. If only I had found it a day earlier! Just twenty-four hours earlier, and I would not be standing beside a hole waiting to see if it is a grave.

A few hours ago, lying in bed (we slept now in separate bedrooms), afraid even to go to sleep, I heard George's wailing even above the sound of rain. It became so loud, so disturbing, that I got up and started outside to quiet him. As I passed Anita's room, she said, "Where are you going?" her voice cold as fog. I told her. "Stay here," she said. I did not stop. As I went out the door, flashlight in my hand, she said angrily, "Don't believe anything he tells you. He's crazy!"

So are you, I thought.

Outside, as I neared George, he jerked up his head. "Mr. Nelson?" he whimpered.

"It's me, George. Tony."

"Oh." The word was heavy with disappointment.

I stopped in front of him and shined the light on his face. I had never seen his expression so calm, so peaceful. A potted plant was in the freshly hoed garden, less than a foot from his knee.

"Where did that plant come from?" I asked.

"I put it there. It's for Mr. Nelson. He's gonna come see me tonight. He told me. It was plain."

"Go inside, George. You'll get soaked out here."

"He's gonna tell me who he wants me to get. Him and me, we been talking a lot tonight. A whole lot. Just him and me, all alone out here." He looked down at the garden and potted plant. "Ain't we, Mr. Nelson? Ain't we, huh? Just you and me, ain't we?"

45

"Okay, okay, George. Just keep it quiet, will ya?" I turned to go back inside the house. I'd had enough of the whole mess. Let him wail his goddamn head off. I could stand it for one more night.

The crazy son-of-a-bitch grabbed me by the arm. "Come on, stay out here with me and Mr. Nelson, Tony. Mr. Nelson likes you. He told me so." His face shone with pride. "He likes you almost as much as he likes me."

"That's good of him."

"He don't like Miss Anita none at all. No more, he said."

I tried to pull my arm out from the grip of his ham hand. His hold tightened.

"Mr. Nelson don't want you to go back inside with her! She's bad. Bad like a snake. Worser!" His fingers bit deeper into my arm.

"Goddamn it, George, let me go!"

"No. Mr. Nelson says no!"

As I swung around, trying to free myself, my foot clipped and broke the potted plant just inside the garden.

"Oh-h-h-h," George moaned, letting me go. He dropped to his knees in garden mud and clumsily began to scrape bits of the broken pot together, sitting the plant upright again. "Oh-h-h-h, all busted. Mr. Nelson's flower, all busted. Now I'll have to..."

His voice broke off. Whimpering, he dropped the bits of pottery and collapsed on the ground, his forehead resting in the garden mud. "Yes, Mr. Nelson," he moaned. "Yes, sir; yes, sir," bumping his head on the ground with each word.

In a moment his "Yes, sir; yes, sir" ceased. He looked up into my flashlight beam, smiling. "That was Mr. Nelson, did you hear him?" I mechanically moved my head. "He said, 'George, let Tony go in the house now.' It was plain. 'Don't hold him with your hands,' he said, ''cause you got nice big hands and you oughten to use them till I tell you to.' It was plain." The man's head went up and down, up and down, childishly happy. "I'm gonna help him get the person he's after, soon as he tells me who it is. It'll be plain."

I had had absolutely enough, too much. A cold horror was penetrating my bones. The sickness of the man, of Anita, of the whole house, the needle... I simply wanted to leave and go somewhere where there was warmth, health. I remember I had turned and started away from George, not sure if I was going to go back in the house and get my clothes and leave, or simply leave without my belongings. Then George said something that made me stop—unfortunately.

"Mr. Nelson is gonna come up out of his grave and..."

As he continued talking, I, at first, thought his words were simply more of his babbling. Yet, something, like a vague itch, made me pay close attention to what he was saying. Perhaps it was because the word *grave* seemed to fit, like a key in a lock.

George mumbled happily on, speaking to the freshly planted garden, unaware, I suppose, that I was even there. As I listened, the horror of what he was saying slowly jellied my soul.

"It don't make no difference if you're dead, does it, Mr. Nelson? You can still come out of your grave down there, can't you? Can't you, huh? That bad ol' Miss Anita, she don't know what she's talking about, saying you're dead and you can't come out of your grave. Saying because I killed you, you could never talk and walk around no more. Saying because I killed you, you don't like me no more. She don't know you have forgive me. She don't know I'm helping you now. She don't know. I don't like her neither, like you don't. She made me do it, you know it. She made me kill you and dig a hole and dump you in it and plant a garden on top. I didn't wanna, honest, Mr. Nelson. She chased me around the house with that needle of hers. She scared me bad. And she told me *you* was gonna kill *me*. It was a lie. She's bad. She's worser than a snake. She's..."

I don't know how long Anita had been standing behind me. Long enough, I suppose, to hear George's words. I heard her when she whirled around and started walking rapidly—almost running—towards the house. I followed her. I don't know why. I don't know whether I went after her in anger, horror, or hysterics, or some of each, or whether I was a puppet and she was yanking me along behind her by my strings, or if I followed her as you would follow a spider that should be squashed. I don't remember the actual following. I remember, vaguely, coming into her—our!—bedroom and seeing her backed into a corner, her lips curled and hard, like an animal, her glittering needle in her hand, its point aimed at me.

"Get away from me, Nelson," she said.

"I just want to get my things."

"They're mine," she said. She took a step towards me, keeping the needle in front of her. "You can't frighten me anymore."

She took another step towards me; this I definitely remember because it brought her within striking range of me. I felt the needle go into my hand before I saw it. I remember its sting. And the white, drawn smirk on her face.

I hit her.

She fell to one knee and started back up.

I hit her again.

"Nelson!" she screamed. "Nelson!" She began to crawl around me, towards the door. "Nelson, don't! In God's name, Nelson, don't!"

I let her go out the door, the needle still in her hand. "Get away from me, Nelson!" she yelled hysterically as she ran downstairs. "Get away Nelson, don't!"

I followed her down the steps and out into the yard. I watched her run towards George, screaming, "Stay away from me, Nelson!" She fell against the man, shouting, "Nelson's chasing me, George! Help me! He's after me!"

"*You?*" George said. "Mr. Nelson...after *you?*"

"Yes. Me."

I heard George say, almost blissfully, "Mr. Nelson, he was looking for *you* all the time. After *you.*"

And in a moment: "Yes, Mr. Nelson, sir. Yes, sir. It's plain."

I remember watching George's ham hands pat Anita's cheeks—tenderly, it appeared. "Mr. Nelson says you're the one," he told Anita, very simply. "It's plain."

"Help me, George."

"I'm helping Mr. Nelson."

His fingers dropped to her neck.

"I'm doing what he says. It's plain."

I watched George's powerful fingers tighten on Anita's neck. She gagged and squirmed and beat at him. I know she hit him at least once with the needle; I saw the blood on his hand when they handcuffed us together.

When I walked up to him he was smiling ecstatically, Anita crumpled at his feet, the needle lying on the ground beside her. "I did what Mr. Nelson told me," he said proudly. "I helped him." Happy tears were in his eyes. "It was plain."

J O H N   D .   K E E F A U V E R

Somehow the police came. I suppose I called them. I remember only the high points. Somehow, I am handcuffed to George and they have finished digging, they have reached the body, Nelson's body. I expected they would. George is radiant about it. He is mumbling, babbling, talking to Nelson. The cops keep telling him to shut up. They are keeping him here to identify the body. His talk does not bother me. When you have been tortured, ordinary pain ceases to affect you.

They are bringing up the body. It will get wet, I think. I turn away. I feel faint. It will get wet, I keep thinking. I cannot stop the silly thought. They lay the body beside Anita's. They have ruined the garden; the body was under it.

I hear someone say, "Look at his hand. His right hand. Look! It's got little holes all in it."

I think of Anita at work with her needle, plunging it again and again into poor Nelson's hand. Probably after he beat her with it. Probably after he was dead.

I hear only rain now. Everyone is quiet, for a moment. George has finally found Mr. Nelson; his babbling has stopped. I hear only rain.

~

NOTES ON "GIVE ME YOUR COLD HAND"

Originally published in *The Sixth Pan Book of Horror Stories*, edited by Herbert van Thal (1965, Pan Books, Ltd. pp. 93-109). Keefauver received $39.20 for this sale ($38.70 after his agent's fifty-cent commission), but according to his records, he resold the story at least twice: to the Norwegian weekly *Alle Menn* for $44.00 in 1972, and as half of a package deal with "How to Say No to a Woman" to Australia's Hampton Press for $32.00 in 1962. A nearly identical version appeared in the July 1968 edition of *Fling* magazine (Vol. 11, No. 3, pp. 8-13) as "Anita and the Needle," so Keefauver must have earned well over $100 on this story. However, that represents only the money he made from *this* version of the story, as we have here another of the core motifs that he revisited throughout his career.

THE LAST EXPERIMENT

I T WAS THE ABSENCE OF noise that bothered him. From the very beginning of his stay inside the soundproof and lightless cubicle, a crushing, total silence had forced him—within the first hour—to make his own sounds.

He did not mind the dark; in a sense, he enjoyed it. For years he had closed his eyes and daydreamed in a private dark.

He had been in the room now for days, it seemed, with only a bed, some cans of food and jars of water and a toilet in the nine-by-seven-by-seven-foot cubicle.

A psychologist had led him inside, smiled, shaken his hand and then left him alone, shutting him into the dark silence, into the waiting. And into his thoughts.

At first he had gone over the incidents of the last few days and weeks that had led to his being in this room. As usual, his thoughts were pegged to sounds—the sound of the voice calling him to the company orderly room a few weeks ago, the sound of the sergeant's words as he was told to pack his gear. "You'll be told what it's all about, Nelson, when you get over there," he had said.

Neff Nelson, unassigned Army private just out of basic training, hadn't waited long. Within a few days he and 24 other young men had been taken by truck to a far corner of the post. There, housed in barracks, they'd been interviewed by two psychologists.

Nelson remembered in particular the voice of one, a soft monotone, almost a purr, that was calm and reassuring. The psychologists had said that because Nelson and the other young men were all healthy and of above average intelligence, they were being offered a role in an important experiment in human research.

The project was to discover the effects of solitude and monotony on human efficiency. What happens to a man when he is completely shut off from society for a number of hours or days; when he has absolutely nothing to do? "What happens when you eliminate all stimulating sights and sounds?" the soft-voiced psychologist had asked. "That's what we're trying to find out; how well a man can perform various skills in such a situation."

The Army wanted to develop tests that would indicate the type of person best suited to man a remote radar, missile or weather station, or any other job—perhaps in outer space—where a man might be alone and doing a monotonous job.

The psychologists had also explained what the volunteers would be getting into. Research assistants in a control room would record all sounds from the cubicles and "they may ask questions of you subjects" through a microphone. The "may" had been emphasized, Nelson remembered. The questions would test the volunteers' ability to think, to solve problems, to retain independent judgment. The answers and reactions of each volunteer would be compared with those he gave before entering the cubicle. He would also be given another test after completing his stay in the room.

"From this comparison," the soft-voiced psychologist had said, "any differences caused by the experiment in the cubicle may be isolated." His voice purred on, explaining that the door of the cubicle would not be locked; that a volunteer could walk out at any time he wanted to, although if he did he would be disqualified. Both psychologists declined to say how long the volunteers would stay in the soundproof, lightless rooms. They explained that if they disclosed the time they would invalidate the test because the men would anticipate the time when they would get out of the cubicle.

"Would you like to be a part of the project?" each man was asked.

Private Neff Nelson remembered the exact tone of his own voice as it had said emphatically, "Yes." He remembered it clearly because the matter of going into a soundless cubicle was a decision he would never forget. He knew he was volunteering for something that might very well drive him insane, and he was afraid.

Not literally all the way off the deep end, he told himself; not to a point where he would go blubbering off to the psycho ward. But all his life he had lived not *with* but *on* sound. The absence of it, if only partial and for a short time, drove him to seek and find a sound, a noise, be it ever so slight. The breathing of another person would be enough, even the sound of a dog walking on a carpet. He had consulted specialists since he was a child but they had never been able to help him. During his waking hours he simply had to be constantly aware of sound.

He had been trying to break himself of the need for years. And when this chance to go into a soundless world was offered, he had jumped at it. Here was an opportunity that would force him to go without—like a dope addict in confinement. If he could survive, his habit would be broken.

Yet when he was actually on the way to his cubicle, his mind had uncontrollably strained to hear, record and store up everything audible in those last moments.

Now he remembered the footsteps of those who went first up the steps of the building that housed the cubicles. He remembered the scurrying sounds of caged rats—also being experimented upon—which they had passed just inside the corridor along which the cells were situated. There were eight cells. Each man received a handshake and last instructions from one of the psychologists as he entered his room. Nelson's cubicle was the last one at the end of the hall. He went in, followed by the psychologist with the purring voice.

The small room, well ventilated and kept at a constant temperature of 72 degrees, was entirely white, corklined and as spotlessly clean as a hospital. A toilet sat in one corner, a food-and-water-stocked refrigerator in another. There was a bed with a pillow and a blanket. That was all.

The psychologist was a tall, stoop-shouldered man, with unblinking owl eyes. He shook Nelson's hand and wished him luck. "Remember, the door is not locked," he said. "You can leave whenever you want, but if you do, you're automatically disqualified." He left with the words: "The light will go out in a few minutes and the one in the corridor, too."

Five-feet-ten-inch Neff Nelson was left alone in a nine-by-seven-by-seven-foot cubicle with water and canned food—each can a balanced meal—to keep his 174 pounds nourished. Suddenly aware of his loneliness, he listened intently for the sound of the psychologist's footsteps in the corridor. But he heard nothing; the room was soundproof.

For the first few minutes he had listened to the hum of the refrigerator, until it had stopped when the light was turned off. "The hum would constitute an audial cue," the psychologist had said. "You would not be completely cut off from society if it were on."

So he had begun a life of fumbling in the dark for food and water, washing with chemically treated washcloths, and lying on the bed. There was nothing else to do. He had no schedule, no wristwatch. Dressed in pajamalike clothes, he could sleep whenever he wanted to—in a quiet that noise could not penetrate, in a darkness that completely blanketed him.

And he could wait. He ate, slept, washed; ate, slept, washed. And waited.

And he thought. In a soundless world his thoughts swirled around sounds. His life had always been one of noises; now there were none.

Once, twice, three times he stuck his head under his pillow and pressed it to his ears in hope that when he released it there would be some contrast, some sound—even if ever so slight. But when his ears came away from the pillow there was no difference. The only thing he could hear was his heart. It pumped on and on, like the pound of a sledge. But this was noise of his own making, an inside sound, like the one he made by tapping his fingers on the wall or the floor. What he needed was a sound from outside, something, anything, to tell him an outside world existed.

And though the darkness itself did not bother him, it intensified his isolation from the outside world and made the lack of sound worse. In addition to hearing nothing, he saw nothing. He could not see the wall or refrigerator when they were inches from his nose. The only way he knew anything existed was to touch it.

Once, after only a few hours in the room, he went to the door and quietly opened it, then shut it, opened and shut it, over and over, listening greedily to the slight noise it made. But, again, it was a sound of his own making and he needed an outside sound. And the corridor was as dark as his room.

At first he had gone over the sounds accompanying the incidents that had brought him into his soundless world. But he had soon used them up. Then he started back over his life, a man on a desperate hunt, searching for sounds he had heard, recalling and listening to them, sucking all noise from them greedily, almost frantically, as his cubicle-stay extended from hours to a day, to days. He clawed into his experiences, going back, back, looking, listening.

He went through the roar of the airplane engines he'd heard on his way to camp, the thump of his foot on a football in high school, the ringing cheer of spectators, the loud ticking of his first wristwatch (a sound that others barely could hear), the squeal of his first car's tires, the scream of his voice when he fell from a tree, the br-r-r-r the cutting tool made in the cast on the leg he'd broken, the screech of chalk on a blackboard (a sound that had almost driven him out of school), his sister breathing on the other side of a bedroom wall...

Yet now his mind kept grabbing onto and holding a sound that had first frightened him—the faint scurrying and nibbling of rats.

The sound had originated on a 30-minute radio show he'd heard when he was a child, a harrowing story of starving rats chewing their way closer and closer to a terrified man.

The man was a lighthouse keeper, and more than a hundred starving rats had drifted to his island in an abandoned rowboat. The keeper had seen them pour off the boat as it touched land, had seen them swarm toward him in the lighthouse. He had slammed and locked the ground floor door but in their frenzy they quickly ate through the wood.

Nelson vividly recalled the panting of the rats and the frightened monologue of the man as the starvation-crazed rodents slowly, relentlessly, chewed their way up to the top of the lighthouse.

Higher and higher, the man had climbed, slamming a trapdoor shut behind him at each floor. But the rats, their feet scurrying, their teeth grinding, maintained a constant background to the man's terrified words. He'd waited at each door until he saw the wood begin to splinter, then with a choking cry of terror he'd sprinted up to the next floor and slammed shut the door.

The rats kept coming, their efforts growing more frenzied at each level, as if they could almost taste the meal so near them. A chewing wave, they washed through every floor until they reached the top, the glass-enclosed room from which the keeper had first seen the rodents. The floor of that room had been made of metal, Nelson remembered; it had stopped the rats—for a while.

Then had come a terrible silence; for the first time since the rats had hit the first door there was no sound of them. The keeper had thought the metal floor had stopped them, that he was saved, and Nelson remembered the strong disappointment he had felt then—and was feeling now—not because he wanted the black rodents to tear the man apart, but because he was left with no sound after having had it with him in long, rich moments of mounting tension.

Then Nelson heard again the keeper's gasp and the scraping of rat feet on the glass enclosing the light room. They had scurried to the ground and then climbed the outside of the building, and two had got into the top room before the keeper could slam the window shut. Nelson remembered the man's scream as the rats sprang at him, teeth bared. But he had desperately kicked and struck at them until he killed them. Then Nelson heard only the sound of claws on glass.

The rats finally left. For some reason they went back to the boat, perhaps because they saw it was moving. Then the shifting tide caught it and carried it away. Nelson could not remember the exact reason for their leaving the glass top. It really didn't matter. What did matter was his reliving, rehearing the program's sounds; when the sounds went, so did his memory of the program.

He had brought it back many times in his life, times when there weren't enough outside sounds, even though the memory sent shivers over him like rat feet. And here, in the lost silence of the cubicle, the radio story was more real to him than it ever had been. Over and over the program repeated itself in his mind. It came back even when he realized he had heard it enough— too much—repeating, repeating, until he couldn't stop the sounds of rats gnawing and scrambling on the lighthouse.

No matter what he thought of, it kept pushing to the surface and began again from beginning to end.

Nelson lay on his bed and tried to sleep. Unable to, he fumbled with food and water and tried to eat and drink. He washed again and again until his body was raw from scrubbing. Still, regardless of what he did, the rats were always with him. He couldn't keep them out. Their noises were part of his life in his noiseless world. They were needed and he welcomed them. Gradually he realized that he was afraid they would leave him. When their sounds faded away for a few minutes, he bit his fingers until he drew blood.

He smiled as he lay on his bed, eyes closed, listening. Noises filled his thinking—it was as if there *were* rats in the cubicle. He was content, he was not afraid. After all, he assured himself, the sounds were in his mind, and he could turn them off whenever he wanted to.

The day grew longer and with each passing hour he became increasingly troubled when rat sounds continued to be the only ones he heard, when they shoved all others back into silence. I wonder, he thought, can I really stop them if I try? If I wanted to? If I have to! Am I capable of even lessening their noise and dominance? If so, what would be the effect on me? I must know the answer.

He concentrated on pushing the rat sounds back. Slowly they diminished; the noise of their feet, their chewing grew faint. Gaps came when there was no noise.

No sound...no sound...nothing. A horrifying block of soundlessness. No noise to lean on, to give him meaning, to give him reassurance that an outside world existed.

No sound! his mind screamed. and he concentrated wildly on bringing back the rats. "Come back!" he muttered, talking aloud to himself for the first time since he'd entered the room. "Rats! come back." He reached out with intense concentration, hungrily, almost frantically, and the creatures scrambled in for a moment. Then they went away; then came back again, but only partially. Slipping, slipping, they were slipping from him; their sounds were leaving him as if they were no longer conceived, controlled by his mind, but separate entities with the ability to go and come as they pleased. They scuttled away from his grasp and disappeared.

Nothing. There was no sound now except the lonely beating of his heart, the gulping of the drink he needed so badly and the sob he couldn't hold back.

The rats and the radio show were gone. *They had gone on their own.* The words flashed like a neon sign in Nelson's mind, repeating themselves. Then the reason for the repetition came.

If the rats had gone on their own, then they could return on their own. His mind could no longer make the sounds the rats themselves could. If there were rats in the cubicle, they would make sounds and he would hear them, even though he wouldn't be able to see them.

Yes, he could hear them if they were here. And immediately he heard them, heard their busy feet in the corner of the room at the foot of his bed. Their squeaky noises were a reassuring, comforting sound. He smiled, relaxed—rat sounds were in his mind and all was right with his world. He listened for a moment, relaxed and satisfied, then sat up on the bed and looked toward the noise. Even in the pitch dark he could see a group of rats in the corner on the white floor.

A dagger of fear slit him. Pieces of his mind flew. He wanted to kick out, to scream. Then he realized he couldn't be seeing rats if it was too dark even to see the wall.

He was remembering the wall, that was what was happening. He was remembering how the wall looked when the lights had been on earlier. And, somehow, he was remembering rats. Of course, "seeing" the rats was something in his mind, like hearing them. It was just a trick of his imagination.

He relaxed again on the bed. But now, instead of closing his eyes and listening, he continued to stare at the ceiling. Creeping into his thinking was an itch, an anxiety, a desire to do something. He fought it, then let the desire out. He said aloud, "I want to go to the corner...feel to see if the rats are actually there."

But he didn't, he stayed in the safety of his bed, wondering: Am I avoiding the corner because I'm afraid rats will be there, or because I'm afraid they won't?

Private Neff Nelson remained on his bed for hours and listened to the scurrying and nibbling of rats. Their noises filled his cubicle. They surrounded him and he was very happy. He eased his foot off the bed once to see if one would nibble at his toe, and he was disappointed when nothing happened. "You little vermin," he said, "you don't know what you're missing."

He didn't bother to eat or wash, and he found he wasn't thirsty. He didn't think about the outside now, or how long he had been inside the room. And he rarely thought any more about when they would come to let him out. He was happy in his dark world of never-ending sounds, soothing rat sounds, like a mother's cooing words.

Private Neff Nelson talked regularly now with the rats in his cubicle. It was a friendly relationship, one of the best he'd ever had. And his mind was doing it all. He had it made, he figured. He had so much that the others didn't have. Who else could spend a week in a dark, silent room, yet have so much company?

His mind was doing it all, he kept repeating to himself. And he had it under perfect control. I'm a pretty creative guy, he told himself. I might even decide to live in a room like this all my life. I'll think it over and let them know.

"What do you think about that, you rats?" he said.

"We don't like the idea," one answered in a squeaky voice.

The private laughed. It was the first time one had answered him, the first time he'd actually heard one talk. It was a wonderful thing, this mind of his: it could make nonexistent rats talk.

"We don't like living with a nut," another one said.

"Oh, you don't," Nelson answered, smiling. "Well, I don't like you either."

"We're not joking," another rat said. "You're losing your mind."

"He's lost it, you mean," another squeaked disgustedly.

"Talking with rats...He's done for."

"Now, come off it," Nelson said. "You know I'm making all this up."

"Yeah," two of them said together. "Sure, sure."

Nelson didn't like their tone. They were getting out of hand.

"I'm in control here," he said, tightly.

Their sarcastic, squeaky laughs seemed to fill the room.

"Goddamn it!" he exploded, sitting up. "When I want to talk to rats, I do! And when I want you to answer me, I make you! That's all there is to it!"

"He's losing his mind. He's lost his mind," they chanted.

"Shut up, you filthy sneaks!"

"He's insane, he's insane," they kept chanting.

"I'm not!" It was almost a scream.

"Insane, insane."

"I'm not! I'm not!"

"Insane, insane," their wailing tone mounted. Hundreds of tiny feet scampered on the floor in a whispering tempo. "Insane, insane, the private's insane."

"No, I'm not! No!" The last "no" was a scream. It went tearing through the room, bouncing from wall to wall. "No!"

"Insane, insane."

"No! No! No!"

And light from the corridor suddenly flooded through the cubicle door.

The two research assistants in the control room had not known the experimental rats caged just inside the corridor had escaped through some defective wire mesh. Nor would they have learned of it until feeding time if it hadn't been for Nelson's screams. The men had recorded on tape his talking to himself from the beginning. They hadn't thought it unusual; they were used to strange talk over the microphone after the subjects had been in the cubicle a while. But when Nelson seemed to be losing control, when he started screaming in terror, they had run from the control room toward his cubicle and noticed, as they passed the cage, that the experimental rats were loose. The researchers knew the rodents had to be in the hall some place.

They had opened the soundproof door at the entrance to the corridor, turned on the hall lights and the one in Nelson's room, and hurried to his cubicle. They saw his door was open a crack.

When they went into the cubicle, a flash of white fur scurried by their feet and into the hall. Nelson was sitting up in bed screaming at the other rats in the corner. The creatures, twitching their noses at the light, were trembling with fear.

One attendant realized immediately what had happened. The rats, after escaping from their cage, had scampered down the dark corridor to the end. There, finding Nelson's door open a crack, they had run inside.

But the attendant didn't know that when Nelson had repeatedly opened and shut the door he had unknowingly left it open enough for the rats to get in. The corridor was as dark as the room and no light had come in to let Nelson know it was open.

The attendant also didn't know why the volunteer kept screaming now.

Private Neff Nelson kept screaming "No! no! no!" because the rats he had seen and talked to before were black, and the ones he saw now were white.

~

NOTES ON "THE LAST EXPERIMENT"

Originally published in *Climax: Exciting Stories for Men*, Vol. 7, No. 2, pp. 20-23. November 1960, then reprinted in *The Seventh Pan Book of Horror Stories*, edited by Herbert van Thal (1966, Pan Books, Ltd. pp. 95-105). Keefauver received $31.53 from Pan for this story and "Mareta" combined (after an agent's commission of $2.79).

The radio performance that plays such an important role in the protagonist's memories in this story must be one of multiple adaptations of the story "Three Skeleton Key," by French author Georges-Gustave Toudouze (1877-1972), which first appeared in a 1927 French anthology as "*La tour d'épouvante,*" then in English translation in the 1 January 1937 issue of *Esquire*. It was adapted for radio at least half a dozen times, first by James Poe (1921-1980) on 14 November 1949. Vincent Price played the narrator in several later versions. Some readers will have recognized the similarity between the plot of that story and Carl Stephenson's iconic 1938 tale "Leiningen Versus the Ants," which also appeared in *Esquire* around the same time. Private Nelson (and presumably Keefauver) misremembers some details of the story, as both the print and radio versions feature three lighthouse keepers.

The experiment described in this story appears to be based on real events that occurred at Fort Ord in Monterey Bay, though whether Keefauver himself was a subject remains unclear. The ending of an unpublished 1,200-word piece in the author's files, "Fort Ord Soldiers Lived in Silent, Dark Boxes 32 Years Ago" suggests that he was.

MARETA

OF COURSE, I DIDN'T KNOW Mareta had killed him until a few days ago. But her admission was negligible—nothing—compared to what I found in her bedroom closet the day after.

I shouldn't have gone into the closet, I know; it was dangerous. As soon as I saw the two bottles and the photographs, I should have left the room—left the house, fled. With the knowledge they gave me, it was suicidal to remain near her. That was her plan, I realize now: to let me discover her secret, then destroy me. But I had had no time to think; I had time only to act, and she had forced me to that.

Now, too late, I realize that she had left the bedroom door unlocked purposefully. Curious, I had gone in. Oh God, if only I had kept out of the place! If your child sucks blood, isn't it better not to discover it? If your wife gives birth to a monster, wouldn't it be better never to know? Now...I am drained.

Drained, like her bottles. Her drinking; I never realized to what an extent it had gone. Drunk, she had told me how she murdered Victor, her second husband, her voice puffed with pride and hate and...and, yes, power. Power! Mareta bragged of what she had done, and she felt power even in the telling of it. Later, I understood something else: by her talk of murder she was purposefully planting fear in me. She succeeded.

It had been his eyes, she had told me, smiling drunkenly, ironically. Victor's eyes. I knew about them; after all, I had been there that night she had killed him, although at the time I, along with everybody else, thought it had been an accident. I had heard the story of Victor's eyes for months after his death. Eyes. I can "see" them now. Bound for the island of Hydra in the Aegean Sea, I was on a boat out of Athens when I met Victor and Mareta. By chance we were standing side by side next to the railing, both gazing at the first island stop of the daily milk-run boat. Toothpaste-white houses, glittering in the summer sun, marched irregularly down to the sea from island mountains. Impressive; but when I turned toward Victor to comment casually on the sight, I saw for the first time his eyes and they wiped out the picture of the storybook houses—forever.

They battered me, these eyes; they hurt. They were pain; they were fear. They were lost; they had been beaten. They were a hungry child.

Sweat, yes. They looked as if they were sweating—too wet, too oily. They glistened with fear, shone with fright.

Mareta, his wife then, had been standing beside him, of course— brilliant in a wind-whipped dress, hair dancing. Even then I felt her power— poised, sharp, penetrating, hard, like a knife. I felt her in my pores. She was small, almost dainty, standing next to her dark-skinned and bulky husband. Yet, even from the beginning I had the feeling, though vaguely, that he and his eyes made up a puppet, and that his wife, Mareta, deftly handled the strings—and that now she was tired, her fingers bored.

By the time we reached Hydra at noon, we had become acquainted enough to have lunch together. Talk came easily. I learned that they too planned on spending a few days on the island of some 3,000 souls, mostly fishermen, the rest tourists and artists, and that Victor, born in Greece, had moved to the United States as a child and was now visiting his parents in Athens. It turned out that the three of us were from the Los Angeles area, where he was in the wholesale fruit business and I taught high school. He told me he had been married to Mareta less than a year. And it was her second marriage, too, I learned; her first husband had drowned, she said. She was years younger than Victor.

In the beginning no one suspected, least of all I, that she was a killer. She did it that first night in quiet, sleeping Hydra, did it efficiently, effortlessly, and with pride. How she smiled in drunken humor months later—just a few days ago now—when she told me how simple it all had been. How easy. How stupid of him.

She had talked Victor into accompanying her on a midnight swim— she did such things with great charm. He did not swim himself, and now I realize that that was one of the reasons she married him—perhaps the most important reason. Did he suspect her? As I look back over my own relationship with Mareta, how *I* grew to suspect her, I think it possible that Victor did, too. But after living with her almost a year, perhaps he wanted to die. Never mind—he died, and was I to be next?

They left their hotel—where I had a room, too—and walked arm and arm (she underlined this point with a chuckle) out of the village proper, up a path along a nearby mountain side. She knew exactly where she was going. Years before she had visited Hydra with her parents; she had gone swimming with them in water beneath a lip of stone that jutted out from mountain rock some twenty feet above the sea. In the lip, out from the mountain enough to be over water, was a large hole. She had remembered the hole, how it would not be seen on a moonless night, how death could easily come there—either by falling on the sharp rocks in the shallow water or by drowning, or by both.

It was clever of her, she admitted. Clever that she arranged their trip to the island on a moonless night without Victor realizing what she was doing. Clever that that same afternoon she had visited the spot alone, measuring her strides from a point on the path to the hole, measuring the distance carefully, so that that night she knew exactly where to stop and give Victor a push over the edge of the hole. He had given one short anguished yell as he dropped; she had heard his body splash into the water..."a delightful sound."

She'd waited. Victor did not come to the surface. Then, an excellent swimmer, she had dived in after him, ostensibly to help him, actually to see if he were dead, she told me. He lay on the rocks beneath the shallow water; he made no living move. She pushed his body into deeper water, she said, then rushed back to the hotel, screaming in wifely agony.

This I knew; for I had been awakened that night by the commotion caused by her announcement that her husband had fallen into the sea. I joined the fishermen and tourists and the village men of the law at the hole in the lip. I watched as they searched for his body. Currents had carried it out to sea. It wasn't found for days, days that I stayed with Mareta, comforting her in my innocence, listening to her talk of Victor, how her love for him had been so strong at first, how it had turned slowly into fear, fear of his eyes. Fear, as she had had of her first husband's eyes, the one before Victor, the one who had also drowned. Neither husband could swim, but it was only a few days ago that I suspected that she had deliberately picked husbands who could not swim. I cannot swim myself, and I became her third husband. And it was only days ago too that she told me that even if Victor had not drowned from the fall, even if he had accused her of attempted murder—it was of no matter; she was the power and the glory and no man and no law could touch her.

Mareta and I had gone out together each day to watch the search for Victor's body. We were on the shore the fourth day, the day his body washed out of the sea. One bystander had vomited, another had stumbled away. I myself cringed in horror at the sight of Victor's eyes—and at the sight of Mareta's when they laid the body out and she was asked, after much hesitation, to identify the body. I saw her expression. My God! how I wish I had not. I still "see" it—more vividly now, even in my present condition. At the time I didn't believe what I saw; I thought my own eyes deceived me. So gruesome, so terrible, the flick, barely perceptible, of happiness on Mareta's face when she saw that both of Victor's eyes had been ripped from his head.

A fish, some monster of the sea, had ripped out Victor's eyes, was the consensus of Hydra fishermen and the law of the island. Some fish with a diabolical mind, they agreed. (Of course, there were cuts and slashes over most of his body, and his clothes were torn in many places.) Yes, the fisherman said, there were fish that could chew out a man's eyes. Perhaps there was a sweetness of a man's eyes that a fish liked. Perhaps they, the fishermen, should protect their own eyes every time they went into the sea. It was something to think much about.

The village shuddered at the tragedy; it was on the front page of the Athens newspapers. And when Victor was buried in the city, a stillness like the Parthenon in moonlight lay like a knot in my heart. I think my memory of Mareta's smile at Victor's eyeless face was poisoning me even then, but I didn't know it. I translated the emotion into love, pity.

Fear. It was to come later, sharp as a knife, after Mareta and I were married. She went back to Southern California after Victor's funeral, and I did too, though later and by a different route. I travelled through Europe for the summer, and by the time I got back to the Los Angeles area she had been there long enough, it appeared, to have forgotten Victor and their marriage. She had rid her home along the coast south of the city of all evidence of him. She had wiped him out, and within a week we were lovers, within a month we were married.

Looking back, seeking a reason why she married me, I can only come to the conclusion that it was mainly because I liked the water—sailing in her Mercury, lying on the beach beside her pool—but did not know how to swim. I had little money, but that was no problem: all her men—her father, her first husband, and Victor—had given her or left her money. My salary as a teacher was hardly needed. Of course, at first I thought she loved me. It did not take me long to find out how bitterly wrong I was.

And why did I marry her? I wonder myself, looking back on the marriage of only months ago. I am perplexed. I think it was because some of her—enough—rubbed off on me on the island of Hydra; her seed grew in me, like a cancer as it turned out. She came through my pores, growing all the time. She had a darling quality about her, a goddess power that said, "If I admit you, you are very fortunate indeed." She admitted me, and I plunged in. And her body. It was golden and sinewy, rich with curves and hunger; it fed on me. Our lovemaking was frenzied, almost combat. But as I look back, I see now that there was no love in her or her body; only hunger; it—she—took and never gave. And when her appetite was appeased, she shoved me away. Within months she was tired of me. And soon fear came.

Fear. First it was disguised, like an itch in the soul; puzzling, like a stare from a stranger you feel you know—like the stare of Mareta that I came to know. Eerie, frightening, powerful, this stare of hers; it thrust itself at me, into me, exploring, prying. It was a power, a weapon—and I began to better understand why I had married her. Power. She was power. Power attracts. And power destroys.

One afternoon beside the pool I became conscious of her stare to such an extent that I knew it was the focus point of my growing fear. I remember how the sun glistened on her golden body and on an opened penknife she held in her hand; she had been peeling an apple. She was lying naked—we never wore suits at the enclosed pool—her head toward me. I was sitting in a beach chair beside her when sun caught the knife blade and a blinding ray hit my eyes. I brought my hand up quickly to shield my face, and she lowered the knife. She knew what she had done. She had done it purposefully, I realized later. Then I felt the full impact of her stare; it hit me harder than the sun ray had. It came shooting from behind the knife blade, slashing my eyes. Then I saw too the flash of her smile, so quick that at that time I wasn't sure she had smiled. Later I realized that her smile was the same as the one she had let flick through her expression the day they brought Victor's eyeless body from the sea.

That night I could not sleep. Lying beside Mareta, I thought I felt her stare upon my face. But it was dark in the room; the mind plays tricks. I shrugged off the feeling and finally slept. Later I awoke and felt her fingers slowly, carefully, lightly, exploring my eyes. "Yes?" I said. Immediately, silently, she withdrew her fingers. All I could hear was her breathing—fast, excited, as if we were making love.

From that day on she seemed to have her knife with her almost all the time. At the pool she used it to peel fruit, in the kitchen to cut vegetables. At night I saw it by our bed, on the bedstand beside her head, the blade always showing. She kept it razor sharp. It was very small, expensive, with a black ivory covering. It had only one blade, which she kept polished. She did not want me to handle the knife. I held it only once. She had left it, forgotten, on the bedstand once when she went into the bathroom; I picked it up. On either side of the blade, worn with age, were carvings of very delicate, probing, powerful eyes.

"Why do you use such a fine knife to peel vegetables?" I asked later.

"A knife should be used," she said. And again I saw the flick of her ironic, secret smile. "That's what my first husband said when he gave it to me."

Fear. We were out in her Mercury one afternoon, a day in which heat waves shimmered like fire off the ocean. The wind had died, and although I could not swim I lowered myself over the side of the boat into the cooling water. Holding tightly onto the gunwale, I dipped my head into the ocean. When I looked up, Mareta was staring down at me, her secret smile escaping her face (too late; I saw!), her open knife near my fingers on the gunwale. When my face titled toward hers, she lowered the knife quickly—too quickly? "I thought I saw a shark," she said.

She began to drink heavily, retreating each day from me into a world of alcohol and silence. I'd come home from work and find her in the bedroom, the door locked, no preparations made for dinner. More and more she kept her bedroom door locked all night, forcing me to sleep in a spare bedroom; and the nights we did sleep together she would not let me touch her and I awoke feeling her stare or her fingers on my eyes. She refused to explain her behavior; she would not answer my questions.

"What is wrong? What have I done? Why are you acting like this?"

She would only smile.

And when I persisted in my attempt to question her, she—never saying a word—moved out of her bedroom. I came home one evening and I could not find her. I searched the house. She had disappeared. Her car was in the garage. Thinking she was at the beach, I walked to the area where we frequently used to go. She was not there. When I got back to the house, she was in the kitchen preparing dinner, using her knife. She was drunk.

"Where have you been?"

She only smiled.

Often when I came home from work I could not find her in the house. Later, though, she would come down from upstairs, an upstairs I had just searched—including all the bedrooms—without finding her. She refused to explain her whereabouts, to even talk, and I soon stopped asking her. I stopped looking for her in the house when I came home after work. I was very tired of it all—and afraid.

But one evening—just a few days ago now—she did not come down from her upstairs hiding place until after I had fixed my own dinner and read the paper. I was watching television, my back to the living room door, when I felt her hand on my neck, a warm caressing touch, like softened butter. I turned. She was naked.

She came around in front of me, blotting out the TV picture, swaying slightly; she had been drinking. Faint light behind me glazed her face; her ironic smile glittered in shadowy mirth. She stepped toward me, her arms came out. Her body touched me, I turned my face.

"What do you want?"

"Let's go out to the pool," she said.

"No."

"Take off your clothes, we'll go in together."

"I'm going to bed."

I stood up. She spread herself against me, like warm icing on a cake. Her arms twined around me. Her lips spread for my kiss.

"Now," she said. "At the pool." I felt her thrust.

I pushed away.

She kept her smile, but it hardened angrily. Spinning, she glided—she walks with the stealth of a cat—out the door toward the swimming pool. I went to the window and watched her stoop at the edge of the water and pick something up. Then she came back into the house and went up to the spare room. As she passed me I couldn't see what she carried in her hand; the object was too small. It wasn't until just a few hours ago now that I understood it must have been her knife.

Then though, the curiosity of what she had picked up at the pool took me into her room later. She was sitting in front of a window, a half-filled glass of whiskey beside her, staring out into the dark. I can "see" her expression now; how can I ever forget it? Her ironic smile was at its ultimate in cruelty—an expression of a mad goddess.

But for the first time her smile and stare were of secondary importance to me. A tapestry hung down one wall, I had seen it many times, but as I came into the room that night I saw that one edge of it, about halfway down, was indented. It was caught on a key that stuck out of a Yale lock. Too, I could see a few inches of an almost imperceptible line of a doorway in the wall. In her drunkenness and anger, she had either forgotten to take the key out of the lock or had purposely left it there for me to see. There was a secret room behind that wall, a hidden closet.

She seemed not to notice that I had seen the doorway. She focused her smile and stare on me. Her anger was now either gone or under control. Very carefully, very slowly, very calmly, her words coming in the quiet between the falling of ocean waves nearby, her voice filled with pride and power, she said:

"I killed Victor."

And then, her cool proud voice cutting me as if she were carving her words out of my skin, she told me, for the first time, the story of leading

Victor to the hole on the island of Hydra. And again—this part of the story I had heard so often—told me of his nightmare eyes—eyes like her first husband's, eyes she feared.

"I killed him too," she said, meaning her first husband, the one before Victor, her voice singing with power now. "He drowned," she chuckled. "All my husbands drown. None know how to swim." She took a long drink.

"Go look in the mirror," she said. "Go look at your own eyes, you'll see what I mean. You're just like Victor and the other one. You're after me, you want to kill me too. I can see it in your eyes." Her voice had lifted into a knot, as if it wanted to scream. "It's in *your* eyes, too!"

I went back to my room on jelly legs. I locked the door. I tried to sleep. I felt Mareta's stare, I saw her smile; in my mind I heard her insane words, over and over. I felt her fingers on my eyes—through the bedroom wall.

I got up and snapped on the light. I went to a mirror.

As I looked into the glass and saw my eyes, I at first felt shock and fear. But the longer I looked the calmer I became and the more I understood. *Mareta* had made fear grow in the eyes of Victor and her first husband. As the men gradually saw her for what she was, fear grew. Mareta, seeing the fear and realizing they *knew* her, translated their knowledge into a threat to her security—her power. And, thus, she destroyed Victor and her first husband.

I understood this because, gazing into the mirror, in my own eyes I saw the surge of living fear.

THE NEXT MORNING I SAW a lawyer about getting a divorce. I planned to move out of the house as soon as I could find a place to live.

But I had waited too long.

As soon as I got inside the house that evening, Mareta came down from upstairs, silently, her smile so strong it seemed to be a being itself. Her stare pried into my eyes before she went out the door, the knife in her hand. I watched her walk across the lawn toward the beach, then I went up to her bedroom.

I suppose I should have known she would come back to the house immediately. If I had thought, I would have realized that she had left the house simply to give me an opportunity to get into her secret closet—especially when, going into the bedroom, I found the tapestry pulled back and the hidden door left open a crack.

Inside the closet I found the bottles. Two of them. Discarded olive bottles, washed and sealed. They were nearly lined up on a shelf, a stool in front of them. Mareta must have sat for hours staring at them and the photographs behind. The three pictures, propped up against the walls, were of her first husband and Victor—and me. A sharp device—a knife?—had been thrust through the eyes of each man.

My mind, of course, at first refused to believe what I saw in the bottles, even though I had come to know Mareta for what she was. The sight I saw in them will stay with me forever, though I've tried with all my being to shut it out these last few days. The sight haunts me. My only consolation is that I know I will never see, actually, such a nightmare again. It is an impossibility.

While I stood in the closet, trying to accept *psychologically* the horror of what I saw in the bottles, Mareta came silently into the bedroom behind me. I did not hear her until she was almost on me. I turned in time to see her plunge the knife at me, silently, her smile bursting with pride, her stare like a goddess. We struggled. She had the advantage of surprise, and I was hurt. She struck again and again before I managed to get the knife from her and, wildly, blindly, stab it into her, blood streaming down my face.

She was dead by the time they got her—and me—to the hospital. They buried her yesterday. I wasn't there. I was in the hospital, where I am now. I'm glad she's dead. I'm glad I killed her. I wish she had been destroyed years ago, before had had time to kill.

My only consolation, as I've said, is that now, blinded by the knife thrusts of Mareta (she had aimed the blade at my eyes only), I'll never again see those bottles, those olive jars contained the pickled eyes of Victor and husband number one, eyes she had cut out with her knife as the men lay at the bottom of the sea.

~

NOTES ON "MARETA"

Originally published in *The Seventh Pan Book of Horror Stories*, edited by Herbert van Thal (1966, Pan Books, Ltd. pp. 106-116). Keefauver received $31.53 for this story and "The Last Experiment" combined (after an agent's commission of $2.79). Readers will notice the similarity between this story and "Give Me Your Cold Hand," which had appeared in the previous Pan volume.

THE MOST PRECIOUS

I HAVE ESCAPED, IT IS true. I am alive—if the condition I am in can be called living. My mouth still bleeds, and I am so weak. Dried blood covers my chin, is splattered down the front of my suit. I cannot speak. No matter; I am alive; I know the secret—worth millions if I can get back to the States.

I have broken from the cords with which Abushalbak the Syrian bound me. I can find a doctor, here in Damascus. And, unlike the girl, Silent One, I can write. She can neither write nor speak. Perhaps never again able to speak, I must write it down—the secret. I must hurry.

Silent One, her father, Abushalbak, called her. Little did I know the reason for such a name that first evening I saw her. The wildest imagination would not have guessed it; certainly not mine. I saw her first as she stood beside her father's sidewalk toothpaste stand on Al Malek Faysal Street near Al Chouada Square in the Syrian capital. A young dentist just out of school in Baltimore, taking a much-needed vacation through the Middle East before plunging into practice, I was attracted and amused by Abushalbak and his toothpaste-selling stand. I had stumbled across his sidewalk business while returning to my hotel on Al Chouada Square from a later afternoon stroll through the nearby bazaar.

The man, dressed in what appeared to be a dirty nightgown, a rainbow-colored towel around his head, was selling the paste by simply rubbing it over an aid's teeth with one rag, then polishing the incisors with another. During the whole process, Abushalbak kept up an almost unceasing flow of sales chatter, disrupting the polishing and *spiel* only long enough to sell an occasional tube of paste from a row of it on top of his stand. At intervals, he would also take something from the boy's mouth—I couldn't make out what it was—and put it in a small jar on the stand. Aside from the comic aspects of the situation, what amazed me was that the aid, a boy, had the most brilliantly white teeth I, as a dentist, had ever seen. They shone like the Taj Mahal in moonlight. If I could make my future patients' teeth shine like this boy's, I knew I'd soon be rich. I edged into the smiling, laughing, dirty-faced crowd around the stand in order to get a better look.

That was when I saw Silent One for the first time.

Silently aloof, she made her way through the crowd and took up a position next to her salesman father, although at the time I didn't know they were father and daughter, nor did I know her name or his. What attracted me about her from the very beginning was her height and carriage, the regal-like tilt of her chin, the strong, clean, sharp features of her face, her dignity, her silence. She was a fantastic contrast to the boisterous, grinning group. She wore a veil as part of her free-hanging, Muslim dress, but whereas the faces of most veiled women in Damascus were completely covered, her veil started below her eyes.

Her eyes. I fell into them immediately. They were great, acorn-colored puddles of warmth; large, luminous, soft lights. The sun was going down; it seemed to set her eyes on fire. I stared too long; she lowered her gaze—not rapidly, though, but slowly, with dignity—and listened as her father spoke a few words to her in quiet, rapid Arabic, his blunt, beard-stubbled chin jumping with the words. He handed her the small jar as he talked. While in the service, I had learned some Arabic at the Defense Language School in California (my ability to speak the language was one reason I was holidaying in the Middle East), but Abushalbak spoke too rapidly for me to understand.

Wordless, dignified, the girl moved—glided—out of the group, carrying the jar, and disappeared into the dusk and maze of the narrow, shop-jammed streets of the bazaar area. I almost followed her that first night.

I went back to Abushalbak's stand the next morning, hoping to see Silent One again, but she was not there. I stayed at the stand a while, again admiring the aid's brilliant teeth. And again I was unable to see what it was that the man took from the boy's mouth and put in the jar on the stand.

That evening, when I returned once more, I found the girl, veiled, of course, beside her father's side. Our eyes joined as she listened to his words. As I think back, I realize that Abushalbak must have become conscious of our mutual stare. He looked up quickly at me with a strange, penetrating, unfriendly gaze, then went on talking to his daughter. He gave her the jar from his hand, apparently the same one, now covered and refilled with something from his aid's mouth, that he had given her the day before. I sensed, even then, that I should not try to speak to her in her father's presence.

When Silent One moved out of the group, I followed her, conscious that Abushalbak was watching me. I kept her in sight for a short while, debating whether I should try to stop her. I suppose I was conscious of the danger then, but I pushed it away and tried to catch her without breaking into a run. She went into the bazaar, walking rapidly, merging into the swirling, moving throng, picking her way through the crowd and the narrow, dirty, shop-littered alleyways as if they were her home. Unaccustomed to slivering through the throng, I fell behind and finally lost her in the vicinity of the Omayad Mosque. A few minutes before she disappeared, she turned and looked at me, her expression, so far as I could make out in the dusk, set in a sort of haughty neutrality. She knew I had been following her all the time.

Of course, I went back to Abushalbak's stand the next day at the same time. Both Silent One and I arrived together, she from one direction, I from another— almost as if she, as I, had planned the meeting. I soon realized, however, that she did not want to see me. As soon as those powerful eyes of hers fell on me from the top of her veil, she went quickly to her father, he spoke a few rapid words to her, gave her the covered jar and she left him, taking the same route as the day before. This time I did not lose her. I followed her through the maze of dirty streets and passageways, and caught up with her in a matter of minutes, brashly putting my hand on her shoulder. She was nearly as tall as I, and when she spun on me, sweeping me with her eyes, I quickly dropped my hand. Pointing back over the route we had just covered, she indicated that I was to return and let her go on alone. She said nothing, and kept the jar behind her, hidden.

I told her in my creaky Arabic that I did not wish to return, that I would be most happy if she would accompany me to dinner.

Although she still said not a word, I could tell by her expression that she was surprised that I could speak the language. She continued to point out my return route, however. Smiling, I repeated my wishes. A flicker of friendliness, of acquiescence, brushed across her face, then abruptly disappeared and she moved on, stopping at intervals to indicate, wordless, that I should not follow her. I smiled, told her I understood—and kept after her.

Near the Omayad Mosque she began to walk extremely rapidly. I, too, increased my pace, and had little trouble keeping her in view: although it was almost dark, the streets became less crowded and her height and carriage easily stood out against others in the narrow passageways. Just outside a wall of Azem Palace, she stopped and glanced back in my direction. Surrounded by a group of people, I was fairly well hidden at that moment; she did not see me. I saw her quickly duck into a doorway opposite the place. When I reached the spot, I hesitated: beyond the doorway I could see nothing, I could hear nothing. But foolishly I stepped inside the door. Of course, I did not know then that Abushalbak, watching me, was standing in approximately the same spot where I had stood as I watched Silent One enter the doorway. I should have realized that he would follow me from his stand. After all, he had seen me start after his daughter twice.

Inside the doorway, I stood still for a moment. At first I heard nothing except sounds from the street outside. Then, yes, I heard quiet footsteps ahead of me. Just a few, then silence. Then, again, more footsteps and, a second later, the sound of a door being unlocked and cautiously opened and closed. Again, silence. I could see nothing.

I slowly moved forward, groping my way, keeping a hand on one wall of the passageway. The floor was earthen. By reaching up, I could touch the stone roof. I shivered. Warmth must never have penetrated the corridor. I rounded a corner slowly. And saw a sliver of light a few yards ahead of me. As I watched, someone—Silent One?—blocked out the light for a moment, from within a room. I increased my pace, cautiously, and went directly to the sliver of light which, I learned, came out from below a rag-shaded window in a lamp-lighted room.

I looked under the shade into the room—and felt, first, an exhilarating joy, then, second, cold horror at what I saw.

Silent One stood in an earthen-floor room containing a few nondescript chairs, a small table, two raggedy beds. She had taken off her veil and was pouring the contents of the jar her father had given her into a great metal pot that reached almost to her hips and sat in the center of the room.

Out of the jar came a gleaming, yellow liquid—not gold. The sight of the liquid left me trembling with exhilaration. There was not a dentist in the world who would not give a fortune for what was in that metal pot.

Then, the pouring completed, Silent One turned from the pot, her veil-less face toward the window outside of which I stood. She had a glass straw between her lips; one end was stuck in a bowl she carried in her free hand. She was eating. At the sight of her face, I felt a horror that froze my very marrow.

I must have recoiled from the sight, actually stepped back, for I bumped into Abushalbak just before he clubbed me.

When I regained consciousness I was lying on the cold floor of the room. My ankles and wrists were tightly bound. A knife and additional cord were on a chair. My lips were not taped, however, and when I saw Abushalbak kneel down beside me, saw what was in his hands and felt Silent One prop my head up with a pillow, I realized why.

"No, for God's sake," I mumbled, first in English, then, my mind catching up with my terror, in Arabic. "Please."

"God watches out for those who watch out for themselves," Abushalbak said in Arabic, or words to that effect. "You have been most unwise in coming here." He bent down over me and brushed his fingers across my lips, feeling their texture.

"Who are you?" I asked. God knows why. The terrorized mind resorts to habit, to routine, I suppose.

The man shrugged. "I am called Abushalbak. I am the keeper of The Most Precious." He nodded towards the metal pot filled with the yellow liquid, then towards the girl. "This is my daughter, Silent One. She also watches The Most Precious." He shrugged again, his great black brows rising and forming almost a straight continuous line above his eyes. "She has failed me before also. She talked then. Hence, her lips are as you see them. As yours will be, too. As others have become when they see The Most Precious, or when they see Silent One, unveiled."

He put one knee on my chest and one on my forehead. Silent One sat on my feet and pushed my bound hands into my groin. Thank God, her father blocked my view of her face.

"But I can *write* it!" I screamed. "I can write, even if the others can't! I don't have to be able to talk!"

"You Americans, you think education means everything." He shrugged once more. "You cannot talk when you are dead."

With that, I felt the needle go into my lip. I lost consciousness.

I do not know how long I was unconscious. Hours, I suppose. When I awoke, Silent One and her father had gone. I was the only one in the room, still lit by the lamp. I was still bound. My mouth was filled with blood; the front of my clothes was stained by it. Without thinking, impulsively, I tried to open my mouth to yell for help. I couldn't of course. And the pain was horrible.

I must have passed out again, from pain, from the shock of realizing what had happened to my mouth. When I woke the second time nothing had changed in the room. The only difference was that now the blood on my clothes had dried.

I lay there for I don't know how long before, looking wildly about. I noticed that the knife, apparently forgotten, was still on the chair. With much pain—any movement sent spasms of agony shooting through my mouth—I inched myself over to the chair and managed to pick up the knife between both hands. Fortunately my hands were tied in front of me, rather than behind. The knife was sharp too. By sitting up and holding the handle between my palms, I was able to saw the cord around my ankles. My feet free, I wedged the handle between the sides of my insteps and was able to cut the cord on my wrists. The whole operation must have taken me more than an hour. I had to stop often because of the pain and weakness—I think I fainted once for a short period—and only fear that Silent One or Abushalbak might return kept me going.

Before I left the room, I found a cup and hastily dipped it into the pot containing The Most Precious. I would need physical evidence of the yellow liquid; otherwise, no one would believe my story. Then, weakly, stumbling a number of times, falling at least once, trying to fix the location of the room in my mind, I made my way back through the bazaar to my hotel. I kept a handkerchief over my mouth, of course. Even in the old section of Damascus, the sight of my lips would have caused alarm, perhaps have brought the police. I didn't want the police; an investigation would perhaps ruin my chances of getting back to the States with my yellow evidence. I wanted only a doctor—and to write the secret down.

I am in my hotel now; a doctor is on his way. I gaze into a mirror. I smile, even though it hurts terribly to do so. Even if terrible scars remain in my lips, I would go through the same thing again to discover the location of The Most Precious.

Joy surges in me. I am king: after all these years of searching, by dental scientists, by the cream of the dental world, I, just out of school, led on by a boy's brilliant teeth and, ironically, by a woman whose teeth were covered, whose lips had been sewn together, as mine are now, have discovered the greatest secret in the world of dentistry.

I now know where the yellow went.

~

NOTES ON "THE MOST PRECIOUS"

Although this story appeared in *The Eighth Pan Book of Horror Stories*, edited by Herbert van Thal (1967, Pan Books, Ltd. pp. 21-27), for which Keefauver received $38.36, this was not its original publication. A slightly different version of "The Most Precious" had already appeared in the August 1965 edition of *Elegant, the Magazine of Fashionable Living* (Vol. 2, No. 9, pp. 29, 66-67). This version, for which Keefauver received $30.00, bears the label "(spoof)" at the bottom of the first short page of text and above the author's name. The author's files also contain an unpublished shorter version under the title "Brush Off in Damascus," in which the protagonist escapes without harm but also without the secret of "the yellow." Readers of a certain age will recognize the ending as a reference to a once ubiquitous toothpaste jingle "You'll wonder where the yellow went / when you brush your teeth with Pepsodent!" Between this obsolete final gimmick and the story's blatant orientalism, I gave serious thought as to whether to reprint it, but ultimately I felt that it necessary to include all of the stories that appeared in the historically important Pan series.

SPECIAL HANDLING

WHEN YATES' HOUSE BEGAN TO shrink not long after the package came for him from *Reduce Today!* I thought at first it was my imagination, or my eyes. But then when I had trouble getting the bills from the same company into his mailbox because it was getting smaller, I knew it wasn't my imagination or my eyes at all. His house, the mailbox out front, a shed on the side, his car parked next to the shed, the trees in the yard, the fence around his place—they all started getting smaller after I delivered him that package from *Reduce Today!*

I'm sure about the name of the company because it was the only mail he ever got. It was the only mail I delivered him, anyway, since I started the route. The first thing that came for him was the package, during my first week on the job. It wasn't a big package; it fitted into his mailbox easy. I wouldn't even have noticed it, except that besides being the first mail I'd delivered to him it didn't have any return address. Just *Reduce Today!* in big letters, and a Chicago postmark. Then about a week later the second piece of mail came for him, a bill from the same company. I thought then the mailbox seemed to be smaller. It sat all by itself—not in a row with others—so it was hard to tell, at first. You couldn't *compare* his house with others either. It sat all by itself, too, hidden from his neighbors by clumps of trees. You could see the house from the road, though. A little bat-and-board bungalow; it wasn't very big to begin with.

When the second bill came, maybe ten days later, I was sure the mailbox was smaller. I could hardly get my hand in it, and it was now lower than my car window. I thought maybe he had put up a smaller box—it was new, like the "other" one—and I was thinking that I might go rap on his door and tell him he couldn't have a mailbox smaller than regulation, it would get me in trouble. While I was sitting there, undecided and looking at his house, half hoping he'd come out, the house seemed to get smaller right in front of my eyes. Not only the house but the shed and his car, too. And the oaks in the yard. I thought I heard something, too, like a ripping or tearing. It made me nervous and I drove away.

Yates didn't get any mail for a while, and since he lived at the end of a dead-end road I didn't see his house for a number of days. I didn't want to either. As soon as I'd delivered to the houses on his road, I'd turn around and head back. His house was around a bend from his nearest neighbor, and he was the only one who had any reason to drive to the end of it, out in the country like it was. It was almost like a private road.

IN A FEW DAYS ANOTHER bill came to him from *Reduce Today!* No return address, as usual. When I delivered it, I had to lean down from my car window to get it in the mailbox, and the envelope just barely fit inside. I still thought, though, that Yates must be some kind of a practical joker who was putting up a smaller box every week or so. Then I looked at his house, which I had been avoiding doing. The bungalow—and car, and trees in the yard, and shed, and fence around his yard—was *definitely* smaller. I was absolutely sure of it. My eyes are good.

I was scared, and I got away from there fast. Even a practical joker wasn't going to tear down his house every week and build a smaller one. Even if he did, how could he make it exactly like the larger one, only smaller? And a smaller car—how could he build one of them? And smaller trees?

I hadn't told anybody about what was going on for a good reason. I didn't want people to think I was nuts. Particularly since I was a new man on the job. And new in town, too, with people not knowing me well enough to even begin to believe such a story. And I had no wife to tell. Also, there was something funny about why the man who had the route before me had left it—so quick, in fact, that he didn't even stay around long enough to break me in. The superintendent of mails had to do it. No one in the post office or in town would talk about it, or even tell me his name. They were protecting him, I guess—or me. I finally did find out, though, that nobody in the post office, or in town, wanted the job I had, although I couldn't find out why. That was why I, an outsider, was finally hired—nobody else wanted the job.

When another bill from *Reduce Today!* came for Yates, I was tempted to throw it away. But I delivered it, and it wasn't easy. I had to get out of my car and lean down to get it in the mailbox. And I had to fold the envelope in order to get it inside. The house—and the shed, car, trees, and fence—was now about half the size that they had been originally. And, like the times before, I didn't see any sign of life around the place. You would have thought nobody lived there. But the bills were always gone from the mailbox. I assumed that Yates got them. None was addressed to anybody except him—Mr. H. L. Yates. And no other mail came at all to the place—to a *Mrs.* Yates, or a *Miss.* I kept asking around the post office and town about him—very casually, on the pretext that I never saw anybody at home and wondered about him, living there by himself—but everybody said they didn't know anything about him. They weren't good liars.

I knew one thing. I wasn't going to go out to his house on my own to investigate.

About ten days later another bill came from the same company for Yates. The mailbox was now about a foot from the ground, and I had to almost roll up the envelope to get it inside. The house, and other things in the yard, wasn't much bigger in proportion. It was as if I was looking at a doll house and yard. Going around the rest of the route, I thought about ways I could quit the job without having to tell why.

When the next bill came from *Reduce Today!* I stopped just before I got to the Yates place and had a stiff shot. It helped. Particularly since I'd been too nervous to eat any breakfast, figuring it was about time for a Yates bill. By the time I got to what was left of his house and yard, I was praying his last bill would still be in the mailbox; that would at least seem more normal, somehow. But the box was empty, as usual, and nearly level with the ground, about as big as a matchbox. I was so nervous I couldn't fold the envelope and just jammed it into the box with the end of my finger, then got the heck away from there, trying not to look at his house. But I couldn't help myself. The house was about two feet tall, maybe less.

I don't remember much about the next week or so. I began to drink hard, and I've never been a drinking man. I could barely pull myself to work. I was so nervous, afraid of getting another *Reduce Today!* bill to deliver, that it was a wonder I got the mail sorted and delivered at all. At night I went home and got right into bed. Hardly ate at all, and I was skinny to begin with.

When another bill came for Yates, I about collapsed. Before I started around my route I bought another bottle; the one in the car was only a third full. By the time I got to his house I was pretty well soused. So soused, in fact, that for a while I thought I wasn't at his house at all. There wasn't any house any more. No mailbox either. No car parked in the yard, no fence, no shed, no trees. There was simply an empty space where his house had been. And where he had been, I could only assume.

I drove directly back to the post office, not delivering one damn piece of mail, gave the latest *Reduce Today!* bill to the postmaster, and told him the whole story—pretty incoherently, I guess, considering the booze I had in me and the wildness of the story. He obviously didn't believe one word of it. I was drunk. I was not only drunk on the job but I was also nuts, batty, insane.

But I do remember one thing very clearly. Thinking I was too far gone to understand, I guess, he turned to the assistant postmaster and said, "This is the same story Yates told us."

"Yates!" I yelled. "Who in the hell *is* Yates anyway!"

"He was the man who had your route before we hired you."

"*H. L.* Yates?"

The postmaster nodded. "We had to let him go after he told us that a house on his route got smaller and smaller until it disappeared."

"His *own* house?"

"No. Another one. He only moved out onto his own route—yours now—after we let him go. Said he wanted to get out of town."

That explained, anyway, why his mailbox was new.

The postmaster coughed. "I'm sorry, Bill, but I'm afraid we're going to have to let you go too."

I could have kissed him.

Then, about a week later, and when I was beginning to wonder why I wasn't getting any mail myself, another package came from *Reduce Today!* It was addressed to me.

~

NOTES ON "SPECIAL HANDLING"

Originally published in *Alfred Hitchcock Presents a Month of Mystery* (1969, Random House, pp. 301-305), edited by Robert Arthur, and reprinted in *Alfred Hitchcock Presents: Terror Time* (pp. 136-140). Keefauver received $50.00 for each of these two publications, but that was only the beginning. He went on to sell not only the U.K. rights, but also permissions for translations into Spanish and Norwegian. Eventually he sold the story to Reader's Digest for $200.00, and in 1988, All Star Readers published a version for middle school students, for which he received $175.00. Shorter versions appeared in other school textbooks, sometimes as "Reduce Today" or "The House that Kept Getting Smaller," and in one case, the story was abridged into a poem in free verse. Over the course of two decades, Keefauver sold this story more than half a dozen times and earned over $500.00, making it one of his most successful and widely circulated tales—and rightfully so. Correspondence in his files suggests that he pitched expanding the idea into a novel, but he could not find a publisher.

The story itself represents the ultimate refinement of one of Keefauver's favorite motifs, the "mysterious elixir." Over the years he wrote many stories using this gimmick—and a gimmick it very much was. In the original scenario, a character receives either free-of-charge or very cheaply some sort of patent medicine that promises to make one grow taller, shorter, thinner, etc. In at least one version, the pills are for penis enlargement. And the medicine delivers. The gimmick is that it delivers too well, and only once the victim has become some kind of freak does the offer of an antidote arrive—for an exorbitant price per-pill. Keefauver worked this gimmick over and over, but curiously it was only when he removed the twist at the end, in this story—and later in "Cutliffe Starkvogel and the Bears Who Liked TV"—that he really wrote something weird and great—and successful. We will see this same sort of progression toward "less is more" for the win in "The Pile of Sand."

GETTING TO LORD JESUS IS A POWERFULLY IMPORTANT THING

H E KNEW WHAT HE WAS doing, Lord Jesus did, else why would He have him, a little colored kid, in this mix-up of getting drug into all that bay water to get baptized? Sure enough, Lord Jesus was sitting right up there in the sky watching it all. Why, Reverend Thomas had said it.

Still, it was a funny-feeling thing coming up to the beach where the white people go, being all mashed in with a busload of the reverend's congregation, all dressed up in white robes and sheets. He had sat next to his mother on the trip from the church. She was like a warm, black pillow, shaking with the bus as it came over Howell's Lane out to the cement road. Pressed up close to her when he thought of what was going to happen at the beach, and pushed his dark hands into her jiggling fat until she pulled him close and whispered, "Now, Ronnie, child, that's all right, now baby child, don't worry."

But it wasn't all right when the bus stopped at the beach and everybody got out, all of a sudden real quiet at the sight of a crowd of white people on the sand, nobody laughing and singing "Jesus, I'm Coming" anymore.

The white people twisted their heads around and stared at the buses. Some pointed, and Ronnie saw some smile. It was sure a funny-feeling thing. He dragged back on his mother's hand, but she said again, "Now, Ronnie, child, it's all right." Reverend Thomas was out on the sand in front of them, stern-looking, saying, "Be quiet, brothers and sisters, be quiet," even though everybody was already quiet. The buses were lined up along the road behind, like a wall, like protection, something they all could run into if they had to, to be safe.

Ronnie wanted to hide. If he could just go right inside his mother and lie there with her all around him. He oughten to be here like this. He was a kid and he ought to be out in the lake swimming with Carl, like you're supposed to do in a lake, not wade out in it with all this white stuff on to get your head dunked.

But it was the only way to get to Lord Jesus, Reverend Thomas had said. He always said that. And now Ronnie was going to have it done to him. He was going to get to Lord Jesus. And Carl was going to see him. That was the worst part—Carl was going to see him.

Just the other day he and Carl were swimming in the lake, just up a little ways from where he was now. That's when he had told Carl what was going to happen to him come this Sunday.

Carl had mostly reddish hair, and freckles, and was the only white kid that Ronnie actually played with. He knew other white guys, but Carl was his only real white friend. Ronnie had played with him as long as he could remember, ever since Ronnie's mother used to go to Carl's house and do the washing and cleaning. They still played together. But they had to kind of sneak out and do it now. Because they were older. That's the only reason they could see. When a colored kid and a white kid got older, they just couldn't play together anymore. It was funny.

"You're going to get *what* in the lake?" Carl had said, stopping his splashing around all of a sudden.

"Baptized." Ronnie tried to say it simple, but it sounded funny. He guessed it was because he had been thinking and thinking the word so much that it must have changed the sound of it.

"In the lake?" Carl acted like he didn't believe it.

"Uh huh."

"Baptized." He said the word as if that was the craziest thing he had ever heard of. "You're supposed to swim in the lake, or fish or go sailing, not get baptized in it.

"How do you get baptized in a lake?" Carl had wanted to know.

Ronnie just kept looking down at the water.

"Reverend Thomas, he pushes your head under."

"What for?" He wasn't slapping the water anymore.

"It's holy. If you don't do it, Lord Jesus will get mad at you."

Carl skipped his hand over a little wave, but not very hard. "We get baptized with just a little water from a saucer," he said. "The minister sprinkles some of it on your head."

Ronnie couldn't think of a thing to say then. He wished he hadn't even told Carl about it.

"Maybe it will be fun," Carl said after a minute, seeing how Ronnie looked so sad. "Just like going swimming maybe."

"I'd rather go swimming."

"So would I."

"It's on Sunday, too," Ronnie said. "All the people will be watching."

"Where's it going to be?"

"Right down there." Ronnie nodded toward Moon Beach, which was just about a half mile or so down the edge of the lake from where they were then.

Carl looked at Ronnie like Ronnie was crazy. Ronnie knew what the matter was. Colored people just didn't go to Moon Beach. Not that there was any law against it, but it just wasn't done.

"That's something I got to see," Carl finally had said. So there it was. He, Ronnie, a colored kid, was going to have to go with his people to a white man's beach and get baptized in a lake that was for swimming, while the white folks—and Carl—watched.

Getting to Lord Jesus must be a powerful important thing.

Judging by the way Reverend Thomas was acting, it was. He had his congregation backed up against the buses and was walking back and forth in front of them, all stern-looking. Sweat was beginning to bubble out on his face. He was a heavy man, with short gray hair, and his stomach pushed out a little bit against his white robe. "Brothers and sisters," he finally said, "follow me."

He left the buses and started down toward the beach, with his congregation shuffling behind him, with Ronnie and the other kids hanging to their mothers' hands, with the white people gawking and coming closer. They walked down a boardwalk to the water. It was like the aisle in their church, Ronnie thought, only the people on either side were white, not black.

He wanted to hide his eyes against his mother's warm black side, and not look at the white people, all gazing and some smiling and some just looking curious. Crowds of white people were coming from both ends of the beach. Reverend Thomas was beginning to sing a song about Lord Jesus, love Lord Jesus, the congregation singing back to him. Mothers and fathers telling the children to sing, children scared stiff. Shuffling and singing and getting closer to the water, the whites crowding in, the reverend singing. It was more than a funny-feeling thing now; it was sort of terrible. Every once in a while one of the congregation would giggle, usually a woman, or a man would laugh, and Reverend Thomas would say, "Quiet, brother," or "Quiet, sister," and they'd be quiet.

Carl. Ronnie wanted to look to see if Carl was there, but he was afraid to. Everybody staring at him and—and it was mixed up—and—and he didn't want to get baptized in the lake, no!

But Lord Jesus was watching. He was up in the sky, He was in heaven, and you had to do it to get to Him.

Reverend Thomas stopped at the edge of the water, turned to his flock, then marched up and down along the edge of the lake in front of them, leading the singing with waves of his arms. Singing words swelled up, and Lord Jesus could hear, Ronnie was sure. He better had hear, anyway, because if He wasn't hearing all this singing, how would He know what was going on? And if He didn't know what was going on, all this baptizing stuff would be a waste of time. Ronnie was sure, though, that Reverend Thomas had a way of letting Lord Jesus know when it was time for his congregation to get to Him.

Waving his arms around, walking up and down, the reverend preached about sin and living right and loving Lord Jesus. "Yeah, yeah!" all his people answered, yeah-ing themselves right in close to Reverend Thomas and the Lord, saying it all was so, smiling as they said it. But the smiling didn't act on Ronnie. He'd still rather be out in the water swimming with Carl, away from all this getting-to-Jesus business.

"That man!" the reverend was shouting, "that man who lives with another man's wife! that man will never get to Lord Jesus!"

"Yeah!"

"Never make it into His loving arms!"

"Yeah!"

"Never will!"

"Yeah, yeah!"

Sweat rolled down the reverend's face. Ronnie could see it glistening bright on his bumpy cheeks. His feet were wet where he'd stepped into the water, and his arms were jerking like that scarecrow's Ronnie had seen one windy day when he was playing with Carl in the field behind the new school.

Most of the time the reverend was smiling now, and as Ronnie looked around he saw that almost all his flock was smiling, too. And so were the white people. Everybody was smiling, like the whole thing was one big comedy show. But Ronnie didn't see anything funny about it—getting baptized in swimming water.

He looked for Carl and found him at the water's edge. He, the white boy, was staring right at him, Ronnie, but he wasn't laughing like everybody else. He looked funny. He looked like he didn't know what was going on, or why it was happening. And he looked kind of sad too—like he was sorry it was happening to Ronnie. It made Ronnie feel even worse, it made him want to run away all the more.

But his mother had him by the arm—he looked up into her face and she was smiling too—and she turned him toward the water as the reverend started into the bay, clothes and all, his helpers behind him, pushing their robes under the water so they couldn't float on top. Two stopped beside each other every few feet, so that they formed a chain from the beach to Reverend Thomas. They were to pass the people along who were going to get baptized, passing them on to the next two helpers. They were sure making certain that everybody would get to Lord Jesus, Ronnie was thinking as the first one, a man, started out into the water. Helped along, he went wading right on out to the reverend and the reverend took his head and dunked it under the water, saying, "I baptize you in the name of the Father, Son and Holy Ghost." The sputtering man was helped back to the beach then and another one, a woman, went out and got the same thing done to her.

Then a whole bunch of people were going out, one by one, and getting their heads pushed under the bay. Some were laughing, some scared and some just looked blank, but they all kept moving forward until the reverend put them under. Ronnie shivered in his mother's grip, whimpering out an

"I don't wanna," but she shushed him and marched him closer to the water with the line of people edging toward the bay. He dug his feet in the sand but she picked him up and flipped him forward, saying, "You gotta be a man, Ronnie, it's time."

When it was his turn, he felt his mother's hands leave him and the grips of two white-robed men take their place. They took him by the arms, they took him from his mother. "Come on, Ronnie, boy, come on, it won't be bad," they said, and passed him on to the next two men. He felt the water getting deeper, felt the black hands on his dark arms, felt their tug, their strength; heard hot in his ears the Negroes chant, "Lord Jesus, Lord Jesus, Jesus Lord-d-d," spilling into him as they passed him on, as if they were angels and he was going to heaven. Dark hands taking him, dark hands passing him on, dark hands taking care of him, showing him the way. He relaxed. He was in a dark-skinned land, he felt it all around him. From dark helper to dark helper he went, leaving his mother far behind, going toward the reverend and Lord Jesus, going away from the white people, the whites going, gone. He relaxed. He didn't think of Carl now, or his words; he was in a dark-skinned lake now, a lake for baptizing, a Lord Jesus lake. And he let it take him.

He let the baptizing take him, he was inside it now. And he let himself go.

The water was up around his chest and Reverend Thomas was waiting for him, black arms outstretched, saying, "Welcome, son, welcome, boy," water and sweat mixed on his smiling face, smiling like a black Lord Jesus. Then Ronnie felt the dark Jesus hands strongly on his shoulders, felt one black arm go behind his head to hold him, to protect him. Just the three of them now, he and the reverend and a black Lord Jesus.

And his head went under as he heard Reverend Thomas chant, "I baptize you in the name of the Father, Son and Holy Ghost," and he knew that he was finally getting to Lord Jesus. It certainly was a relief.

~

NOTES ON "GETTING TO LORD JESUS IS A POWERFULLY IMPORTANT THING"

Originally published in the Spring 1970 issue of *The North American Review* (Vol. 255, No. 1, pp. 48-50).

A BUSHEL OF FROGS

I DON'T REMEMBER ANY MORE why we put a bushel-basketful of frogs on Old Man Waligora's front porch, just as I don't remember why we tied a goat to it another night, or put some milk—twenty-two quarts—on it another time. Or dumped catsup all over Charlie and put him alongside the road in front of the old man's house, as if he was a hit-and-run victim.

Don't ask me why. All I know is that we did it. Maybe it had something to do with keeping up with your peers.

But I do know that Old Man Waligora sure was popular. He had this talent for cussing and yelling and bellowing and firing his shotgun (at us) and nailing up posters all over town that offered a reward for our "terrorizing" skins. We appreciated him. It was a fine relationship.

There were about ten or twelve of us—all boys, except for one girl named Myrtle. She was chubby, and she wore a girdle. We called her Girdle Myrtle, to which she'd scream, "I'm not wearing a girdle! I'm wearing elastic pants!" She was the only peer I knew who wore a girdle claiming it was elastic pants.

The story was that Old Man Waligora had a silver plate in his head, which was supposed to have had a lot to do with his anti-peerness and other strange behavior, like blinking his front porch lights on and off every time a plane flew over or a train went by on the Baltimore & Ohio track a mile or so away. One thing, anyway: he only blinked the lights at night, which was something. He told us once he was signaling to the pilots and engineers.

Anyway, he was a funny old duck, big as a crate. Sometimes I used to think they had never taken him out of it. He had cotton hair, balloony cheeks, and a stomach like a pillow.

But the thing about him that impressed us the most was his voice, his yell. It was like a cannon. When he let it loose, it was enough to shake all the windows in our town's two hundred houses. It wasn't a yell; it was an instrument of war.

The night we tied the goat to his front porch, for example. We stole it out of a pasture, which happened to be the town's baseball diamond, tied it to the railing of his porch, rang the doorbell, and ran like madmen.

Now, a stranger might have thought the important thing was that he charged out of his door with a shotgun. But to us this was mere routine. When he raised the gun and pulled the trigger, we merely shrugged. The goat, it's true, buckled a bit, but the poor fellow hadn't been exposed to Old Man Waligora's shotgun the way we had. What we were waiting for was his yell.

It came. He peeled back his lips as if they were on rollers, opened up a cavity any hog caller would have been proud of, and let loose a bawl that Joe E. Brown couldn't have come close to. It shot past us and into Washington like a shell—and Washington was nine miles away.

"PO-lice!" was what he bellowed.

Well, the police didn't come, but the goat left. The old man's yell did what his shotgun hadn't been able to: the poor animal snapped the rope that was holding him and cleared the railing by a good three feet. Nobody ever saw him again.

That was the sort of man Old Man Waligora was.

We returned, though. With skyrockets. (We never did actually hit the house.) And with twenty-two quarts of milk. (What a mess! The only thing that disappointed us was that his shotgun, not his yell, shattered the bottles.) And with burning tires.

We used to sleighride down a hill near the old man's house. For warmth we made a fire of old tires on top the hill—phew! One night we rolled one, burning and smoking like a garbage dump, into the old man's front yard. We intended to put it on our favorite spot, his front porch, but before we could get it up to the steps—it was uphill—he came out of his door as if he'd been shot out of a cannon and diverted it with his shotgun. It hit the corner of the house, wobbled against a tree, and then started back toward us. It chased us a half a block before it died in its own stink in the middle of the street, paralyzing traffic for a good mile.

Which gave us the idea of putting a "new" tire in the street—or, at least, on the side of it. So the next night we wrapped up one of our old tires with new wrapping paper so that it looked as if it had just come out of Western Auto or Sears. Then, tying one end of a piece of wire to it, we put it on the side of the road across from Old Man Waligora's house and hid in some bushes next to the street with the other end of the wire in our grimy hands.

Action came with the first car! The driver, seeing the "new" tire, stood on his brakes and smoked to a stop. Back he roared. Out of the car he jumped. Up to the tire, swish! He jerked it up and started back toward his car at a fast trot. He never made it. We yanked the wire and out of his hands the tire flew. Snickers. He got back into his car and sheepishly drove away.

This sort of thing went on for many a rich night. The best nights were when a driver, instead of driving away, would stay there and start bellowing. This usually tied up traffic and brought Old Man Waligora out of his house, shotgun at the ready, sometimes firing, sometimes bawling and firing both. God knows why they never arrested him.

Interesting, too, were the nights when drivers refused to give up their tire. Of course, we always won the tug of war: there were more of us. And I'll never forget the night we jerked loud-mouthed Mrs. Mersley, all two hundred pounds of her, through the night air, until she landed at our feet like a slab of beef, still shrieking. Myrtle almost lost her girdle laughing that night.

After Mrs. Mersley we gave up tires and started in on dummies. God knows why. Our young creative minds needed new fields, I suppose. Dummy-making didn't require any big expenditures, either, like buying brown wrapping paper. We didn't spend a cent on the dummies. One peer, Alex O'Brien, borrowed a pair of pants from his father's closet, another threw in an old shirt, and we found a pair of shoes and a hat at the town dump. Leaves for stuffing were picked up, and I supplied the catsup (blood) out of my mother's cupboard.

Our first dummy, though a flimsy, amateur, falling-apart job, was a bloody success. We had cars lined up for a block the very first night, with a good two dozen drivers and passengers examining our hit-and-run "victim," while Old Man Waligora bellowed from his front porch. Even an ambulance came that night. Cops, too. It was glorious. We watched the whole show from under my father's big front porch, which was catercornered across the street from Mr. Waligora's house.

We were scared to death. Especially when my father came out of the house to see what was going on. He passed within three feet of us.

In a few minutes he came back into the house carrying Charlie—or most of him, anyway. Charlie had broken in half when my father picked him up. Actually, as it turned out, my dad had brought home only the bottom half of Charlie.

I suppose the bottom half of poor Charlie would still be in my father's basement if Alex O'Brien's father hadn't gone looking for his pants a couple days later. When he couldn't find them, he got Alex in a corner. Alex weakened after a while and told him his pants, were on Charlie.

"And *who* is Charlie! And what is he doing wearing my pants!"

Alex told him.

"Well, young man, you just go and get my pants *off* Charlie!"

We really felt for Alex when he told us what had happened. And we agreed with him, although very reluctantly, that the only thing for him to do was to ask my father for Charlie's pants.

Which is what he did. He knocked on my father's door that very night. When I heard him at the door, the little blood in me turned to sludge. I felt as dead as Charlie.

"Evening, Mr. Taylor," I heard Alex say. His voice sounded as if he'd lost most of it.

"Good evening, Alex. You want to see Mike?"

"Ah ... no, Mr. Taylor. It's about something else." Long silence.

"Yes, Alex. What is it?"

"Well..."

"Yes?"

"Well... Well, Mr. Taylor, my father really needs his pants."

"His pants?"

"They're on Charlie."

"Charlie?"

"Charlie. You can have everything except his pants, Mr. Taylor. Honest. But I just gotta have the pants. They're my father's *best* ones."

After that the peers and I decided we wouldn't put any more dummies on the side of the road. There wasn't much left of Charlie anyway.

But that's not to say we didn't do anything. What we did do, in fact, was put a bushel-basketful of frogs on Old Man Waligora's front porch. It seemed like a splendid idea at the time.

For years we'd been hunting frogs at night in a pond not far from the ball diamond. We caught the ugly things partly for fun and partly for humanitarian reasons: the rascals croaked so loud that hardly anybody in town was getting any sleep. Frog hunting was the only thing we did in those days that the townfolks went along with.

We caught them by shining a flashlight in their eyes, paralyzing them, or at least blinding them; they wouldn't move anyway, and we'd scoop them up by the dozens and put 'em in a potato sack. On the night of The Great Frog Caper, though, we put them in a bushel basket and started, hip boots and all, toward Old Man Waligora's front porch. What a racket they made! Porch lights flashed on and people came out to look. They must have thought the whole damn pond was moving in on them.

We made it up onto Old Man Waligora's porch all right. And we dumped the frogs in front of his door okay. I mean, there were frogs all over the place. They must have been a hundred, all croaking. And we made it back out to the street—just in time.

The porch light flashed on, the frogs let out an extra barrage, the door flew open, and there was Old Man Waligora, shotgun in hand, a nightgown around his belly. He just stood there a minute or two, not saying a word, just listening to all the ear-mashing noise. Just staring and listening. He must have thought he had wandered over to the pond in his sleep. In fact, he stared and listened so long at those frogs, not paying any attention to us out in the shadows, that we got a little fidgety.

Then he came back to form. He opened this excavation he called a mouth, sucked in half the air in town, and out of him, like screaming fiends, came: "SHUT UP, DAMN YOU!"

And they did.

I mean, like that, zip—silence. Not a croak.

And without another word, Old Man Waligora, Napoleon himself, turned around and walked—strode!—back into his house. He even shut the door proudly.

Not one more croak!

I guess you'd call us stunned. Then, slowly, without saying a word ourselves, we also turned around and went back to wherever we had come from. Only *we* weren't striding. I remember I walked home in a great silence, as if I'd seen a miracle.

Maybe I had. I dunno. I'm sure of one thing, though: none of us peers ever pestered Old Man Waligora again. Any man who could shut up frogs just by yelling at them oughtn't to be pestered. This was a man to be respected. And from that night on he was.

~

NOTES ON "A BUSHEL OF FROGS"

Keefauver wrote at least 10 versions of this story, and it may have been his personal favorite. These versions differ primarily in the number of pranks and characters and the names of the characters. In some versions, Keefauver gender-swapped the main character (usually Old Man Waligora or Old Man Barker) for "Aunt Gert," the female version of the eccentric uncle figure that was one of his mainstays. The text here follows the most complete published version, from the Spring 1971 issue of The North American Review (Vol. 256, No. 1, pp. 70-72), with one minor addition.

Thanks to the Keefauver family, I was able to confirm my suspicion that at least some of the events in this story actually occurred, and I have seen a map showing the actual location where "Old Man Waligora" lived (the name probably derives from the name of a giant in a Polish fairy tale). I will leave it up to the reader's imagination to decide which events are verifiable.

THE GREAT THREE-MONTH SUPER SUPERSONIC TRANSPORT STACK-UP OF 1999

I T WAS ON THE THIRTY-FIFTH day of The Great Three-Month Super Supersonic Transport Stack-Up of 1999—a Fourth of July weekend, when the thousands of SSSTs stacked up over Hole, Wyoming, actually began getting higher instead of lower—that Henry J. Littlefinger began to have serious doubts that he would ever get back down to the ground again, safely.

Earlier, on the twenty-ninth day, when the captain of the SSST that Henry and 3,333 other passengers were on had said over the public address system that "some damn Piper Cubs are sneaking into the bottom of the stack," Henry had foreseen trouble ahead. And two days later when the captain of the 3,006-foot long, 306-foot wide jumbo-jumbo named Super Speed had shouted, "There's a crack in the stack!" Henry had begun to shudder.

But only he. For Henry, of all the passengers and ninety stewardesses aboard, was the only one who was not gulping Fly-Cheerful pills, the issuance and gulping of which was required by the International Aviation Agency during extended stack-ups, i.e., those lasting more than fifteen days. Henry, clutching his parachute, refused to take the pills offered him, though they came in attractive Speed-Ho Pink. "I'm a flying dropout!" he muttered, thrusting aside the capsules. "A landnik. Leave me sulk and sweat, cheerlessly."

Henry spoke the truth. Refusing to fly, he had been labeled a landnik and flying dropout some years before by the IAA, and had been sentenced to scrubbing SSSTs for a living—which was what he had been doing (while wearing his parachute, which he refused to scrub without or even to enter an airport without) that Memorial Day weekend of 1999 when the Super Speed had taken off from the East Coast to fly to Hole. He, forgetting to bring along a map of the interior of the SSST when he went to work, had got lost in the jumbo-jumbo. ("Six feet longer than ten football fields! Six feet wider than three football fields!") It had taken off before he could find his way off the thing.

Henry didn't even have a picnic basket to sit on. Except for him, every passenger had a basket to use as a seat (instead of the usual suitcase), for the Super Speeders were en route to Hole for a picnic at one of the few remaining sites in the United States. Long before the Fourth of July weekend arrived, however, they had eaten all their picnic goodies, including the apple pie, and had to stand cheerfully in one of the nineteen Super Speed chow lines as they circled over Hole, grateful to the IAA for all the free meals they were getting for their $2.98 Zip-to-Hole plane ticket. After The Great Two Month Stack-Up of 1994 five years before, over Tourist, Arizona, during which 14,049 passengers in twenty-one SSSTs (jumbos were smaller then) starved to death, the IAA had decreed that all SSSTs store enough food aboard to last three months.

Little did the Super Speeders—and Henry J. Littlefinger—know, though, what was ahead of them when they took off from the 17-mile-long runway at Zip, New York, that Memorial Day weekend of 1999.

In 11:43.18 minutes their SSST (pronounced "sssssss-t!") was over Hole.

One month later it was still over Hole, for, unfortunately, a large portion of the country's population of close to 200 billion had decided to take a picnic that weekend at Hole. By actual count, 7,007 SSSTs were in stack-up circles over Hole, along with seven Piper Cubs.

By the Fourth of July weekend, when the Super Speed was getting ever higher, instead of lower, there was some muttering among passengers, albeit cheerfully, since by the Fourth the picnic season in Hole had passed. And by the middle of July they had sent a message, via a stewardess who had a steady wink, to the captain, requesting that he land anywhere, even if back in Zip. In minutes his answer came back, on the public address system, from behind the three-inch steel pilot compartment's door, guarded by a machine-gun nest:

"If the SOP (Speed Or Perish) Airlines says it is going to land you in Hole, it *will* land you in Hole! After all, we're only number two. We try harder. Besides, flying there is only half the fun. The other half is landing. There."

So, fueled periodically by Hole-based Seek-Out Flying Hoses, which honed in on the SSST and other planes by smelling out fuel tanks, the Super Speed continued to steadily go up in the stack-up, while its passengers, gulping Fly-Cheerful pills by the thousands (except for Henry J.), settled cheerfully back on their twenty-two rows of three "seat"-wide picnic baskets, separated by twenty-three aisles. As suitcases ordinarily would have been, the baskets had been tied to each passenger during ticketing back in Zip, a process called "Ticket & Tie," which had solved both the pesky problem of losing baggage and seating passengers on SSSTs. Of the two problems, however, seating was by far the lesser; for, flying at 18,000 miles per hour, eighteen times as fast as the earth rotates, it didn't take long for Super Speed or any SSST to get anyplace. "Standing to there is half the fun!"

Although the Super Speeders were Fly-Cheerful, residents of Hole weren't. For sonic booms following thousands of overhead SSSTs were speedily destroying the town-and picnic area, which was the community's chief tourist attraction. SSSTs, unfortunately, couldn't fly under 1,300 miles an hour without stalling—unlike back in the 1980s when wings could be extended (and retracted) for slower speedier flying. Moving wings had to be abandoned, Henry remembered with a shudder, when a few moved all the way back through the airplane—in error—and didn't work properly when they came out the other side.

Fortunately, Super Speeders couldn't see what was going on below; the portholes were too small. Shaped in the form of a mini-SSST, the windows were so tiny that if a few blew, pressure in the plane could still be maintained, although it was admitted that it would be somewhat drafty inside at 18,000 mph. The glass was too thick to see through, too. No matter. A film—in slow motion—was constantly shown on the inside of the windows, depicting various parts of the earth, to let passengers know that it was still there.

Eating Fly-Cheerful pills as if they were popcorn, Super Speeders (except for Henry J.) availed themselves of the many entertainments provided by the SOP of the convenience and cheerfulness of stacked-up passengers. As the weeks went by, they watched dozens of concurrently shown movies, all edited down to fifteen minutes (the time it took to fly over the United States). The films were shown in the dance floor during the day, and in the five bars, nineteen chow lines, and library all the time. If they didn't want to watch movies, passengers could pull down mini-TV sets from the ceiling to a position in front of their eyes—one for each eye—or, when they felt a need to get away from it all, they could go to the Special TV Rooms on the 14th floor, where they could plug a unique Stick-In Set into their navel for Contemplative Viewing.

Also included by SOP airlines for added passenger cheerfulness were ponies for the kiddies; a rock 'n' roll band, "The Dow-Jones Averages"; three physicians; seven nurses; and nine psychiatrists. And a map of the Super Speed.

The map, issued to each passenger as he entered the plane through one of twenty 33-foot-wide doors, along with a plate of food with the admonishment to "Eat harder!" was decreed by the IAA after The Passwater Case of 1996. Passwater, admittedly not an intellect, got on an SSST in Go, Florida, bound for Stop, Florida, only a 93-second flight away. Seventeen weeks later he finally found out how to get off the thing. ("Six feet longer than ten football fields! Six feet wider than three football fields!") He had flown around the world, by actual count, 432 times, making some 14,004 landings in seventy-three countries and picking up a smattering of sixteen languages. And, although never proved, one couple was reported to have conceived and *had* a baby while lost on an SST for eleven months. This had been vigorously denied by the IAA, however, but only because the couple was not married.

Toward the end of their third month on the Super Speed with the SSST still going up in the stack-up, muttering, although cheerful, reached a point where another stewardess (also with a steady wink) was again sent to the captain with a request that the plane land somewhere—anywhere.

Back came the reply, cheerfully: "It's like this at all 17-mile-long runways all over the world, particularly now with the Labor Day weekend coming up. What has happened is this: Memorial Day weekend SSSTs, merging with

Fourth of July weekend SSSTs, have now merged with Labor Day weekend SSSTs. The result is one gigantic worldwide stack-up." Laughing cheerfully, he added, "If it's like this over Hole, you can imagine what it's like over, say, Chicago. But hold on—and stay Fly-Cheerful! Speed Or Perish Airlines will get you down—somewhere, sometime! Landing is half the fun! Wherever!"

Next to getting down, Henry was worried about what would happen once he got down, assuming he got there in pieces bigger than Fly-Cheerful pills. If the Super Speed made a successful 17-mile landing, it would taxi, at 173 mph, into an underground hangar built to withstand hydrogen bombs. He and the other passengers would then be shot at 760 miles an hour in a subway rocket to the terminal, also underground, from which they would arise, if all went well, to step once again on mother earth. From the terminal to the city, though, their speed would be reduced somewhat: according to the latest IAA report, the average speed for a commuter between city and airport was three and a half days.

Speed Or Perish Airlines, and others, had often denounced this ridiculous jumbo ground delay in the age of ssssssss-t, but when suggestions for speedier movement on Moveways, i.e., what used to be called freeways, were suggested, such as building hangar-terminal subways all the way into cities, or, O radical thought! from cities to cities themselves, SOP, and other airlines, always came back with a plan to make terminals into cities, arguing that people should simply live in terminals. "Terminalize!" SOP cried. So, long ago Littlefinger, and others, had given up fighting Terminal Hall, although there were some diehards who continued to push a proposal whereby the 17-mile-long runways, many of which went from city limit to city limit anyway, be used as Moveways instead.

On Labor Day, 1999, with the world one gigantic stack-up, the IAA gave up and decided to use its Ultimate Plan. The agency was swayed to the decision, too, by a newer and bigger plane coming off the assembly lines of Loeing and Bockheed, one so big that it need never leave the ground when in flight. Made of a rubber-like compound, called Snap There, the front end took off and reached its destination before the rear end left the ground. Once the front end was safely on the ground, the rear end was debolted from the origin airport and, destretching, rejoined the front end. A trial ride on the new plane, named Stretch Super Supersonic Transport

(SSSST), was described as "thrilling" by the first passenger, who was picked by a nationwide lottery restricted to mental hospitals. "Snapping there is half the fun!" he cried.

As the only noncheerful passenger aboard the Super Speed, Henry J. Littlefinger was the only one who noticed the Seek-Out-And-Stick rockets approaching from Hole and, indeed, approaching planes from all airports over the world with stacked-up planes overhead. He immediately recognized, uncheerfully, the rockets for what they represented—the putting into effect of the Ultimate Plan—and, screaming, "Seek-Out-And-Sticks are coming, jump!" jumped. As he soared out the emergency exit airlock (ordinarily used for garbage), parachute strapped on, fingers crossed, all Super Speeders cheered, then gaily went into *For He's A Jolly Good Fellow.*

Down-going Henry narrowly missed many of the thousands of up-coming rockets, but since he didn't smell of fuel, they passed him by. Shuddering, he watched each hone in on an SSST (some on Piper Cubs), fasten upon it with a hearty, if not cheerful, *slurrrrrp!* and stick; then, its mighty rocket roaring, scream up, each carrying an SSST (or Piper Cub)... up...up...up, into the stratosphere, all to become, eventually and permanently, Super Supersonic Satellites (SSSSs) ...up...UP...the Ultimate Plan.

Leaving Henry Littlefinger to float safely down onto Hole.

Just before Henry touched ground he thought of something that made him smile. Cheerfully. Sort of.

Then he dismissed the thought as being too ridiculous: that the SSSSs sometimes come back to earth, but, after having a look while hovering over the ground, decide they're lucky to be rid of the place and fly off.

Flying saucers, indeed!

~

NOTES ON "THE GREAT THREE-MONTH SUPER SUPERSONIC TRANSPORT STACK-UP OF 1999"

Originally published in *Alfred Hitchcock Presents: More Stories to Stay Awake By* (1971, pp. 217-223). Keefauver only received $35.00 for this printing, but he later resold the rights for a Spanish-language edition of the book for $20.00, and went on to earn $100.00 for an abridged version that appeared in *Another Way Out: A Thematic Reader* from Holt, Rinehart and Winston. This aerial variation of his perennial traffic jam story is one of his most dystopian stories, and the ending of this tale presages that of one of his greatest works, "The Great Moveway Jam," which appeared several years later in *Omni*.

SCREAM!

A<small>ND YOU SAY</small>, M<small>R</small>. A<small>NGLOS</small>, that in these nightmares you turn into a cock?"

"That's right. Just before I kill each man I turn into a cock. Rip him to death, like fighting cocks do."

"I see." The psychiatrist moved back in his chair. Unconsciously, he lifted a small-boned hand, fragile as new snow, and flitted it through hair the color of fog. "I see." Manicured nails caught mid-morning sunlight plunging in from office windows behind him. Twenty-two stories below was downtown New York.

Anglos, with cheeks the color of crushed cherries, watched the nails as the doctor's fingers smoothed down his long, tenderly-combed hair, once, twice, three times, the snowy hand rising, in an arc, each time he returned it to his forehead. Watching, Anglos thrust his own hand, his left, farther under the psychiatrist's desk, hiding it. His right hand lay on the desk, nickel-shaped fingernails incongruously dirty against the mahogany shine.

Then Anglos' right hand clenched in a spasm of anger: "I wish you wouldn't do that, makes me nervous!" His voice was fist-hard.

"Oh, sorry." The doctor dropped his hand into his lap. "Habit of mine. Do it when I'm thinking."

Anglos let an understanding grunt work through his lips, yet his eyes still seemed to sizzle, frying in a face worked up to the color of flame. His hair, nearly as red as his cheeks, looked as if it had been kicked instead of combed. A wart perched on the side of his chin, as if ready to jump off; fatigue made him look older than his late-twenty years.

He had come into the psychiatrist's office less than fifteen minutes ago, and he was still nervous: the doctor, so rich-looking, so clean and educated and *bossy*. His office rich too; all them fancy rugs and pictures, leather chairs and stuff. Money. He, Anglos, was sure out of place here, him and his beer joint ways. Ought to never have come here, like that ordinary doctor had told him to. But he was so tired, so tired; he just had to come, go somewhere.

The psychiatrist's nose was aimed beaklike at his patient now. Thrusting cheekbones seemed to point. Fresh bullet-colored eyes, older and wiser, shot into Anglos's sleepless ones.

"Tell me about the cockfight, please."

"Hell, doc, you know what a cockfight is? Two cocks fixed up with knives on their left legs, clawing each other until one can't go on any more. Usually he dies."

"Yes, I know. But *your* cockfight, the one in Manila, what was it like?"

"Same thing. Blood all over the place, dead cocks on the ground." Anglos's voice burst. "It was horrible!" Below the desk his fingernails pressed into his palms. "Horrible! But the men were worse. The men who were betting, all crazy nuts, all around me, throwing their hands up, betting with their fingers, some kind of code. Like claws. That's what their fingers looked like. Like claws! Like the knives men tape on the cocks' left legs. More I thought about it, the more they looked like knives."

"Easy."

"Easy, hell! I've been thinking about this, dreaming about it, ever since I left Manila a month ago. I was on my way back to New York from a construction job in Vietnam when I stopped to see this cockfight in Manila. Worst thing I ever did.

"Easy, crap! You see what happened? You see it? Men are animals! Knives for fingers, ripping the air, yelling, screaming, betting. You see it?

Men are animals! They're worse than the cocks. Day and night, that's all I can think about."

"All right, all right. I understand. So the nightmares started then."

"Yeah, yeah. Always the same. I'm in an arena ripping a man to death. The place is always jammed, and the men—the men watching—aren't men. They're cocks. All of 'em. Cocks. They're all yelling like mad, happy as hell that I'm killing a man."

"Yes, yes..."

"Like I say, just before I kill the man I turn into a cock myself—sort of. Least, I think I'm a cock. I rip the man to death with my fingers, rip his throat with 'em, like my fingers are knives, like the kind on a cock's leg. Cock's left leg. They always tie the knife to the cock's left leg. I always use my left hand, too. Like a cock. And I'm righthanded ordinarily."

"Logical," the psychiatrist murmured. His hand was again smoothing his hair.

"After I kill the man, I always fly away. Like a cock. Fly right away. I feel swell. Guess I've killed thirty, thirty-five men, all told."

"But..." The doctor was frowning.

Anglos interrupted. "Another thing: I only pick a man to kill after I see him raising his hand. You know, like the men did at the cockfight when they were betting. As soon as I see a man raise his hand, any man, anywhere, I go after him, I want to kill him. If he doesn't raise his hand, I leave him alone. I dunno how it happens. I just see a man raise his hand, and next thing I know I'm in this arena ripping his throat with my fingers.

"Every morning since the nightmare began, I've been hardly able to get out of bed. Up until I came to see you, I thought it was simply because I wasn't sleeping good, as you can imagine. The other morning, though, maybe a week ago, I woke up and found blood on my clothes."

Anglos dropped his head so that he was staring at the wrist and upper part of his left hand. He could see the fingers; they were still stuck under the desk, as if he wanted to hide them from himself, as well as from the psychiatrist.

"Of course, at first I refused to believe..."

"Of course."

"But after I had seen more blood on the clothes I had worn the previous nights... And when I read in the newspapers morning after morning of murders—throat cuttings, always men—in my neighborhood..." He shrugged. "I understood. I had to admit it to myself. Especially when one of the places where I always found blood was under my fingernails—my left-hand fingernails, the long ones."

Anglos pulled his left hand out from below the desk and put it on top of the shiny wood, palm down. The fingernails, except for the thumb's, were almost an inch long—filed, glistening, deadly. Giving the psychiatrist only a glance at them, he quickly withdrew his hand and put it back under the desk.

"Right after I saw the cockfight I had a compulsion to let my fingernails grow—only on my left hand, and only my fingers, not my thumb. Compulsion—ain't that the word?"

"But it's not possible to kill a man with your fingernails," the doctor put in. "I don't care how long you let them grow, or how sharp you file them."

Irritation came like anger on to Anglos' face. "Don't tell me it ain't possible! *I'm* the one who found the blood. *I'm* the one who has read of the murders in the papers. *I'm* the one who hasn't slept for I don't know how many nights, afraid to go to sleep, afraid I'll kill somebody else. You understand! It's *me* it's happening to! It's *me* who has to fight the urge!"

"Easy. I understand. And you must try to understand, too. You must try to realize that it is impossible to kill a man with your fingernails. They would snap, they would break, they would bend before you could do it."

"Listen, doctor..."

"You must also try to realize that your nightmares are simply just that—nightmares, and nightmares only. You have not killed anybody. Blood can get on anybody's clothing by any number of means. You may have got blood on them in the past and simply forgotten about it. Perhaps you only imagine blood on your clothing. The mind plays tricks."

"Doctor, there's one thing I haven't..."

"Especially *your* mind," the psychiatrist interrupted again. He was slowly smoothing his hair. "A mind that's been filled with guilt the last month—and probably before, for that much. First, guilt you feel in being a member of a mankind that will set two innocent animals against each other in a fight to the death; second, guilt you feel as a murderer, a supposed murderer.

"Let me see those fingernails again."

"No."

Anglos watched the psychiatrist dismiss his request with a slight wave of his hair-caressing hand. And he only vaguely heard the doctor say, "Here's something else, too: you said earlier that you, as a cock, flew away after each killing. This is a violation of what I would call external logic, as opposed to internal, or psychological, or *your* logic. In other words, flying cocks violate day-to-day reality, and as such are in violation of a reality, or logic, apart from your inner psychological reality. This you must understand."

Anglos heard the doctor cough. He watched his hand fly to his mouth.

"This all adds up to another fallacy," the psychiatrist went on. "You must simply understand that it is impossible for cocks, in external logic, to fly for more than a few feet."

Anglos was not looking at the doctor's face now, at his eyes or his lips. He was watching the psychiatrist's hand play with his hair, rubbing the strands back, over and over, his fingers arching up high every time he brought his hand back towards his forehead.

"You're simply the victim of a very severe, very traumatic, very real nightmare, Mr. Anglos, not that I want to take anything away from its importance or internal reality. If you can only understand this, we can proceed from that point very satisfactorily, I'm sure.

"First, let me see your fingernails again, please. I'll begin by demonstrating to you their fragility."

The words of the doctor bounced off the mind of Anglos. He was busy with his own thought—and with the doctor's hand, moving, rising, getting higher and higher each time he wiped at his hair. Almost soaring, the fingers were; almost soaring.

"Please, Mr. Anglos, your hand, your fingernails."

The psychiatrist never did see the fingernails. They came out from under the desk so fast they were only a blur. He felt them go into his throat. And he died without hearing the crow.

The crow came after Anglos got up on the windowsill, a great joyous crow to all the world.

Time to fly.

He was a cock, and it was time to fly. He jumped over the street, twenty-two stories below. And crowed. Anglos flew.

When he hit the pavement only one of the four slivers of razor blade came uncemented. The other three remained secure in their hiding places under his left-hand fingernails.

~

NOTES ON "SCREAM!"

This story first appeared in a magazine called *The Mrs*. (Vol. 1, No. 1, March 1967, pp. 42-44). However—and more prominently—it was also published in *The Fifteenth Pan Book of Horror Stories*, edited by Herbert van Thal (1974, Pan Books, Ltd. pp. 107-112), marking Keefauver's return to the Pan series after a seven-year hiatus. Although the series continued for another ten years, twenty-five volumes in all, this was also Keefauver's final appearance therein. Why van Thal did not publish him for so long, and never did again after this brief return, must remain a mystery.

Keefauver sold "Scream!" again to the South African Broadcasting Corporation for £22.50, where it was adapted for radio by Brian Squires as episode 168 of *Twist in the Tale* and broadcast on 31 March 1979. A copy of the script survives in the author's files.

THE HUNT

H ER HAND DARTED FOR THE bottle under the counter as soon as she heard the voice from the shortwave radio crack, "Car eighteen. Six-eye. One-twenty-three Fowler." And she had thrown half an inch of whisky into her mouth before the splintery voice stopped; had gulped it as, "Daniel, Daniel, it's going again," came moaning out of her. Through the broken front window of the garage she could see him putting gas into a car, his shoulders already flaky with snow.

She stretched a palm out toward the radio, as if to ward off any new voice, then slid off the hip-high stool behind the counter and walked toward her husband outdoors, went away from the radio holding tightly to her half-filled glass. "Cold outside," she murmured. She stopped. And drank.

She stood now under a single bulb that dangled from the ceiling. Its light smacked one side of her face, causing a thumb-size scar on her left cheek to shine grotesquely. Graying hair hung in disarray down over both ears.

"Daniel, it's cold for you," she said, then hurried past the shelves of nuts and bolts and hanging fly belts, the greasy overalls which dangled from a nail on the wall, past the stack of secondhand tires, the tool box, the portable jack, and walked to the front door, drawing her sweater tight around her child-thin figure at the sight of the falling snow.

"Daniel, come on back in here where it's warm." She gazed at the spurting gray smoke from the car's exhaust, at her husband now going to the car window on the driver's side. "But it's not very warm," she said, shivering beside the broken garage window.

"Pretty," she said softly to the floating snow.

She backed from the door as the car drove off and her husband walked through the snow toward the garage. He came in, brrring! big shoulders hunched, a jacket stretched tight around his pillow-big stomach. His cheeks were red, heavishly firm and rounded. Large freckled hands adjusted his cap, sausage fingers first rubbing through his hair.

"Daniel, it's cold in here."

He looked down at his little wife, at the drink in her hand, and said softly, "Nellie, now go on back in the house and go to bed," trying to smile through the sadness in his voice. "It's late."

"You said you were going to fix that window, Daniel," her words a whining reprimand.

"I am. Now go on."

Turning, she started back toward the counter, Daniel beside her.

"Ann's not home yet," she said.

"Stop it, Nellie."

"Worries me, Ann not in yet, all this snow." She worked herself up onto the stool behind the counter. "You shouldn't've let her go out tonight, Daniel. Your own daughter. Snowing like it is."

"Nellie..." his eyes had tumbled below the counter to the whisky bottle "...where's the top?"

"Maybe I ought to phone that girl's house, see if Ann's still there. All this snow, ought to never gone out."

"What did you do with the top, Nellie?"

"Coming down like it is."

"Nellie?"

"Haven't seen the top, don't know where it is."

"Give me the top, Nellie." He was looking at her left hand, clenched tight at her chest against her red sweater.

"Just took it off to hold it," she mumbled.

"Nellie."

She opened her fist and gave him the top and he screwed it back on the bottle.

"Go on to bed, Nellie. I'll be back in a little while."

"Going to wait up for Ann."

"Nellie, please. You know Ann's not coming home." He reached for her glass but she held it away. "Go to bed. I'm going to stay open a little while longer. With this snow, we ought to get a call," nodding at the shortwave radio.

"Oh, Daniel, please turn it off. It scares me, you know how it does. All those wrecks it says about. Throw it away, please, Daniel. Throw the goddamn thing away, Daniel!" came shrilly, almost shrieking, out of her before her husband's hand clamped on her arm and squeezed her bursting voice quiet.

The radio broke silence. "Ten-four, eighteen, on your ten-eight at two-forty."

And Nellie's head went shudderingly into Daniel's chest. He put his arms around her, melting her shudders against his keglike chest. "If only it wasn't snowing, too, if only that wasn't happening, too... I mean, both at once, it's awful," her voice a whimper.

"Nellie, Nellie, we have to keep it on, it's our business. How would we get any wrecks hauled in here if we didn't have it going?"

"Don't want to see any wrecks, don't want to see anymore," she was saying when the radio burst, "All cars. Be on lookout for gray '69 or '70 Pontiac sedan. Pennsylvania tags, one-oh-three-six-seven-one. Wanted for eleven, apparently six-eye." A repetition and the voice stopped.

"Please, Daniel, turn that thing off."

Nellie's voice was quietly cold now. She had drawn away from her husband, and he did not try to stop her as she drank from the glass.

"I *can't*, Nellie, you know that."

One corner of the woman's mouth arched with scorn. "I could make you, if I wanted to. Be easy."

"Be easy," she said again as a car stopped at the gas pumps outside.

Daniel hurried to the door, zippering up his jacket. Nellie reached for the whisky bottle under the counter, her lips in a twisted smile. But her hand flew from the bottle as Daniel stopped, as he backed toward the counter.

Two men were coming in the door, gripped guns in their gloved hands pointing at Daniel's broad, round, sticking-out stomach.

"Easy," one said.

His eyes were level with Daniel's chin, his overcoat too long, low below his knees. He gruntingly cleared his throat before he spoke again, tight-thin lips barely moving in the shadow beneath the brim of his hat

"Take care of the door," he said to the second gunman behind him. The second man wore a red turtleneck sweater. A few flakes of snow sat damply on his plastered-down hair. More flakes had settled on his humpback, like snow on a mountain peak; bare bulb light added to his grotesqueness. He glared at Nellie, who was still perched on the stool, her expression a steady stare, bewildered, uncertain, yet faintly and gigglishly amused.

"Turn off the outside lights, Fatso," the small man said to Daniel.

"Don't call Daniel Fatso."

"Be quiet, Nellie," Daniel said.

Daniel walked to the switch on the wall by the door and turned off the outside lights.

"All right, Fatso, let's you and me go out and change a tire. And hurry it up, what d'ya think we came in here with these guns out for. Action, Fatso, action, that's what we want. And cash."

"Don't say that name, it's..." Nellie began, her voice splintering under the impact of the exploding radio, "Car twelve, signal eight. Two-one-oh-six Eleventh Street. Car twelve..."

The small gunman spun toward the sound, his gun hand whirled, pointing. The humpbacked man had half opened the door, tense and ready to run.

"Make 'em turn that thing off, Cy," the humped man whined.

Cy whirled toward Daniel. "What street is this, Fatso? Quick!" His gun jumped at Daniel's stomach.

"Reese."

"That signal eight, what's that mean?"

"Disturbance."

Cy relaxed and with his gun waved Daniel toward the door. "Okay, Fatso, let's go."

"Don't you keep calling Daniel that."

"Cut it, momma," Cy spat.

"I'm not your momma," she mumbled. "Ann's momma."

Daniel picked a lug wrench out of the tool box near the door and got the portable jack next to the wall. He started toward the front door, the small gunman behind him.

"Let me go out with him, Cy," the big man said. "Cold don't bother me none."

"I'll take him out," said Cy.

The humped man glared at Daniel. "I can take care of him."

"Unpth!" Cy grunted harshly. "You couldn't even take care of the car. Couldn't even put a jack in it." Cy's voice began to rise. "Couldn't even put a stinkin' lousy jack in the goddamn car! I got a good mind to make you change the tire!"

"I'm sorry, Cy."

"Don't yell at him," Nellie said. "Everybody yelling all the time." She had got the bottle out from under the counter and was filling the glass as she frowned at the small gunman.

"Shut up, momma."

Cy prodded Daniel with the gun and they went out the front door toward the sedan, leaving the larger man inside.

"Calling Daniel Fatso," Nellie mumbled. As she raised her glass to her lips, she stopped, she glanced at the inside gunman, and with her crooked grin said:

"Want a drink?"

"No."

She gulped at the whisky and put the glass back down on the counter, bubbling a small chuckle at the gunman as his head spun, his gun hand jerked, as out of the radio a monotonous voice rolled, "Car nine. Signal three. One-four-five-three, Sixteenth Street. Apartment sixty-two. Employ caution. Car nine..."

"That scares you," Nellie giggled, as if her past fear of the radio had gone into the man.

"Don't neither."

"You was scared, I could tell. Everybody's scared. Daniel. You. Everybody 'cept me."

"Nothing to be scared of." He swaggered toward the counter, carrying his hump in rolling bounces. "Me and Cy, we won't hurt you none. 'Less you start something."

"You ought to have a drink."

"Can't now. Working."

"Come on."

He glanced out the front window at the sedan, which had been moved, its headlight now swinging toward the end of the garage.

"Cy'd see me."

"He won't mind."

"He would."

"Just afraid," she murmured.

A quick glance at the car, and he walked rapidly to the counter, grabbed the bottle and gulped, no chaser, smiling at the admiration in Nellie's gaze.

"I can't drink it that way," she said sadly. "I'm just a sissy." The moving part of her bottom lip puckered. "Sissy."

The gunman shrugged. "It's all in the way you're used to," he said, giving her a swaggering smile.

"What did you rob?" Nellie asked, staring at the gunman's back.

Still smiling, "Something."

"Something big?"

"Maybe."

"I bet it was. You wouldn't rob nothing little, I bet. Like I would," she said sadly. "Or Daniel."

She fingered her scar.

"I'm sorry about your back," she said.

The gunman's smile broke.

She murmured, "Both of us are the same. Ugly."

"Not neither," he muttered.

"Just alike," she said. "Were you in a car wreck, too?"

The sedan had pulled up to one end of the garage, horn honking, headlights flashing bright through the large garage door windows.

"He wants you to open the door," Nellie said before Pete could answer. "I could have told them to fix the tire in here all along. But nobody asked me."

Pete shuffled toward the large door, his gun now almost despondently swinging at his side.

"Nobody ever does," Nellie murmured.

Daniel drove the sedan into the building. Cy sat on the seat beside him. The shortwave radio barked as the car stopped. Cy quickly opened the car door and got out.

"What did that thing say, Pete?" he snapped at his partner, who was closing the garage doors.

"What?"

"The radio."

"I didn't hear it."

"You didn't hear it! You dumb bastard! Why didn't you?!"

"Don't yell at him," Nellie whimpered.

"Was opening the door," he said meekly.

"Christ!" Cy drew his hand up, as if to backhand Pete. "Aah," he let the hand fall, "get the hell out and get the jack. And hurry it up!" as Pete went toward the smaller front door. "We don't got all night!" Turning to Daniel, "Come on Fatso, get out of the car and get this tire off!"

"Don't call Daniel Fatso."

"Nellie, be quiet," Daniel said softly.

Pete brought in the jack and gave it to Daniel, who rolled it under the car and pumped until the tire was off the garage floor.

"Calling Daniel Fatso—my husband." Her voice rose. "He's my husband, I got a husband."

Cy did not turn to her or look from Daniel, who was now unscrewing tire lugs. But Nellie saw Pete staring at her, saw his look of admiration because she was talking back to Cy. She heard, "Be quiet, Nellie," come again from her husband. "No," she answered, and kept looking at grinning Pete.

Daniel swore once softly as he yanked with no success at a rusty lug. He looked up within his anger and saw Nellie, weaving, taking another drink. "Don't drink anymore, Nellie," he said, tone harsh and rusty, like the lugs.

"Come on, come on, hurry it up!" Cy cracked.

"Can't even get that wheel off," Nellie mumbled to Daniel. "Sissy." Smiling twistedly, she turned to Pete. "You're not a sissy, are you, Mister? You just wear a sweater. Like me." She began to unbutton her sweater down the front, gazing at Pete.

"Keep your sweater on, momma," Cy said. "Don't have to."

Daniel, who had got the spare on, looked up from the tightening of lugs. "Nellie!"

"It's not cold," Pete murmured.

"Goddamn it, Pete," Cy bullied, "mind your own business. You need something to do, you can finish tightening up these lugs. Fatso here is getting a little tired."

"I'm not going to tighten no lugs," he grumbled, glancing quickly at Nellie.

"You're getting snotty as hell, Pete!" Cy snapped. "Suppose you just put this wheel back on, you know so much. Fatso, get up and let big mouth here get down there."

"He can do it," Pete mumbled.

"Yeah, and so can you. Come on, Fatso."

Daniel got up from kneeling at the wheel and gave Pete the wrench. "Take your gloves off," Cy said to Pete. "You'll get 'em dirty."

"Don't give a goddamn about the gloves. Never needed 'em anyway, not cold."

"Take 'em off."

Nellie watched Pete take off his gloves; watched him—her head going up down, up down, pleased—pull his tough-man sweater over his head, doing it easily, professionally; watched him drop it to the floor; watched as she weaved toward him; watched as her fingers finished unbuttoning her own sweater; watched him as she took it off and dropped it to the floor, too, pimples popping out on her bare arm.

"Nellie, put that sweater back on," Daniel said.

"No."

Daniel picked up her sweater and gave it to her. She threw it down beside Pete's.

"We're alike," she said. "Alike. Him and me."

The radio cracked, "Ambulance two-oh-nine, are you calling this station?" and Cy spun nervously toward Pete.

"Hurry it up, let's get the hell out of here."

"No," Nellie said. "Don't go. We're alike."

Pete was banging with the palm of his hand on the hub cap. "Goddamn it," he muttered.

"Leave it off," Cy said.

"Don't go." Nellie had taken a step toward Pete. She stopped as he straightened up from the wheel. "Don't go, Mister."

"Get in," Cy said to Pete, opening the car door.

"Mister..."

Pete walked around to the driver's side, carrying his sweater. He got in under the wheel next to Cy.

"Open the garage door, Fatso," Cy said.

Daniel went behind the car and opened the large doors.

"Don't go," Nellie moaned to Pete.

Pete began to back the car out of the garage.

"Wait a minute." Cy ran the glass down in the car window. "How 'bout the dough in your cash register, Fatso."

Nellie began to cry. She dropped her drink to the floor as her voice mounted into a wail.

"Don't go, Mister! Don't go!"

She lurched around the front of the car and went to Pete's window and put the palms of her hands on the glass. And pressed. And pressed.

"Mister, don't go. Please!"

"Shut up, momma. Fatso, I asked you..." Daniel started around the car toward Nellie. "Wait a minute, Fatso!" Cy pointed the gun at Daniel. Daniel stopped as Cy got out of the car. "Come on, Fatso, let's you and me go over to the cash register."

Daniel and Cy walked to the register. Cy grabbed the paper money from the drawer and stuffed it quickly into his pocket. Behind him Nellie wailed.

"Jesus Christ!" he said. "You sure got a nut for a wife, Fatso, wanting to go with Pete, ugly as he is. What's the matter, don't you treat her good?"

"Yes, I..." Daniel's voice sighed "...treat her good."

"Don't sound like it, way she wants to go."

"She's hunting for something, outside of here. Away someplace."

"What's that?"

Daniel's head made sad movements. "I don't know. Ever since our daughter, Ann, was killed in a car wreck, all she talks about is she's gotta find something. Nellie was driving the car Ann was in. It was Nellie's fault, the accident. Nellie was drinking. That's how she got the scar, the accident. It happened when there was snow. I hauled the car in myself."

"Yeah, but this stuff she's after, what's that?"

"I don't know, but I guess Pete's got some of it, whatever it is…"

"Jesus, wait 'til he hears that!"

They walked back and Cy got into the car.

"Jesus, Pete, back this thing out of there. Jesus!"

Nellie clung to the handle for a moment as Pete shot the car back.

A sob, and she let go. Pete turned the car around in the snow-covered front; back wheels spun as he gunned it down the street.

"Mister!" Nellie screamed.

Daniel had started toward the phone on the wall but stopped at Nellie's scream and hurried to her and put his hands under her arms.

"No," she moaned. "Leave me alone."

He lifted her and, arm tight around her waist, started to close the garage doors.

"Leave them open," she mumbled. "Keep it cold in here."

Daniel closed the doors and led Nellie back toward the counter. She lurched away from him, ran to the counter and grabbed the bottle.

She saw Daniel coming toward her, slowly, his expression hurt and angry. She backed. Backed until she was behind the counter.

"Give me the bottle, Nellie."

"No."

Pressed herself against the wall.

"No."

But he kept coming closer.

"It's mine," she said.

He reached for the bottle and she drew it away from him.

"Mine."

She saw him turn from her then and go across the floor and pick up her sweater where she had thrown it. He came back toward her, the sweater held in front.

"No," she said.

"Here's your sweater, Nellie. Give me the bottle. Time to go to bed."

"No."

The police radio shrieked as her husband spoke. She could not hear him.

"I don't want that sweater."

"You're cold, Nellie," softly.

"No," she weakened.

"Your own sweater, Nellie. It's warm."

"Warm," she intoned.

"Yes."

"It's cold in here, Daniel. You ought to fix that window."

"I am."

She sighed and gave Daniel the bottle and took her sweater and let him help her put it on.

"Daniel," she said, "let's go back in the house where it's warm. Ann ought to be home soon."

~

NOTES ON "THE HUNT"

Originally published in 1972 in *Wascana Review* (Vol 7, No. 1, pp. 79-87).

THE PILE OF SAND

THE EARLIER ARRIVALS AT THE beach saw the pile of sand and assumed it had been made by someone at dawn who had left it to go, perhaps, to have breakfast and would be coming back later in the morning to sculpt it into an entry for the sand-castle contest that day. That seemed like a good explanation, anyway (it was later agreed), for the existence of the gigantic pile of sand, at least twenty-five feet high, maybe thirty, with a proportionate base, sitting on the beach not far from the ocean's edge at 9 A.M. with not a soul near it. It appeared to have been thrown up hurriedly, or without design, anyway, as if it were the first step toward a giant sculpture, although it was puzzling that there was no dug-out area around the pile, from which the sand would have come for the mound. Not puzzling at first; later, when the whole town was talking about the sand hill.

At first no one had paid much attention to the mound (other than to wonder who had such a gigantic sculpture in mind, one which he must have had to start building at dawn) because everybody was intent upon building his own entry. But as the morning wore on and nobody came back to continue work on the mountain of sand, there was more talk about the strange pile, particularly after the judges arrived about noon and began to ask around if anybody knew whom the hill of sand belonged to. Was it an entry? Of course, no one knew any more than the judges. So the thing just sat there, unattended and unworked on, as the hours passed, with parents telling their children not to climb on it or even touch it because it might be the beginning of a sculpture. Which was a difficult order for the kids to abide by, for the great mountain of sand was a most tempting play hill. One boy, in fact, did scamper up the hill, to come tearing down, frightened when his father bawled at him. The father then tried to smooth out his son's footsteps on the pile, muttering all the time about the nut—most likely nuts, from the size of it—who made the thing and then went away and left it unguarded.

By 2 P.M. the judges began making their rounds through the more than a hundred sand creations up and down the beach for about a quarter of a mile: the castles, of course, of all sizes; the animals—the crocodiles and turtles and whales; the offbeat creations—the VW, the hamburger and piece of pie ("Lunch"), a bathtub with a woman in it, kelp used as plumbing, a mouse approaching a trap with a piece of cheese in it, the pyramids, sculptures connected with the space program. And the pile of sand. By three-thirty the judges had compared notes and awarded the first-prize ribbon to "Apollo 12." Second prize went to the VW, and the mouse and trap and cheese won third. The judges ignored the pile of sand; they considered it the work of kids who had tired of it.

Traditionally, after the ribbons had been awarded and people started to go home, children were allowed to destroy the sculptures. The incoming tide would cover them anyway, and the kids might as well have the pleasure. The children jumped savagely on the creations, screaming with delight, while the parents watched with almost equal pleasure. Occasionally an adult would join his child in smashing a sand design.

There wasn't much the kids could do about destroying the mountain of sand. They ran up and down it and kicked it, but they would have had to have a mechanical shovel to have knocked it down. Either that, or have worked hours with shovels to flatten it. Adults ignored the pile.

As the evening fog drifted in and the weather turned cool, there was a rapid departure from the beach, which now looked as if a battle had been fought over it. Only the great pile of sand remained unbroken. The evening high tide would take care of it, though. What nuts went to all that trouble and then never showed up to finish their job? What fools?

By dusk the tide was lapping at the base of the pile.

An early-rising beach-front resident noticed the police car parked in front of his house shortly after dawn, and when he went out to investigate, he saw the officer down on the beach looking at the pile of sand. When the officer came back to his car, he said to the resident, who had walked out to meet him, "That damn hill is still there. Looks like the tides didn't take an inch of sand off it." And sure enough, as the resident went out onto the beach himself, he saw that the high tides during the night and at dawn had flattened and smoothed the beach of all remains of the previous day's sculptures except for the giant pile of sand, which, if anything, appeared to be larger. The bottom three or so feet of the mountain were smooth where the tide had encircled it but, strangely, the water appeared to have washed away none of the base.

By midmorning a number of children were playing on the pile, but it was of such size that the only damage they did to it was to puncture it with footstep holes. Adults looked at it curiously, but none tried to keep the children from climbing on it now.

While the same beach-front resident was eating lunch he saw the car with the press sign park on the street in front. A photographer went down to the beach and took some pictures of the pile, and in that evening's local paper there was a photograph of the "Mysterious Mountain of Sand that Challenges the Sea." The story beneath the picture was written with much tongue in cheek.

That evening about a hundred people (the resident estimated) were around the pile waiting for high tide to reach it. Children played on it, including some older boys now. One man, though, yelled at his son to come down from the hill. "Why?" the boy wanted to know. "Don't argue with me! Come down from there!" As the tide gradually circled the pile, all the parents, though, made their children get off the mountain, leaving only the older youngsters, those whose parents were not with them. They whooped and laughed as the tide rose around the pile, until one boy, a younger one, became silent and finally jumped from the mound into the water and ran in to a dry part of the beach. Then the other boys followed him, one by one,

127

until the scarred mountain of sand sat by itself in the onrushing water, which climbed inch by inch, foot by foot as darkness came on. Some onlookers had brought flashlights, but as they were forced back from the mound their lights gradually lost their effectiveness. When a patrol car on the road above the beach shone its spotlight on the pile of sand, though, they all could see that the mountain remained, as if while one wave was taking sand away, another was bringing it in.

The next day a larger crowd surrounded the pile of sand. The beach-front resident himself had seen the report of the "Sand Mountain" that "survived the night" on the early local television; the pictures clearly showed that the mountain was as big that morning as it had been the day before. And that afternoon another picture and story of the mound were in the local paper, this time on the front page. The story was still written with a light touch, and an oceanologist was quoted as saying that the mountain remained because of the "press's molehill," while the story quoted a geologist: "The sand of the sea speaketh in diverse ways—especially with the help of some local wags with many shovels and much true grit." During the evening the crowd was larger than the one of the previous evening, although more parents kept their children off the pile. There was some talk of digging into the mountain in order to flatten it or at least to see what the hell was inside it. None of the talk was serious, though. It would be a lot of work for nothing. Would be silly. Let the water wash it away.

As the tide rose around the pile, what talk there was quieted down, and as it became apparent that once again the mountain was going to withstand the evening high tide, the onlookers, including ones now along the road that rimmed the beach, became silent. A spotlight from a patrol car stayed on the mountain as the water rose, as if the mountain were a monument. Many spectators stayed even after the tide peaked, and just before dawn, when the tide peaked again, two old men stood beside the police car that had come up and stopped and turned its spotlight on the beach. The mountain still stood. As if, one of the men said, it were the only real sculpture that had ever been there.

By the fourth day of the existence of the mountain of sand only a few parents would allow their children to play on it. Of course, there were older children, on the beach without parents, who climbed up and down the mound, but by the fifth day there was only a total of seven children who ascended the mountain, although it was a beautiful, sunny day and the beach was crowded. One man had brought a shovel and wandered up and down the beach, half-heartedly asking if there were any volunteers with shovels. There was none. So the man went to the hill by himself and jokingly started to plunge his shovel into the sand, then stopped as one of the younger boys on the mountain started to cry, then ran down the mound to the beach, still bawling, to be followed by the others, one by one, as if each were afraid to be left on the mountain alone. "What's the matter?" the crying child was asked. But all he did was blubber that he had become "scared." And the man with the shovel went back to his family on the beach and turned his back on the pile of sand.

On the seventh day of Sand Mountain, a Saturday, three carloads of men with cases of beer set up camp near the hill in midafternoon. Each had a shovel. Immediately a crowd gathered around them, to ask if they were going to flatten the mountain, to urge them to. "We sure as hell are!" said a man who apparently was their leader, a burly, hairy loudmouth in his early thirties. "Soon as we have a few beers."

The crowd waited impatiently as the men, bantering among themselves, lolling on their backs looking up at the mound, slowly drank their beer. To cries of "What you waiting for!" and "Come on!" and "Can't get anything done lying there!" they laughed and grinned and their leader said, "No hurry. That pile of sand ain't going no place. And if there's anything inside it, it ain't going no place either." Then seeing that a half a dozen or so men, men not in his group, had gone off and returned with their own shovels, he stood up and said, "Stay away. This is our baby." And then seeing that the six men with shovels weren't in any hurry to start digging on the mountain, he sat back down and opened another can of beer, the others with him then doing the same. As each drinker finished a beer, he carefully put his can on a stack which, crudely and in miniature, resembled the mountain of sand. None of the drinkers offered a beer to anyone outside his group, and none wore a bathing suit.

By early evening, with almost all the beer drunk and the tide beginning to lap around Sand Mountain, the leader got up and deliberately, dramatically, looking around first to see if he was being watched, destroyed the hill of cans with a kick. "Okay!" he bawled. "Let's go get that damned pile of sand!" And cheered on by some (most onlookers were silent), the men grabbed their shovels and charged up the mound.

They began to dig furiously, throwing the sand as far out from the mountain as they could. About twelve of them, they ringed the pile at various levels, led by their leader, chanting as they worked, "Mountain, mountain, dig it *down*! Mountain, mountain, tear it *down*! Mountain, mountain, get its *heart*! Mountain, mountain..." Onlookers came as close as they could to the pile, to a point where the thrown sand landed just in front of them, while behind them, seeing the attack on the mountain, others streamed toward Sand Mountain from up and down the beach and from the road along the ocean. Cars were stopping now, the occupants getting out to watch. "...tear it *down*!" the onlookers now picking up the chant "...get its *heart*!" Until after only moments spectators with shovels were asking the beer drinkers if they could help, and receiving the go-ahead, climbed onto the mountain, too, and began to dig. "...dig it *down*!" Then men without shovels climbed the hill, to scoop into the mountain with their hands, and stand and throw, chanting. Then women were climbing the mountain, then teenagers and children. "...tear it *down*!" The pile of sand was covered finally with chanting, furiously digging, clawing, throwing, nonlaughing people, becoming packed even tighter as the original beer-drinking diggers kept moving down the mountain as the top of it was flattened. "...get its *heart*!"

The water was rising now around the beheaded mountain, washing over the sand thrown down from the height of the remaining pile, flattening the thrown sand, drawing it back into the ocean. Rising inch by inch, foot by foot, as the sun dropped lower and lower, the water encroached until some men and women picked up their smaller children and waded from the base of the mountain to the dry beach. One woman fell and her child screamed in terror when she, hit from behind by a shovelful of sand, fell into the water. A policeman quickly grabbed them and pulled them out. His patrol car stood ready with its spotlight if it should get dark before the mountain had been destroyed. Its light was already on, aimed at the mound.

Gradually the mountain came down, until only the original shovelers were digging, slower now, panting, chanting less (although the onlookers were still chanting strongly, angrily). Then as the ocean began to lap over what was left of the mountain, the workers straggled off the slight rise and out of the water, until only their leader was left, sweating, panting hard, his chant now down to "dig, tear, heart!"

He waded out of the water the moment the ocean finally covered the mountain, disappointed, muttering, "Hell, there wasn't a *damn thing* in that pile of sand."

Out of habit, the beach-front resident was up at dawn. When he looked from his living-room window at the beach, he didn't know whether to feel disappointment or relief that the mountain was gone. Some of each, he guessed. But mostly relief.

From the distance he was not able to see the beginning of a new mountain not far from the one destroyed. Later in the day, though, he and others would see it as the morning high tide piled up more and more sand. And he would see the second baby mountain, too, near the first one, both growing at equal speed. By 9 A.M. both were larger than old Sand Mountain.

~

NOTES ON "THE PILE OF SAND"

Originally published in 1973, in *Alfred Hitchcock Presents: Stories to Be Read With the Lights On* (Random House, pp. 133-139). As with "Special Handling," we can see here Keefauver perfecting a gimmick he had worked on through multiple stories, including "The Smile of the 30-Foot Woman" and "Giant on the Beach" (to be sure, "The Pile of the Sand" was the first of these three to appear in print, but I suspect it was the last to be written). Just as with "Special Handling," Keefauver finally gets it right by eliminating the gimmick part of the gimmick and letting the mystery prevail. In doing so, he created not only one of his greatest stories, but a subtle masterpiece of Weird Fiction.

PASTE A SMILE
ON THE WALL

HE LET HIS EYES SOAR now, let them climb high and proud up to a window of the house he was walking to. For there, behind that window, in that room, was something better than sleep—and much better than smiles pasted on a wall.

He had almost run up the hill toward the house, at dusk, his back to Monterey Bay and his daytime dishwashing job in a restaurant on Cannery Row. Washing the last pan, scouring the last pot, he'd pulled his head out of steam and, with a wave or two, had hurried, face up and even trying to smile, out of the kitchen, leaving cooks and waitresses wondering what it was all about. Dobby never used to wave, you know; Dobby never used to lift his face up off the floor. Never had before, until the last week or so. And everybody knew he couldn't smile.

But they didn't know about the new secret something in his room, something that could easily change a man. He called her Peggy Ann—but he knew she wasn't real.

They all knew him along the Row, skinny, bent-over, bluejeaned Dobby, always looking at the ground, plodding to and from his dishwashing job. Dobby, face down, face always in dishwashing steam or on the ground; only dirty dishes and pots and pans and his feet ever really got to see his face, they said. Without a hunchback, he was the Hunchback of Cannery Row. That's what they all said.

Dobby was ugly, his face grotesque. A bucket of boiling water on a stove, his reaching hand, his boy face tilted up then; a pull, and down over his head and face the water had come. The screams. Only the memory had faded; the scar remained; it had grabbed all his face, like cement, or glass, and long ago, long before his now late-twenty years, he had given up trying to smile: when he'd tried, something else had come out, something that made people turn and look away and hurry off. They thought, "Poor Dobby," but they kept on walking by. No wonder he likes a bent-over job, they said; lets him hide his face in steam.

Only thing better about Dobby was that he didn't have to shave. That's what they said along Cannery Row.

Yet worse—for him and for the people who looked away and kept on walking by—was that *they* couldn't smile at him, except for the quick kind, the kind that really didn't count. Dobby couldn't give a smile, and he couldn't receive one. He had even given up trying to smile for only himself.

He'd learned to find his smiles in magazines, in pictures there; many nights, at first, he just sat in his room and looked and looked at all the painted smiles, looking so much he wore the pages down. But he never tried to smile back; it didn't seem right.

Then, later, he'd got a pair of scissors and begun to cut the best smiles out of his magazines. He put them—his smiles—in little boxes he'd covered with pink paper, like Christmas. Cutting them out and putting them away made smiles seem more like his own, something to have, like other people. But he didn't tell a soul about what he did; it just didn't seem right to tell it. He was ugly, but he didn't want to be thought crazy, too.

And then, not too many months ago now, he'd gotten a better idea. He thought of something he could do with his boxfuls of smiles, something that would make it much easier for him to look at them all the time whenever he was in his room. Without even asking his landlady, he'd pasted his smiles all over the walls of his room—all kinds, big and little ones, ones in between, men and women's; he even had a horse's smile. All over the old wallpaper he pasted them until he had a roomful of smiles.

But still he didn't smile back; it didn't seem right.

When the landlady finally came into his room and saw what he had done, she puffed up until her face turned an angry pink. She was a big woman, bigger than Dobby, chunky, nearly square, twice the age of him, worn, widowed, toughened by it all, seemed like to Dobby. He was scared of her. He would have moved out a long time ago—but the room was cheap, she kept it clean, and when he had first moved in, she had tried to smile at him, tried more than once—then gave it up. Now she was like everybody else: she looked the other way and kept on walking by.

"Dobby," she had said, "you'll have to tear that paper off those walls." Paper, she had said. Paper, she called his smiles.

So he had torn them off, very carefully so that they wouldn't be hurt. And he had put them back into the boxes, those that weren't ruined. It was a sad thing, a bad thing, and he would have definitely moved away that time except that…well…that room was his home. Other people had homes; oughten he to have one, too?

Even with his smiles now off the wall and back into his pink boxes, Dobby still stopped every once in a while to hunt through trash cans for magazines with smiles. He'd stop at cans on his way from work to his room in the old, paint-faded Victorian house and rummage through the trash.

Which was what he was doing at dusk one day when he found behind a Lighthouse Avenue department store a mannequin with a smile.

He saw her smile first. She was sticking out of a trash can smiling at him. And as he came closer and looked and kept on looking, she *kept* on smiling, she didn't pinch her smile off and look away like everybody else.

"Hi," Dobby said; he was playing a little game.

And even better, Dobby found out that he could smile back at her and smile his smile that never came out looking like a smile, and she *still* didn't look away, she *still* didn't go away. *She kept on smiling.* Smiling and smiling and smiling. A big happy baby doll, that's what she was.

But most important was that with her he could smile back and it seemed all right.

"Hi," he said again, still playing his little game. He knew she wasn't real.

Oh, he had seen other baby dolls—mannequins—in windows of stores, and he had seen that they were smiling. He had stopped and looked at them many times, glad they were able to smile, jealous, too, and they had been nice to look at. But they were different, the ones in store windows, all dressed up fancy and proud and glittery and new, impersonal, for the public. The smiling doll he'd found, now, it was cold and naked and one leg was broken off, all by herself in a dirty trash can with night coming on, discarded.

And she was smiling at *him*; nobody else was around. At him!

So Dobby took her home with him, he smuggled her inside his plain-furnished room. He went out and bought a dress for her, a red dress, like Christmas, too, and a hat; he got a brand new mop head, dyed it black, used it for a wig. Then he propped her up behind a bureau in a corner; this way her broken leg wouldn't show. When he'd leave his room in the morning to go to work, he'd hide her in his closet; the landlady mustn't ever know. And as soon as he got home at night he'd bring her out where he could smile at her and she'd smile back. He called her Peggy Ann; there was no doubt at all that she ought to have a name.

Along Cannery Row they could see the change in Dobby, although they didn't know why it had come about, all in a few days, too. And Dobby wasn't about to tell them, tell about smiling Peggy Ann. Everybody would have laughed at him—not smiled—and thought that he was crazy. Dobby seemed to have more grit in him, everybody agreed; he didn't go slinking around all the time, looking the other way; he didn't bend over so much when he walked. he looked up sometimes from the ground. His hat brim wasn't pulled down so low over his face, you know, and he even waved at you sometimes. And Dobby himself was considering quitting his dishwashing job and getting a better kind.

It was a good feeling, it was—damn—hurrying home to a Peggy Ann like everybody else, nearing home and looking up at his window with eyes high and proud.

Then one evening, like all the others during the last week or so, he'd rushed home from work and climbed the stairs so fast that by the time he reached the door of his room he was panting bad. He opened the door smiling—it seemed all right to smile now—and hurried to his closet and looked, then reached, then looked and reached again, and then—letting what was left of his smile go—*again, again,* calling, "Peggy Ann?" and louder, "Peggy Ann!"

Peggy Ann was gone.

He heard the heavy steps of the landlady coming up the stairs, but he kept on calling for Peggy Ann, looking under the bed, looking behind the bureau, looking in the closet, calling, "Peggy Ann!"

"I took your Peggy Ann, if that's what you call her," the landlady said as she came lumbering into the room. "I took her, I threw her out. And you're getting out next. Pack up and leave."

Her words like an icicle jammed into his brain.

"Keeping a...a half-woman, half doll in my room. Why, it's immoral, it's wicked. It's perverse!"

Turning the icicle in his brain.

"Where is she! Where is she!"

"She's out back in the trash can, where do you think? You'll never bring her in here again. A slut she is, the way you dressed her up, keeping her in your room. A slut! I fixed her good. Peggy Ann, indeed!"

But Dobby was past her now and going down the stairs, running, tearing out the front door and around to the back, eyes not even looking once at the ground.

He saw her before he reached the can. Her face was smashed, she was sticking out of the can. Smile, smashed, sticking out of the can. He stopped in front of her, icicle still working in his brain.

He felt her broken lips and murmured, "Peggy Ann." He felt again; he tried to make them smile. They crumbled. "Peggy Ann." Plaster from her lips stuck to his hand.

He did not know the landlady was behind him until she said, "Into the trash can with her, good riddance. I hit her with a hammer just to make sure."

And Dobby screamed and swung with all his might, and felt the knot of his fist thud into the live woman's face. And screamed and swung again, again; he beat her to the ground, unconscious, or dead.

And then, before he gathered up what was left of Peggy Ann and plodded off across the backyard looking at the ground, he tried—and failed—to set the landlady's lips into a smile for him and Peggy Ann. It seemed the right thing to do.

But now the landlady couldn't smile either. And on second thought, this seemed the right thing, too.

~

NOTES ON "PASTE A SMILE ON THE WALL"

Both the history of this story and its position in Keefauver's oeuvre are complex. Although it was originally published in the fifteenth and final issue of *The Smith*, (May 1974, pp. 153-159), "Paste a Smile on a Wall" had already won seventh place in the 1968 *Writer's Digest* Short-Short Story Contest. Keefauver received $100.00 for this honor even though none of the judges selected the story for publication. He then went on to sell the reprint rights to *Alfred Hitchcock Presents: The Master's Choice* (1979, pp. 173-177). He received an additional $80.00 when that volume was translated into French, with his story appearing as *"Un Mur Plein de Sourires"* (with the promise of an additional $80.00 if the book went into a second printing, although that does not seem to have occurred). In 1983 he received an offer to reprint the story in the Polish journal *Fikcje i Fakty* for 1,500 zlotys ($17.24 in the exchange rate at that time), although there is no check in the file. At the time, *Fikcje i Fakty* was seeking to republish seven stories from two different Hitchcock volumes. Altogether he earned at least $242.24 off this story, perhaps more.

But wait, there's more: Keefauver wrote at least three other versions of this story, one with only slight differences, and two that are longer and more complicated, with additional characters. The longer versions appear to incorporate elements from his unpublished novel *Noodles*. The story also shares a number of motifs, and a similar protagonist, with "Harvey's Smile," a story Keefauver published in the June 1981 issue of the *Mike Shayne Mystery Magazine* (Vol. 45, No. 6, pp. 81-88), although this version (called "Diz's Smile" in the typescript) draws heavily on elements from another unpublished novel, *Shell*, a.k.a *Spook Ship*.

As a final note, also in 1981, Keefauver submitted "Paste a Smile on a Wall" to the annual *Writer's Digest* Short Story Contest (a different one than the Short-Short Fiction Contest), and received an "Honorable Mention"...but no cash award.

HOW HENRY J. LITTLEFINGER LICKED THE HIPPIES' SCHEME TO TAKE OVER THE COUNTRY BY TOSSING POT IN POSTAGE STAMP GLUE

HENRY J. LITTLEFINGER'S TROUBLES BEGAN when he got the major role in a plan by Hippies, Incorporated, to take over the United States. His job: Tossing pot in postage stamp glue.

Up until he was handed the starring role by Large Daddy Throckmortan, the eighty-five-year-old original hippie and current boss, Henry J. had been a simple, happy, lazy, lovable, loyal, dirty hippie. But he had even a better quality, as far as Large Daddy was concerned, one that had caused the old man to pick him for the job of slinging pot-laced brownies into the glue pots of Sticky & Sons, biggest stamp-making contractor for the United States Postal Service.

Henry was a diabetic.

"Thus, Henry," said Large Daddy grandly, flinging his beard over his shoulder, "you won't be tempted to eat a brownie yourself."

And with that, Large Daddy had infiltrated Henry J. into Sticky & Sons as an employee in the glue department, given him a week's worth of the special brownies as a starter, whacked him heartily on the back, and said, "Upon your shoulders, Henry, rests the salvation of the United States—pot.

If you succeed, we'll take over the country and make it into what it ought to be—simple, lazy, happy, lovable, and dirty!"

Large Daddy's reasoning was simple: With pot on postage stamps, and with almost everybody in the country licking them, nearly everybody in time would be helplessly high, thus allowing the hippies to take over. Of course, Large Daddy knew full well that his hippies were already helplessly high, but he also knew that, being used to it, they had an advantage. Nevertheless, he ordered all hippies to stay off stamps for the duration, unless they wetted them with water, which was unlikely.

So Henry J. Littlefinger shaved off his beard, borrowed some clothes and shoes, took a bath, and, his lunch box filled with zapped-up brownies, went off to work as a glue man for Sticky & Sons.

He was successful the very first day. With no trouble at all, he threw a handful of brownies into a pot of glue while all the other glue men were on a coffee break. And as days went by, he, a former pitcher for the Hippie Nine, became so skillful that he could get rid of a dozen cookies, unnoticed, on underarm, backhand, over-the-shoulder, and under-the-leg shots while simply strolling past a pot.

The world first knew that something strange was happening in the United States after Nixon, having written the first letter to be mailed to Mars, licked a stamp for it. The next morning he appeared at his office wearing sandals, beads, bells, jeans, and a turtleneck sweater and, after noting that since the Air Force had first started bombing Vietnam in order to make peace, he commanded it to stop bombing the place in order to make war.

THEN, IN QUICK SUCCESSION, AS more and more people licked more and more stamps the following days and weeks, the editors of *Reader's Digest* ran a fold-out nude; Hugh Hefner and Billy Graham traded jobs; General Motors announced plans for a car that wouldn't exceed five miles per hour—frontward—which had no connection with the dynamiting of all freeways by highway engineers; television sets, all with bullet holes in them, overflowed ashcans—and, in general, all citizens discovered slower relief, goodness that didn't crunch, and started bowling overhand.

And no one knew how and why it was happening—except Large Daddy Throckmortan and Henry J. Littlefinger. And no one was in condition to care.

Large Daddy, reflectively picking his beard, hadn't expected such a gigantic turn-on. In high glee, he sat back on his throne of old orange crates to await the day, soon to come, when he would be carried into the White House, wherever it happened to be at the time, on the shoulders of Madison Avenue sandal shoes.

Henry J., meanwhile, stuck to his job, although he was getting pretty tired of tossing brownies into pots of glue day in and day out. To relieve the monotony, he began bouncing them in off the side of his foot, top of his head, and bottom of his elbow, and angling them in off the ceiling.

There came a day, however, when he couldn't think of one new way to get a brownie into a pot of glue—except one, which he was afraid to try: spitting it in. A diabetic shouldn't put a cookie in his mouth, he reasoned, even if it was a spitting cookie. Besides, Large Daddy had told him not to.

But Henry J. became so bored one day that he tried it anyway. Into his mouth he threw a brownie; it soared out immediately, beautifully spat, to splash into the pot, a perfect shot. And he had received only the slightest taste of sugar. So, born anew, he tried again and again. In and out of his mouth the cookies flew, even faster. Each time he did it he tasted a little more sugar, which tasted pretty damn good to a sugar-starved man. Ever faster— until, unfortunately, his spitter went into reverse, his swallower took over, and down into his hippie belly...slid the zapped-up brownie.

FROM THAT SWALLOW ON HENRY J. LIttlefinger was a different man.

On his way home from work he, hardly knowing what he was doing, bought a new wardrobe, two television sets (one for each eye), and some washday miracle. Before he had dinner that night he scrubbed his skin, then sprayed it with chemicals. Then he sat down to a meal, chockful of heartier flavor. Afterwards, he enjoyed some smoking pleasure. And the next morning, of course, he enjoyed crispier and crunchier goodness.

All the things I've been missing! he thought.

For, of course, Henry J. wasn't a hippie any more. And it was all because of pot. It had caused non-hippies to go hippie; therefore, logically, it had caused him to go non-hippie. Or so he thought. For he had never had pot before; since smoking of any kind had long been banned, everybody ate it in brownies, and he was a diabetic.

And—suddenly!—he, a new non-hippie, realized in horror that he was the cause of the hippies' possible takeover of the government.

With that, he immediately phoned the FBI and told them about the pot in the postage-stamp glue. The agents to whom he talked (they kept passing him around for laughs) either didn't believe him, or cheered, depending on how many stamps they had licked that week.

But now Henry, although nervous, was not discouraged. He would lick the problem himself. He would simply stop throwing brownies in the glue.

Nervously throwing another cookie into his belly, he, avoiding anybody who wore a beard, beads, bells, jeans, or turtleneck sweater, went off to work at Sticky & Sons. He thought he ought to appear to avoid suspicion.

Henry J. Littlefinger's Program for Survival worked. As the glue on stamps became progressively potless, stamplickers gradually went back to normal. Nixon, wearing shoes and a tie again, his beard shaved off, commanded the Air Force to resume bombing Vietnam to make peace; the *Reader's Digest* began running fold-out urban renewed images; television sets were installed in navels for happier contemplation; Graham began a chain of Soul Clubs, and Hefner went back to converting bunnies; General Motors brought out a car that wouldn't go under ninety-three miles per hour—backward; and highway engineers started building freeways into backyards.

Henry J. was in high glee. But Large Daddy Throckmortan was in high wrath and suspicion—as crafty Henry had foreseen.

Thus, when Large Daddy himself got a job as a glue man at Sticky & Sons to see if Henry was still tossing pot in the postage-stamp glue, Henry was ready for him: He had some real brownies, containing nothing but shortening and sugar and chocolate and the rest. These, instead of the zapped-up ones, he threw in the glue.

The zapped-up ones he threw in his mouth. He really didn't know what else to do with them. Besides, he liked his new non-hippieness, pot induced; it was something he'd never had.

Besides that, he liked sugar very much.

Unfortunately.

For, although Henry J. Littlefinger was well-equipped to be a simple happy, lazy, lovable, loyal, dirty hippie—and to save the United States from going hippie—he was cruelly cut down when he got a taste of the sweet life.

Diabetes killed him.

~

NOTES ON "HOW HENRY J. LITTLEFINGER LICKED THE HIPPIES' SCHEME TO TAKE OVER THE COUNTRY BY TOSSING POT IN POSTAGE STAMP GLUE"

Originally published in *Alfred Hitchcock Presents: Stories to Be Read with the Door Locked* (1975, pp. 109-113). In this story, Keefauver finally sacrifices his fictional alter-ego, after roundly abusing him in multiple tales, although he would soon resurrect him at least once more.

THE JAM

THE JAMMER SAW THE TOUGH just after the bally had begun, but he hadn't seen the knife then. The tough wasn't showing it then. It was after the jam came inside the tent and the jammer had taken over that the tough had begun to threaten him with the knife.

The jammer had stayed inside the tent as the flaps had been opened and the two floor-men had carried out the counter for the bally and set it down on the mall. And, as was his habit, he had watched through a slit between the flaps as the bally had begun; he usually watched only long enough to get some idea of how many marks he was likely to get inside later on. Tonight, though, he watched longer because he saw the tough, a mark he'd taken for close to two bills the night before. That happened sometimes; the mark came back, and it could be ugly. The tough's wife had been with him last night; she had talked him into buying the sewing machine and some other junk. That happened sometimes, too—a lot really, the wife talking the husband into buying. Tonight the mark was alone though, and he looked mean. A big young sneering tough. So the jammer stayed just inside the entrance where he couldn't be seen, and watched the tipman start the bally, hoping that the tough would leave.

"Watch! Watch! Wa-a-a-a-tch!" the tipman shouted as he stepped out into the carnival's main mall and tapped a glass with a paring knife. A thin tall man dressed in a striped shirt and slacks, he wore a microphone around his neck. "Watch it! I'm going to do it on the pineapple! In three seconds, I'll fill up this glass with luscious juice. If you don't have a pineapple, take a grapefruit..."

He was up behind the high counter now, and as he talked he stuck a spiral slicer into the top of a grapefruit, then into an orange and a pineapple. "If you've never seen this demonstration, you're in for a treat." He partially filled a glass with pineapple juice and handed it to a small girl standing next to a woman, then began to slice a potato with the same slicer. "Look! Look! This is the most incredible thing I've ever seen." Quickly he was working on other vegetables and fruit. "Look! Apples for slicing, carrots for creaming, beets for pickling, potatoes for frying—isn't that remarkable? I get so excited every time I do this! Look, every slice, cut to perfection. Look!"

The jammer kept watching the tough as the tipman went into the story. The tough was staying back on the rim of the crowd, still with his sneering smile. "The reason I'm here telling you all these things," the tipman was saying, "is that the Wilkinson Company, who makes these slicers, has instructed me to give everybody out here one of these *free*, so you can try them, tell your friends and neighbors about them, and they can go out and buy one for ninety-eight cents. That's called *advertising*. They gave us ten thousand of these, *free, free!*"

Some people who had started to saunter away turned and came back when they heard the word.

"Ten free samples!" He was pulling a knife out from under the counter. "Now look at this. This is the world's sharpest knife. Guaranteed never to get dull. It's going on sale in every Sears store in the country on Labor Day for three-ninety-five. These are made by Wilkinson, too. Watch this, unbelievable." He was cutting up an apple, then a banana. "Look! Look how thin these slices are! One apple can last you all summer. This knife is so sharp you can cut a cow in half, and that's no bull!"

Some laughter, but the tough's expression didn't change, and the jammer ran a finger around the inside of his collar. The jammer was dressed in slacks and a sports coat, not as loud as the tipman's.

"These knives are going to be sold for three-ninety-five, but I want somebody here to take a big chance and give me a quarter and then advertise it," the tipman was saying. "*Advertise it.*" He quickly sold one to the woman with the girl he'd given the glass of pineapple juice to. "Who else will give me a quarter? Who else will advertise it?" He sold three more, then said, "Now everybody who bought a knife—I have ten free gifts to give you. Everybody's going to get ten free gifts!

"Look at this juicer. Watch!" He pulled a small boy out of the crowd and squeezed the juice from an orange into his mouth as he kept talking. "Governor Jerry Brown of the great state of California calls this the most amazing thing he's ever seen. Look at that, unbelievable! You're all going to get one of these free. I promised you all ten free gifts, and I'm going to give them out right now. I'm going to give you the juicer, the extractor, the corer, the cutter, the slicer, the rosette cutter, all this stuff, *free, free.*"

He's finally got that down right, the jammer was thinking: using six words to describe two things. The tough had moved in closer to the counter, and the jammer was sure now that he'd be coming inside. Well, he could handle the bastard, just like he'd handled all of them through the years. This one was a big son-of-a-bitch though, a lot bigger than him, a lot younger.

"Here's what I want you to do," the tipman was saying. "Take a nickel out of your pocket, and *don't give it to me.* Just hold it up in the air. Hold a nickel up." About a dozen nickels went up, and at the sight more people stopped in front of the tent. "All right now, who wants to take a big chance and give me his nickel?" Laughter as the nickels were passed to him. "What a bunch of big-time gamblers I've got, what a bunch of big-time gamblers," he kept saying as he collected the coins, counting them out loud. He counted more nickels than he received. Then he told the two young men who had carried out the bally counter to pass out paper bags. "Everybody gets a bag whether you passed up a nickel or not. I'm going to fill those bags with free gifts."

The tipman was off the counter now and tossing a few juicers and cutters into the crowd as he slowly backed toward the entrance to the tent, talking all the time. At the same time the jammer left the entrance, crossed the inside of the tent, and went out a rear exit. Most of the crowd followed the tipman into the tent. "Take a seat, folks," the tipman kept saying, still handing out gifts— trinkets now, not juicers or cutters. "Take a seat. There's no charge."

147

Rows of folding chairs could seat about a hundred, and the crowd filled about a third of them. On one side of the tent ran a makeshift stage with various articles on it, including a number of black and white boxes. Behind the stage was a sign: ALL SALES FINAL.

As the jammer came back into the tent through the rear exit, he saw that the tough was sitting in the front row, still with his sarcastic smile. The smile turned into a look of anger when he saw the jammer. The tough wore a dirty white T-shirt and jeans, and as the jammer came close to him to get some trinkets from a box on the stage, he saw the knife. Holding it low in his lap, the tough was palming it so that only the jammer could see it. He'd sold the tough's wife that knife the night before.

"Here's a free gift, sir," the jammer said, offering the tough one of the better trinkets, a screw-out pencil.

"I brought my own junk." With his free hand the tough reached into a pocket and pulled out a handful of trinkets—small china figurines, combs, key chains. "I got this crap last night—my wife and me. I'm going to sell 'em back to you. You're going to pay this time." Showing the knife. "Plenty." His voice was so quiet—a hard quiet—that only the jammer could hear it. "But I'm going to watch your show for a while. Then I can show these people what a crook you are."

The jammer ran a finger around the inside of his collar, but as he heard the tipman say to him, "Oh, Jack, there you are," he went into a big smile. "I want you to do me a favor, Jack. I promised all my friends here some gifts." He turned to the crowd. "This is my friend Jack. Let's give him a big round of applause."

As the crowd clapped, the jammer took the mike off the tipman's neck and said: "Isn't he wonderful! Do you know why he's so happy? 'Cause today's his birthday! Give him a hand." The crowd clapped again. "Jack," the tipman said, "treat these people right. Favor 'em! Give 'em the gifts!"

As the jammer gave away more trinkets, talking all the time, the tipman left the tent through the front entrance. "Do you need some money?" the jammer was saying to a woman.

"Sure." A big grin.

"Well, here's a pencil. Write home for some. Anybody else need some money? Here, sir; you look like a writer... Here's a comb I'd like to give

away. These combs are guaranteed never to break; absolutely unbreakable."
He snapped it in two and threw it on the dirt floor, grinning. "Sure am glad
I caught that one in a million that's no good."

He kept passing out trinkets, talking. "Each article I give away is going
to be more expensive than the last one. Who likes that stereo up there on
the stage? We are going to get rid of a couple of them tonight... Who here
is from New York?" Some hands went up. "How about L.A.?" More hands.
"I understand you L.A. people got a freeway all the way from there to here
in Vegas to help you haul your loot home... Who's seen Monty Hall on TV,
giving away furniture and appliances like mad?" Hands went up. "Does he
pay for that stuff he dishes out? Of course not! His sponsors do. Well, we get
this merchandise to distribute to you from our sponsors, so you'll take them
home, use them, and advertise them."

"We could just put a big box of merchandise outside with a big sign
that said *free*, but you know what would happen? One guy would get five
or six articles, and some old lady would get five or six bumps on the head,
trying to get them. That wouldn't be advertising, that would be paralyzing.
So we do it this way. I know how to tell which ones are the snatchers and
grabbers, and which ones are my responsible advertisers who'll really make
good use of these articles, like the stereo or the sewing machine, and show
them to their neighbors."

Up on the stage now, not looking at the tough even though he was
sitting almost in front of him, the jammer held up three lighters. "I got three
lighters here to give away free. Who wants one? Everybody. Who'd give
me one dollar for one of these lighters? Uh huh, not as many hands up this
time. Okay, you, you, and you. You three people, I want you to dig down
into your pocket, your purse, your shoe, and hold up one dollar. Don't *send*
it up, just *hold* it up. If you need change, one of my assistants will make it for
you." He nodded at the young floor-men who had carried the bally counter
outside; each held up a fistful of money.

Two women and a man held up dollars. "Are you satisfied to spend a
dollar?" he asked each. After each said yes, he tossed the lighters to them.
"I wasn't really going to sell those lighters for a dollar. I said I was going to
give them away free, and I am. I just want to see who my good advertisers
are. If those three people were sincere enough to spend a dollar of their

hard-earned money, that shows me that they're the type of people who will take these products home, use them, and advertise them for us."

"Sure," said the tough, sneering. "Sure." He again spoke just loud enough for the jammer to hear. "I'm gonna advertise *you.*"

The jammer ran a finger around the inside of his collar as he, ignoring the tough, went to three medium-sized black boxes on a table on the stage. He put his hand on one. "I have this box here. As I said, each article gets more valuable, so naturally the price has to go up. This box is two dollars. But this box comes with two guarantees. First this box is worth a lot more than any one of you will ever actually pay me for it. Second you're going to get a lot more than this box and what's in it. That's my guarantee. Now for the box and its contents—and the two guarantees that go with it—who'd say two dollars?"

Three people offered him two dollars, but before he took it he asked each if he was satisfied to spend the amount for the box. After each said he was, he took the money. Then he showed a necklace that was in each box. "This is worth more than any one of you will pay for it because you're actually going to pay *nothing*! And you're going to get more because I'm giving you the two dollars back. I'm backing up my guarantee a hundred percent, and I'm finding out who my responsible citizens are.

"Now look at these. Look at this. Who likes this Snoopy dog? The special advertising price of this is a penny. Who likes this electric toothbrush, with its own waterproof carrying case? It's a nickel. We have to sell certain articles. This salad set is going to go for a dime. How about this knife set that you see the Galloping Gourmet use every day on TV, or you used to, before he retired. I'm going to sell that for a quarter."

The tough sneered. "Quarter, hell!" The jammer had sold his wife the knife set the night before, and what he was palming now was one of the smaller knives.

Ignoring some marks who wanted to buy the articles at the cheap price, the jammer turned away from the black boxes and pointed at a number of white boxes on the stage. "I'm going to form me a little advertising committee. I need about twenty-five good, honest, responsible citizens who are not too proud to get a little something for nothing, not too proud to say 'thank you,' and not too proud to show these things to ten or twelve of your neighbors and do a little advertising, that's the main thing. From now on anybody who gets any advertising merchandise at special prices—like a knife set for a quarter—is going to be somebody with a white box. The lucky person who takes home a stereo or a sewing machine is going to be somebody with one of these white boxes.

"Lady, do you want to be on my committee? Okay, I'm going to call you advertiser number one. Remember your number. If I take this watch and say, 'This belongs to advertiser number one,' and you forget your number, you may as well forget the article. Everybody who wants a number raise up your hand."

Except for the sneering tough and a few others, everybody in the tent raised his hand, and the jammer gave them numbers. "Now to prove that you're sincere I want each of you to hold up three dollars. Don't *send* it up. Just *hold* it up. My assistants here can change money for you." Gradually hands with money in them went up. "I see some people who raised their hand before but aren't holding up their three, so I'm going to have to separate this crowd one more time. If you said three, if you meant three, but most important if your *word is worth three dollars*, send up your three."

About a dozen sent up the money, and the jammer put each three on the top of a white box, as if a person receiving the box would also receive his three dollars. "Now I must ask those people who did not have enough interest to send up three dollars to please leave. I have nothing else for you. You just can't see what I'm trying to do here."

About half the crowd left the tent, and the opening was closed. The tough with the knife sat fast, sneering.

"Sir," the jammer said, "I must ask you to please leave."

"I ain't going nowhere till you buy this junk back from me." He reached into his pocket and again pulled out the handful of trinkets. "I want fifty dollars for all this crap. And I want a hundred and fifty for your no-good sewing machine that's in my car." His voice was tight, hard, still so low that only the jammer and a couple of marks on either side of him heard what he said. Only the jammer saw the knife, held deep between his legs, as the tough gave it a little jerk toward him, blade first.

The jammer saw one mark next to the tough turn to his companion and whisper "Fifty dollars," and the jammer then watched the woman scowl at the tough.

The jammer pulled his fingers out from under his collar, thinking hard, as he said to the crowd: "There—we've gotten rid of all the snatchers and grabbers. Now I know that those who are left are responsible advertisers. You're the people I will treat and favor."

"Sure," said the tough. "Sure."

The jammer watched another mark, one on the other side of the tough, scowl at the tough; and he heard a mark behind the tough whisper to the tough to keep quiet.

Of course, the jammer was thinking. Of course. The tough was so obnoxious. That was—made—the difference. And if he got louder, worse...

"Now, who'd give me a penny for the Snoopy dog? Everybody will. Who'd give me a dollar? You would? Send up your dollar." When it came up, he put it with the dog and then gave both back to the mark. "I didn't want your dollar. I said I was going to sell it for a penny, and I always back up my word."

He then went through the same process with an electric toothbrush, except that five dollars was collected and returned. Then he picked up a large paper sack from the table. "Now, I'm looking for a sport, a speculator, who'll offer me ten dollars for this bag. Is there a sport in the house with ten dollars?"

"What's in it?" a man asked.

"Crap," the tough said.

The jammer showed his irritation with the tough to the marks, but with a large grin he said: "A mystery. A big mystery. Everybody loves a mystery, right?"

The man, who seemed to have been drinking, grinned widely, winked at the woman with him, and handed up ten dollars. "You've got yourself a sport here, buddy."

As he took the money without giving him the bag, the jammer said, "Okay, you sent up ten dollars for this bag. It's my ten dollars, it's your bag, right? Satisfied? You're not going to come back later and say that that was the baby's whiskey money, are you? If I give you the bag and nothing else, you can't complain, because that's all we bargained for, right? See that sign? It says ALL SALES FINAL. A bargain is a bargain. Satisfied? Okay.

"Now, I'm going to give you some time to think about this, so I'll hold your bag and my money up here while I tell these people about this stereo and sewing machine. These are the big deals of the day, folks, like on TV, like on *Let's Make a Deal*. I guarantee you won't have any trouble advertising these..."

He talked about them until finally he put the drinking man's ten dollars, a salad set, and a number of trinkets into the paper bag and gave it to the man. "Here you are, sir, just like I said I would."

"Sure," the tough said. He suddenly got up and moved two seats down so that he was directly in front of the jammer. "Sure. Just like you said you would." His voice was louder now, and as he glared at the jammer, the jammer could see that almost everybody else was glaring at the tough. The woman whose girl had received a glass of pineapple juice during the bally said, "Keep quiet" to the tough. "Shut up," somebody else said to him. One of the floor-help, after going behind the crowd, said "Go on home!" as if a mark had said it.

The jammer, ignoring the tough but showing his irritation, picked up another paper bag and started talking about it, raising the price from ten dollars to twenty dollars. When a woman said she'd pass up twenty dollars for the bag, the tough turned to her and said: "You're crazy, you're going to get taken." He turned to the crowd and said: "You're all going to get taken."

"Sir," said the jammer, "I must ask you to leave."

"I ain't leaving until I get my money back."

The woman was now hesitating about passing the twenty dollars up, and the jammer quickly said, "Ma'am, just pass your twenty dollars on up, you're a sport, too, aren't you, don't let this fellow ruin your evening. Just pass it on up."

She did as the tough sneered at her.

Ignoring the tough, the jammer, quicker than he had done with the ten-dollar bag, put the woman's money in the bag, along with a knife set and a handful of cutters and slicers, and gave it to her. "Here you are, ma'am, just like I said I would."

The jammer was silent for a few seconds, to let *just like I said I would* sink in. Those words impressed them. They always did. But from now on out it would be different, and it was time now to get rid of the tough while the marks were on his side.

"Sir, I must ask you again to leave. You're disrupting the people here."

"I ain't going no place till I get my money back, what you took off my wife and me last night—two hundred dollars! For this crap!" He almost jumped out of his seat and, turning to the crowd, showed them the handful of trinkets and the knife. "Look at this junk! I paid two hundred dollars for this junk, plus a no-good sewing machine, plus some knives. Here's one knife here!" He held the knife high. "And unless I get my money back, I know it will cut something—this crook here!"

The jammer spoke quickly, pretending anger: "Listen, buddy, if you don't leave, I'm gonna have you escorted out by my friends here."

"Try it!"

"Which of my friends here will help me escort this gentleman out of the tent so that we can get on with the advertising?"

The man who had got back the ten dollars and the man who had earlier told the tough to shut up stood up. Seeing them, another man got up too. Then they, along with the two floor-help employees, started toward the tough. "Just go on out peacefully, sir," the jammer said. The tough did not move. When the five got up to him, one grabbed his knife hand while two others held him. A fourth man got the knife away from him. All then started pulling and shoving him toward the entrance as he began to scream that he wanted his knife back. He jerked free long enough to whirl and throw the handful of trinkets at the jammer as the jammer called after him: "You can get your knife back later, sir, when the police are here to guard me."

After they had pushed the tough out the entrance, the three marks and the two floor-men acknowledged the smiles and words of praise from the crowd. The mark who had grabbed the tough's knife started it through the crowd; each mark passed it on to his neighbor, and most had something good to say about its quality.

"Now that we've got rid of that crazy man, let's get on with the advertising," the jammer was saying. "Thank you, gentlemen, for your help. Every once in a while some drunk wanders in, and I have to call on responsible citizens like you to help me out... Now I can only advertise one more article, favor one more person. I have here..." and he described with glowing words an electric razor, a wristwatch, a hair styler, and a whiskey-decanter set. "Now for any one of these four articles I want someone—first hand up gets it because I can only advertise one—who'll say...thirty dollars!"

One of the men who had got rid of the tough raised his hand... "I want the razor."

"You got it. Send up your thirty dollars." As he took the money, he said, "Some articles we give away, some we sell. The price of this razor is thirty dollars. Are you satisfied to spend thirty dollars?"

The man grinned and said "Sure" as he took the razor. His grin disappeared though when he heard the jammer say, "Wait a minute! Give me back that razor! I'm sorry, sir. Would you trust me with your razor up here for a second?" The man nodded, puzzled, as he returned the razor. "Good. Then I'll trust you with my thirty dollars."

As the jammer handed back the money, he suddenly moved his eyes over the crowd and said angrily: "I just heard something, and I don't like it. I'm not going to stand for that. Somebody just whispered that this man works for me. Is that crazy man back in here?" The crowd looked each other over suspiciously as the jammer said to the man he'd just returned the thirty dollars to, "Sir, do you work for me?"

"No."

"I'll show you all that nobody here works for me. Whoever wants one of these four articles, raise up your hands."

"But Jack," one of the floor-help said, "you said only one article."

"Shut up! I know what I'm doing, you don't! You just mark it down on the sheet and I'll sign for it."

Eight hands went up, and as each person chose an article, an assistant put it on the table on the stage as the jammer, anger still in his voice, said: "If I asked you to send up thirty dollars, would you?" Each answered yes.

When all choices had been made and put on the table, the jammer said, "Now, just to show that you're sincere—and to show that whispering busybody that nobody here is working for me—I want everybody who chose an article to hold up thirty dollars. We're going to collect your thirty dollars and give you this card as a receipt."

Quickly the floor-help collected the money.

"Now some of you might be a little short of cash today, so I'm going to give everybody a chance to get in on this one." His anger was gone now. "Who's ever gambled and lost? Everybody, right? I want ten people to take a gamble with me. I'm thinking of something. It could be a stereo, or it could be—" (a grin) "—nothing. I want ten people who have faith to say—not thirty dollars, not twenty, or even fifteen—I want ten people who have faith to raise up their hands and say ten dollars!"

Quickly he collected the money from four people with their hands up, after he asked each if he was satisfied to spend ten dollars. He put the money on the table with the money for the thirty-dollar articles. Already on the table were the articles themselves and the white boxes.

"Now let's leave that aside for a while and get to the real reason I'm here. This is what I get paid for..." And he began to speak glowingly and at length about the sewing machines and stereos on the stage. Finished, he took a manila envelope from the table. "For the first two lucky people who take away a sewing machine or a stereo I have a special bonus that's worth at least as much as the stereo or the sewing machine, plus the extra added bonus that Monty Hall gives away every day—forget four hundred for the stereo; forget three hundred for the sewing machine; forget three hundred or two hundred and fifty or even two hundred. If I were to say one-seventy-five, it would be the best deal you ever made in your life. You know why? Because the *dealer* can't even get it for that! I want some people with the sense that God gave to a six-year-old to raise up their hands and say one hundred and fifty, and leave the rest to me! If you don't have cash, we'll take credit cards, Spanish pesetas, Russian rubles, or Italian lire. We'll even take Chinese money, if you have a yen for it. If you're ever going to buy a sewing machine or a stereo, now's the time to do it!"

When no one spoke up, he got down from the stage and began going through the crowd. "Treat your wife to a sewing machine." "Treat your husband to a stereo." "We'll take a deposit." "We'll take personal checks." "Treat your wife..."

Finally selling a sewing machine to a woman and a stereo to a man, he went back on the stage and opened the manila envelope to show a certificate good for a trip to Florida for four days and three nights. He gave one to each buyer.

His voice was slower now, folksy. "Now it's time to give you what you paid for and send some money back with you." He then began to give out all the merchandise on the table. In the white boxes were pen-and-pencil sets or perfume. Those who sent up ten dollars got "a genuine Royalite Gem manmade diamond necklace, which sells for one hundred and ten dollars at all the fine jewelry stores."

Quicker now: "Who thinks I've worked hard up here?" Hands went up. "Who thinks I deserve a tip?" Everybody. "Who would give me a dollar so my helpers and I can go out for a drink tonight?" Almost everybody gave a dollar. "Thank you, folks. That's it."

One assistant stood at the entrance as people filed out. He gave each a small good-luck charm. One woman, whose husband was carrying a sewing machine and Snoopy dog and other articles, said almost apologetically to the attendant: "Can we have one of those potato-slicers the man promised us? That's all we came in for."

As the assistant was telling her, with a sour look, that she'd have to stand aside until all the people were out of the tent before he could go get her a slicer, the tough, who had come to the entrance from the mall, yelled at her: "You silly ass, all you came in for is a free potato-slicer, and look at the junk you paid good money for!"—the veins in his face pink and protruding, his nose inches from the woman's frightened face. Her husband tried to nudge the tough away and go by him, but the tough kept getting in the way, yelling about "that crook stealing all of you blind!" as he glanced at the other marks trying to file out of the tent. He was blocking their way. Helped by the two floor-men, two of the men who had grabbed the tough earlier took him by the arms and waist and began pushing and pulling him away from the tent. The tough swung at them, and they, hitting back, knocked him to the ground as the jammer, drawn by the cries, came to the tent entrance and gazed quietly, almost reflectively, at the scene. The tough was now screaming that he wanted his knife back.

Maybe he ought to actually hire a guy like that, the jammer was thinking, considering the hand this one had given him. First off he could actually have a guy whisper during the jam that a mark was working for him, instead of the way it was now—nobody saying it. Then let the marks back him up by kicking the guy out. On the other hand a guy like this could help out if a mark got troublesome, like if one noticed that travel and transportation weren't included in the Florida trip. And, yes, let him come back to the tent like now, obnoxious as hell. The fact that he was so obnoxious kept the marks on the jammer's side when it was normal for them to start having some doubts, now that their money was gone. Well, he'd think about it.

As the tough got up and staggered up the mall, watched by the marks who had beaten him, the jammer closed the flaps over the entrance. Then, as the attendants started to sweep the tent floor, he began to count the money he'd taken in. It came to $621, including tips; and quickly, out of long habit, he figured his expenses were about $200—about $55 each for the sewing machine and stereo, about nine dollars for the thirty-dollar items, a buck for the ten-dollar articles. Take off a buck or so for the trinkets he'd given away, and it wasn't bad for less than two hours' work. Not bad at all. His smile grew, triumphant. No, not bad at all. And what always struck him about it all—every time—was that the marks were greedier than *he* was. Even the tough wanted his knife back.

Ten minutes later, as the jammer watched from behind the entrance, now hoping that the tough would come back after his knife, and feeling almost certain that he would, the flaps were opened, the tipman appeared, and the jam started again.

~

NOTES ON "THE JAM"

Originally published in July-September 1980 issue of *The Sewanee Review* (Vol. LXXXVIII, No. 3, pp. 383-398). At 5,500 words, this is one of Keefauver's longer stories (in a note attached to the check for $200.00, editor George Core actually wrote that the story "can be very tedious in parts"), and also one of his most realistic, lacking any elements of the fantastic, the macabre, or the whimsical. The closest examples of such detailed realism focused on society's twilight side in his published work are probably certain scenes in his novel *Tormented Virgin*, such as the beach party or the visit to the strip club.

THE ROCKS
THAT MOVED

WHEN OLD KIRBY NESON CAME into town that first time and told everybody who would listen that rocks—boulders—were moving around on their own out in the scrub, nobody, of course, believed a word of it. Everybody knew Kirby was a little funny in the head. But, as it turned out, it wasn't long before the whole town was talking about those moving rocks.

That first day, though, Kirby couldn't even get anybody into his old pickup to take out to where he said—bragging about it—they were moving. He was *proud* of those moving rocks, as if they'd done something he knew they were going to do all along—not that he'd actually seen them move. He was very careful to say that he'd only seen that they *had* moved from one place to another, as if we'd be more apt to believe that. More than once it had happened, he claimed. He said he could tell they'd changed position because he'd marked some of the rocks with a chalk and then walked off the distance to where he'd driven a stick in the ground. When he checked the rocks a few days afterward, they'd moved. He showed how he'd done it, once he finally got Burt Kolodzie and Fred Knotts out there after they'd got tired of listening to him every time he came into town. Kirby knew that if Burt and Fred said those rocks were moving, everybody, by God, would know they were.

Problem with Burt and Fred, though, that first time, was that *they'd* never seen where the rocks had been before, and so there was no way they could really tell if they'd moved. They saw the chalk marks that Kirby had put on them, and they saw how flat everything was all around, like everybody knew would be the case in that part of Texas (there wasn't any hill for the rocks to roll down, that is), and they saw of course how big the rocks were, each of them weighing at least a few hundred pounds. But what they couldn't see were any tracks to show the rocks had moved, which wasn't unusual, though, seeing as how the wind was almost forever blowing out where they were and would have covered up any tracks. Besides that, it had rained the day before, this being the rainy season.

Kirby finally convinced Burt and Fred, though, to do their own marking with the chalk—writing their initials on the rocks—and walking off the distance to the stick he'd put in the ground. He had them dig their own design around the stick so that he couldn't be accused of moving it on them. Then he said he'd bring them on back to the place the next time the rocks changed positions. They did all this and said they'd come back, maybe to humor him, maybe not. Maybe because they were just curious. Because, funny or not, old Kirby could be very convincing when he was talking about his "communing with Nature," as he calls it. And it turned out, so Burt and Fred said, that old Kirby thought the rocks were moving because Nature was fed up with being tampered with by men and their atom bomb and going to the moon and all that, and that she was showing her anger by "flexing her rocky muscles," as he put it, secretly amazed at his own wit.

Of course, in a way, whether the rocks were moving or not was secondary to the fact that the rocks were there in the first place, which was actually the biggest part of Burt's and Fred's being curious—at first, anyway. Ordinarily in this part of the country you didn't see rocks the size of Kirby's. You might see one once in a while, but not a dozen or so grouped together. All you'd see were mesquite and cactus and maybe some scrubby oaks, and some little patches of scrawny grass in January and February when it rained, and with the wind blowing the way it does in these parts, nothing stayed still unless it was tied down, not that the wind could move rocks big as Kirby's, of course.

Anyway, Burt and Fred promised to go back to the place—it was about thirty or so miles out of town, in the middle of nowhere—the next time Kirby told them the rocks had moved. Kirby lived someplace out there; he wouldn't say exactly where his shack was. He didn't want any visitors interfering with his communing with Lady Nature.

Well, in a couple of days or so, sure enough, old Kirby came into town and told the two of them that the rocks had moved again, and out there Burt and Fred went, along with some others, and, as Burt was to say, the rocks he'd marked had sure enough moved—one of them, in fact, about two hundred feet, and it must have weighed close to five hundred pounds. And this time he and Fred could see the tracks the boulders had made because there had been a rain so heavy, before the rocks had moved, that the wind hadn't had time to dry the land enough to blow away the tracks—any tracks. Tire tracks of Kirby's rock-pushing pickup, say. Or tracks of a bunch of practical jokers doing the pushing. Because, you see, there wasn't a rock small enough that Kirby could have pushed by himself, by hand; in fact, as old and scrawny as Kirby was, he could hardly push a marble, not that he wasn't tough. He was about ninety pounds of meanness, getting meaner the older he got... In other words, the only tracks there were those left by rolling rocks. There were about a dozen of them, all weighing into the hundreds of pounds, and they had all moved.

Well, now, when Burt and Fred got back to town and told it around that rocks were moving on their own out there, it got a different reaction from old Kirby's telling it, you can bet. Besides looking respectable, both of them *were*, and they weren't a couple of kids, either. People believed them, and most everybody wanted to see for themselves, but by then it was too late in the day for rock watching.

That evening Kirby came on into town, proud as a scrubby peacock, but when he heard how most everybody was planning to go out and see his moving rocks in the morning, he got mad. "Leave them rocks alone!" he said, and kept saying. "Somebody's gonna get hurt out there if you don't!"

Some, making light of it, asked him if he thought the rocks would jump on them. He got madder at that. "If you don't want nobody there, why'd you tell us about it?" Sue Weibacher asked him. (She's been the postmistress ever since her husband died three years ago of gout.)

"Because I didn't know then what I know now!" Kirby said, getting even madder.

"What's that?"

But Kirby wasn't saying. He jumped into his battered pickup and bounced out of town in the direction of the rocks.

It wasn't long before Ed Furrow, who runs a weekly paper over in Gilroy, came nosing around, asking Burt and Fred a lot of questions and trying to find Kirby in town. Kirby wasn't to be found, though. So Ed and Burt and Fred and a bunch of others, including me, went on out to the moving-rocks place. Ed took some pictures, but it was plain that he, not knowing Fred and Burt the way we did and being of a suspicious nature anyway, didn't believe that the rocks had moved by themselves. He wanted to talk to Kirby, but Kirby wasn't to be seen there, either, and, of course, like I say, nobody knew where his shack was.

So the next issue of Ed's paper had a front-page picture story about "Moving Rocks Puzzle Progreso," which is the name of our town, not that there's any progress going on, in my opinion. All of it was written up in a tongue-in-cheek way, and that was how it was treated, too, a day or so later in the Houston paper, which had sent a reporter and photographer to the place after they read the story in Ed's paper, I guess. That, in turn, led to a geologist driving out from the space center there in a few days, and it was raining to beat hell. This was all happening just after we'd started bringing rocks back from Mars, and so there were some geologists at the center.

The geologist didn't believe it, either, as you might imagine—at first, anyway. But he did decide to do his own tests. He made his own markings on the rocks—chipped the boulders—and measured their distance from each other and then took some pictures of them to set their location, too. He estimated their weights with some measuring gadget he had and then said they were all too heavy to be moved by human hands unless you used some big mechanical mover, which would give itself away by tearing up the land.

About a week passed before he came back, and maybe we wouldn't have known if he hadn't stopped in town en route from Houston and asked Fred to show him the place. He didn't think he could find it himself. When he and Fred and some others got there, including me, you could tell right away that the rocks had moved even if there weren't any tracks to see—some of them hundreds of feet. And somebody, most likely Kirby, everybody thought, had tried to cover up the chipped-out markings the geologist had made by slapping some cement on the scars. Kirby still wasn't to be seen, though. Nobody had seen him, in fact, since the day he'd shown Burt and Fred the rocks, which wasn't unusual, considering his ornery ways.

Well, this geologist measured the distance the rocks had moved and looked at a book and some charts and did some calculations and used more gadgets. When he had finished, he told us that the wind was moving the rocks. "Winds funnel through here pretty strong," he said after saying that the rocks were actually in a dry lake bed so shallow you'd never know it. We *had* realized, though, that the soil was sandier and harder here than most soil in the area. "When the surface gets wet from rain, the ground gets extremely slick, and when conditions are just right, movement occurs," he said.

Well, some believed and some didn't, and, as you'd expect, among those who didn't was Kirby.

Just as everybody was getting into cars and trucks to go back to town, Kirby came gunning up in his beat-up pickup. He jumped out of it before it had hardly stopped and started yelling and cussing and screaming soon as he saw the blue NASA sign on the side of the geologist's brand-new white truck.

"Get the goddamn hell out of here!" he yelled at the man from Houston. "You bastards can tear up the moon and Mars and bring Nature's rocks back here where they ain't supposed to be, but you leave these earth rocks alone!"

"But, sir," the geologist said, turning nearly as white as his truck, "we haven't bothered these rocks. We haven't moved them an inch. Wind and rain have done it."

"Wind and rain!" old Kirby roared. "Wind and rain! Nature is doing it!" He was pointing into the sky. "Nature! God!"

I believe if Kirby had had a gun, he would have shot the man right there. As it was, he suddenly ran toward his truck, and everybody got out of there fast. When we looked back, he sure enough had his old rifle in his hand.

Fred and I and some others made trips out to the area in the coming days, regardless of Kirby; we didn't think the old buzzard would shoot *us*.

We never saw him, as it turned out. But we did see that the rocks moved most every time it rained (we were still in the rainy season) as long as the wind was blowing hard, just like the geologist had said.

And they always moved in the same direction the wind was blowing. Still it was hard for us to believe that wind and rain were moving those god-awful big rocks. But, unlike Kirby, we never thought God was doing it.

We began to wonder, though, as time passed. First of all, we went out there once and saw that the rocks had moved a lot more than they ever had before. Although there was a wind, it wasn't a particularly strong wind. It had rained just before, though. More and more we'd go out there and discover that the boulders had moved one helluva distance with hardly any wind. Finally, one time one of them moved about a quarter of a mile and there'd been no rain for at least a week and the wind hadn't amounted to a damn thing. And this was the *biggest* rock—a monster, big enough to knock down a house. You knew that rock really had to be moving to cover all that distance in such a short time, and I say short time because it just so happened that I saw the movement the boulders had made on consecutive days because I happened to be passing by the place both days, and I'd driven off the road to the site both times.

Also, it seemed that the rocks—all of them—were getting bigger. Of course, I thought this was my eyes or imagination. But when I got Burt and Fred to go out there with me in a few days, they thought the same thing, but, like me, they couldn't believe it.

Another thing: There were more rocks moving now. We were positive of that because one of the first things we'd done was to count the rocks that were moving. There were fourteen of them to begin with. Now there were twenty-three. The extra ones had just appeared out of nowhere, it looked like.

Then the strangest thing of all happened. We went out there one day after it'd been dry for a long time—we were getting into March now. The rocks—there were now thirty-seven—had *all* moved at least three quarters of a mile; we were sure of that because there had been—and was—such a small amount of wind that the tracks weren't blown over by sand, especially those made by the big rocks, and they were all big now. The tracks were so deep that there didn't have to be any rain-softened ground to show them up. Big, deep grooves!

But what I'm getting at is this: All the rocks had changed direction. They were now going in just about the opposite way they had been for months—*against the wind* now.

When we phoned the geologist at the space center, he said he'd meet us at the site the following day.

WHEN WE WENT OUT THERE the next day to meet the man, the rocks were gone. Not a single one anywhere. They hadn't been gone long, though, because we could still see their tracks leading off in the dry soil and there was a very stiff wind that day. The rocks were heading right into it.

We got in Burt's four-wheel-drive and started after them. We figured the boulders had gone maybe just out of our sight, and that the man from Houston would find us and the rocks easily enough by following the tracks.

Well, we drove and drove without seeing any rocks, and Burt started giving the truck more gas until we were going along at a good clip, just about being bounced to the roof because, of course, we weren't following any road. It was all desolation for miles and miles, all the way into Progreso and beyond. A good ten or fifteen minutes passed, and we still didn't see the boulders. We saw more rock tracks, though. A lot more. New ones came in from either side. Then we began to hear a strange sound at about the same time we saw what appeared to be a cloud of dust ahead. As the size of the cloud grew, the sound began getting louder—a rumbling, a crashing. The ground began to shake.

In less than a minute we saw them, or at least the tail end of them. After Burt gave the truck even more gas, we could see more of the dozens of boulders making up the rear end of the rolling mass, and although we were now traveling at about forty miles an hour, we were just barely gaining on them—hundreds of boulders, maybe thousands, with more coming from either side all the time, all monsters, all heading in the same direction, as the crow flies, straight toward Progreso!

Burt, who was driving, must have thought the same thing I did at the same time, because as I yelled, "Let's get on the road!" he had already started to whip the pickup to the left toward the road into Progreso, the idea being that we might reach town before the boulders did and give a warning. But even before we were halfway to the road, we could see that the rocks were over the highway and beyond as far as we could see.

And then a horrible thought made me look to the far left and then behind us, and I saw hundreds more of the huge monsters bearing down on us, aiming right for us. Pointing at them, I screamed for Burt to turn right and speed up.

He did. But now the rocks ahead of us were rolling faster, leaving us, while the ones behind were gaining. In minutes we would be crushed flatter than a couple of cockroaches.

Then, as if on command, the direction of the boulders changed, both those in front of us and those behind. They began to split—some to the right, some to the left. And I realized what was happening. They were going around Progreso, and in the process, as far as I could guess, they would miss us. The town was saved because the rocks had a different purpose in mind.

On the far side of Progreso, though, they converged (we would learn) and without ever changing direction again they headed directly, ever faster and growing more monstrous at every mile, toward the space center in Houston.

~

NOTES ON "THE ROCKS THAT MOVED"

Originally published in the July 1979 issue of *Omni* (Vol. 1, No. 10, pp. 102-106). A color illustration by artist De Es Schwertberger accompanied this story; appropriately, this image typifies his "Stone Period." The story also bore the tagline: "Who would believe that the rocks not only moved but had a goal in mind?" As with "The Great Moveway Jam," Keefauver also wrote a version of this story for young readers, which he does not appear to have sold. Although he never gives the name of the narrator in this version, the protagonist of the middle-school version is his perennial alter-ego, young Henry J. Littlefinger.

THE SOAP CAT

STANDING BEHIND THE COUNTER IN a soiled apron, he'd seen her drive past out front, then park, and he'd had an impulse to hide the Ivory soap before she got in the store. Then, though, before he could make up his mind, he'd seen the cat go to the screen door to greet her. He watched her stop to pet him as she came in, and he thought that anybody who liked that cat the way she did, you couldn't help but try to like her, too. Especially when the cat made so much over her as well. Look at him, the devil, rubbing up to her like that; it reminded him of…well, it was more than any fish smell on *her* hands, he bet. (Smiling a little now.) He'd always suspected that devil cat of liking *him* more because of the fish smell on *his* hands than for anything else. At first, that is. He'd been handling fish the first time the devil came meowing in the store, years ago now, and he'd never been able to get rid of him, not that he wanted to now, of course. The cat liked him now whether he was handling fish or not, and Lord knows he didn't handle it much nowadays, or hardly anything else, for that matter, the way his business was.

"Good morning, Father," she said, still stroking the Siamese's fur as he rubbed against her legs and sandaled feet.

That "Father" jolted him, as usual. He just couldn't get used to it, no matter how often she called him that. He wasn't her father, whether she was his son's wife or not—if she *was* his wife. This day and age, who could tell? Sure, they said they were married, and she wore a ring, but that didn't mean anything. She wore a lot of rings; all kinds of jewelry, handmade stuff. And he knew his son—or thought he did, anyway; sometimes he wasn't so sure. Fred marrying a young girl like this? Only twenty-one, she'd said. She looked more like seventeen to him. Did she know how old Fred was? Thirty-nine, wasn't it? Or was it forty?

He wished she'd get away from that door. Little she was wearing, you could see right through her dress, the light behind her like that. He could see why Fred had tied onto her, all right, the lecher. Well, Fred had been a lecher all his life, along with everything else. But it looked like she was getting the best of him now, sending him off to school at his age like she was.

She was coming toward him now, the cat in one arm, a small paper bag in the other. She'd probably ask him for another bar of soap right off. That quiet grin on her face as she strode (what a long-legged one she was!) past the vegetable stand on her right, the fingerprint-smeared candy counter on her left. Stopping then at the stand, to finger the tomatoes. "How about a nice tomato salad for your lunch, Father?"

He didn't answer. That "Father" again. It irritated him, that was all there was to it. Her moving into the house, taking over. Not really taking; she wasn't that type. It was as if she thought she should—now that Millie had passed on. When Fred had brought her home for the funeral last month, saying she was his wife, she'd said, "I'll do the best I can, Father," even though he hadn't asked her to do a thing. Trying to please. That was all right, but she tried too hard.

She repeated her question, glancing at him, never losing her smile. He couldn't remember ever hardly seeing her without that smile. Was it real? Or did she paste it on every morning? Was this part of her forever trying to please?

"That would be nice, Karen," he answered, "if you can find one that's not spotted. This is the middle of the week, you know."

She nodded. He'd explained to her before that the way his business was nowadays he ordered fruit and vegetables only once a week, on Fridays.

The wholesaler wouldn't bring a truck out from the city more often for a piddling order like his, and he couldn't get that lazy Fred to go in with his car to pick up some things for him during the early part of the week. They'd had some hard words about that, Fred and him, and Karen had heard it all. She'd taken Fred's side, of course, saying he had "school work to do."

He watched her put a bruised tomato on the counter in front of him, still holding the cat and paper bag, and waited then for her to ask for some soap.

"What would you like with your salad, Father? Fred said he didn't care."

"Oh, anything. Fred up?"

"Yes, he's studying."

She never quit smiling even though she knew, all right, what he thought of that. Studying. Pottery, art, *the*ater (as Fred called it nowadays—courtesy of Karen?). He gave her a little nod. "You think Fred would like a pork chop?"

"He *adores* pork chops."

"Well then, I guess we better have a chop. You adore them too?"

"Oh, Father, I just like them." And as she laughed, he was once again struck by her eyes. Sort of speckled green, they reminded him, in a way, of the cat's, except that they weren't slanted. And they were darker. Too bad she put all that black stuff around them. Fred had said he liked it, that paint around her eyes. Well, he must have liked something to up and marry her, if he had, after the life he'd led, running all over the country, one girl after another, one job after another. Could he actually have finally decided to settle down? But why this girl? Oh, she was nice enough, all right, but... Well, he'd always hoped that Fred would marry somebody more stable if for no other reason than that he needed, Lord knows, somebody stable. Her and her "arts," as she called them. Her THEater. She seemed to be on a stage, all right, and all the time. Like calling him Father with a capital F. Even dad with small d would be at least better.

Well, he'd brought it on himself. He'd told Fred that they could live at the house. Of course, he'd hoped then that Fred would help out in the store. He should have known better than to have hoped for that, though. What it amounted to—no use to deny it—was that Fred and her were living off him while they took their pottery classes, and art, and THEater and Lord knows what else, none of it the sort of thing either of them could expect to earn a living from, and all because of her. She was more irresponsible than he was.

And Fred at his age! Good Lord, did he think he was still a teenager? It looked like it. Why, when he was Fred's age, he owned a store—this store.

When he got back from cutting the chops, the cat was gone from her arms and she'd put what had been in the bag on the counter. She just stood there then, waiting for him to say something about it, it seemed, her smile busting out all over the place. It looked like some new kind of soap: funny shape; no wrapper on it. That was a switch, all right, her bringing soap *into* the store.

"Oh, Father, don't you know what it is? It's a carving for you. I made it for you."

He really didn't know what to say to that. A carving. Looked like soap to him.

"A carving?"

She nodded, still smiling. "In soap. Ivory."

So that's what she'd been doing with all that soap. Good Lord, he should have known. Well, maybe it was a carving. Looked like some kind of animal: a cat, that was it. Maybe it was supposed to be his cat.

"It's real nice, Karen. Thank you. Thank you very much."

Yes, it must be his cat. That was nice of her, and he was grateful. But the main thing he kept thinking about was her using up all those bars of soap for this, this thing (she must have practiced on a million bars), and not paying a cent for any of it. Not one bar. She'd been coming in the store and getting bar after bar of Ivory for days—weeks, it almost seemed like—and he'd almost asked her what in the name of God she was doing with all that soap. Were she and Fred eating it? Was Fred selling it at halfprice to that damn new chainstore? Who did she expect to pay for it? She didn't think that Fred was going to, did she?

"I did it at school," she said. "From a photograph. I did *them*, I should say. I ruined a lot of them."

"I wondered why you were getting all that soap."

"I knew you did. Aren't you surprised?"

She just never thought about buying the soap, he guessed. Never thought about paying for it.

"I bet you thought I was really on a clean kick," she giggled.

"I thought you and Fred were eating it. What did you do with the bars you ruined?"

"Oh, I threw them away."

Threw them away, had she? Just like that.

"You do know who it is, don't you, Father?"

"The cat?"

"Yes. It's Don Juan—a white Don Juan."

That was *her* name for the cat. He just called him cat.

"He's the most beautiful thing I've ever seen," she said, "and, well, I wanted to sculpt him. His grace, his dignity. And I wanted you to have it. Do you like it?"

"Of course I like it, Karen. Thank you."

Now he was feeling a little ashamed of himself about being upset about her not paying for the soap, and as he picked up the Ivory-white, umblemished sculpture to examine it and say something nice about it, he was very conscious of his old, dirt-lined, scarred hands, greasy now, too, from the pork. He put the carving down as soon as he thought he could.

"I don't see how you did it, Karen."

"A lot of work, that's how." Her smile at full force. "And you have to be some sort of a weirdo."

He nodded at that, all right. "I'll—I'll put it in my—room."

Caught himself, just in time; he'd almost said bathroom.

"Don't you want it in the store, Father? This is where Don Juan lives."

"All right, I'll keep it in the store."

"Good."

Funny thing to have in a store, but he didn't care one way or the other. Maybe he could sell it. No, he couldn't do that. That would be terrible. Besides, a crazy thing like this was the sort of thing a chainstore would be likely to sell.

"What would you like me to make for you next, Father—the store?"

"You mean in soap?"

"Of course. But I'd need more than one bar for the store. Maybe I could stick a few bars together. Three, maybe."

Good Lord, she was going to clean him out of Ivory, and not paying a cent for it. And after the store, what next? He'd been running a store for more than forty-five years in this town, the biggest merchant in it at one time, before the chains started coming in; selling everything through the years from coal to coal oil, from T-bone to pigs' feet, but he'd never thought he'd see the day when a teenage daughter-in-law, so-called, would clean him out of soap, and not paying a nickel for any of it. Had it come to this? A lazy, middle-age son living off him, a son who didn't want to take over the store from his father, who wanted him to sell it! ("Sell out, Pa." Those were his actual words, a lot of times. "Sell out before the chains eat you up. Sell out while you have at least one customer left.") And now Fred being egged on, made worse, by this green-eyed, black-ringed, grinning teenager, his so-called wife, carving things out of tons of his soap and thinking it was grand. Why, they'd soap him to death! He'd be the laughing stock of the town, he who had at one time been the biggest... Now, enough of that. Stop it.

"What are you frowning at, Father? Would you like me to sculpt *you*?"

"Me? Good Lord, girl, no. Why me?"

"Because you deserve it. You deserve to be immortalized, too."

Her smile all over the place.

He couldn't help but smile himself at that. Immortalized? Well, if there was anything that deserved to be immortalized, it ought to be the store—to survive all it had. Sell it? Why, he'd sooner cut off his hands.

"I'll decide later what I want next, Karen—in soap, that is—and let you know."

"Good. See you at lunch."

He watched her go out the door with the chops and tomatoes, and it was plain the cat would have gone out with her if she hadn't blocked his way. Then he gazed down at the soap cat on the counter and wondered what to do with it. He wanted to put it someplace where she wouldn't see it and be reminded of making more soap things. He was sure of that, all right. Well, he knew where to put it temporarily, at least, until he could think of a better place.

The cat followed him as he left the counter with the soap carving; stayed right on his heels, meowing, until they reached the cat's feeding place; stopped there, meowing louder, as the old man kept walking toward a farther corner. "No use meowing, cat," he said. "You've already been fed. Just because you've been immortalized now doesn't mean you're going to get fed twice a day." Smiling now himself, a little. "I suppose you'll want salmon now instead of fish-heads, too. Well, forget it, Mr. White God. I'm still the boss in the store."

He had no sooner got rid of the soap cat than Karen came back into the store and said she'd tripped over that old, cracked sidewalk near where she'd parked, and fallen, dirtying and scraping a knee. "Can I wash it off, Father?"

He knew when he heard that that he was going to have to find some way to stop her—but couldn't for the life of him think of anything to say except "Wait!" saying it more than once, each time louder. "Karen, wait!" But she was at the sink by then and had seen what was in the tray, and as he walked up to her she turned to him and her green eyes were blazing. "I just put that there temporarily," he said, and it was the truth. He knew that wasn't enough, though. And making it worse was that he hadn't realized how dirty the soap tray was until now, with that damn pure-white cat sitting in it and Karen reaching for it with her lily-white hands.

"For anybody to use!" she hissed at him. "For the whole town's dirty hands!"

Dramatizing it, blowing it all up. On stage.

Picking it up then, her face looking almost as white as the cat. "It was for *you*, not your hands!" she nearly screamed. "Yours or anybody else's!"

Then, her smile now, finally, all the way gone, he was watching her fly out the door with it in her hand. The cat trotted out with her, too, this time, and he found himself wondering if he would have to put fish on his hands to get him back again. Had it come to that with the cat, too?—like with Fred—and his old customers—all wanting out of the store. And her—he'd have to face her at the house. Would she smile for him then? Again? Ever? Did he want her to?

Or was it now him who was blowing it all up?

Well, he was sorry about what had happened, but... But what? Well, for one thing, if she'd made the carving of him instead of the cat, things might have been different. Or even made it of the store. That didn't seem so far-fetched now, come to think of it, either of them—the store or him.

~

NOTES ON "THE SOAP CAT"

This version of the story originally appeared in the Winter 1979 issue (Vol. VII, No. 2) of *green's magazine (Fiction for The Family)*, for which Keefauver earned $20.00. A typescript of this same text in the author's files bears the title "Carved Surprise," but no correspondence survives to indicate whether the title change in the published version was his decision or the editor's, although an entry in his sales journal for 1967 suggests he may have sold a version of it as "Soap Cat" to a magazine called *Pet Fair*(?) for $200.00. I have been unable to find any other record of this publication, however. Nonetheless, the entry implies that Keefauver may already have been using this title by that time. Keefauver later attempted to sell the reprint rights to this story, but there is no evidence he was successful.

However, even if "The Soap Cat" had appeared in 1967, this would not have been the first time the story saw print, or at least the central narrative of this story. A completely different version entitled "Thanks..." appeared in the Third Quarter of 1950 edition of *Decade of Short Stories* (Vol. 10, No. 3), making it by far Keefauver's earliest identifiable professional sale. In that version, the central scenario is largely the same, but the woman is a local artist and not the storeowner's daughter-in-law, so there is some suggestion at the end that the protagonist is missing out not only on a potential commercial opportunity but a romantic one as well. Although the language is completely different between these versions, the climax remains the same: the soap-sculptress returns to use the store's sink after injuring her knee, and sees her rejected carving there.

Both versions obviously draw on Keefauver's experiences working in his family's general store in Maryland. The space of almost thirty years between the two publications illustrates beautifully how he continued to revise some of his ideas throughout his career, like an itchy oyster polishing its pearls.

As "Thanks..." is a very short story (occupying only three pages in the original publication), I include the entirety of the story below so that the reader can compare both versions:

THANKS...

THE SCREEN DOOR OF THE grocery store opened and she came in, her back-stretched hand catching the door, easing it shut noiselessly. A cat purred and rubbed against her leg, and she bent over to pet it. "You beautiful thing," she said.

The man in the apron looked down at her. Above the pencil behind his ear, his hair was thin. He watched, smiling.

"I brought you one of my animals," she said, placing her bag on the counter. He gave her a puzzled look. "You remember, those pictures I showed you last week? Of the animals, I mean?"

He looked away for a moment. Then his face lighted, and he turned back to her. "Oh, you mean those soap things?"

"Yes," her face brightening. "I knew you wouldn't forget." She looked down at the bag on the counter. "You remember I told you when I showed you the pictures of them that I was going to bring in one? My soap animals, I mean?"

"Yeah." She was looking into the bag when he smiled to himself.

"So you could see one, actually."

"Uh huh."

"Well, then, here it is." She reached into the bag, carefully bringing out a sculptured soap miniature of a cat. "I hope you don't mind, Mr. Winters, but I used your cat as a model. I did it from memory."

"Why, it's a pleasure. I had no idea you were going to do that old cat of mine."

"I wanted to surprise you." She smiled and looked down at the sleeping cat. "She's beautiful." He did not answer. From the rear of the store a radio blared out a baseball game. He looked over his shoulder toward the sound and quickly turned back to her as she said, "Don't you think so? Look at her lines, so clean and—fine. See how they flow when she's asleep See how they—melt together." Her voice tightened, and she looked first at him and then at the carving. "I tried to catch that— her lines—in this, Mr. Winters. I could see her so clearly in my mind as I worked. I think maybe I did, even if it was from memory. What do you think?"

"It's pretty, Miss Roberson, real pretty." He studied the soap statue. "Looks something like her, too."

"Just something like her?" Her voice was low.

"I mean," he said quickly, "something like her because it's—the soap thing is smaller than the cat actually is." He drew his lips taut, "You know the difference in size is what I meant when I said it looked something like her."

"Oh, I see." Her laugh was strained. "I couldn't make her life-size. That's impossible. I couldn't get soap that large. It takes a lot of soap as it is. A lot, of it."

"I guess it does."

"Yes, sometimes I use half a dozen bars for one carving."

"What kind you use?"

"Ivory. The large size."

"You do? Why, I handle that kind, Miss Roberson. See right here."

He moved to his right a few steps, pointing. "Three for forty." His eyes searched hers inquiringly.

Without hesitating, she said, "No, I don't need any right now."

"I got a good price on it."

"Well, I don't know, Mr. Winters. Martin's sells his cheaper."

He flicked his hand at some spilled sugar on the counter. "I might make you a special offer."

She shook her head. "No, I don't need any."

Avoiding her eyes, he looked down at the cat, which had risen and was purring a deep rumble against the girl's legs. He picked the soap model from the counter and fingered its lines. His hands were deeply lined, dirty, contrasting with the fine white strokes or the sculpture.

Finally he said, still studying the model, "I don't see how you do it. How you can take a square of soap and make this real-looking cat out of it. Why, it almost looks like it's living."

"It is living, Mr. Winters," she whispered. He looked at her quizzically. Her fingers were white where she gripped the counter.

"It's living?" He looked at the carving. "What do you mean, it's living?"

"Oh, I shouldn't have said that. She bit her lips. "I'm afraid you wouldn't understand, Mr. Winters."

"I might though, if you would tell me," his voice was strangely soft.

She looked away. "No, it wouldn't make sense to you. If you don't see what I mean, I can't tell you. I shouldn't have said anything."

He was silent, picking at a splinter in the wood of the counter. Finally he said, "Well, if you don't want to say anything, that's okay, only," looking up at her intently, "I would like to have known, that's all."

She smiled. "Some day, perhaps. I hope so." He nodded his head knowingly. "You just have to know things like this without—by yourself. You understand, don't you? She spoke softly, searching him with her eyes.

"I think so. Yes, I think so."

"Thanks," she said quietly. Her gaze shifted suddenly to the stacks of soap. He was instantly alert, waiting. "You know, I think I will get some soap. I'll need it anyway. Might as well get it now."

"You want the Ivory, don't you?"

"Yes, about a dozen bars, I guess."

He put the soap in a bag. "That will be a dollar sixty plus four cents tax."

She paid him and started out, leaving the soap cat on the counter.

"That's yours, Mr. Winters. You keep it. I want you to have it."

"Why—uh—thanks, Miss Roberson."

She strode briskly up the street, face flushed, eyes glowing. A hundred yards from the store she looked back but did not stop walking. "A beautiful store," she said to herself. "A warm store." As she turned she did not see the rough place in the pavement.

Mr. Winters gave her a surprised look as she pushed the door open. "I tripped and fell. You won't mind if I sponge my knee?" She started toward a sink in the corner.

"Wait!" he shouted. She kept on walking. Then she saw it. She picked it out of the soap-tray. Holding it gently, she walked to the grocer. Her face was white. "It's alive yet, Mr. Winters. See." Her voice cracked. Weeping, she ran out. Under the dripping faucet sat the dozen bars of Ivory Soap.

THE GREAT MOVEWAY JAM

EDITOR'S NOTE: THE MAJORITY OF readers will remember, of course, the Great Fourteen-Month Moveway Jam near Moveway City, California, during 1998-99, which, at the time, was the longest and largest traffic jam in the history of mankind. But what most readers do not know is that if it were not for an unassuming, prim, and frightened little man—Henry Littlefinger—the world today would not now have the opportunity to learn of at least part of the terror of Jam-ees who were inside that prairie of unMoving automobiles on an unMoving Moveway in a jam that extended from San Diego to Santa Barbara, and from the Pacific Ocean eastward to points reaching some seventy-nine miles inland. Carefully, patiently, calmly, Jam-ee Littlefinger for more than a year jotted into an ever-thickening notebook the incidents that went on around him in Jamland. The world should well be thankful that he, as a stationery salesman, had in his Jammed-in blue panel truck an ample supply of paper, pens, and ink that fateful day in May 1998, when all traffic stopped for fourteen months.

What remains of the Littlefinger Notebook was discovered quite by accident when the only known survivor of the Great Jam tried to pawn it in a shop in downtown Des Moines in 2002, three years after the Jam was brought to its gruesome ending by Moveway Engineers. The man, who carried no papers and was never identified, was one of the worst cases of Jambreakdown, or Jam Psychosis, on record, according to the U.S. Board of Jam Surgeons. When taken into custody, he was in such a state of advance Jambreakdown that, unfortunately, he was unable to answer coherently the simplest questions.

It should be noted, however, that officials of the Moveway Historical Society and other interested parties never had a chance to question the man, since while he was being taken from the pawnshop to the Des Moines General Hospital the ambulance became snagged in a routine jam (three days), and he died before it could be broken up. Thus, it has never been learned how he came into possession of the last pages of the Notebook. Many think, including P. T. Townsend, Chief, U.S. Bureau of Moveway Investigation, that the short, skinny, middle-aged man took it from Littlefinger's outstretched, lifeless hand immediately after the "end" of the Jam. This is pure guesswork, of course. That the man was a Jam escapee has been verified, however, largely on the testimony of Jam Surgeons; they reported that his body, upon examination, demonstrated overwhelming physiological characteristics of complete Jambreakdown, including symptoms of exhaust fumes in the blood, gasoline in the urine, and oil in both. In any event, the Jam escapee, evidently not realizing the value of the pages from the Littlefinger Notebook, failed to bring it to the attention of the authorities. It is indeed sadly ironic to note that if a Jam-crazed man had not needed money, the world today would not now have the opportunity to read such a startling report of life as lived in the last few days of the Great Fourteen-Month Moveway Jam.

The unknown possessor took excellent care of the few pages of the Notebook, however. They were well wrapped in strong brown paper when he brought them to the pawnshop. Only a few pages were in any way damaged; although rain soaked, they were legible and shed much light on the final days of the Jam when Moveway Engineers arrived in Jam Helicopters and put into effect their chilling solution to the massive problem.

Unfortunately, the vast bulk of the Notebook was never recovered; Littlefinger left it behind when he and a group of Jam-ees began their march to The Wall, which Moveway Engineers had built around the Jam in order to stop motorists from deserting their vehicles and escaping the Jam on foot. Fortunately, however, the part of the Notebook recovered contains the account of the march.

According to the Moveway Historical Society, Littlefinger and other Jam-ees began their march from the only part of the Jam where there was some semblance of order and civilization, an area which they had ironically named Moveville. Stretching ahead of the ragged, hungry group (made up of about twenty-five percent of the population of Moveville) were about thirty miles of what they called Unincorporated Jamland, where wild, starving Jam-ees roamed, as the notebook shall reveal.

By the time they began their march, Jam-ees were in a state of insurrection against Moveway authorities; after fourteen months of frustration, they were in no mood to accept any further announcements from hovering Moveway Engineer helicopters that the Jam was about to be broken, especially when the copters gradually decreased the number of emergency food deliveries and began dropping more and more suicide capsules. Out of desperation, then, they decided that some of the stronger Jam-ees would try to reach and climb over The Wall and at least let the world know of their plight.

Who was Henry Littlefinger? Little is known. Fragile yet tough, unimpressive yet of a nature that attracted people and their confidences, small, wiry, downright skinny toward the end, with a beaklike nose and steadying owllike eyes, he was born about 1950 on a Moveway (in those days, of course, called a freeway) in the middle of Moveway City (then with the name of Los Angeles) while in a car going eighty-five miles an hour. From that day on, according to his parents, Harry and Hilda Littlefinger, now of Fairbanks, Alaska, he was scared to death of, and had a hatred for, Moveways.

And ironic, too, is that Littlefinger never knew the cause of the Jam that killed him: A little old lady, signaling for a right turn in Ventura, made a left turn instead.

ಀ

THE LAST PAGES OF THE LITTLEFINGER NOTEBOOK

JULY 10, 1999—We are now camped an estimated eleven miles from Moveville, our group of 167 exhausted men sprawled about in an area roughly the size of half a city block. I write this by shaded flashlight; fortunately, among my provisions in my blue panel truck when the Jam began was a large supply of batteries. (Unfortunately, I left my Notebook in Moveville; I write on pages scrounged from the men with me.) We did not light campfires. We are wary. This morning as we "marched" away from Moveville at dawn a Moveway Engineer helicopter darted in over us, fluttered there a moment, then sped back toward Moveway City. And twice during the day we were observed by other copters. We ran for cover, squirming under and in the rusting cars all about us; I'm afraid, however, that we were seen.

Although the Boy Scout movement in the United States has in recent years been severely handicapped because of the absence of wooded areas, they being covered by cement, we are fortunate in having with us an Eagle Scout, George Barnstrong, who with his trusty compass and other directional gadgets, of which I know absolutely nothing, has mapped out the most direct route to that point of The Wall which we *think* is nearest Moveville. We have no way of knowing exactly, of course, since our sole source of information has been the two scouts we sent out, a few weeks ago, neither of whom returned and we assume are dead. However, we are of the opinion, based on pre-Jam observation, that Jams are usually longer than they are wide. Thus, we are moving in a southwesterly direction, mostly across, over, and through cars. from side to side—sometimes actually opening the door, sliding across the seat, and leaving by the other side, often to the surprise of the "uncivilized" motorists who make up the inhabitants of the unincorporated areas of Jamland. This, plus the fact that most cars are Jammed-in bumper to bumper, plus that today was frying hot, plus our weakened condition, has resulted in our exceedingly slow rate of travel. Too—and with great sadness I report this—we lost three men today: Adobe James, William Funhouse, and Nicholas Funk. They collapsed one by one during the day. We could not bury them, of course. We could hardly dig our way through at least a foot of Moveway without proper tools even if we had the strength. We placed their bodies on tops of deserted autos; we hope that helicopter hearses will pick them up, thinking they are the "uncivilized."

We move in more or less a westerly direction—like pioneers of old, we tell ourselves somewhat grimly—because in addition to hoping that it is the shortest route to the Jam limit, we hope that Moveway Engineers have not built The Wall along the Pacific. (We hope to reach the ocean at a point about four miles north of Laguna Beach.) Certainly they think the *ocean* will retain us! Too, I suppose the sea attracts us, just as it beckoned to those plodding pioneers of a bygone era. (Bygone?) How joyous it will be to see something—water!—besides automobiles! How lovely it will be to see girls wearing something—bikinis!—besides Jam Survival Suits.

The unincorporated area of Jamland that we passed through today was in chaos. Rusting cars of all descriptions, windows broken, tires and seats missing—for "firewood." More ghastly, though, are the skeletons—the human skeletons. They are everywhere: in, under, on top of, and beside automobiles. Bones of children are extremely pathetic.

JULY 11, 1999—We made only about six miles today and are now camped, by rough estimate, about seventeen miles from Moveville. Our progress was slowed considerably by helicopters. We saw the first one about 10:15 A.M. as we were passing through desolation similar to that which I wrote about yesterday. We saw the copter before he saw us; as soon as we sighted him in the distance, we dived beneath the rusting cars until he flew over and away. He was flying very slowly and low, obviously looking for us. As soon as he disappeared, we came out from under the cars and continued our march. The second copter delayed us considerably, however. He saw us. We had stopped for lunch, were sprawled about, when suddenly one of the smaller and speedier Moveway Engineer helicopters—fitted with a noise abater—

darted over us hardly ten feet off the Moveway. We clearly saw the pilot looking down at us through the bottom of the control bubble. Nevertheless, we dived under the surrounding automobiles, staying there for exactly one hour and forty-seven minutes before we crawled out and continued on our way. A number of our group had fallen asleep under the cars, and another fifteen minutes were wasted waking them up. One, James Lupo, was dead.

We had hardly started our weary march again, though, when another copter, the speedier type again, zoomed over our lunch stop and dropped a small parachute, the kind used for communication purposes. It was a communication, all right! Bill Smitt and I rushed to the chute, opened the small pouch attached, and read the following letter, which I copied in full. It read:

Federal Bureau of Moveway Engineers,
Western Division,
12643 Moveway Avenue
Moveway City, California 90029
July 11, 1999

To: The Insurrectionists
SUBJECT: Insurrection

Gentlemen:

You are hereby notified that by departing your vehicles in Moveville on or about July 10, 1999, you are in direct violation of Federal Moveway Law 73, Section 3, Paragraph 14, which reads: "Any operator of a motor vehicle, or person capable of operating a motor vehicle in which he is a passenger, who leaves said vehicle without express authority of the Federal Bureau of Moveway Engineers, while said vehicle is entering, within, or leaving a Moveway Jam, shall be executed by the means most available."

You are also hereby notified that by the power vested in me as Chief of the Bureau of Moveway Engineers, Western Division, I am obligated, and do cheerfully accept the obligation, to enforce all laws under my jurisdiction.

You are observed, gentlemen. You are in danger. Return to your vehicles at once or be prepared to accept the consequences.

Very truly yours,
(Signed) P T. McSniffle,
Chief Federal Bureau of Moveway Engineers,
Western Division
cc: Hdqrtrs., ME. Washington, D.C.
File, 1-14
Moveway City Mortuary, Jam. Div.

JULY 12, 1999—Five more men died the day before yesterday (William Snofly, Norman Mendicat, John Brumfield, Peter Downey, and George Moundtop) and seven died today (Harry Flow, Nathan Foulpine, Samuel Week, Philip Dugan, John Downdike, James Peters, and Mike Thomas). Fifteen dead so far. Our original 167 men are now down to 152; we have lost nearly a man a mile.

We voted on what action to take after we received McSniffle's letter yesterday. I'm proud to report that to a man we decided to continue the March, which we did immediately, our eyes on the sky as much as on the Moveway. We saw only one more helicopter, and that from a distance. Knowing we were observed, we did not attempt to hide.

This morning (I write this, as usual, at our overnight campsite) we started out as soon as it was light. Most men did not sleep well. They are wary, they are afraid. We had hoped to reach the Pacific—or The Wall—today; our scout leader had estimated it to be about thirteen miles from last night's campsite. We didn't make it. It happened this way:

A few minutes after three we heard the roar of approaching helicopters; a glance showed us that there must have been at least a dozen and that they were coming from all directions. We shot under and into any vehicle within reach. They roared overhead in a thunderous armada. Cautiously I inched my head out from under the auto I was under. The first thing I saw were the guns. Each copter had at least two, front and back. They pointed Movewayward. After roaring over us, one by one, their guns. still silent, aimed at us, they flew outward about 100 yards, grouped, and then in a great circle flew around the area where we were hidden—as if they were flying Indians and we were in a circled wagon train.

Then we heard the guns.

At their first chatter I—and I'm sure every man—ducked back for protection. Then, not seeing—or feeling—any bullets around me, I got up enough nerve to inch my head back out from under the car. The copters, still flying their circle, were shooting not at us but in an area directly below them—sort of a Jamland version of firing over your head. They were literally tearing up that portion of the Jam with machine guns. This went on for about four minutes; it was an extremely terrifying experience. At any moment I expected them to move in over us with their guns.

Then, abruptly, the firing stopped. They all flew off except one. The one made a dart over us, and as he sped off I saw a parachute floating down toward us. I was one of the first to reach it. It was another letter from McSniffle. In somewhat flowery language, it warned us that if we did not immediately turn back, we could expect "the same murderous fire that you have witnessed today to be directed unerringly at your insurrecting bodies."

We voted at once. We decided to go on.

We waited until darkness; then, after a cold meal we continued the March. Although there were no casualties from the guns, two men had died during the firing, probably from heart attacks (Pete Snick and Joe Newhouser).

We stopped a little after midnight. I write this by shaded flashlight from our moonlit campsite. Around me men sleep fitfully.

Tomorrow the Pacific!

Or The Wall.

July 13, 1999—We started out this morning before dawn, hoping to reach our destination by daylight. A count in the darkness revealed that three men were missing. A hasty search uncovered only one—dead (George Hoston). We moved on. To track down the others would have taken up our so important time. They are probably dead anyway (Nick Appleton and Francis Bowen).

By dawn our hopes had been smashed. As we neared the Pacific just north of Laguna Beach, as we began to actually hear the surf, and as the darkness faded, we saw It—The Wall. A monstrous thing of gray stone at least a dozen feet high, with barbed wire along the top. And as we reached it, we saw one…two…three…four skeletons along its base, evidently poor wretches who had tried to scale the thing.

I say our hopes were smashed. Not actually, for we would climb The Wall. Yet we had so hoped to see the Pacific. It seemed to be right behind The Wall. The Moveway, of course, extends right up to the waterline (as it does on the Atlantic and Gulf coasts, too), so there was no sand beneath our feet even though we were probably standing where sand ought to have been.

With the immediate prospect of finally being on the Outside, plus that it was dangerous to tarry, we soon overcame our initial disappointment and eagerly began to roll the closest automobile—a rusty Chevrolet Whoosh!— up to The Wall. With some 140 men trying to lend a hand, the task was over before it had hardly started. The car hit The Wall with a great rusty, dusty crunch. Immediately Bill Smitt and Lawrence Lardicart climbed up on its roof; this put them about seven feet below the edge of The Wall. "Come up one by one, men," said Smitt. "We'll boost you over. You, Hank, first. Use your clippers on the wire." (Hank Lawnsdown, a metal smith.)

What we would have done once over The Wall I don't know—swim, I suppose. As it turned out, that problem never plagued us.

Lawnsdown had got on the car and was being boosted up toward the edge of The Wall when the helicopters came—by the dawn's early light. Their machine guns began chattering immediately. The first few bursts ripped into Smitt and Lawnsdown. They fell to the Moveway. More bullets poured into the cluster of men waiting to climb onto the car. Many fell, screaming. Some dragged themselves off toward the surrounding automobiles. Most did not move. The remainder panicked; they ran in all directions. The helicopters continued firing—there must have been five or six of them. They pumped bullets into the running men mercilessly. It was pure slaughter. They fell like flies. I was some seventy-five feet from Smitt and Lawnsdown—maybe more—when the firing began, and somewhat apart from the men grouped around the car. This is what probably saved me—and that I was, by pure luck, standing next to a flatbed truck still partially loaded with concrete blocks. I don't remember actually jumping under it, but I watched the slaughter from under its protection. The whole area was filled with screaming, cursing, groaning, and blood. If any of our men fired what weapons they had, I did not see it. Bullets, of course, went right through the automobiles that most of the men flung themselves under. The copters came back again and again; they raked the area without letup. One man crawled under the truck with me. Blood poured from his foot. He groaned, looked at me with eyes glazed with shock, then collapsed, dead. Then I saw blood spewing from his chest.

Suddenly the firing stopped. A great moaning silence took its place, except for the clatter of choppers. I peeked out from under the truck. The sky was thick with copters; more had arrived. And guns protruding from their bellies, they began to settle down toward what was left of us.

How I escaped undetected I'll never know. God must have been with me. I simply crawled out from under the truck, in the direction that took me away from The Wall, and wormed my way under a car, then left that car, picked the one closest to it, and crawled to and under that one, avoiding open spaces as much as possible, for I felt sure that the copters would land in them. How long I kept this up I'm not sure. I only know that I stopped only when I was too exhausted to go on; and when I could no longer hear any sounds from the Moveway Engineers, I lay there panting.

I must have dozed, because the sun was high when I looked out from under the car. My hands were scraped and bruised from my flight; the front of my Jam Survival Suit was torn. The sky was clear of copters. I heard not one sound. I crawled on aimlessly, staying under vehicles as much as possible. I saw not one living soul, although there was an occasional skeleton. I suppose the firing scared all the "humans" of Unincorporated Jamland away. My thirst was terrible; a blazing sun had broken through the usual smog. My weakness was nearly overpowering. I had lost all food and water. I had to stop after having crawled only a very short distance.

I must have dozed again. The next thing I remember was that the sun was nearly down. Quickly, before darkness fell, I began to write the day's horrible happenings, which I now have just done. Now I am trying to think what to do. Shall I try to make it back to Moveville? I doubt if I could make it, with no food, no water, and nothing in between except a prairie of rusting automobiles and childlike "savages." If I went back to The Wall, how could I get over it? I cannot bring myself to return to the scene of the massacre, even if the Chevrolet is still next to The Wall, even if I had strength to climb it and somehow go over the top of The Wall. Probably the Moveway Men have Moved the car away, anyway. And they would certainly be there for the next few days, cleaning up the mess they made. I think the best thing for me to do is to head back toward The Wall to a point some distance from where we first encountered it. In the morning I shall risk a climb to the top of a car here, find The Wall (I have not crawled far from it, I'm sure), and start crawling toward it. Perhaps I can find some method to get over it.

Or under it?

JULY 14, 1999—This will be hard to read. (*Editor's note:* This portion of Littlefinger's Notebook was almost illegible, the reason for which will be shortly known.) I am hardly in a position to write well-formed words and well-formed sentences. I write feverishly. There is so little time left.

To go back—

I was awakened last night by the clattering sound of many helicopters, some passing over me and others some distance away. At the same time I heard a different noise, a mystifying patter similar to the sound of falling hail, although not as intense. Crawling out from inside the automobile I was sleeping in to investigate, I was immediately struck by two or three small, lightweight objects. I heard others hit the Moveway around me: one bounced from a fender and landed right in front of me; I could see it in the moonlight. When I picked it up I was chilled to my very soul; and after I had examined it by the best angle of moonlight and noted its color, I knew I was not mistaken. although I swore to God that I might be.

Moveway Engineers were showering Jamland with thousands of suicide capsules!

And by morning I knew why.

I barely slept from that point on. At dawn I crawled out from inside my car. All around me were suicide capsules—dozens of them in my immediate area, in all their green malevolence. I was seized with an indescribable fury. Cursing, I began to grind every capsule I could see underfoot. It was as if fourteen months' worth of frustration burst out of me, concentrated into one minute of fury. I was soon exhausted. I am very weak. As I sprawled out to rest I saw one capsule nearly hidden behind a wheel. At first I thought

I would mash it, too, as soon as I had regained my strength. But when I got up in a few minutes, I found myself putting the capsule in the pocket of my Jam Survival Suit reserved for just such pills of instant death. (*Editor's note*: These suits were dropped from helicopters in the early days of the Jam.)

When with painful effort I climbed to the top of the car I had slept under I saw that The Wall was about a mile away. I was about to climb back down to the Moveway when I took one quick glance in the direction of Moveway City. I saw a dark mass and then heard the beginning of a deafening roar. Then—I could not believe what I saw. Approaching Jamland were hundreds of helicopters.

I hurried down and scrambled under the automobile. The ground literally shook as they approached. The roar was overpowering. I risked a peek out. The sky was black with the whirling monsters. They were all the large KILs—the biggest helicopter made, large enough to lift two tanks. As I watched, and as they passed over The Wall, I saw a stream of something fall from the leading copter; and then as each machine passed over The Wall it, too, dropped a stream of what appeared to be a grayish, mucky substance. As soon as each copter dumped its load, it turned back toward Moveway City. In following the return of one for a second, I saw a second great cloud of helicopters approaching. Then, looking off to north and south, I saw more gigantic clusters of the machines, all coming toward Jamland. And as I watched, each of these copters also dropped something—a load of something—onto the Jammed cars as soon as it passed over The Wall.

Jamland was being covered up by something dropped by hundreds— thousands—of helicopters! No wonder suicide capsules were dropped during the night.

In a matter of minutes the copters were dropping their loads a goodly distance from The Wall—in my direction. Each dropped load easily equaled that of a large dump truck. In the spot where each load was dropped a mound of a gray, mucky substance appeared, then settled a bit until it was nearly level with the tops of the cars. I watched, horror stricken. Closer and closer they dumped. I could not stay under the car; I would be covered by the muck. There was no firing. In fact, I saw no guns protruding from the copters.

Then I realized what I was seeing. These copters were the specially made ones used in Moveway construction. They had probably been assembled from various parts of the United States for the job they were doing now.

And as one dropped his load scarcely fifty feet from me I realized what they were dropping and what they were doing.

They were dropping wet cement. They were making a new Moveway over the old Moveway.

I quickly climbed from beneath the car and got inside it. Fortunately it was a sedan and in relatively good condition. I ran up all the windows but one—and just in time. With a tremendous slushing thump, a load of cement hit the top of the car and the surrounding area. As it mounted up the side of the car, I shot through the open window and onto the roof again, just ahead of the rising wet goo. It leveled off just below the top of the car. As I reached my new position, another copter dropped a load so close to me that I was splattered and nearly knocked over by it.

I whipped out my Notebook and began to write furiously. It was obvious that a second assault would put the cement over my head. They probably intended to make the new Moveway level with the top of The Wall. I thought fleetingly of trying to make it to The Wall by jumping from car top to cartop. There were many spaces, though, where no tops showed, where the spaces were too great to jump over. Those damn sports cars! Could I swim in wet cement? I decided I couldn't. So I sat on top of my car and wrote and wrote and wrote—which is what I'm doing at this exact moment.

Thousands of helicopters are now overhead, coming and going, dumping their loads and flying back for more. Such a gigantic effort (it looks as if they want to finish in time for lunch) must have been the result of a congressional investigation. After all, this Jam has been the longest on record, and something just had to be done, and done fast.

The cement is creeping over the roof of my car now. I am now sitting in it. It feels most disagreeable. I stand up. I write while holding my Notebook on my chest. It is the only thing I have left.

In the distance I see a few Jam-ees also on tops of cars. Not many. A half a dozen or so. The other poor creatures are probably too weak to climb onto the roofs. I try not to think of my friends in Moveville.

By the thousands! Never have I seen so many helicopters. The sky is a black fury of them. Tons and tons of cement falling.

Another wave approaches me, dropping cement as they come, peeling back. More coming.

The cement is rising, constantly finding its own level. There are so many tons of it in this area of Jamland now that every load, no matter where dropped, raises the level a fraction. And tons are being dropped.

The level is now just below my knees. What can I write? There is nothing new. I just saw a man who was on a car some 100 yards from me disappear. A load of cement hit him squarely.

And another just toppled over. Suicide?

Here comes a load. (Editor's note: This sentence was scrawled out so badly it is assumed Littlefinger wrote it as he was actually ducking. Spots of cement were found on this page.)

It hit about 100 feet from me. Cement is now at my waist. I must raise my hands to write.

Suicide?

Another load is approaching. Here it comes.

Just missed me. Hit about fifty feet a

Cement up to neck now.

Write with Notebook over head.

At chin.

Can't die like this.

I am going

At lips.

I have taken the capsule.

It is gone.

Good b

(*EDITOR'S NOTE:* It may well be assumed, although there is no supporting evidence, that Henry Littlefinger died holding the pages of his Notebook over his head, above the cement; and that, some time later, it was thus found in his death grip. One must imagine that that unknown man, that finder of the Notebook pages, that only known survivor of the Great Fourteen-Month Moveway Jam, somehow escaped the onslaught of the "dump-truck helicopters" that fateful day. One must also imagine him for some reason cautiously creeping out over the just-hardened, or hardening, cement the next morning, or later that same day, and coming upon Littlefinger's Notebook pages and hand. As readers may know, Moveway Engineers ceased dumping cement at a level corresponding roughly to the height of a man standing on the roof of a Jammed car, plus about one foot. And since the Notebook pages were not encrusted with cement, it would appear that they were not buried in it. Later, of course, after the original cement had entirely hardened, Engineers dumped the final layer, which brought the level of the new Moveway up to the edge of The Wall—and covered Littlefinger's hand, wherever it may be, that hand that wrote so much for the enlightenment of so many.)

~

NOTES ON "THE GREAT MOVEWAY JAM"

Originally published in the March 1979 issue of *Omni* (Vol. 1, No. 6, pp. 70-73, 114-116: "For months they waited to be rescued from the mammoth traffic jam. Then the copters came!"), with artwork by the American photorealist painter Don Eddy. This story marks the dark apotheosis of Keefauver's obsession with traffic jams—but not its end. In 1992, Simon & Schuster published *The Three-Day Traffic Jam*, a (short) novel for young readers, Keefauver's only standalone hardcover publication. Although that novel, whose protagonist is *also* named Henry Littlefinger, is much less bleak than the story, it does mention the Great Moveway Jam of 1999, and thus represents a sort of sequel. Note that Keefauver kills off his friend and colleague "Adobe" James Moss Cardwell (1926-1990) in this story. Cardwell is another author whose stories have never been collected but deserve to be.

BODY BALL

EVERYTHING SEEMS TO BE IN order, Mr. Wellington. You may now reserve the Body Ball at your convenience."

"Very good. I'd like it on the seventeenth, at eleven."

"It's available then, sir. If you care to read through the contract, and sign it, we can proceed for that night."

"That's not necessary. As long as the major points are the way we agreed, I'll sign."

"They're as agreed, sir. If you win at Body Ball, you collect one million. If you lose, all your financial assets go to the syndicate, and..."

"Never mind. I know the second part of it very well."

"Of course, sir."

"That's the only thing that concerns me, frankly—the disposal of the body."

"There is absolutely nothing to worry about on that score, sir. It will be disposed of per our agreement. We stand on our record, and I'm sure you are aware that we have been in business long enough to have an excellent one."

Wellington nodded. "Well aware. I'll sign."

At precisely eleven o'clock on the evening of the seventeenth, Wescott

Wellington pulled his Mercedes to the curb in front of one of a number of undistinguished row houses and turned it over to an attendant who had been waiting there. As the man drove the car off, Wellington rang a doorbell at the house. The door opened automatically, and he was ushered inside by a voice coming from a wall speaker.

"Good evening, Mr. Wellington. Welcome to Body Ball. You may hang your coat on the rack to your right, sir, and then enter the room directly in front of you."

Wellington was surprised as he walked into the room. The Body Ball machine was gigantic. He'd known it would be large, of course, but had not imagined it as stretching nearly wall to wall and being ten to twelve meters wide. They must have torn down almost all the walls in the house to make the room large enough for it. On the other hand, aside from its size, nothing about it was different from the hundreds of pinball machines he'd seen for almost as long as he could remember—nothing different on the outside, that is; the inside, of course, the part immediately below the playing surface, was far different—deep enough to hold a body.

The giant pinball machine was the only thing in the room except for a chair in front of it and a few steps that led up to its lower end. As for the room, around the upper meter or so ran a strip of mirrored, one-way glass, behind which, he'd been told, would be spectators, both official for verification and some simply there to enjoy the show.

He eased himself into the chair slowly. His age and his paunch would be against him when he played the machine, of course, but otherwise he was a healthy man. Deeply tanned, impeccably dressed, gray hair darkened, fingers manicured, and already feeling an anticipation, a thrill that he had thought he had lost forever, he smiled when an attendant approached.

"May I be of service, Mr. Wellington? Something to drink?"

"No, thank you. The Body Ball is ready for my use?"

"Yes, sir. May I help you with it?"

"If you will."

Wellington got up and slowly walked to the giant pinball machine and climbed the steps at its lower end. On the top step he bent and went through a small doorway into the machine as the attendant hurried up the stairs behind him.

Inside, still in a crouched position because of the glass above him, a pane that extended over the playing area, he edged onto a bucket seat that was attached to a wheeled scooter. The back of the seat rose to head level and was resting against the machine's giant plunger.

"Now, sir, if you will permit me—"

The attendant, crouched beside him now, buckled and locked the seat belt carefully, and then did the same to belts at his ankles and wrists so that, besides being made safe against being thrown from the scooter, he was unable to guide it by using his limbs outside it, although he was allowed to use all the body English he was able to muster.

"There you are, sir. All ready to go."

"Thank you."

"As soon as I get out and close the door, just call when you're ready and I'll send you on your way."

"Right. It will be a moment. I want to relax some first."

"Of course, sir. If I can be of more service just give me a call. I'm here to help."

"Thank you."

As the attendant left, Wellington mused with a faint smile that it was only proper that he should be offered "service" at this time, the pinnacle of his career. God knows, he'd earned it. All of it. Service came with the good life, the rich life. The gambling life. Millions won; millions spent. He'd had it all. He'd been everywhere, done everything, bought everything. And all because of dice, cards, horses, the wheel, you name it. He'd always been a winner. Always. And he didn't have the slightest idea why. He had no system, no nothing. It was uncanny. He'd been barred from many a place through the years because of his continual winning; he'd had to disguise himself, use a phony name.

He'd resented having to do that at first—the subterfuge—but gradually he had learned to look forward to it. Because when you won almost consistently, gambling became—there was no other word for it—just plain boring. To him, anyway, and getting into the places he'd been barred from was a challenge and knocked the boredom for a while. Boredom, in fact, was his greatest problem now, and he might even have gone into some other line of work except for the style of living he'd become accustomed to, and, boring or not, gambling was his life.

When he heard of Body Ball, he was attracted immediately, thinking it impossible to be bored by the game since he could never be certain that he was going to win—in the long run that is. One loss when playing Body Ball was the final one; there was absolutely no chance to recoup, to win. He'd be dead.

He knew the backers—casino people. They were reliable. He applied to play and as he expected, was quickly accepted not only because they thought he had enough money to make it worth their while if he should lose but, far more important, because he was a winner and because casino owners wanted to get rid of winners—legally. That was why they had invented the game, he suspected, with its extreme penalty for losing.

But why would winners play Body Ball in the face of such a penalty? Well, he didn't know what motivated the rest of them, but he knew about himself. He was here for the ultimate thrill, the greatest challenge, with absolutely no possibility of boredom. One loss ended it; if he lost, he lost his life.

He had "practiced"—a joke. He hadn't even liked pinball when he was a kid; it was a game played by addicted robots—numbskulls, in his opinion. And, of course. there had been no money in it. But during the last few days he had wearily played dozens of times, always winning. of course. Even so, he suspected that the correlation between playing ordinary pinball machines and playing Body Ball was infinitesimally slight, if existent at all.

Now he would find out for sure.

Taking a deep breath, he called out to the attendant that he was ready to start.

"Very good. Sir"

He felt the scooter move as the plunger behind him was drawn back by a powered device. Slowly he rolled backward until the plunger was released abruptly and he was shot up an inclined corridor at stomach-jolting speed.

Ahead of him, rising vertically at the higher end of the machine, a blinding array of colored lights began to flash spasmodically on a huge board; in the board's upper center brilliant green lights spelled out BODY BALL, and under the lights was a clock. Activated by the plunger's release, the clock's second hand was already moving. If he stayed on the playing area four minutes—one minute for each letter in BODY—the exit slot at the lower end of the machine would automatically be closed at the end of that period of time by a device triggered by the ticking clock, and he would win his million dollars.

If, on the other hand, he failed to stay on the playing area four minutes and dropped through the open slot, a device, triggered by his falling body, promptly slid the metal covering over the slot and him. With the covering closed, and with the rest of the lower part of the machine equally sealed— the part, that is, into which he had fallen—cyanide pellets were dropped into acid, releasing killing gas.

His speed gradually lessened as he approached the top of the playing area. Even so, the speed was great enough to jolt him harshly when the scooter hit a padded obstacle shortly after he rounded the top. The scooter, which had an inflated tire-like rim, bounced back with a jerk to the top of the playing area, and from here he would begin his all-too-speedy descent toward the exit slot at the bottom.

Just below him now were two raised, parallel corridors. Hurtling backward, he went through one of them, bouncing off its sides and triggering a barrage of blinding lights and a deafening cacophony of bells and buzzers on the vertical board and playing area (something, he was to learn, that happened every time he struck anything). Coming out of the corridor at a slight angle, he crashed into a giant mushroom-shaped protrusion that, with its springy edge, spun him off to another mushroom and he smashed against a rectangle-shaped padded obstacle near the left side of the playing area. From here he dropped alarmingly until he crashed into a flipper about halfway down the machine. The flipper, activated on contact, shot him to the far side of the machine, toward the top, where he crashed into another mushroom, which smashed him into the bottom of one of the raised corridors.

From here he rolled straight down the center of the machine toward the exit slot, skimming past two mushrooms and not even getting close to a flipper, even though he savagely yanked at the arms of the scooter with his belted wrists, He zipped past two padded obstacles, another mushroom, and another flipper, gaining speed all the time. Ahead were two more raised, parallel corridors directly in front of the slot; below the corridors he saw there were only two flippers that could stop him from going through the hole.

With desperate yanks of his wrists and body against the belts, he was able to jerk the scooter to the left enough to smash against the top of one of the corridors, which sent him back up the machine about three meters. Right back down toward one of the corridors he sped, though, zipping through it cleanly and setting off an even more horrendous barrage of lights and noise. But again, using savage jerks, he was able to hit the last flipper before the exit slot; it slammed him to the far side of the machine, where he hit another triangle-shaped padded obstacle with such force that he thought his head would be thrown from his body. Rolling backward, he crashed viciously into another mushroom. This one shot him against another tire-rimmed obstacle. Then he bounced off it and landed against another flipper, which smashed him against the side of the rubber-rimmed machine with such force this time that his head crashed into the back of the scooter, stunning him. Groggy, he hit a rubberized, fingerlike obstacle.

And then he was speeding down again. A flipper jolt, and he was moving crossways, and then up once more. He was spun backward and came up heavily against a mushroom. Then he caromed off into another. Lights exploding before his eyes. Noise hammering him. Body spinning, jerked. Thuds. Crashes. Belts into gut, wrists, ankles. Up. Down. Across. Down. Up Across. Up...

He was near the top of the machine when the covering slowly slid over the exit slot. He had won—again.

HE FELT THE OLD BOREDOM within days after he collected his million. And it wasn't long before it was unbearable again; worse, because now, having won the ultimate gamble, what was left? It was impossible for him to really win, it seemed—win freedom from boredom. *Quit? Quit gambling?* That thought itself was depressing enough to lead, finally, to thoughts of suicide. Gambling was his life.

Was death better than boredom? He was beginning to think so.

As he was getting ready for bed one night, he gloomily came to the conclusion that it was, and he decided to play Body Ball again...and again... and again...until he must lose.

It seemed that he had no sooner got to sleep, though, than he woke up with a start, his boredom gone and his whole body tingling with life.

He'd bet the Body Ball owners—with suitable odds, of course—that the cyanide pellets wouldn't drop into the pail of acid. How could he lose?

~

NOTES ON "BODY BALL"

This little story did very well for Keefauver. *OMNI* originally published it in their January 1981 issue (Vol. 3, No. 4, pp. 73-76), with an illustration by [Gérard] Di-Maccio and the tagline: "It was the ultimate gamble. The stakes? His life." The editors and/or the readers must have liked the story, as the magazine purchased the reprint rights for *The Best of OMNI Science Fiction No. 5* in 1983, for $225.00 (where it appeared alongside such heavy hitters as Philip K. Dick's "Rautavaara's Case"). *OMNI* went on to purchase nonexclusive world rights to this story for $300.00, for publication in their foreign language editions. Keefauver received $1,000.00 for the original 1981 printing, so "Body Ball" earned him at least $1,525.00 altogether. No wonder writers miss *OMNI*...

SNOW, COBWEBS, AND DUST

BEAUTIFUL ISN'T IT DARLING?" THE man whispered, standing on the boardwalk, his eyes half closed against snow that fell lazily onto the beach. White fluffs crouched on his moustache, gray and newly trimmed, before melting down cheeks crinkled now in a wan smile.

"Give me your arm, Martha." He crooked his arm, the palm of his hand up, his fingers slowly curling. "Wearing gloves now, aren't you." A chuckle. "A little different from the last time we were here—that summer." He bent quickly and kissed an inch above his palm. "You'll have to forgive me for being such a romantic old fool, dear, but it's been so long since we've been together. Like this."

His chuckle seemed incongruously loud in the floating snow-quiet. "I know it's ridiculous, Martha, walking the boardwalk in the winter. But then, we always did do ridiculous things."

He listened, then quietly nodded. "Yes. A long time, forty-three years. Forty-three years ago today, we were married."

The feet of a policeman crunched dry snow, slowed, hesitated, then crunched on down the boardwalk.

"Let's hurry, darling," the man said anxiously. "It's cold, and I want to get inside with you. Again."

He walked over snow-matted boards, past shops and restaurants boarded up for the winter, his left arm crooked at his side. He slipped once and nearly fell, but caught himself and laughed and walked on again, the crunch-crunch of his footsteps loud in the quiet of the falling snow.

"It'll be nice and warm when we get to the club," he said reassuringly. "I saw Christy yesterday. He gave me a key to the place. See?" He pulled a key from his pocket and held it to his left. "I didn't tell Christy you were going to be with me." He grinned wryly. "Didn't think he'd understand. Just told him I was going to look around on my own. Told him I was a sentimental old fool. Don't you think that was the right thing to say?"

The man's face lighted as his listened. "You're lying," he said, "but I love it. Keep talking—I love to hear you talk, it's been so long; go ahead, please."

Chuckling, he crunched on until he stopped at the door of a restaurant that fronted the boardwalk, its windows now dark and salt-crusted. Jutting out from the building, the unlit neon tubes spelled *Christy's*.

"We're here, Martha."

He unlocked the door and went inside, snapping on a wall switch. Sheets covered stacked tables and chairs, like grotesque diners huddled in silent conversation. Cobwebs patterned corners. Unmelted, the man's snowy tracks led back through the dust to the door.

He quickly took off his hat and coat and hung them on hangers, and, shivering as he walked toward a table, said with eagerness, "Look at the crowd, Martha. Christy always did pack them in. Remember? Remember?

"Waiter! Table for two, please. In the corner. Over there."

He walked to a table and pulled the sheet off it and two inverted chairs. "Comfortable, darling?" he asked when he had arranged the chairs.

"Good," he answered.

He glanced at the dance floor. "I wish the orchestra would hurry. We haven't danced in years." His voice sagged into a husky whisper. "But let's have something to eat first—the same thing we had the last time we were here."

He snapped his fingers and ordered steaks and wine—"With candles, please."

He held a package of cigarettes over the table after he watched the waiter leave. "Martha?" He waited, smiling. "Cigarette, Martha?" His chuckle spilled into the quiet club. "You haven't changed a bit, have you. Still gaping at women's clothes." He burst into a laugh. "But go ahead and look."

His laughter broke. A match scratched loudly in the silence and through its flare he said, "Because even if you don't look at me—" his hand was trembling now, "—I'll be able to see you." He stared at her chair. "Let me. Please."

Then, with a resolute swing of the head, he turned toward the dance floor, his lips taut. "Let's dance, Martha. Now. Like we used to."

He got up and hurried to pull out the other chair; its legs made clear lines in the dust as it moved. He walked quickly, as if afraid he would stop and turn and come back, to the dance floor, his footsteps loud-thumping and hollow on the cold boards.

He hesitated when he reached the raised floor. "In each other's arms," he whispered. He stepped up onto the floor and walked to the center and stopped, standing like an old forgotten mannequin in a closed-up store.

He was trembling now as he forced his arms up, reaching for Martha. Then he let them fall. Sweat began to bubble on his forehead. His tongue flicked out over drying lips. A shiver spasmed him. His hands were knuckled at his side now.

Up came his arms again. Slowly. Slowly. Up. They reached out in front of him. Searching, they cupped. Cupped, feeling for her.

They felt. They held. His arms tightened; they held.

He felt her. He *felt* her.

"Martha," he whispered. "My God," he whimpered.

"My God. My God." And he jerked his arms down, he snatched them away. "My God." Backing, backing.

Backing from the floor and the covered tables and chairs; backing through the dust and the unmelted snow his tracks had left. Backing, and he yanked open the door and burst out onto the boardwalk, leaving his coat and hat hanging.

Outside, snow settled lazily onto his footprints, and after a while quietly leveled them.

~

NOTES ON "SNOW, COBWEBS, AND DUST"

Originally published in *Shadows 4* (1981, Doubleday, pp 142-144), Keefauver's only appearance in Charles L. Grant's prestigious series.

ESCAPE

HE CAME WITH A GENTLE stagger out of the Waltzing Matilda, almost waltzing himself, sort of, as if he were trying to make a partner out of Waltzing Matilda booze. Waltzing out of publand into the nighttime mist of a Kowloon street. It was sobering. Strange. Like an icicle up a nose.

The icicle kept moving until it chipped his brain, nearly straightening his stagger out, while neon street signs, spitting mist, began to suck the waltz out of him, blowing warm, friendly publand smoke away.

Frightening, almost—and he wanted very much to go back inside the warm, familiar Matilda.

"Steve, dammit, hell!" he bellowed to a little Chinese man inside his arm, "this is no night to go hunting for no damn Dreamland!"

Besides, he remembered what the bartender had said. Men who go off to Dreamland with Steve never come back.

The drinking man took a long, wobbly look down at Steve's face; cleaned by mist, the color of oleo, it shone up at him, cheeks looking as if they were pumped with air. Head like a basketball, the big man thought. A Chinese basketball with hair.

Steve answered the American man's stare, basketball face grinning from atop a night-colored tailor-cut suit, young, steady eyes pushing mist aside. He'd come into the Matilda just a few minutes ago, pushing smoke aside then, come in after his big American friend. They'd hit the street together, arm in arm, with only the big man full of drink.

"Every night, Paul, can be a Dreamland night. Come," the little Chinese man said.

The words were big with friendship. They made the six-footer feel small. They made him shake a big laugh out of a fog-colored face and throw it out of work-wearied eyes. There were thirty-some years of working muscle behind his laugh; it seemed to shake the suit he wore, a Hong Kong special bought very cheaply with the help of Steve's knowing ways.

Damn that bartender, anyway! He, Paul, had come into the Matilda early, by himself, and got to talking with the drink-serving man. Told him after a while that he was waiting for Steve. Steve was gonna take him to a special place over in Hong Kong, a place called Dreamland. It was a bit of old China, you know. A mystery place of beauty and strangeness, where ordinary tourists didn't get to go, where Steve took only his special friends. A place for Escape from everything like home.

Sure, sure, the bartender knew. Knew Steve and had heard of this Dreamland place. Every so often a tourist—always English or American or, of course, Australian—would come in and tell him, the bartender, the same story. Steve would come pick the tourist up and off they'd go, bound for the Dreamland place. He'd never see the tourist again. Never again. Was enough to make a man wonder, wasn't it?

Well, maybe it was at that, Paul had said, throwing down the booze. He'd known Steve only a few days, met him on a Kowloon street. Turned out Steve was a freelance guide. Could show you anything, take you anyplace. Steve had taken him by the hand and shown him around. They'd seen many a sight together; he'd eaten many a good inexpensive meal. And all Steve's services came at a bottom price. The last day, in fact, Steve hadn't charged him a cent. "He took me around free," he'd told the bartender.

Sure, sure, the bartender knew. All the other guys had told him the same thing.

Hmmmmmmm. Paul wondered about it. Maybe he ought to chuck the whole thing. Can't tell about these Chinese. Liable to do you in, them and their mysterious ways. But dammit, he ought to see at least one Dreamland before he headed home; a man's gotta have some pleasure on a business trip, something to *really* tell the home folks about. Something really different, something tourists didn't ordinarily see.

Sure, sure, he was like every other tourist in a faraway land: all wanting to shake off hometown dust—but only temporarily. A fellow can't get all the way off the beaten track *permanently*, you know. Gotta Escape—but only for a little while. Always gotta come home again, even if it's a substitute home, like the Waltzing Matilda. It was an Australian place, but it was close enough to remind him of home.

And he kept on throwing down the booze until Steve came in with a doorful of mist. When they went outside, publand smoke stayed far behind, rolling off Paul's back like an old suit at bedtime. He stepped into the mist in Steve's new suit. The Waltzing Matilda door closed, separating smoke and mist.

"Least we could do is take a cab."

"No cars can go to Dreamland," Steve came back, quick.

"Why not?"

"Dreamland is for people."

"Hell, we can *get there* in a cab."

But Steve spun his head and, with him leading the way, they walked over to the main drag, turned left, and went on down to the harbor and the Star Ferry, Dreamland-bound. Paul tried a Matilda song. It came sagging off his lips; it fell no-good on Kowloon streets, wet and limp, crushed by smokeless mist.

Side by side they sat on the ferry, hip to hip on the crowded boat. Long benches, like pews, were bumpy with the Hong Kong-bound. Steadily the ship nosed through its ten-minute ride. Steadily Paul fell into a mood. He didn't even hum a Matilda now, and waltzing was blue-lawed out. Funny thing: he began to think of home. House in suburbia, mowing the lawn; scotch and apple pie. And a wife waiting to kiss him back in from his Escape—a chunky wife. Chunky kisses, too, and Karo eyes. Made a fellow wonder if he wanted Escape at all, even the temporary kind.

BUT DAMMIT, HE WAS GETTING old, and he needed a taste of something different before it was too late. Just a taste would do, and just this one time.

That was why he'd jumped at the opportunity to come on this trip. For years—all his life, it seemed—he'd been selling for the company, tied down, indoors, and always broke, in debt. Then they'd picked him for this Hong Kong trip. Because of his record, his dedication, they'd said. *Buying* for the company now, instead of selling. A business trip, sure.

But that wasn't the real reason he'd said yes to them. Business was just the excuse, far as he was concerned. The real reason was getting away— Escape—before it was too late. Just once would be enough. He'd dreamed about it for years back home while boozing around in the bars. Seemed like every time he went into a bar, that was all he thought about.

Bernice wasn't like him. "You go," she'd said when he'd asked her if she wanted to come along. "It's not important to me, me going. Besides, the company won't pay my way, and I don't think I can take off work at the restaurant now anyway."

He was relieved when she'd said she didn't want to go. Escaping is easier, better, when you do it by yourself. Part of it was getting away from everything at home, including your wife.

So actually the whole trip was a dream, and going to Dreamland was the frosting on the dream cake. He just had to be sure that he was going to get back from this Dreamland place.

"Something I've been meaning to ask you," he said then to Steve, sucking on his mood. Dammit, he felt like a fool, but he just had to ask.

Steve's whitewashed teeth disappeared. He had caught the mood.

"I was talking to the bartender back in the Matilda," Paul plunged on. "Told him about you and Dreamland. He said you've been meeting tourists in the Matilda off and on for a long time. He seemed to know all about it."

Steve's smallness shrugged. "I always meet my friends there, ones I'm going to take to Dreamland—ones who have asked me many times to take them, like you—if they are Australian or English or American."

"How come?"

"Dreamland will be better, more different, if you come direct from a place like your homeland first. What you call it—contrast?"

"But why did I have to ask you so many times?"

"Because I must be sure you really want to go. It is a very special place. You must be sure."

Yes, the words were right, the idea true. It satisfied Paul, but...

"But the bartender says a man who goes to Dreamland with you never comes back to the Matilda. How come?"

Teeth flashed back on, lighting up a peanut-butter face. "You will see. Dreamland not far." The ferry had nudged Victoria Pier.

And Paul followed the little man. Followed because Escape was boiling in his blood, and, by damn, he would see this place, a place to take home with him, to talk about, to pet and pat, to chew. A dream is to chew. To chew for the rest of his life, the frosting on the cake.

Mood flew. And by the time he and Steve had started climbing Victoria Peak maybe ten minutes later, he was almost waltzing again, although he was panting too much to try a tune.

The going got steep. Streets turned into stairs. On either side of the ladder street, markets screamed their wares. Buildings sprouted overhanging signs, neon and otherwise, most in Chinese vertical characters; from the middle of the street, if you looked up its length, their color looked like Fourth of July explosions frozen on the way up. The chatter of Mah-Jongg blocks came bursting out of windows; the playing of this domino-like game sounded like soprano machine-gun fire.

They climbed on, and soon Paul waltzed around a corner.

Into a different world.

"Dreamland," said Steve, as if no one knew, tilting up his face at Paul so that laughter ran out over his lips. "An American friend named it for me one time many years ago. He said it was like a dream."

Paul let out a whistle. It tunneled easily through the mist.

"It is only Dreamland in the night," Steve warned. "In the daytime it is something else."

They stood on the edge of an area perhaps half the size of a city block, leveled, dug into the side of the mountain so that it was flat, crazy flat, against the climbing all around. Flames from oil lamps lit it up in tender, licking light, painting yellow movement on everything they tongued.

Faces. Peanut-buttered faces. Hundreds, dancing with the flames.

Clanging, tonky, wailing music singsonging out.

And Paul waltzed in. Nobody knew he was coming. He didn't know himself.

Waltzing in, into Chinese in native big-sleeved pajama-clothes, eating fishy, stringy, eely, fingery things off boards slung over boxes, and soup, too, all cooked in big black kettles over open fires. Not like any restaurant he'd ever seen. Waltzing in, past crude drawings of hands and palms on canvas spread out on the ground, leathery-skinned old men sitting on boxes beside them. A palmist reading a hand, stuck out by a pajamaed customer who seemed to have a steady wink. Next door a face-reader telling a customer in singing musical language what the hell his face was telling him.

Old Chinese mamas and old pelt-faced papas, and some young ones, too, flitted over their merchandise, patting their piles of rice, petting their watches and tie clasps and trinkets, lovemaking over rolls of silk, hawking it all. Lovemaking all over the place.

What you might call a bazaar.

IN THE CENTER OF THE dream a platform came off the ground. On it were two women and two men, all wooden-shoed, all dressed in silky, fancy-colored robes that glittered like eyes. They were singing, sort of, sometimes talking, everything coming out in high-thrown squeals. Behind them was a three-gong band. Every so often somebody gonged a gong: the Devil was a-coming, but they were a-gonging him out. Can't get into Dreamland, Devil! Get out!

Up and down Dreamland's narrow paths Paul went, waltzing without a Matilda in sight. Paths seemed to widen as he floated through, making room, taking him in.

Escape: getting farther in.

In deeper, right into the middle, mist parting at every step, Escape peeling it away.

In front of him then, almost suddenly, a bunch of Chinese playing drums and horns and stringy instruments, all putting waily, singsongy music into Paul's exploding ears. He was the only one around with yellowless skin.

Near the band a seven-foot wall nuzzled up against a building. Chinese up there, too. One reached down to offer the wall to Paul. Others put their hands under his feet and rear. And up he went onto the wall, seven feet closer to heaven. Grinning butter faces took him in. Angels. There ought to have been a harp.

Maybe there is, inside every man.

A wailing number ended, and Paul let out a thunderclap; his hands exploded. No one else clapped. Was he breaking a Dreamland rule?

The bandleader heard; he turned and saw. Saw a white man in Western clothes sitting on a wall clapping with quiet Chinese. Never saw it before— well, only once in a while, when Steve the Tourist Man brought 'em around on his Special Tour. The leader bowed; a string of wispy hair under his lower lip fluttered in Dreamland air; his sleeve ballooned. He knew what to do.

And he nodded. Not at Paul; at someone, or something, off in mist. Then he raised his baton. A wand? And as the Dream Quintet wailed into another tune, Paul heard a voice, not near, not far, or thought he did—a voice warm as sin, yet cool, too, crisp as a brook that suddenly tumbled out of his memory from some long-ago boyhood fog.

"Escape, sir?" it said. "How much do you need?"

Escape? Well, that was why he was here.

And as if being pulled, he slid. from the wall to the ground...

As waltzing toward him out of the mist came a young woman, golden hair tumbling down like a waterfall, the strands licked by lamps so that they danced on their own—or to the Dream Quintet. She wore a kind of robe, yellow as fool's gold. Straight down to sandaled feet it hung, only winking of what was underneath: boulders or butter, song or dirge? Not even a hint.

"How much do you need, sir? And in what denominations, please?"

She stopped in front of him, and then he felt it—a soft brushing of what he thought was the wind. But an unprotected oil-lamp flame beside him had not moved. Then again. And again.

"Seconds," she said. The flame seemed to be climbing up her nose. "Seconds rushing by." Then the flame cupped her face: a beauty, unlike his wife. Not like his wife at all.

"In a minute, now..."

And then he felt a harder brush, stronger. One, then two.

"Minutes," she purred. "Minutes going by. You're losing them all, sir. Seconds, minutes, hours of Escape. All passing you by."

And before he could answer, or laugh or cry, he felt a bump, much harder than the rest.

"An hour," she explained. "Lost forever. Gone. Let me help you," she murmured, "as I've helped the rest. All the others that Steve has brought here. All of you who are looking for Escape."

Then, as more seconds brushed him and the band wailed on, she reached into her robe, into a secret fold, and pulled out a handful of gold-colored bills. She handed him one from the top; ONE WEEK was printed across its face. And below it, IN ESCAPE: PAYABLE TO THE BEARER ON DEMAND. On another was ONE YEAR and below it the same words. On another, ONE DAY; and ONE MONTH on another.

"Big bills, you see." Smiling softly. "I don't bother with small change—seconds and minutes." Then she murmured, "There's a special place where you can cash them in."

Special place? Well, that was for him. "Where?" he asked her.

"Just stay here," she said, "and you'll see." And after another brush: "May I help you Escape, sir?"

And Paul answered, "Sure."

And with a laugh that burrowed like steam through mist and dreams, she reached into her robe and brought out handful after handful of bills.

"Now," she said. "The exchange."

"Exchange?"

She nodded, giving him a golden smile. "My bills for yours. Escape for whatever is in your billfold. Fair, I think."

Fair? Who cared? He could always get more money. And he gave her all the bills that were in his wallet as she dumped all hers into his upturned palms, until he seemed to sink down as if under their weight. He began to count them—a joke at first—one by one, adding up his wealth. Years! Years of Escape! (But he could always go home.)

"There's a lifetime there, sir." A smile. "But if you need more, I'll always be here."

She seemed to be leaving him, but he didn't mind now.

He counted, first slowly, then in a sort of frenzied greed, Steve now forgotten. He hadn't seen the little Chinese man since he'd waltzed into this screwy place. He counted years! a lifetime!—until, boozewearied, eyelids heavied, greed-dulled as if drugged by the bills, his fingers lost their beat. Until dreams now led him away into a private land...

While the Dreamland Quintet played on and on their timeless wail.

And while, some distance away, the girl in the robe the color of fool's gold split his money with Steve.

SOMETHING TAPPING ON HIS SHOULDER. Somebody saying, "Wake up, sir. I'll be back in a minute. Wake up." It was all he could do to open his eyes and see a man walking away from him. Looked like he was wearing a sort of gray uniform.

So sleepy. And he would have tumbled back into his dreams except that, even half awake, he noticed the change. There was no more Dreamland—although he had no doubt that he was in the same place. The Dreamland Quintet had blown itself away. Singers had sung themselves into air. Restaurants had eaten themselves up. Palmists and face-readers had rolled themselves up in their canvases and rolled away. Gongs had gonged themselves into mist.

Only thing left was the mist now, it seemed. And it was lighter now. Gray.

Then he noticed, through bleary eyes, that sitting beside him, about five feet away, was a man leaning against a short metal pole, head in arms. And beyond him was another man in the same position. And beyond him, another figure: a woman. And so on, as far as he could see, in either direction. And in front of him, too. Lines and lines of sitting men and women, their backs against short metal poles protruding from the pavement. None looked Chinese.

Funny. But none of his concern. So sleepy.

Then he saw the man in the gray uniform walking from pole to pole, glancing at each one, coming closer, militarily erect, gun on hip, carrying what looked like a riding crop. At one pole he stopped, looked again, then briskly tapped the shoulder of the man who sat in front of it. The sitter— incredibly old—looked up. They exchanged words. The sitter nodded, gave something to the uniformed man, and the attendant went on to the next pole.

And finally got to Paul.

"Well, I see you are awake now, sir." Voice brisk. "Just arrived, I see." He glanced at Paul's pole. "You haven't been informed?"

"What's that?" So sleepy. When he tried to look at the attendant's face, all he could see was a blur, a shadow. It was as if the face were covered by mist. "Informed?"

"About the meters. About your meter, in particular."

"Meters?"

"The meter you're leaning against, sir."

And so he was. He, too, was leaning against a pole—or a meter, if you wanted to call it that. It felt very comfortable anyway.

"You must feed it, as you Americans say."

"But I have no car parked here."

The man laughed, not unkindly. "These meters have nothing to do with cars, sir. They are for people."

Strangely, the man's words did not seem funny or even incongruous.

"Oh," murmured Paul, so sleepy, the meter so good against his back. "For people."

"You must pay for your time here, sir. And it's my job to see that you do."

"Of course. I understand."

"Now, if you will give me a bill, I shall exchange it for a proper meter coin."

Paul fumbled for his billfold. All he wanted to do was satisfy the man and get rid of him: So sleepy. So nice here with his meter...

"Not the money in the billfold, sir—if there's any there. That's no good here. I must have the special meter money. The money there that you're sitting on, that's under your legs and feet."

Oh yes, so it was. Funny he hadn't noticed it before. So sleepy. He reached into the pile of bills and gave the attendant one without looking at it.

"Thank you, sir." The man glanced at the bill, put it into a leather container attached to his belt, and took out a coin, which he put in the meter. "Now you're all set for a day, sir. That was a *ONE DAY* bill you gave me. I'll see you tomorrow."

He started away, toward the next meter, then stopped. "If you should not wish to be disturbed so often in the future, sir, just give me larger bills. You should have some *ONE YEAR* bills there, I believe."

"Check," murmured Paul, as he settled back against his meter. As the mist parted a second, he hardly noticed or cared that the man was Steve. "Thanks much."

"You're quite welcome, sir. Nice to do business with you."

But Paul had fallen asleep.

~

NOTES ON "ESCAPE"

Originally published in *Rod Serling's The Twilight Zone Magazine* in July 1981 (pp. 74-79), for which Keefauver received $235.00, a nice sum for a short story even today. At that time the editor of *TZ* was the great Weird Fiction author TED Klein, and his correspondence with Keefauver survives in the latter's files. The original title of this tale was "Escape: Payable to the Bearer on Demand," which was shortened at Klein's request. "Escape" bore the tagline: "For the tourist, Hong Kong was just too close to home. He wanted a ticket to Dreamland." The layout of the story also made use of a "wonton font," which unfortunately accentuated its orientalism.

THE SMILE OF THE THIRTY-FOOT WOMAN

FROM THE BEGINNING THE MEN had trouble deciding about her: whether to kill her; whether to push her back out to sea; whether she was even alive. To start with, she was so large—at least thirty feet long—that in a way you could hardly think of her as a woman. But, she *was* a woman, or at least looked like one, no matter how large, and very attractive. Alive? She had no pulse, no heartbeat, no movement, as far as they could tell. She didn't seem to be breathing. Her color wasn't that of death, though, and she had a smile. There were no cuts or bruises on her, no bites; she must not have been in the water long.

They had found her on the beach at the water's edge that morning, early—beached was the only word to describe her—on her back, naked, with her tantalizing smile. She never lost it, dead or alive, and that was one point made by those who thought she was living. She could hardly keep smiling if she were dead, could she? As far as her nakedness was concerned, though, there wasn't anything unusual about that. Most women were going naked, the last they'd heard, when the weather was suitable for it. And they'd heard they were all larger now, although they hadn't any idea they'd be thirty feet tall. But the men had been on the island a long time.

Those who thought she was alive wanted to kill her immediately. The hate in them was still overwhelming; they hadn't been on the island that long. Still, she *was* a human, a few argued—mostly younger men and those who had never been married—whether thirty feet tall or not, whether a woman or not, and as such she should be spared. This brought on a number of threats, and the bachelors and young men shut up and drew back. Everyone agreed, though, that if she were already dead she should be pushed out to sea immediately. They did not want the work of burying her.

Regardless of her size, regardless of whether she was dead or not, she was an extremely attractive woman and they had not seen a woman for a very long time. Therefore, along with the matter of hate, there was the matter of sex. Perhaps this was why no one made a move to kill her or shove her out to sea. They would first look upon her awhile.

She seemed to be in her mid-twenties, and she was well-shaped for her size. Her breasts, for example, were vast when considered alone, but considered along with the rest of her they were in proportion. The nipples were almost the size of grapefruit. Her pubic hair stretched for at least three feet, and within minutes of finding her, one man had climbed atop her and lay down in the hair with an expression of hatred and fear but also, at times, of bliss. He just lay there on his back, staring into the sky, his face working. Two more men eventually climbed upon her; each sat on a breast. They began to bounce up and down on it, laughing between obscenities. They couldn't seem to decide whether they were having a good time or punishing her. Another man lay between her breasts with a kind of haunted look. Two more then got upon her stomach. No one got upon her face, though, and she continued to smile—or, more exactly, her smile stayed. Her eyes were closed. Her brownish hair floated in the water around her head; her hair was the only thing that moved. Her arms were at her side, palms up. One man kept fingering the sharp edges of her nails.

WHEN THE MEN HAD FIRST come to the island—years ago now—they had been prepared to survive. Their ship was well stocked with food, water, seeds, farming implements, and other necessities, and the island had been chosen as one that would be ideal for them in terms of tillable land, water source, weather and, of course, safety. It was not on any map, and its existence was known by only one man when they had set out for it—or so they had thought. In time, more men had arrived, and kept arriving, until the island's capabilities for survival were unable to support so many and the disintegration had begun. The potential for chaos had been there from the beginning, of course, the same potential—the bickering, the warfare among themselves—that had caused the defeat of men by women (although they had arrived on the island before the defeat was complete, and before they knew about the extent of the physical growth of women). They did not learn about the growth until the later-arriving men told them, but even then most of the island's old-timers did not believe it. That women had become more powerful was understandable; the men had seen it happen, certainly. But that women had become larger physically to the bewildering size reported—up to twelve feet in height—was something that a clear-thinking man could not accept. It must be a fantasy on the part of the newer arrivals, brought on by the horrors of intersex warfare. In any event, as more and more men had arrived on the island, bickering had begun over food, shelter, and land. Quarreling had started and continued over the matter of leadership, too. Homosexual jealousies had entered into it. Eventually chaos had come—fighting, killing. And so now, together with the fact that it had now been many months, perhaps years, since any men had arrived on the island, along with there being, of course, no births, there were relatively very few men left.

And so, typically, bickering had begun about the thirty-foot woman, and as the morning wore on they began quarreling even more. Those few wanting to help her argued that she must be one of the female rebels they'd heard about from some of the last men to reach the island. The rebels were unhappy with living in a society where associating with surviving men was prohibited, where the only way to bear a child was through the use of frozen sperm; and so some women had set out to find freedom with free men, a few in small boats. This woman must be one of them, they argued; her boat had sunk and she was the only survivor, pretending to be dead because it was safer. Even though she was thirty feet tall, there were so many more of them—men. Besides, she must've been weak from being on a boat and in the sea for God knows how long. Those who argued these points said that once she realized the majority of them wanted to help her, she would let them know she was alive. So they must feed her.

These men were attacked, only verbally at first. Men who had been married and seen their wives and daughters turn against them were the most vicious. Finally one of the latter grabbed the smallest bachelor and threw him against a fingernail of the woman and sawed his neck against the nail until the jugular was severed. He bled to death.

There were some who said the woman's smile momentarily disappeared when the bachelor was being killed, but they were hooted down and threatened, too. It was clear that an overwhelming majority assumed the woman was alive and wanted her killed. It was almost as if they wanted her alive so that they could kill her.

Yet even within the majority there was an element of reluctance because of her beauty and youth. Although they hated women, they had not seen one for years, and now seeing such a specimen, they were reminded of, or even felt, old desires. And so each man hesitated to start the killing. Each waited for another to begin. All carried at least one knife; those without knives had long ago perished.

And so they waited, gazing at the woman. Her smile, if it had indeed disappeared momentarily, had returned.

Nevertheless, they would have killed her soon if another of the unmarried men, foolheartedly taking their reluctance as a mass change of mind, hadn't spoken up again in favor of sparing her. This time they were upon the sympathizer with their knives; and afterwards, perhaps sated somewhat by two killings within such a short time, their interest in killing the woman immediately slackened. They decided to tie her to shore with vines, and the next morning they would do the job.

After she was tied, they lolled on the beach side of her. Some climbed upon her; they said she was warm; but others said she was warm only because of the sun. The man who had lain between her breasts earlier was chased away by a larger man, who took over his place, snarling at anyone who tried to come near. Two men climbed upon her, so that eventually she was covered by men except for her face and other bony areas. They said they were upon her so that in the morning they would be in the best position to be the first to sink a knife into her. Yet the longer they stayed on her, the less severe their expressions became.

Her smile remained. It may have become even larger. The men who were unable to get upon her claimed it was, but by then it was growing dark and no one could be sure.

In the morning, it was clear. Her smile was larger.

Two men now lay between her breasts, and a third man lay alongside the others on her pubic hair. More were on her stomach. Her legs had spread during the night, enough to let a number of men lie between them, and many men were now cradled between her arms and her sides.

As the hours passed, more men climbed upon her, while others, of those remaining, clamored for space there. Some men had left during the night, and it was first thought by those who slept on the beach that they had gone to their huts.

As more men climbed upon her, her smile grew even more pronounced. Even the men were smiling now, especially those between her legs waiting their turn to worm their way inside her. Only her smile was triumphant.

~

NOTES ON "THE SMILE OF THE THIRTY-FOOT WOMAN"

Originally published in the Summer 1983 issue of *Pulpsmith* (Vol. 3, No. 2, pp. 166-169). This story and "Giant on the Beach," which appeared in the April 1980 issue of *Omni*, are both obvious, and, I will argue, inferior versions of "The Pile of Sand." What order Keefauver wrote these stories in, we do not know; my theory is that "The Pile of Sand" was the last written but first published, as it represents by far the most polished version of this motif. All three stories exhibit Keefauver's interest in mob psychology, which is also in evidence in his traffic jam stories. Unlike "The Pile of Sand" however, both "The Smile of the Thirty-Foot Woman" and "Giant on the Beach" address obvious social issues of their time. I have included this story here because I feel that it does so in an interesting way, and although it is cringeworthy at moments, I feel that is deliberate also, whereas "Giant on the Beach" ends with a highly dated play-on-words, and is better left behind.

CUTLIFFE STARKVOGEL AND THE BEARS WHO LIKED TV

I DIDN'T THINK IT WAS out of the ordinary when Cutliffe told me that black bears had taken to watching television through his cabin window. After all, he was a bear lover as well as an all-around woodsman and freelance shellfish consultant—and a bit odd generally, anyway. Like his idea, for example, that there were only fifty-nine people left living in the world, and saying it without a bit of a smile.

He didn't smile, either, when he told you about the bears looking at TV through his cabin window. They were very particular black bears, it seemed; he could get only two channels, and if they didn't like either program they'd rip shakes off the top of his place. Not that he was worried about his cabin. What worried him was that the TV habit would ruin the bears' social structure.

"It purely ain't normal for a fine, clean-living California bear to stay up all hours watching the *Late Late Show*," he told me not long after somebody gave him a television set. "Next thing you know them bears will be riding a horse, wearing a vest, driving a pickup to town, and honky-tonking on Saturday night and bowling Monday."

Then he gave a fierce scowl.

"Why, already there just ain't no satisfying them. They don't like *Beverly Hillbillies*, *Star Trek*, or *Tic Tac Dough*. Ain't much left except *Bear World*, which, of course, we all enjoy."

"*Bear World*? I've never heard of that one."

"If you like bears the way I think you do, you will."

Cutliffe and I lived way back up a canyon along the coast south of Carmel Valley, a good hour's drive or more inland through fine ranchland from the Monterey Peninsula. His place was a lot farther in than mine, and although I wasn't required by the post office to deliver his mail all the way up to his ranch house, I took it to him rather than put it in a mailbox at the entrance to his property because I like the old codger. I had to walk the last few hundred yards to his house; that will show you how he'd let the road (and about everything else) go to seed; seems like he was more interested in bears than what was left of his cattle, sheep, and horses. But he hardly ever got any mail until he started getting the weekly packages from Hair Growers, Inc., which surprised me, because even if he was bald, he wasn't the sort to worry about it, especially at his age.

"Cutliffe," I said, handing him that first package, "don't tell me you're trying to grow something on that lunar rock of yours."

He never answered me. He just stood there looking down at the package, his old leathery face wrinkled up in pure joy, acorn eyes shining. "Well, what do you know, it's finally come."

"You been waiting long?"

"All my life."

"All your life? When did you order it?"

"I never ordered it. It just came by itself."

"You mean this is junk mail?"

"Junk! The fifty-nine people left say it ain't junk, and I'm one of them."

And that's all he would say about that, except to add that I could sure use some of the stuff myself, which is true, since I'm as bald as he is even if I'm younger—and generally more presentable, too, I might say. Cutliffe ain't one to dress up for nobody. Only thing he ever wore were old overalls, and they were always too big for his skin, bones, and orneriness.

It was plain he wanted to get in his house with his hair grower, by himself, so I left—wanted to get inside so bad that he didn't even mention bears while I was there, which was unusual for him. Bears are his favorite subject. He talks to them, which isn't unusual if you get back in the valley far enough. Not that he talks to them much. "You got to realize," he told me once, "that there ain't one bear in ten that's really got a helluva lot to say."

I've always agreed with him on that. Not that I've ever talked to bears—or sung to them. Cutliffe tried once. I came up to his place, and there he was on one of his horses singing away as if he thought he was an old Gene Autry. Oh, it was horrible! He told me he was singing to the bears!

"What bears?" I asked him.

"Those behind that clump of bushes yonder."

I didn't see any bears, and I told him so.

"You will," he said. "You will."

He quit the singing, thank God, after a few tries. He told me it was driving them away when his whole idea was to get them to come closer and sing along with him.

Me, now, I haven't even talked to 'em, like I say. I haven't lived around them enough, I guess, like Cutliffe and some of the others back in the valley have. I've got me a little spread (I used to cowpoke until I got thrown and broke a hip and had to do some other kind of work, like deliver mail), but I've never seen bears on my place. Cutliffe says I'll be seeing 'em and talking to 'em in time because I'm basically a bear lover, too—and he's right about that—and that's what it takes, according to him. Maybe that's what he really means when he says there're only fifty-nine people left living in the world. They're all bear lovers, and they're the only ones who count. After all, he sees more than fifty-nine in one week of watching TV, even if he can't get more than two channels. That's two more than I can get. I don't own a set.

So, even with the extra work they cost him nailing shingles back on his ranch house, Cutliffe, being a bear lover, was awful worried about their TV habits—except for their watching Bear World, which he thought was healthy.

Anyway, old Cutliffe Starkvogel and I were friends, and so I was a bit put out when he wouldn't even open the door when I made a special trip to deliver him his second package from Hair Growers a week later, on a Friday. He just yelled from inside, "Leave it by the door. I'm busy." He didn't sound busy; he sounded impatient for me to leave so that he could get the stuff.

The same thing happened the following Friday. He wanted me to leave it outside. "Are you all right, Cutliffe?"

"Sure I'm all right, damn it! I've always been all right, and I always will!"

The fourth Friday, when he yelled from inside for me to put the package by the door, I asked him how his hair was coming along.

"Fine."

"Well, aren't you gonna give me a look?"

"Not until it's finished. Nobody sees me until it's finished. I don't want to be the laughing-stock of the neighborhood."

Which wasn't like Cutliffe at all. Like I say, ordinarily he didn't give a good damn how he looked to anybody, hair or no hair, clothes or no clothes.

The next Friday I admit I walked up to his house quieter than usual and stood real close to his door for a moment before I knocked. I heard him talking to somebody. Or at least somebody was talking, or it might have been his TV going. I couldn't hear what was being said, anyway, and I couldn't hear anybody answering. That wasn't like Cutliffe, either, because about the only time he ever had a visitor was when somebody came to consult him about the mysteries of shellfish. Anyway, if somebody was in there, he had lost me as a friend, that was for sure, after not letting me see him for weeks.

When I called out to him I got the usual impatient answer, and I left in a huff.

The following week I tried hiding behind some bushes close to his house after I'd left the package at his door. I wanted to at least see him when he opened it to get the box, to see if he looked okay. He *sounded* all right, God knows, what with his always bellowing at me to leave the hair grower outside.

I had no sooner got behind the bushes than he bawled from inside the cabin, "I see you behind them bushes, Ned Sturny! Get out of here before I fill you full of shot!"

"Damn it, Cutliffe, this ain't no way to treat a friend!"

"Friends don't squat behind a man's bushes, spying on him!"

"Damn it, Cutliffe, I'm not gonna bring you any more hair grower! From now on I'm gonna put it in your mailbox!"

"Don't make a damn to me. I've got enough now anyway."

"You mean you finished with growing your hair?"

"I will be, when I've used up this boxful."

"You're gonna come outside your house and act normal then?"

"Not for a while. I like it in here mighty fine. Gets me away from people."

"People! What people?"

"Somebody's always coming around here every three or four months, you know that."

I fumed all week. Him treating me like that, me a friend for years. Next to him, I was the longest-living man in the valley since my friend Hiram Walker went away last year. I got so riled up at Cutliffe that that Friday just the sight of another one of his damn hair-growing packages made me lose all control. I threw the damn thing down on the post office floor hard as I could.

Well, a glass bottle inside broke—one of seven bottles in the package, as it turned out. Soon as I had seen what I'd done, I got control of myself, got a rag, and began to wipe up the mess. It was a clear liquid, and, God, did it stink. Smelled like it would grow warts on a horseshoe. Just for the hell of it I wiped my fingers, wet from the stuff, on my bald head. If it would grow hair on Cutliffe's noggin, it ought to grow trees on mine.

The labels on the bottle weren't like any I'd ever seen. Only thing they said was that the stuff was made by Hair Growers, Inc.—that was all. Just "Made by Hair Growers, Inc." And there was no mention of what was in the stuff or how much there was of it or if it had been patented, or any other thing that labels usually have on them.

I didn't take Cutliffe the six bottles on my regular run that Friday. I made a special trip, at night, walking very quietly.

As I crept into his yard, his cabin was dark except for the light made by his TV. I shushed a dog but one of his horses neighed. I froze. But no light went on and Cutliffe didn't come to the door. Then I knew why. As I got closer to the ranch house, I could hear the set and hear Cutliffe laughing. Now I wasn't about to knock on his door this time and go through all his yelling again. I headed for a window, the one that he'd told me the bears used when they were watching his TV. If there were any bears there tonight watching, they'd have to go find another window. But as I got close I could see that there weren't any there. Must not have been anything on they liked.

Well, when I looked through that window I saw something that, even considering the likes of Cutliffe Starkvogel and what he stood for, was enough to send a sane man out of the woods forever.

Watching TV were Cutliffe, wearing an overcoat, and three black bears wearing what looked like skullcaps. Cutliffe had grown a beard, and I had a hard time not to laugh out loud at that, because his noggin was still barer than mine. If he'd put that stuff on it, it hadn't done him any more good than it had done me. It had made my fingers burn a little, is all, the ones I'd used to put the stuff on with.

On the screen was what looked like a zoo, except that people were inside cages, behind bars. Bears were outside, throwing them what looked like peanuts. And laughing and pointing.

That was what Cutliffe and his three friends were doing, too—laughing and pointing—except they didn't have any peanuts. First time I'd ever heard a bear laugh, but, after all, they were Cutliffe's friends.

"Boy, I sure am glad I'm on the outside," Cutliffe said with a big ha-ha.

And then, so help me, I heard one of the bears say in perfect English, "I am too. Now there're only fifty-eight more to go."

Not only that; the voice sounded familiar.

"But it's a damn shame," Cutliffe muttered, "that hair will grow everywhere but on a bald head. That's civilization for you. Getting hair to grow on a bald head is something that even we haven't been able to do yet."

"But we keep trying," the same bear said. "It's the challenge of it."

Then Cutliffe said something I couldn't make out—it sounded like a question—as he looked away from the screen and at the bear who had spoken and then at the other two. I understood what he said next, though. He said, "what do you think, Fulton...Sledge?"

Fulton!? Sledge!? I had known a Fulton and a Sledge. And then I knew who the bear who had spoken reminded me of—Hiram Walker. He had lived not far from me until he disappeared last year. So had Fulton and Sledge, except they had disappeared even earlier. And all three had been bald. They'd been my best friends; it had broken me up pretty bad.

I decided I'd had enough of the whole screwy business when I heard their answer and Cutliffe agreeing with it. "That sounds logical," he said. But before I could get the hell out of there the show came to an end and its title flashed across the screen. It read "Bear World."

What really stopped me from leaving, though, was when Cutliffe then turned on the lights. When he did that, what I saw would have turned my hair gray if I'd had any.

Cutliffe wasn't wearing an overcoat. He was covered with hair, except for the top of his head. Even his face was covered with it. And he was bigger and thicker. He had a snout and paws and everything else a black bear has.

Cutliffe Starkvogel had turned into a bald-headed black bear! So had Hiram. And the other two bears—who used to be Fulton and Sledge—were bald, too. They hadn't been wearing skullcaps at all.

I got out of there fast.

THE NEXT MORNING THERE WAS a big box sitting outside my front door with a card tied to it. I figured what the card would say even before I read it. Because during the night I'd kept waking up, and every time I had I'd thought about that "logical" answer to Cutliffe until I'd figured out what his question to the bears must have been. And when I read the card I was sure. "Compliments of *Bear World*," it said, followed by "Sponsored by Hair Growers, Inc." Inside the box was a TV set.

Because, you see, what had woken me up during the night were my fingers. They were really burning. And when I'd woken up this morning there were some little black hairs growing out of them—but not out of my head.

Cutliffe must have asked the bears, "Who's next?" Because their answer had been me.

And, sure enough, the following Friday the package that came from Hair Growers, Inc., was addressed to me. By that time I'd thought everything over pretty good and had a change of heart. I mean, when you're a bear lover and your best friends have become bears, what's an old cowpoke to do?

~

NOTES ON "CUTLIFFE STARKVOGEL AND THE BEARS WHO LIKED TV"

Originally published in *The Best of the West* (1986, Doubleday, pp. 52-58), edited by Joe R. Lansdale, for which Keefauver received $100.00. Lansdale's brief introduction to the story stands as an astute and accurate description of the author:

John Keefauver is a highly original author of wacky stories. Fantasy. Horror. Mystery. Mainstream. You name it, he can write it. He's one of those rare things—a professional short-story writer, a species that is rapidly going the route of the passenger pigeon and the dodo.

Keefauver is perhaps the only author I know (maybe Philip Jose Farmer or Neal Barrett) who could mix an old rancher who sings to bears, television, a mysterious elixir, as well as a number of other unlikely elements and make them jell. A mad jell, mind you, but a jell, nonetheless.

Within this "mad jell," we can recognize one of Keefauver's core motifs, the "mysterious elixir," which also provided the basis for "Special Handling." A comparison of the two stories will quickly demonstrate Keefauver's ability to spin endless fresh variations out of a single basic idea, as if he were not just a single author, but a sort of Kwisatz Haderach of all human storytelling ability.

Curiously, a much-abbreviated version of this story appeared in several major newspapers in November 1967, after being shared by the UPI (United Press International) wire service. This version lacks the "mysterious elixir" motif and only extends as far as the description of Cutliffe Starkvogel and his concern that television-viewing would disrupt the bears' natural social structure. Papers that printed this short filler piece included the *Arizona Republic*, the *Cincinnati Enquirer*, the *Long Beach Independent*, the *New York Daily News*, and *The Ottawa Journal*, mostly on their TV listings pages. In all cases, the story bore the dateline "OCEAN SHORES, Wash. (UPI)," but the *Long Beach Independent* also included a byline attributing the piece to journalist Eldon Barrett (1921-2009). This must be an error, as the piece had already appeared in several other papers the day before. Keefauver frequently recycled his own material, but not the work of other writers.

CANDY SKULLS

THE LAST THING I SAW of the kid was his look of both terror and hate just before we hit him with the bus. Duke, who was driving, saw it, too.

We were south out of Mazatlan heading for Mexico City—driving too fast—when it happened. It was still light enough to see without headlights when we came up on a bunch of Mexican kids alongside the road in a village. As usual, Duke didn't slow up. Just as we got up to them, two kids jumped out in front of us, almost as if they were doing it on purpose to taunt us. One got back to the side in time. The other one didn't. Duke swerved and hit the brakes, but the right fender hit the kid and knocked him off to the side. Cussing, Duke gave the bus the gas.

When I saw what he was doing, I yelled, "For God sakes, Duke, stop!"

He was bent over the wheel, his face stretched into a frightened mask. Right then he looked twice as old as twenty-four.

"Duke, for God's sakes!"

He didn't slow up.

I looked out the back window. A car was coming up on us fast. The old school bus—Duke had bought it in L.A. at sort of an auction—wouldn't do much more than fifty.

"Duke!"

"Shut up!"

The car behind us swerved out to pass, then came up beside us. I could see four or five faces—some kids'—all glaring at us as it went by. Then the car went on, disappearing around a curve. It had a Mexican license plate.

"Man," said Duke, his foot still all the way down on the gas pedal, "you don't stop in Mexico when you hit somebody. They'll throw you in the can until you rot."

"But he may be hurt bad, or dead."

"All the more reason to keep going. You want to get us killed, too?"

"You can't just drive off!"

He began to sulk, not saying a word, keeping his eyes straight ahead, the bus at full speed. It was about ready to fall apart. He'd bought it on impulse, cheap, a small-size job. It only seated about twelve kids. He'd thought it would be funny—and fun—driving through Mexico in an L.A. school bus. The bus was sluggish, though, especially on the hills we were now running into. I kept looking behind, still scared.

"Hand me the bottle, will ya."

Duke took another long swig—straight—and tucked the rum between his legs. "Maybe we can make Tepic tonight."

He kept swigging at the bottle and sticking it back between his legs. I finally had to ask him for it to get a drink myself; I mainly wanted to help get the bottle empty. "If you get tired, Duke, I'll drive." I hadn't known him very long, so I didn't know how well he could drive and drink. I'd planned on bussing it into Mexico, but when I'd got into L.A. from Oregon I'd met Duke at the Y. We'd got to talking. He'd told me about the bus he'd just bought and said he needed somebody to share driving and expenses. Some woman who was going to go with him had changed her mind, and he'd asked me to go along. It had taken me a while to make up my mind. There was something funny about him.

"I'm doing all right," he said.

He didn't let up on the speed, and he kept on drinking, silent, moody, answering the questions I threw him every once in a while only with a grunt. I wanted to get him talking, to keep him from thinking whatever he was thinking, to keep him awake—but he wasn't having any. At least he started to slow down now, whenever he saw somebody walking alongside the road. But he always took another drink right after and jammed the gas pedal down.

We were balling into a town when our headlights picked up a bunch of people walking toward us, right down the middle of the road. I yelled at Duke, but he had seen them and was putting on the brakes, cussing. He came to a dead stop. Kids were leading the mob. They were all carrying what looked like paper lanterns with flickering candles inside. Then I heard wailing and singing, and saw what were supposed to be skeletons, I guess, dancing toward us, behind the kids. I heard Duke take in a long breath. The skeletons, it turned out, were men dressed in skeleton costumes. The women were dressed in rebozos and serapes, and carrying candles, flowers, and earthenware jars.

Laughing and singing and wailing, they all turned off the road just before they got to the bus, not paying any attention to us. But after they were out of our way, Duke didn't make any move to start the bus. He was still breathing hard.

Then, with the help of the moon, I could see where they were going— the village cemetery. And I suddenly knew what was going on, although I doubted if Duke did. I'd been reading up on Mexico, and realized that today must be what they call the Day of the Dead. This was the night part of it— the vigil—when the living go to visit their friends and relatives who were buried in the graveyard. Everybody dances and sings and drinks and has a good time, and men with guitars play the dead's favorite tunes. But they're also sad and do a lot of wailing. Kids eat candy in the shape of skulls and coffins. It's sort of a feast to the dead eaten by the living.

And that's what they started doing. All of it. Right there in the graveyard! All around the tombstones and between them.

Duke got out of the bus.

"Where are you going?"

He didn't answer. He started walking toward the cemetery. I put the parking lights on and got out and followed him. He walked right into the crowd. I walked up beside him, hoping to God that they hadn't heard about a school bus hitting a kid back in the other village. "Come on, Duke," I whispered, "let's get the hell out of here."

He didn't pay any attention to me.

Most everybody, even old crones and scarecrows of men, were dancing and crying and laughing and wailing in there with the tombstones. The kids, too—sucking on their grisly candy. It was as if they were all dancing with death but, because of the fun they were having, without quite touching it— not quite in its arms. Death was that old friend, that old joke.

"Come on, Duke. Suppose they've heard about that kid we hit." Not that anybody was paying any attention to us, but I kept picturing that kid's face. I put my hand on his arm. He shook it off easy, being a lot bigger than I am. He seemed to be in a trance, just staring. I didn't know what to do. We sure didn't belong here.

"Duke! Please."

Then, so help me, he started to dance himself. Very seriously, not smiling. He must have been drunker than I'd thought. His eyes looked like they had sweat in them. Thank God he didn't try to grab any woman. He just wobbled around, all by himself, around and around one little tombstone. But nobody paid any attention to him.

He might have danced there all night, for all I know, if the headlights on the bus hadn't gone on all of a sudden. Then the horn started blowing, off and on, off and on. The horn was loud, but I don't think Duke heard it. I had to yell at him that somebody was in the bus, and he finally came with me, not saying a word. The Mexicans hadn't paid any attention to the horn or lights.

The bus was full of kids, all yelling and laughing and sucking on their damn candy skulls and coffins, a lot of them holding paper lanterns. One was blowing the horn, having himself a ball. There must have been twenty of the black-haired little rascals in there, some sitting all over our gear and on the floor. When they saw us, they started making more noise and offering us candy. I declined. Duke didn't say a word, but he didn't take any either. Then they let us know they'd like a ride. "*Vamos, por favor! Vamos!*" Let's go, please. And yelling a lot more Spanish as they made gestures with their hands to reinforce what they wanted. It looked like none of them had ever had a ride in an L.A. school bus before, and they thought that it would top off their Day of the Dead.

I didn't care for the idea at all—I'd had enough of the Day of the Dead, and I didn't much care about having an accident with the bus loaded with kids. With Duke's driving, I didn't even want to get in the bus myself.

But Duke, he was all for it. Shooing the kid who had been blowing the horn from behind the wheel, he yelled, "*Vamos,* okay, *vamos!*" and got in the driver's seat.

"Damn it, Duke, you can't take these kids away from here."

"Shut up, let's go, let's go!"

The kids were laughing and shouting like mad, knowing they were going.

"But, Duke, their folks will be worried sick about them."

He started the engine. "You want to go or stay here?"

"Let me drive."

"No, I'll drive."

I pushed a couple of kids over on the seat, right behind Duke, and sat down. If I'd had forty more pounds, four more inches and a few more years, I might have tried to get him from behind the wheel. But I wasn't about to stay there, be there when the parents found out their kids were missing.

As we started to move away, somebody out in the dark—I guess it was a kid—threw something through the open window on the driver's side. It hit Duke on the head, then bounced onto my lap. He didn't say a word; I doubted if he felt it. I brushed it to the floor after I felt what it was—a candy coffin.

Instead of going on in the direction the bus was pointing, Duke turned it around and headed back toward where we had been. I had hoped he'd drive on into the center of the town—slowly—and then come back.

"Where you going?"

He didn't answer. And he was flooring the gas in every gear. The kids were whooping it up like mad. Then, in addition to all the laughing and yelling and waving of lanterns, they started throwing those damn candy skulls and coffins at each other. The things were rolling all over the bus. The L.A. school system probably never had a load like this.

It didn't faze Duke. He acted as if he didn't know the kids were there; hunched over the wheel, rigid; the only thing moving about him were his hands as he took the old jalopy around curves as fast as it would go.

"Duke, for God sakes, slow down."

"Where's the bottle?"

"Man, you don't want any more to drink."

"Hand me the bottle."

I took a swig myself to get rid of some of the stuff, then handed it to him. He took a big pull, and kept the bottle.

"We've gone far enough, Duke. Let's go back."

But he wasn't talking anymore.

Duke took the bus back over that winding road as fast as it would go, silent, swigging on the rum, acting as if he didn't know the kids were there—as if he were making the ride for himself, as if he were doing it alone. Then, through the noise of the laughing kids, he suddenly yelled, "It happened to me before, I hit a kid. Hit him with my car, killed him, I think."

"Yeah? When was that?" I wanted to keep him talking. "Where?" At least that way I knew he wasn't asleep. Or in his own world entirely.

"Here. Last time I was down here, couple years ago. I didn't stop then, either. You don't stop in Mexico. I drove right back to the States without stopping after it happened."

I made a neutral sound. I didn't want to irritate him. I just hoped that none of the kids understood English.

"Maybe I ought to have stopped though. It might have made it easier on me, no matter what they do to you. I've been hurting ever since it happened."

"But, hell, Duke, you did the same thing today—kept on going."

"Yeah," he mumbled. "Yeah. That's why I'm going back this time. Maybe I can do something."

"Back...? You mean back where you hit the kid?"

But he had finished talking again.

The nightmare ride finally ended. The first thing I noticed was that all the cars were off the road. There hadn't been many, but then they stopped altogether, and it wasn't that late. Suddenly the kids got silent. They even stopped throwing the candy skulls and coffins at each other. They didn't put out the lanterns, though. Then Duke began to slow down. He got slower and slower, as if he was looking for something. Now the kids began to come up to the front of the bus, as if they were looking for something, too. They weren't laughing anymore. They weren't even grinning. Very serious now, intent.

Duke screamed, "He's in the road!" and jammed on the brakes, at the same time jerking the wheel. The bus went off the road and stopped.

I had been looking straight ahead when Duke had yelled. There hadn't been anybody in the road.

While the singing and wailing and a sort of screaming kind of laughter came from the darkness around us, from outside the bus, the kids, all together, threw their candy skulls and coffins at Duke as hard as they could. Then they were upon him, lanterns held high. Some of them held onto me, while the others, in sort of a dance, dragged Duke out into the road to finish the job.

~

NOTES ON "CANDY SKULLS"

Originally published in the Spring 1987 issue of *Pulpsmith* (Vol. 7, No. 1, pp. 98-120). Keefauver had published in this journal at least three times before, with "Neutron Warhead vs. Mustard Gas" in 1981, "The Ventriloquist" in 1985, and "The Smile of the Thirty-Foot Woman" in 1983.

KILL FOR ME

NOW THE GUN IS AIMED at him as he sleeps so peacefully there, and all I have to do is pull the trigger and the whole horrible thing will be finished. Finally finished. Years of it, over. And I'll be the only one left. Not that I deserve to be the one surviving. But if Irene had told me what she was going to do, there would have been two of us left. I would have killed him then instead of now.

In a way, of course, she's the one who will be killing him. Not that she would want it that way. Still, there's the irony of it. Her note to me after I found her: "Tell him you did it, that it was your idea. He will think I'm the 'somebody' and he will stop. He will be satisfied…"

Satisfied? *Him?* Him, stop? Whatever possessed her to think that he'd stop! Why should he stop after all these years? To my mind he's just getting started. A bullet will be the only thing that will stop him.

She was always the optimist, though, Irene. She always said he would grow out of it. From the very beginning, she was the one who gave in to him, thinking he'd stop. And what she has just done was her final giving-in. Now that I didn't think the same way she did, too, at first, that it was simply a baby thing on his part. After all, don't all babies go into a tantrum at some time or another, at least once, in order to get their way? Like holding their breath until you give them whatever they want. Like he did, although I don't remember what it was he wanted anymore. But that was the beginning. And I suppose if we hadn't given in to him then, and all the childhood years afterward, I wouldn't be standing here now in his bedroom with a gun aimed at his head, my finger on the trigger. Can I really do it? If I hadn't lived through it, I would think of myself now as a monster. Can I really do it?

It's not a matter of whether I can, but that I must do it. For Irene's sake. And for all the others he will destroy if I don't destroy him. I won't give in to him again. If I—and Irene—had only stopped years ago. If we'd let him hold his breath until he turned blue. He couldn't hurt himself—we knew it then—but he scared us and we gave him what he wanted. Scared us... Little did we know.

That time when he was six or seven and he wanted to see that movie and we wouldn't let him and he said he was going to jump out of a tree if we didn't let him go. We wouldn't, and we found him not long afterward with a broken leg at the foot of the elm in the backyard. He hadn't made a sound. No screaming or crying, lying there I don't know how long with a broken leg. Just lay there until we found him. All he said then was, "I demand to be allowed to go to all the movies I want to go to." Demand. Allowed. That was the way he talked, even then. As if he was reading the words out of a book.

So from then on we let him go to the movies he wanted to. Wouldn't you? No?

That started it, anyway. We were afraid, although Irene for a long time didn't entirely come to stop believing that he simply had fallen out of the tree. She asked him more than once about it, at first: "Now, Billy, you *must* have fallen out of that tree." He'd simply say, "I jumped. I deliberately jumped." I believed him. After all, hadn't he been building up to it with his other threats from the time he'd learned to talk? The time he said he was going to burn himself with the birthday candles if he didn't get a bicycle for his birthday. Not a small boy's bike; a big one, one he couldn't possibly ride. Of course, he didn't get it—and he deliberately waited until it was time to blow out the candles, and we were all watching, to stick his hand over the flames and hold it there until Irene jerked it away. I felt sorry for the kids at his party. Of course, that was before we stopped inviting his friends to the house. He didn't mind. It wasn't long after that he didn't have any friends, not at school or anywhere. He didn't care.

Even Irene had to admit that he had deliberately burned himself, since it happened right in front of her eyes that way. I think he did it in front of her to make her understand that it couldn't possibly have been an accident—especially when, about a year earlier, he'd fallen down the cellar steps after we wouldn't let him go ice-skating one day. (He had a bad cold.) Even I thought it had been an accident. He was furious with us for thinking he had simply fallen. "I told you I was going to do it!" he kept yelling. When he jumped out of the tree, I guess he just got tired of waiting for us to come out and watch him. He claimed he had yelled for us to "come see." We didn't hear him.

He got his bike, and when he eventually asked for another one, an expensive racer type, we gave it to him, even though he couldn't possibly ride it. He told us he would drown himself if he didn't get it. What would you have done? Irene was very frightened. She kept saying that he "might accidentally drown himself." I argued against it because I could see what was going to happen to us for the rest of our lives if we didn't take a strong stand, although I admit I never thought it would come to this. I told her there wasn't any body of water large enough for him to drown himself in for miles around. How could he get to it? (He was only seven or eight.) Then she mentioned our bathtub...

When I heard him running the water for his bath that night, on his own, I gave in. Especially considering that we'd always had to drag him to the tub.

From then on we gave in to all his demands that were halfway reasonable. When we balked on some of the more outlandish ones, he threatened to do himself bodily harm. Always bodily harm. I began to dread hearing him open his mouth for fear of another demand. He got everything he wanted.

Three or four years went by like this. Why didn't we take him to a doctor, a psychiatrist? We tried to. We told him he was going to the "doctor for a checkup." He thought he was going for a physical examination—until, unfortunately, he saw the word "psychiatrist" at the entrance to the doctor's office as we walked up to it. He darted from us, pulled a penknife out of his pocket, and told us he would stick it in his stomach if we didn't promise never

241

to try to make him see a psychiatrist again. Or any kind of a doctor. Or—he was a smart one—if we ourselves ever tried to see a doctor *about* him.

The worst thing, for then, was when a year or so later he told us he was going to jump in front of a car if we didn't buy him one—a VW. "A car!" I yelled at him. "You're only twelve years old!"

"I *demand* a car. Do you think I'm only a child because I'm twelve?"

We argued about it until he made me so mad that I told him he could jump in front of cars for the rest of his life before I'd ever buy a twelve-year-old kid an automobile.

I had not sooner said that than he ran out of the house. I went to the door, but I didn't realize he was running toward the highway until he was too far away to hear me. I screamed then that he could *have* a car and began to run after him. From a distance, still screaming, I saw him reach the highway, wait a moment, then jump right in front of an oncoming sports car.

I had the VW waiting for him when he got out of the hospital—a new one. That's what he'd demanded.

I'd hoped that he'd be content just to own the car, to sit in it, to pretend he was driving it. But as soon as he was recovered enough, he demanded that Irene or I drive him wherever he wanted to go whenever he wanted to. We did. Wouldn't you? I was particularly anxious not to displease him. Irene had told me that if I ever did anything again that might cause him to do something on the order of jumping in front of a car, she would leave me. I also felt guilty about causing his injuries, if you can believe it.

He soon tired of being driven, though, and demanded that we buy him some property, a field large enough for him to drive the car in himself. He wasn't old enough to drive legally on public streets, of course, and the fact that he insisted on not breaking the law amused me in an ironic way—until I came to the conclusion that he was not really interested in not breaking the law, or even in driving. His interest lay in making another, a larger, demand on us. He well knew that I couldn't afford to buy a field. But I did it.

He'd had the VW less than a year when he told us that he'd cut his finger off if we didn't buy him a Porsche. I borrowed on the house for it.

I thought he was tiring of the game when he didn't make a major demand—there were many minor ones—for more than a year. Then out of the blue he said that unless we swore to give him anything he wanted for the rest of his life—*anything*—he would kill himself.

We agreed—what else was there to do?—and he said the first thing he wanted was for us to kill somebody for him.

He said this at dinner. Sitting at the head of the table, saying it very calmly, as if he were asking for the mashed potatoes (which he liked very much and which we therefore had every day), very composed, his face calm. He's a skinny, pimply kid, hardly someone who looks forceful. Yet right then he spoke with the assurance of a President of the United States—a mad president. And very seriously, just as he always was, incidentally, in asking for the potatoes.

In the morning, I thought, I'd go to the authorities and commit him to a mental institution. He was still a minor.

"Kill somebody for you?" I was afraid to look at Irene.

"That's what I said."

"Why?"

"Because I demand it."

"Well, then, who?"

"Anybody. It makes no difference. I demand that you kill for me."

"When?" I had to have until morning.

"Within twenty-four hours. If you don't, I'll kill myself."

There was no doubt in my mind that he would carry out his threat. And there was also no doubt in my mind that if we killed once for him, he would demand that we kill again—and again. How far could he go? To, indeed, the President of the United States?

With that, he rose and we were dismissed.

That night in our bedroom I told Irene about my plan to go to the authorities in the morning. In fact, I told her a number of times; she seemed to numb, so uncomprehending, so withdrawn, that I didn't seem to be getting through to her. She never answered me. She made no reply—except for a low moaning sound. As I tried to go to sleep I kept hearing her moan. She wouldn't let me hold her. And she wouldn't take a sleeping pill.

Toward dawn I awoke to find her gone from the bed. There was a light coming from our bathroom, and when I went in, there she was lying on the floor, dead, an empty bottle of sleeping pills beside her. The bottle had been nearly full.

Beside the bottle was a note: "Tell him you did it, that it was your idea. He will think I'm the 'somebody' and he will stop. He will be satisfied. It will shock him into sanity." And then a P.S.: "Hide the pills. Say you suffocated me with a pillow. Put me in bed."

Wild grief first. Then a fury. Calling the police simply wasn't enough.

I went into our bedroom and got my gun. Then, into his bedroom.

The gun, aimed at his head. What could be more fitting than he be the "somebody," that within the time specified his last demand be fulfilled?—by me, as always.

Now that the police and everybody else have gone, I suppose I ought to tidy up a bit. If nothing else, clean up the blood. That's what Irene would do, God bless her soul. (Oh, God, how will I ever get along without her?) At least I got her into bed before the police saw her—she wouldn't have liked to be seen on the floor—although I didn't do anything else for the rest of the day except wait for dinnertime. I wasn't up to it. I thought a lot, though—about not killing "somebody" for him, putting it into the right words. And once more I thought about all of his threats, especially the last one, and how he'd followed through on every one of them. Had I made the right decision? Including telling him the truth about Irene, that she had committed suicide?

I had. He'd done exactly what I knew he was going to do. As soon as the twenty-four hours were up, at dinnertime, and I'd said, I-don't-know-how-many times, that I hadn't killed "somebody" and that I wasn't about to, he'd taken the gun I'd offered him—the same one I was going to shoot him with until I came to my senses, and thinking of his final threat, changed my mind just before I pulled the trigger—and he'd blown his own brains out.

~

NOTES ON "KILL FOR ME"

Originally published in *Masques III: All New Works of Horror and the Supernatural* (1989, St. Martin's Press, pp. 285-292), edited by J.N. Williamson. Williamson reprinted this story twice: in *Fleshcreepers: Startling New Works of Horror and the Supernatural* (1990) and *Darker Masques* (2002). Keefauver received $75.00 for the original publication.

A typescript of this story in the author's files bears the title: "I Demand...Or I Will

Kill Myself," but "Kill for Me" is the title in the contract, so probably this was Keefauver's decision. Williamson's intro to the story is worth sharing:

> Like Adobe James and Paul Dale Anderson, John Keefauver is a living secret editors should want to expose. To acclaim. I knew of neither John nor "James" before Ray Russell confided their existence. But "Kill for Me" was (like "Motherson") once meant to be part of an anthology I edited to advance new and "undersung" greats, like this Californian whose book appearances include several *Hitchcock Presents* anthologies, Joe Lansdale's *Best of the West*, and *Shadows 4*. John's fiction and humor have also made *OMNI*, *Playboy*, *National Review*, and *Twilight Zone*. Whereas my other anthology never made it into print, the tales by the likes of McCammon, Kisner, R. C. Matheson, Winter, Paul Olson, Castle, Tern, and Wiater have. And now, at last, this existential corker too!

"Motherson" was a story by Steve Rasnic Tem; "Adobe" James (James Moss Cardwell) and John D. Keefauver were friends, and they frequently published together.

UNCLE HARRY'S FLYING SAUCER SWIMMING POOL

U NCLE HARRY HAS DONE SOME screwy things in his time, like living in a bathtub one winter because he said it was cheaper to heat the water than the house, and another time collecting unemployment checks while he was in jail. And for a while there he was identifying himself as "a retired informed source." He wasn't what you'd call an average fellow. His latest, for example, was this flying saucer made out of a swimming pool.

He claimed that Unidentified Flying Objects were portable rubber swimming pools he'd filled with helium and launched—not that anybody actually believed him, of course. Well, *we* didn't, anyway—Mom, Dad, and me. We knew better—or thought we did.

We first heard about his flying saucer swimming pool when he let out a bawl from the roof of our ranch house. He'd been sleeping up there for days, but he never would tell us why. We thought it was because he'd just come in out of the scrub and that he wanted to still live out of doors even though it was on top a house. Dad had felt sorry for him and invited him in late summer to live with us on the ranch in exchange for some work, like keeping the snakes out of the pea patch and cattle inside fences he was supposed to keep mended. Uncle had reluctantly agreed to try it for a while; he must have been broke, or maybe his age was telling him that living in a lean-to wasn't smart anymore, especially during another Wyoming winter, which he knew was coming up.

Anyway, we didn't find out why he'd really moved up on the roof until one night when he let out a howl from up there. We ran up and saw him dancing around and cackling and bellowing, "There she goes! See it?" He was pointing off into the sky.

"See what, Uncle Harry?"

"My flying saucer swimming pool! Are you blind?"

We thought for sure he'd gone all the way off this time.

"Flying saucer swimming pool, Uncle Harry?"

"That's what I said—flying saucer swimming pool. I've inflated it with helium. You don't think a swimming pool can fly without being inflated with helium, do you?"

We said we guessed not.

He gave us one of his special dumb looks; then, real quick, he moved his finger a little bit, off toward a new direction. "Ain't she pretty! The only flying saucer in the world made out of a swimming pool! I'm going to use it to round up the cattle. I won't charge you a cent."

I looked where he was pointing. Don't ask me why. All I could see were stars and maybe a jet. I looked at Mom and Dad. They shook their heads—sorrowfully. They didn't see any flying swimming pool either.

"Do you need glasses!?" he bawled when we didn't turn handsprings.

"But it's dark, Uncle Harry."

"Dark! Of course it's dark! That's why I've got it lit up with a red light. You think I want to get into trouble with the FAA? There! See that red light? That's my special flying saucer swimming pool navigation neon tube!"

We didn't see any flying navigation neon tube either.

"Don't you think you better get it down a little so the cattle can see it?" I said, carefully.

"I will when I learn to aim it better. After all, this is my first one."

God help us if he went into mass production.

That was the beginning, and gradually we got the story. Uncle said he'd bought a rubber swimming pool, taken it to "my flying saucer lab on the roof," where he had attached an electrical gimmick to it that lit up a circular neon tube. Then he'd inflated the thing with helium instead of air and launched it in high glee.

That's what he told us, anyway, very seriously, and awful proud.

We didn't believe a word of it, of course. We're used to Uncle Harry. Although it's true we hadn't been up on the roof since he'd moved up there. He wouldn't let us.

Now, it didn't cause much commotion in town when Uncle started driving his beat-up pick-up into town and going from door to door asking for cash donations. The local people all knew he was a little bit funny. But when he told them he needed the donations to buy swimming pools to make flying saucers out of, they thought they'd underestimated him for sure, especially when he started running up and down the main street, his finger pointed toward the sky, bellowing "There she goes!" Then often as not, he'd saunter into the local department store and say casually, "My last order for rubber swimming pools come in yet, Moe?"

"Not yet, Uncle Harry," owner Moe would say. (He knew what to say.)

"Well, when it does let me know. I'm running short." And he'd saunter out of the store as if he owned the place.

And we didn't mind his running up and down the street yelling so much. We figured it was better to humor him than to fight him. But when he nailed a big sign on the side of the ranch house—after first putting an ad in the town's little weekly, *Cowpoke Gazette*—that read, "See flying saucer swimming pool on inventor's launching pad—$1," we kind of revolted. We didn't much care for all kinds of people—mostly strangers, too, because the town people knew better—banging in the house and up the stairs and onto the roof, especially when the only saucer they saw was the dirty one under Uncle Harry's coffee cup. We objected, and we let Uncle know it, too.

He got all up in a huff about our objecting. Said we were just jealous because we didn't have any flying swimming pools of our own. Getting so a man couldn't even make an honest living anymore, he told us, drawing himself up to his full five-foot-three and trying to flatten his gut inside his jeans.

Well, our relationship went on for quite a time like this—sour—with him trying to get people on the roof and us trying to keep 'em off (and with snakes probably swarming through the pea patch), and it might have gone on for the rest of our lives if Sweetbread Monroe hadn't come to town.

Sweetbread was a gigantic fat woman, about mom's age, and every time I saw her she was dressed up in tons of jewelry, big jangly things dangling from her arms and back. She looked like The Queen of Garage Sales and smelled like a gallon of perfume had been spilled over her. Her face was painted up like a barber's pole, only more, especially her eyes. First time I saw her—at the front door—I backed up.

"I want to see the man who makes jewelry out of wisdom teeth," she said.

"Beg your pardon?"

She said it again—I'd heard her right!—but before I could tell her she was at the wrong place, Uncle Harry came busting down from the roof, which he was in the habit of doing when he suspected we were trying to keep a flying swimming pool customer from coming up. "Step right in, madam," said he, all smiles. "If you'll follow me up to my launching pad you may see, with your own eyes, the only flying saucer swimming pool in captivity."

"Are you the man," said she, sort of gushing, "that makes jewelry out of wisdom teeth? I saw your ad."

That stopped him—but only for a minute. "That was last week," he said.

"Darn!" she said. "I've been saving mine for years for something special, and now I'm a week too late."

Then she gave our uncle a certain look and smile that made *him* back up.

He started to close the door but she barged right in, sort of giggling, and did everything but throw her arms around him. "Flying swimming pools! How delightful! I've always wanted to meet a different man. Let me *see!*"

Right then was the first time I'd ever seen Uncle Harry show any reluctance about his invention. "Closed up for the day," he told her. "Locked up tight."

She didn't make a move to leave. "Aw, come on, show Sweetbread."

Then she sort of cooed and grabbed him by the arm, and the next thing I knew she was pushing him toward the roof. Mom and Dad weren't home, and there was no way I could stop them by myself.

From that day on Uncle Harry would duck whenever he'd see Sweetbread Monroe coming. He'd bolt the door, run out the back. He even took down his $1 sign—which made us root for Sweetbread, all right. But she didn't give up. Even if she never got inside again, she came jangling up to the ranch almost every day—sometimes more than once—always with her wisdom tooth in her purse; she couldn't seem to get it through her head that teeth were last week. Hardest on Uncle Harry, though, was that he couldn't run up and down the street hardly at all anymore, yelling and cackling and pointing toward the sky, without running into her and having to have to run the other way.

I guess the battle between Uncle Harry and Sweetbread Monroe would have gone on into the fall, or forever, if she hadn't made the mistake of coming to the ranch one night with a bald wig for him.

Now, our uncle has pounds of thick, red, shiny hair on his head, of which he is awful proud. So when Sweetbread, at the door, gave him this bald wig to cover up his red glory with, you could tell she had made her final mistake as far as Uncle Harry was concerned.

"I like bald-headed men," she tittered, not noticing that his eyes were beginning to smoke and his face was turning as red as his hair.

"You do, huh?" he muttered.

"Uh huh," she giggled. "It's something about the shine."

Uncle Harry's eyes got as black as poison. "You want to see my latest flying saucer swimming pool?" He didn't smile once, much less cackle. "It's the biggest one yet."

"I'd love to, Harry dear."

Without a word, and looking right through us, he took her elbow and, as she tittered and squealed, led her up to the roof. He was almost solemn. We didn't try to stop them. By now, Sweetbread was hardly a stranger.

We didn't go up, of course. We never went up. We knew what the roof looked like, and we didn't want to encourage him with any show of interest toward a swimming pool or flying saucer or whatever he had up there, if anything. Besides, he wouldn't let us.

We listened, though. A peaceful and solemn Uncle Harry puzzled us. It was quiet on the roof for maybe ten minutes. Then we heard this awful shriek from Sweetbread. "Harry, don't! EEEEEeeeee!" Then her voice gradually quieted—to be replaced by Uncle Harry's cackling and laughing and bellowing. He was back to normal, and we relaxed.

In a minute he came down from the roof by himself, all smiles.

"Where's Sweetbread?" we asked.

Grinning like a madman—or saint—he led us onto the empty roof and pointed toward the sky, awful proud. And, sure enough, in the distance there was a red light moving away.

~

NOTES ON "UNCLE HARRY'S FLYING SAUCER SWIMMING POOL"

Originally published in *The New Frontier* (1989, Doubleday, pp. 29-31), edited by Joe R. Lansdale. This was the second of three Keefauver stories that Lansdale anthologized, and his payment was presumably similar to the first, but the only check in this folder was one for $75.00 from the *Weekend* edition of *Monterey Peninsula Herald*, which published an alternate version of the story as "Unicorns, Saucers, and Uncle Elmer" on page 17 on 27 July 1986, three years before the Lansdale volume. This earlier version ends in much the same way, but it begins with Uncle Elmer running around with a plumber's helper stuck to his forehead and pretending to be a unicorn until Sweetbread Monroe (whose "real name" here is given as "Merrily Willing") enters the picture about halfway through. Unlike Uncle Harry, Elmer is bald, so Sweetbread's ultimate provocation in the 1986 version comes in the form of a final supplication for her wisdom tooth to be made into some sort of jewelry, rather than the insistence that the protagonist don a bald wig. Several other typescripts of this story also exist in the author's files, including one in which the protagonist is female: "Glynda's Aunt Malphasia" and the doomed suitor's name is "Roscoe Monroe." In this version and at least one other, the reason the protagonist had "come in out of the brush" was because black bears had taken to watching television through his cabin window, an anecdote that became the centerpiece of "Cutliffe Starkvogel and the Bears Who Liked TV."

Joe R. Lansdale's introduction to this story is shorter than the one for the latter tale, but is worth sharing nonetheless:

> John Keefauver is unique. I said that last time, and I'm saying it again. The man is whacked-out—well at least his writing is. John himself sounds like a pretty normal guy—almost. He lives out in Carmel and is not a personal friend of Clint Eastwood, the former mayor. He is that rare bird a professional short-story writer, and a good one. His story in *The Best of the West* was one of the more popular ones, and I have a feeling the same will be said of this. Who else can mix ranch life, rubber, inflatable swimming pools, and flying saucers and make it work?

DEAD VOICES LIVE

MARK HAD NUMBLY GOT OUT of his car and started across the rain-dark yard toward his living quarters above the old grocery store when a light flashing on in his mother's room there stopped him. Robotlike, he stared up at the window; it seemed to stare back at him like an unblinking square eye, or like a spotlight pinning him to the soggy yard. Through the glass he could see the ceiling of the high old-fashioned room and part of a light fixture, and he thought that if he listened he would hear the squeak-squawk of her ancient rocker begin. Or if he watched long enough he would see her come to the window with a needle in her hand.

Then, still numb, he began to move across the yard toward the back door of the store again. A quartered moon, momentarily appearing between ash-colored clouds, deepened the shadows beneath his eyes and sharpened the line of his nose and the high cut of his cheekbones. It made him look older than his twenty-seven years.

He was almost to the door that led upstairs to the living quarters when a rhythmic chant came from the shrubbery near a fence that enclosed the yard. "Yes-s-s-s, Mr. Nelson," the voice wailed. "Yes-s-s-s, Mr. Nelson." Mark shook his head in disgust and, turning, started toward the wail. George was at it again. And as he approached the fence he saw the man jerk up his cabbagelike head. "Mr. Nelson?" George whimpered, his voice piously simple.

"It's me, George. Mark."

"Oh." The word was heavy with disappointment.

Mark stopped in front of him and he knew immediately that George had entered a new phase with Nelson. He had never seen the man's face so calm, so peaceful. Then, as he watched, George's gaze dropped and he began to pat a small mound of earth near the fence, at the top of which was a potted plant.

"I thought you was Mr. Nelson 'cause he's gonna come see me tonight," George mumbled. "He told me. It was plain."

Slowly the man stood up. He was taller than Mark, and burly. "And he told me that Mrs. Gribe was after you." The peacefulness in his face had disappeared. "But I already knew that. She's all mad 'cause you didn't stay home." His sausage fingers dug into his shaggy hair. "He don't want you to go in the house."

"Mother's not after me, she's asleep. Or she was."

George's cabbagelike head spun. "Not asleep. She's been running around the house with that needle in her hand, yelling at me, like she does when the devil's talking to her."

"Oh, come off it, George."

"The devil *does*, too! Like Mr. Nelson talks to me. Like now."

"Oh, for God sakes, George. I've got enough on my mind without having to listen to you and your Nelson talk again."

And Mark started toward the door. It was times like this that he'd like to kick George out of the house. But the stoop had been living with him and his mother for years now as sort of a handyman. He was almost part of the family...if you could call what they had a family. Actually, though, of course, he couldn't *let* George leave. He might talk.

"Don't go in there, Mark, don't go!" George lumbered after Mark. "No!" He grabbed Mark's shoulders with his huge hands. "She's acting just like she used to when Mr. Nelson was here."

Mark whirled. "I've told you to shut up about dad! It's hard enough as it is, without your yelling his name around."

254

"But I heard him," George whimpered. "I hear him all the time. He just says, 'George, George, George.' He won't stop, Mark. No time! He's trying to tell me something, something he wants me to do. He's gonna tell me tonight."

"For Christ's sake's George, shut up." He watched the man sink to the ground again, hands to his head, whimpering. "You and your voices! You'll drive us all crazy. Crazy enough now." Audry was gone, he was thinking. Audry...gone.

Gone. He had driven to her apartment tonight, but she wouldn't let him in. Wouldn't let him in, and they were supposed to get married in less than a week. He had knocked on her door...knocked and knocked...until she had finally said from behind it, "Go away. Go away, Mark."

He had thought he had misunderstood her, of course, and he'd said, "Audry, it's me...Mark."

"Go away."

"What?"

"Go away. I don't want to see you again. Go away. Don't come back."

He still thought he was hearing things, but she had kept saying, "Go away," and when he'd finally asked her why in the name of God she was saying that, what in the name of God was going on all she would say, finally, was, "I know what happened," half a whimper, half a sob.

That was when the numbness had begun. And he had asked her, "You know *what* has happened?"

But all she would say after that was, "Go away, don't come back." And then she wouldn't even say that. She wouldn't say anything, and she wouldn't open the door.

He had gone to the nearest phone and tried to call her. She wouldn't answer. And so he had driven home, thinking, his mother must have told her. His mother must have phoned her. His mother would do anything to break them up. Yes! After all, he had told his mother just this evening that he and Audry were going to get married.

But she wouldn't have told Audry *everything*.

Or would she? Was she that insane?

All he could do was hope until, confronting her, he found out, one way or the other.

He said to George, as calmly as he could, "Was Audry here tonight?"

She could have come between the time he'd left the house and the time he'd arrived at her apartment. He'd been to a two-hour class at the college during that period.

"Just me and Mr. Nelson here. Me and Mr. Nelson, that's all. And Mrs. Gribe."

"Are you sure?"

"Yes."

His mother must have phoned her. He turned toward the door to the store and living quarters again. "Come on, George, let's go in. You'll get soaked out here."

"Don't act like Mr. Nelson. Only he tells me what to do. Just him."

"Oh, George, shut up that talk! Let's go in."

"I can't help it," he whimpered. "He talks to me, and I got to talk back to him, else he'll get mad at me again." He stared up at Mark, his face once again peaceful. "Mr. Nelson ain't mad at me no more. Him and me been talking a lot tonight. Just him and me, all alone out here." He looked back at the fence. "Haven't we, Mr. Nelson? Haven't we, huh?"

"You better get that plant back in the house before mother finds out."

"I was inside at first. But I couldn't hear Mr. Nelson good in there. So I come out here where him and me are closer together."

"Yeah, I know all about that, George. Now, let's go in."

"No."

Mark made a movement toward the store. "Okay, stay out here all night if you want to, but I'm going in?"

"No!" He lifted up straight on his knees. "Don't go in there!"

George was up on his feet as Mark started for the house. He grabbed Mark by the arm, his huge hands like a vise.

"For Christ sakes, George, stop acting like a maniac."

"Stay out here with me and Mr. Nelson, Mark. He don't care. He likes you now." George's face shone with pride. "He likes you almost as much as he likes me. He told me so." His voice rose, excited. "He told me! He don't like Mrs. Gribe at all. Don't like her at all, he said. He don't want you to go in there!"

He began to yank at Mark's arm, jerking him back toward the fence and the potted plant, pulling the lighter man behind him.

"Stop it! George. I'm not in any mood to play around!"

256

"Mr. Nelson don't want you to go in the house!" he shouted. He held Mark tight at the fence, arms around his waist.

"Goddamn it! George, let me go!" He kicked out and jammed his elbow in George's stomach, almost slithering away.

"No! Mr. Nelson says no!"

Mark's foot slammed around and clipped the potted plant, scattering broken parts on the ground.

George moaned and let Mark go. "Oh-h-h. All busted. Mr. Nelson's flower, all busted." He dropped to his knees and clumsily began to scrape bits of the broken pot together and tried to set the plant upright. He moaned again and looked accusingly up at Mark. "You ruined it for him. Now I'll have to..."

His voice broke off. As Mark watched, he whispered and dropped the plant and the bits of pottery, and collapsed on the ground.

"Yes, Mr. Nelson," he moaned. "Yes, sir. Yes, Mr. Nelson."

"George?" Mark said, irritated yet worried.

George stirred, and his head came up from the ground. A moan, and he looked at Mark, his face glazed and trancelike. "Did you hear him?" he mumbled.

"Come on in the house, George."

"Did you?" quickly, eagerly.

Mechanically, Mark's head moved in a no.

"That was Mr. Nelson." He smiled happily and slowly nodded. "He said, 'George, let Mark go in the house *now*,' That's what he said. 'Let Mark go in the house now.' It was plain. You didn't hear him at all?" Incredibly.

"No, George."

"You ought to have. It was plain. He said to let you go in the house now so he can go looking out here." He glanced at the remains of the plant, childishly happy. "He won't tell me who it is he's looking for. But when he does I'm gonna get that person for him. That's how I'm gonna help him." Quickly, he swiveled his head up toward Mark. "He didn't tell you who he was looking for, did he?" he said anxiously.

"No, George," softness in his voice now. "Mr. Nelson didn't tell me."

He smiled, relieved. "He won't tell nobody 'til he tells me." He shook his head in emphasis. "Nobody!"

"All right, all right."

"I bet I know Mr. Nelson better than you do. Or Mrs. Gribe. I bet that. He won't talk to you or her, I bet. None at all." He proudly puckered his bottom lip. "Just me."

"Okay, now come on, let's go in."

"I'm going to stay out here, Mr. Nelson told me to."

"Aah, for God sakes," Mark said as he went toward the store.

"I'm not aah!" Mumbling, mad, he puffed out his lips. "I'm not aah 'cause I'm really helping Mr. Nelson find somebody and he comes up out of his grave and tells me, too. Every night. It's plain! And he don't want nobody acting like him, neither. Like that ol' girl did tonight."

Mark was nearing the porch when he heard George's words. He stopped and spun around. "What girl, George!?" His voice shot across the yard.

"Nobody."

George lowered his head. He began to moan and whimper as Mark ran toward him.

"You told me Audry wasn't here!" he yelled, grabbing the man by the shoulders.

George whimpered. "Don't hurt me, Mark. I didn't mean to do anything bad."

Mark felt his nerves snap and twitch. He had an almost overpowering desire to scream, to ram his fist into George's face. Everything seemed to be crushing him—his mother, Audry, George. He raised his hand to slap George, but at the man's flinch, his frightened expression, he calmed himself, he lowered his arm.

"I didn't mean to tell her," George whined. His head whirled. "I didn't mean it, Mark. Honest I didn't."

"Tell her what?"

George groaned. "Bad. Awful. Oh-h-h-h." He gagged. "Bad."

He had George by the collar now and was shaking him.

"Tell her what! George?"

"I didn't mean to, I didn't mean to."

Mark stared at the anguished man. He had to be calm now. He had to relax. He had to be sure of what George had told Audry. He felt weak and syrupy. Everything was drained out of him now. Everything, gone.

"George," he said, "when Audry came here tonight you told her something. Is that right?"

George shook his head in a moaning yes.

Mark steadied himself. He heard his voice come whisper-dry out over his lips. "You told her about dad's murder, didn't you? That I was...involved.

"Didn't you?"

George sobbed.

"Didn't you!"

George nodded.

Mark turned, he felt himself move, the store was in front of him and he was putting one foot down, then the other, moving toward the door. Walking over the yard, walking up to the porch. He felt his hand move out and turn the door knob, and then he was inside the house, the dark stairs reaching up over his head. He heard the sound of his feet on the steps. Up. He was so tired, he wanted to drop down and go to sleep. Sleep. If he could just go to sleep. Just sleep and sleep and sleep.

When he came up over the head of the stairs and saw the white splotch of light in the hall from his mother's room and heard the squeak! squawk! of her rocker, he stood still for a moment. The light seemed almost friendly now, beckoning. It was somehow calling to him, it seemed, this puddle of light from his mother's room. His mother was in there. She was waiting for him. Always waiting. He pondered, his face in a twisted smile, then shrugged and walked toward the light, squish! clump! squish! clump! rainwater coming out of his shoes. He'd leave tracks, he thought, and wanted to laugh because that was a crazy thing to be thinking about, when really what he wanted to think about was Audry. Audry was gone. Audry...gone.

He walked into his mother's room and said, "Audry's gone," and it sounded so natural and the right thing to say that he said, "Audry's gone" again.

Squeak!

Her staring eyes, rocking with the motions of the chair.

Squawk!

He gazed at her, this thing, this rocking mother. She was a funny thing. He wondered if she were alive and how she would be if she were dead, and at that he had to smile, for in a way he was dead and so was Audry, and his mother might as well be, too. He felt a second smile curl through his lips; but this one twisted into a smirk.

Squeak!

He saw the thick, blue-veined ankles and dark-striped skin at the top of her bedroom slippers. And the twirling darning needle rolling between her forefinger and thumb. The needle that she always had stuck in the front of her blouse or dress or sweater, ready to be pulled out and played with, or worse. Her needled eyes. She was smiling at him. Smiling. Ugly-pretty smile, layered on her face, a gloating smile.

He took a step toward her.

His voice sounded strange to him when he spoke; it seemed to come from a distance. Hollow. Empty. As if he were hearing it from someone else's lips. Audry's lips. Audry. Heavy on his mind, he felt her.

"Mother," he had murmured.

"I heard George and you screaming out back. Was Nelson after him again?" The needle spun.

"It must be awfully frustrating;' she said, "sitting out there on a grave trying to talk to a corpse. But George can be quite a conversationalist. At times." With a quick flick of her hand, she straightened her housecoat over her knee. "I heard you shouting Audry's name at him." Smirking, she glanced up at her son. "Tell me, Mark, did you actually expect to marry that Barrow woman?...as if you think you're a grown-up man?"

The mole on her cheek was withered and brown; it danced obscenely in the light from the lamp at her shoulder as she talked. Her face was the color of wet ashes now.

"If I was that hard up, I'd just pick up one of the local whores. But I suppose Miss Barrow had something special about her. She was pregnant, I suppose. You either had to marry her or pay for an abortion."

"Shut up!"

"Sharp wires are effective, Mark. Much cheaper, too." Her eyes glittered. "I wish I had known about wires and such when I was carrying you." She shrugged. "But I suppose Barrow knows all about that sort of thing."

"Audry's gone!"

"Gone? My word, where? To heaven?" She chuckled. "Too bad Nelson isn't there to enjoy her company. He'd enjoy that—sleeping with an angel." She sighed. "His soul might be enjoying hot females, but what's left of his body surely isn't."

Mark heard her chuckle splinter into a shriveling laugh—an insane laugh.

"But at least Nelson's good for something," she went on. "Fertilizer. Did you see how well the grass next to the fence came up this spring?"

"Shut up!"

Squeak! squawk! sang the rocker.

"Don't talk to me like that, Nel...Mark," she said in pretended fright. "I'll sic George on you."

"You mention dad's name again, mother, and so help me God I'll kill you!"

"Kill me. My word, how horrible. Kill your own mother?" She snickered. "But if you do, get George to help you. He's good at it, with the hands he has. As you know. As Nelson knows. As George knows—after I told him about what they could do, what they had to do if he wanted to keep living here, if he wanted a home, if he wanted to eat."

Mark felt a dry hard laughing knot begin at the bottom level of his stomach, then snowball up as if it were something separate from him. The laugh exploded, short and piercingly shrill.

"Mark, stop it. And sit down," she said coldly. "You remind me of Nelson with that insane cackle of yours."

The darning needle whirled as she smiled and motioned for him to sit beside her. He didn't move.

"That woman of yours isn't going to come here anymore, Mark." Her voice was restrained and concise, yet with cutting strength. "I've had enough of her sucking around you."

"You have?" The words were flat.

"She puts her foot in this house again, I'll mash that pretty face of hers in. Or have George do it. Or worse. The bitch will find out about George's hands, too."

"Shut up, mother," he said calmly.

"Don't tell me to shut up. Your father used to do that. I just told you not to remind me of him that way."

"So you did."

"You know just the thought of him frightens me—in certain ways... his...his hysterics."

"I know."

A flush swept her face. "I don't like your attitude, Mark. You held your tongue until that Barrow woman started influencing you." Her voice snapped at him. "From now on you're going to stay in your place!"

Mark felt another knotted laugh burst out of him. He saw his mother recoil from its shrillness.

"Mark, stop it! And sit down."

He did not move.

"Stay in my place," he murmured bitterly. "Sure. Stay in my own little hole." He laughed again; he couldn't stop it. "If I try to climb out you'll push dad's murder in my face. You'll go to the police. If I move out, you'll go to the police. You don't care. You don't care if it's found out that you planned to have him killed, arranged it, that George killed him. You don't care if I'm found guilty of hiding it, of not going to the police myself. If only I had gone right after it happened. But I wanted to protect you. *You!* You who just don't care one way or the other. I realize that now. The only thing you care about is making my life miserable. And you can do it either way: by going to the police or not going. One way I go to jail, the other way I live with you the rest of my life. I'm miserable either way, which is what you want—just why only your screwed-up mind knows, but I bet a...needle it's because I was fathered by a man you came to hate. You're insane!"

A squeak and the rocker stopped, and he saw her come up toward him, then hesitate, then reach out for his arm. "Mark," she said softly.

"Yeah, Mark. That's all you have to say and I'll come running. But I'll never do enough running, enough of anything. You've made sure of that with your threats to turn me in. And there's nothing I can do about it?"

Deliberately he brushed her reaching hand away. She stiffened. The rocker began to move, rapidly. The needle spun.

"Of course there isn't," she said.

"When someone else tries to get into my life, you'll get rid of *her*."

"No," she said, so soft, so cuttingly soft. "I won't. *You* will."

He bent over her and let his fingers flick through her hair. "You're so sweet and kind."

She knocked his hand away.

"Why, mother, am I upsetting you?"

"Go to bed," she snapped. She spun the needle once, then glared up at him. "You won't be able to get up in the morning...to open up the store." She smirked.

"That son-of-a-bitching place!"

Squeak!

He jumped. He grabbed the chair and held it still.

"Old gray-haired mother," he said.

"Don't make fun of me, Mark," Her smirk and sarcasm were gone.

"How can I?" His fingers were playing with her hair. "You're much too sweet...and kind."

"Mark! stop it!"

He chuckled. A strange chuckle. He listened to it a moment, his hand on her arm, squeezing the old flesh, slowly, so soft between his fingers. Insane old mother, it would be better if she were dead.

"Mark! stop it!"

"Don't tell me *I'm* scaring you? Only dad could do that."

She twisted. "Please."

"Please. What a strange word for you. Say it again."

"Mark, don't."

"You're sure you're talking to Mark? Remember that dad was the only one who could..." he squeezed "...scare you." The needle, glinting in the lamplight, caught his eye. "That goddamn thing. I'd like to run it through your neck," and he gave a short, brittle laugh and grabbed for it and missed.

She half rose out of her chair, her arm still in Mark's grip. "Let's go in the kitchen and have a cup of coffee," she said.

But his hand was on her forehead, pushing her back.

"Mark!" She jerked her arm free and sprang up and ran for the door.

He caught her by the wrist.

"I believe you're afraid, mother." he said, softly sarcastic. "*I* couldn't hurt you. Only dad could do that. Only dad could make you scream. You remember dad, don't you? Dear, sweet dad?"

She whimpered. "Mark, stop it! Get away from me! Stop! You're hurting me!" She twisted and pulled at him.

"Just like dad?"

He hit her.

She fell to the floor and he stood there staring at his fist, puzzled at the sting in his knuckles. Then he looked down. She was twisting up on one knee and trying to get up. He pulled her to her feet.

"Son," she whimpered. Her head flopped as he shook her. "Son."

"Son," he echoed, then exploded a laugh. "I'm not your son!" shouting now, flopping her head back and forth. "I'm not your son! I'm Nelson now, your husband!"

She sagged against him, whimpering.

"You understand! I'm *Nelson* now!"

"Nelson." she moaned. "Nelson." Her eyes flew wide. "Nelson!" she screamed. "Nelson, don't..."

"NELSON!

Nelson!

Nelson.

"Stop it! My dearest husband, don't! In God's name, Nelson, don't!"

She tore out of Mark's arms and ran, the needle still in her hand; stumbled out into the hall and down the back stairs, screaming hysterically, "Get away from me, Nelson! Get away..."

Huddled next to the fence, George looked up at the sound of her screams. "Stay away from me, Nelson!" he heard her shout. She was running toward him through the rain. Ponderously, he rose to his feet. "George!" she screeched, "Nelson's after me!" She stumbled and almost fell, then swaying, sagged against him and clawed at his shoulders. "Help me, George," she moaned. "Nelson's chasing me!"

"You?" he mumbled.

She nodded, making frantic bumps on his chest. "He's after me," she whimpered.

"Mr. Nelson ... after *you?*"

"Yes. Me."

George's face was puzzled and amazed and frowning; then slowly his expression began to clear. "Mrs. Nelson, he was looking for *you* all the time," he murmured, smiling in understanding, nodding up-down, up-down. "After *you.*"

Then, suddenly, he tilted his head, attentive, listening, his face tranquil and trancelike. "Yes, Mr. Nelson, sir," he mumbled. "Yes, sir."

He felt Mrs. Gribe trembling against his chest, her head so little on his shoulder, her hair so soft. He lifted his ham hands and patted her cheeks. "Mr. Nelson says I got to," he said, voice cloud-soft. He clumsily caressed her arm. "Got to do it, he says. It's plain."

"Help me, George." She glanced back at the house.

"I'm helping Mr. Nelson."

His fingers rose to her neck.

"He told me to, and I got to do what he says."

His fingers tightened on her neck.

"George!" she sputtered. She tried to jerk away. But his hands like hooks held her.

His face lifted. Rain splattered on his forehead and ran down his thick jaw, his bristled chin. "Yes, Mr. Nelson, yes, sir, Mr. Nelson," he chanted, voice humbly pious.

His fingers squeezed.

Mrs. Gribe gagged and squirmed and twisted; she clawed at George's fingers, she jabbed at his hands with the needle; but his huge hands only tightened and squeezed as his blood trickled down to his wrist.

"Yes, Mr. Nelson, sir, I'm doing it, sir."

Mrs. Gribe choked, she weakened; her weight sagged against George.

His face was glowing, mystically ecstatic. Mrs. Gribe, rag-limp, dangled from his hands.

"Yes, Mr. Nelson."

His fingers loosened.

"Yes, sir."

He let her go and she crumpled onto the ground.

A tear of happy pride rolled down George's cheek as he turned and walked toward the house. His hands had done it. His big, strong hands had helped Mr. Nelson and he was happy with them—now, this time. His own hands. Mrs. Gribe had told him about them, how big they were, how strong. Yes, they were very good hands. He was very proud of them now.

He went up the steps talking to Mr. Nelson. When he got in the hall he saw the light coming from Mrs. Gribe's room. He ought to turn off the light. Ain't no use having a light on now.

He was surprised when he saw Mark flopped on the bed. This wasn't his room. This was Mrs. Gribe's room.

"Hullo, Mark," he said.

Mark stirred and opened his eyes.

George smiled. "Mr. Nelson told me to do it, Mark." His voice was kind and proud. "Mr. Nelson told me to help him." He nodded in quick jerks. "Yes he did, he told me."

Wearily Mark turned on the bed, his back to George. "All right, George."

"He was after Mrs. Gribe tonight and he told me to help him. That's what Mr. Nelson said, Mark, that's what he told me. He was after Mrs. Gribe all the time. All the time, he was."

"All right, George. Now go on in your room and go to bed. I'm waiting for mother to come back."

"It was plain, Mark, what Mr. Nelson said."

"I'm simply going to tell her that I'm going to marry Audry, regardless. If she'll have me now, that is."

George bubbled happily and looked down at his hands.

"It was plain."

~

NOTES ON "DEAD VOICES LIVE"

Here we have John D. Keefauver's last story published in a major anthology. It originally appeared in the 1992 anthology *Dark at Heart*, edited by Karen and Joe R. Lansdale, in the company of such luminaries as Norman Partridge, Steve Rasnic Tem, Lewis Shiner, and Andrew Vachss. Keefauver received $378.00 for his contribution. The editors' introduction is a bit briefer than for his two previous stories in Lansdale anthologies, but still on the mark:

> John Keefauver is rare in that he is a professional short story writer. No novels. No films. Just short stories. And he survives. His work has appeared just about everywhere. He is primarily known for his off-the-wall tales of fantasy and satire. The following is a bit more traditional, but lacks none of the wild Keefauver imagination.

Of course, Keefauver actually had published two short novels by this time—one in the soft-core porn market, and one for young readers. He also had at least half a dozen unpublished novels in his files.

Readers who have gone through the stories in this volume in order will recognize the similarities between this tale and "Give Me Your Cold Hand" and "Mareta," all the way down to two characters having the same names as in the former story, as well as certain repeated motifs, such as the needle and the potted plant. The major difference here is that the protagonist is the son of the manipulative woman, rather than her husband or lover. This arrangement most closely resembles the dynamic in Keefauver's unpublished novel *Shell* (a.k.a. *Spook Ship*).

THE TREE

N O ONE IN TOWN COULD remember how the tradition of nailing death notices to the tree began. Even John Martin, the oldest person in the village, couldn't remember. All he remembered was that, when he was a boy, the notices were being nailed to the tree, and his folks acted then as if it had been going on forever. It had always been important. It gave a person a good feeling, John impatiently explained to outsiders, to know that when his time came, his name would appear on the elm along with the names of all his friends in town who had died before him, all together then, on something that was living.

It was only natural that John was the first to notice that the tree was dying, seeing as how he was the one in town closest to his time, by age. Also, he could remember the other elms dying, one by one, and because of that he paid a lot of attention to the only one that remained. About a dozen elms used to line the main street. Some hadn't died, though; they had been chopped down because of the building going on then. Of course, building had stopped a long time ago: the town itself had been dying for years.

John and the other older folks in town (which meant almost everybody because most of the young had moved away) refused to believe that the sickness of the tree was caused by the nails driven into it. They said it was diseased. Dutch elm disease had killed the others, and it was killing the last one too. It wasn't until they got an expert in from the state agricultural college that they changed their minds, and some didn't even change them then. It was just too hard for some of the townspeople to take.

Four nails were used to hold each death notice, and since a notice was never removed, the tree was nearly covered by the two-by-four-inch metal strips. It had become harder and harder to find space for the black-bordered notices. Years ago the undertaker, who traditionally had the responsibility of putting up the notices, had to ask the town to buy him a ladder since the only space left to nail the notices was fifteen feet up the trunk of the nearly 100-foot-tall elm. In more recent years there had even been some talk of removing the oldest notices and replacing them, as needed, with those of people recently passed on. That talk hadn't gotten far, for, after all, the point of the tradition was that a townsperson continued to live on the tree. A notice that came loose was either nailed back on the elm or replaced with a replica—replaced, that is, as much as possible, for lots of times parts of the older notices couldn't be made out because some of the strip had rusted away, often the part including the date of death, which was one of the reasons no one was sure how old the tradition was. In a way, the notices themselves were dying too.

Back when the tree first began to be crowded with notices, some of the younger people still left in town argued that since a notice far up the trunk couldn't be read by people on the ground, the whole idea of the tree was nullified because a person lived on only if he could be *seen* on the tree. They argued that the tree had become a death monument, like the town's cemetery. At least in the cemetery you could read the headstones.

Led by John Martin, the angry elders had replied that, unlike the cemetery, the elm was living, and a person continued to live because he was *on* the tree. He didn't have to be seen there anymore than the tree had to be seen to be alive. Additionally, didn't the young realize that the elm was a tree that had been associated with the growth and development, the very life of the village? That had to be taken into account too.

What John ultimately emphasized, though—his eyes especially fierce, his face a weathered pelt—was tradition. There had been no town newspaper during the early years of the village, and the news of the town's deaths had had to be announced somehow. The elm was in the center of the village, and in the course of a day almost everybody went by it. What better place could there be for the announcements?

At first, any type of notice was nailed to the tree. Eventually, though, only death notices appeared there, on metal strips made by the blacksmith, traditionally a Martin. How this restriction came about no one knew anymore. But it was thought by most that the stately elm with its gracefully arching vaselike crown, its glory, should not be tainted by news of mundane events. What greater memorial to the town's dead could there be than this majestic living elm, symbol of the village's life?

The tradition became so firmly established that even when a weekly newspaper was started in the town around the turn of the century (when the town was at its largest and busiest, with farmers bringing their produce to the railroad for shipment to the city), the notices still appeared on the tree. It was said that the editor himself checked the tree to see who had died.

Of course, the town had been without a newspaper and train service for years. The twice-a-day train roared right through town, as if the place didn't even exist.

Through the years, the village, cut off from the more populated parts of the state, fought an increasing problem: out-of-towners. As automobiles and pickups became more and more popular, people found it relatively easy to reach the village on a narrow, rutted road that ran through the bleak mountains surrounding the town, a road that the elders insisted remain just as it was. As news of the tree spread, more and more gawkers came to see it. The problem became so serious that John Martin and some of the other old-timers threatened to build a wall around the village to keep the tourists out. As it was, about all they could do, besides ignoring the gawkers and generally refusing to be helpful, was keep out anybody who wanted to make money off the tree. They all remembered with disgust, for example, the man who wanted to build a motel by the tree. Another wanted to build a souvenir shop in town. Some of the younger townspeople (Brills, Nickersons, Summers) got so sick of the tourists they actually began muttering about cutting the damn tree down.

And now it was dying—an impossible thought. Simply impossible to think that the majestic elm, at least three hundred years old, could die, and harder yet to believe that a tradition could be responsible. No, the nails couldn't be the reason, said the elders. It had to be disease. No, said the young. It was the nails. Look at the tree, the young said. Covered by pieces of metal, many in various stages of decay, it didn't even look like a tree. Indeed, it was a ghostly sight under a full moon. And under the sun it reminded many of a Christmas tree decorated with silver ornaments. Or of the head of a gray-haired old man, John Martin said softly.

They got an expert to look at it, a man from the state agricultural college. But even after he told them, after making many tests, that the nails were killing the tree—had killed it, nearly—the elders refused to believe him. They brought in another expert, from out of state. He told them the same thing. No disease was killing the tree; no bug; no virus. It was the nails. The thousands of nails. The only reason the poor, mistreated tree had lived that long was because it once had been so healthy. If you pulled out all the nails, *maybe* the tree would live, but he strongly doubted it. It was too late.

That evening the town met in the church. Even David Neidson closed up his general store early, and nobody could remember him ever doing that before. As usual, John Martin led the meeting. He summarized what the tree experts had said: the nails would have to come out or the tree would die. They'd have to decide right then whether to pull the nails—if they believed the experts were right, that is.

Of course, it was not the nails themselves that bothered most. It was the death notices. If the nails came out, the notices would come off (except for some of the ancient ones that had become embedded in the wood). And if that happened, they might as well cut the tree down. Wasn't there any way to attach the notices to the elm without using nails? No one could think of a way that wouldn't damage the tree. Maybe some kind of cement? Maybe. But why go to all that trouble if the tree was likely to die anyway? Wasn't it already dead?

It was Jake Mills, who was almost as old as John Martin, who finally yelled, "The hell with the tree! I've been waiting all my life to get on that tree, and now it's dying! To hell with it! Let's cut the damn thing down!"

Jake was known for his crotchetiness, and no one paid much attention to him. Yet it was obvious that almost everybody thought the same way he did. Waiting all their lives only to find out that they were going to outlive the tree. It wasn't fair. They led a tough life: working the land from near dawn to dusk, broiling in the summer, freezing in the winter, isolated from the outside, one of the few places in the country that was cut off even from television because of the surrounding mountains. The same life basically as their forbears. Their forbears were on the tree, but they wouldn't be? It wasn't fair. It wasn't right. It couldn't be allowed to happen.

They would say later that poor old Jake Mills never lived to see the solution. His heart gave out not long after the meeting, and his notice was dutifully—hurriedly—nailed on the elm in one of the few spaces remaining. It was spring then, and some of the more optimistic townspeople thought that just maybe the season of growth would keep life in the old battered tree, would even, perhaps, allow it to keep ahead of the notices that would continue to be nailed to it week after week, month after month, year after year. For they had decided that since it wasn't certain that they could save the tree by pulling out the nails, they would continue nailing death notices to it. Perhaps the tradition itself would somehow keep the tree living. Or perhaps they could slow up the death rate in the town and thus hammer fewer nails into the tree, allowing the elm a better chance at life. One thing was certain: the notices would continue to go up as long as the tree remained.

The one good thing about Jake's passing on was that there was still room, if just barely, on the tree for him. Although just driving four more nails into it seemed to kill the elm a bit more.

And there was still room for David Neidson a day or so later.

But when John Martin was found dead the day after that, it was obvious that the tree couldn't take any more nails. And that was the night when, almost frantically, people began to die in the town by the dozens.

IT WAS ONE OF THE Nickerson boys, Roy, who tried to "stop the dying," as he would say later, by chopping down the tree, but he was stopped by Fred Daniels after he'd only struck a few blows. By pure luck, Fred had been standing, unable to sleep, at his bedroom window overlooking the tree, worrying about things. Under an almost full moon, he saw Roy approach the tree, and, suspicious from the beginning because he could see what looked like an ax in Roy's hand, Fred had stumbled down to the elm before Roy could really get started. Considering his age, the only thing Fred could do to stop Roy was to get between the boy and the tree and bellow at the top of his lungs. Roy had to run. In minutes a good portion of the town was at the elm. Where Roy had hit the tree there were only a few superficial scars.

Roy was to say later that the main reason he tried to cut down the elm was because his father had begun to wonder if he, the father, would ever get on the tree. Roy was afraid his father might "die on purpose," and he wasn't even what you'd call really old. No matter what he said, Roy was shunned by almost everybody in the town and was told by what was left of the elders to get out of town and never come back.

Even though Roy hadn't done much damage to the tree, most elders feared his cuts would cause the tree to die sooner and they would be deprived of what was rightfully theirs. And so, hurried along by this added fear, they began to go about dying at an even faster rate, no matter how hard the young argued against it.

It was young Nason Brill who set off dynamite at the base of the tree— dynamite, the elders were to say coldly, he'd brought in from the outside, from a construction site where he had a job, "not content to work here in town with the people he lived with." "And die with, if they had their way," muttered Nason from jail. The dynamited tree hadn't hurt or killed anyone as it fell onto a house unoccupied since its elderly owner had passed on, but Nason was jailed because the explosion had sent jagged pieces of death notices flying like shrapnel through nearby parts of town. One piece had sliced into Fred Daniels, who, still having a hard time sleeping, had heard Nason at the tree and had gone to the window overlooking the elm.

Fred was the first to die without being able to have his notice put on the tree. To the elders, that was almost life-threatening in itself. But a rising tide of the middle-aged (close to the majority now, with so many elders dead) joined the young, thinking differently, grumbling that when you considered what the tradition had led to, they were glad the tree of death was gone, although they were, of course, horrified at what Nason Brill had done.

But an even colder horror wrenched them when Elliot Summers, who was only in his fifties, dug in a stout transplant next to where the old elm had been.

~

NOTES ON "THE TREE"

Keefauver's last great story—how many writers have ended their career on such a perfect note? Originally published in the Winter, 1997 issue of *Mānoa*, from the University of Hawaii Press (Vol. 9, No. 2, pp. 86-90, subtitled: *Century of Dreams: New Writing from the Philippines*).

ACKNOWLEDGMENTS

Firstly, John Pelan, who set these wheels in motion, like so many others. Alas, John passed away on 12 April 2021, during the final editing of this volume. Marina Westfield (pictured left), who saved her great-uncle's work from oblivion. Margaret and Michael Westfield, who provided support and hospitality—and copious cups of coffee—at every step and every level. Christine Boccella Santangelo, whose assistance has proven invaluable. Kay Allan, John's landlord in Carmel, who took the crucial first steps to preserve his legacy. Steve Berman and Lethe Press, the *sine qua non*. Anya Martin, indefatigable proofreader. Joe R. Lansdale, who *gets it*, and who took the time.

CPSIA information can be obtained
at www.ICGtesting.com
Printed in the USA
BVHW081340130921
616672BV00004B/289